ENDEAVOUR

(ARK ROYAL, BOOK XVIII)

CHRISTOPHER G. NUTTALL

The characters and events portrayed in this book are fictitious.
Any similarity to real persons, living or dead, is coincidental and not
intended by the author.

Text copyright © 2019 Christopher G. Nuttall

All rights reserved.

Printed in the United States of America.

No part of this book may be reproduced, or stored in a retrieval system,
or transmitted in any form or by any means, electronic, mechanical,
photocopying, recording, or other-wise, without express written permission
of the publisher.

ISBN: 9798848809206

Cover by Justin Adams
http://www.variastudios.com/

Book One: Ark Royal
Book Two: The Nelson Touch
Book Three: The Trafalgar Gambit
Book Four: Warspite
Book Five: A Savage War of Peace
Book Six: A Small Colonial War
Book Seven: Vanguard
Book Eight: Fear God And Dread Naught
Book Nine: We Lead
Book Ten: The Longest Day
Book Eleven: The Cruel Stars
Book Twelve: Invincible
Book Thirteen: Para Bellum
Book Fourteen: The Right of the Line
Book Fifteen: The Lion and the Unicorn
Book Sixteen: Fighting For The Crown
Book Seventeen: Drake's Drum
Book Eighteen: Endeavour

http://www.chrishanger.net
http://chrishanger.wordpress.com/
http://www.facebook.com/ChristopherGNuttall
All Comments Welcome!

Contents

Author's Note ... vii
Prologue I: The Sphere, Virus Prime ... ix
Prologue II: London, United Kingdom ... xv

Chapter One: London, United Kingdom ... 1
Chapter Two: London, United Kingdom ... 10
Chapter Three: HMS Endeavour, Sol System ... 19
Chapter Four: HMS Endeavour, Sol System ... 28
Chapter Five: HMS Endeavour, Sol System ... 37
Chapter Six: HMS Endeavour, In Transit ... 46
Chapter Seven: HMS Endeavour, Virus Prime ... 55
Chapter Eight: The Sphere, Virus Prime ... 64
Chapter Nine: Research Station, Virus Prime ... 73
Chapter Ten: HMS Endeavour, Virus Prime ... 82
Chapter Eleven: HMS Endeavour, In Transit ... 91
Chapter Twelve: HMS Endeavour, In Transit ... 100
Chapter Thirteen: HMS Endeavour, In Transit ... 109
Chapter Fourteen: HMS Endeavour, Dyson System ... 118
Chapter Fifteen: Dyson One, Dyson System ... 127
Chapter Sixteen: HMS Endeavour, Dyson System ... 136
Chapter Seventeen: HMS Endeavour, Dyson System ... 145
Chapter Eighteen: HMS Endeavour, Dyson System ... 154
Chapter Nineteen: HMS Endeavour, Dyson System ... 163
Chapter Twenty: HMS Endeavour, Dyson Two (Interior) ... 172
Chapter Twenty-One: HMS Endeavour, Dyson Two (Interior) ... 181
Chapter Twenty-Two: HMS Endeavour, Dyson Two (Interior) ... 190
Chapter Twenty-Three: Shuttlecraft, Dyson Two (Interior) ... 199
Chapter Twenty-Four: HMS Endeavour, Dyson Two (Interior) ... 208
Chapter Twenty-Five: Near South Gate, Dyson Two (Surface) ... 218

Chapter Twenty-Six: Near South Gate, Dyson Two (Surface) 227
Chapter Twenty-Seven: HMS Endeavour, Dyson Two (Interior) 236
Chapter Twenty-Eight: Near South Gate, Dyson Two (Surface) 245
Chapter Twenty-Nine: HMS Endeavour, Dyson Two (Interior) 254
Chapter Thirty: Near South Gate, Dyson Two (Surface) 263
Chapter Thirty-One: Near South Gate, Dyson Two (Surface) 272
Chapter Thirty-Two: Near South Gate, Dyson Two (Surface) 281
Chapter Thirty-Three: Near South Gate, Dyson Two (Surface) 290
Chapter Thirty-Four: Near South Gate, Dyson Two (Surface) 299
Chapter Thirty-Five: HMS Endeavour, Dyson Two (Interior) 308
Chapter Thirty-Six: Near South Gate, Dyson Two (Surface) 317
Chapter Thirty-Seven: Near South Gate, Dyson Two (Surface) 326
Chapter Thirty-Eight: South Gate, Dyson Two (Surface) 335
Chapter Thirty-Nine: HMS Endeavour, Dyson Two (Interior) 344
Chapter Forty: London, United Kingdom 354

Afterword 361
Appendix: Glossary of UK Terms and Slang 365
How to Follow 369
Bonus Preview 371

AUTHOR'S NOTE

Endeavour is set roughly a year after *Drake's Drum*, and draws on characters established in that cycle—*The Lion and the Unicorn*, *Fighting for the Crown* and *Drake's Drum*—but it is intended to be as stand-alone as possible.

As always, I welcome reviews (hint, hint). I've also been broadening my social media presence—please check the list at the rear of the book, then follow me if you are so inclined.

CGN.

PROLOGUE I:
THE SPHERE, VIRUS PRIME

RACISM, Doctor Athena Gaurs told herself, *is a mental illness.*

It didn't help. Her heart began to race as she drifted through the Sphere. She had spent most of her professional life working with aliens, studying their cultures and technologies in the hopes of promoting interspecies cooperation and harmony, yet the Sphere was just too *alien* for her mind to process. It was so huge, built on such a great scale, that she felt like a fly crawling across a cathedral window, something so far beyond the poor creature it couldn't even begin to comprehend what it was crawling on. The other alien races humanity had encountered, in nearly a hundred years of contact and conflict, had all been understandable. Whoever had built the Sphere was not.

She tried to calm herself as she glided onwards. The Sphere was inert, powerless, and yet it wasn't. The xenospecialists had noted and logged everything from strange lights, with no discernible source, to faint flickers of energy and gravitational pulses that came and went so quickly that even the most sensitive equipment in the known galaxy was barely capable of detecting their presence before they were gone. Athena had read the reports, when she'd been assigned to the project, and she'd had trouble understanding why so many of the exploration team had managed to get lost in the structure.

She knew now. The interior seemed purposely designed to be confusing. There were even hints it restructured itself when humans weren't looking.

And some of us are sure we're being watched, she thought, grimly. *What if we are?*

The thought taunted her. It had been nearly a year since HMS *Lion* had stumbled across the Sphere, during the final days of the Virus War. Since then, a covert project had been mounted to explore the alien artefact and unlock its secrets, a project that—so far—had produced precisely nothing. Athena had read the reports from the first teams, brimming with excitement and enthusiasm until they'd started their work. They'd drawn a series of complete blanks. They didn't know what material had been used to produce the alien artefact, let alone what it was intended to do. They didn't even know why it had remained undetected in the system for so long. There were even people who wondered if the Sphere hadn't been detected because it simply hadn't been *there*.

A shiver ran down her spine as she drifted into the next chamber. It was hard, sometimes, to avoid the sensation she was being watched. They hadn't found anything to suggest they *were*, but that was meaningless. Whoever had built the Sphere was so far ahead of humanity that their surveillance tech, assuming they even relied upon something as primitive as *tech*, might be completely undetectable. The human race could produce bugs so small they couldn't be located without the proper equipment. Who knew what the Builders could produce?

She frowned, turning slowly to take in the entire chamber. It was a bare sphere, within *the* Sphere, the bulkheads utterly unmarred by even the slightest *hint* of writing. The bronze material had defied everything humanity had thrown at it, from pens designed to leave marks on everything to laser cutters capable of slicing through a battleship's hull. It was maddening to think of all the secrets waiting for discovery and exploitation, if only they could figure out how to unlock them. And yet, they'd found nothing. There was a small but growing consensus amongst some of the scientists that there was nothing to find.

This installation was clearly not abandoned in a hurry, she reminded herself, grimly. *They had all the time they needed to strip it bare, taking everything save for the shell itself.*

It was possible, she'd been assured. The Sphere might be nothing more than a hollowed-out asteroid, as far as the Builders were concerned. They might have abandoned it, secure in the knowledge they'd taken everything that could be used to unlock their technology or leave a trail of breadcrumbs to their homeworld. Athena would have believed it herself—she knew how carefully warship datacores were swept for sensitive information, then rigged for destruction if there was even the slightest chance the warship would fall into enemy hands—if she hadn't seen so many oddities surrounding the alien structure. It just didn't *feel* dead and cold, abandoned like so many mined-out asteroids. It felt as if it was watching and waiting as the team probed its innards.

Perhaps it's an intelligence test, she thought, as she proceeded into the next chamber. *And we're failing.*

Athena keyed her sensors, taking a reading and comparing it to what she saw. The results made no sense. They never did. Some suggested the Sphere was bigger on the inside, some suggested it was imploding…she gritted her teeth and looked at the nearest bulkhead. Her sensors insisted the walls were closing in. Her naked eyes told her the bulkheads weren't moving. Athena sighed, inwardly. There was no way to *know* if the Sphere was spoofing their sensors deliberately or if the structure was just too *alien* for the sensors to handle. Athena wasn't sure, sometimes, if *she* could handle it. The Sphere was just too big.

We've seen larger structures, she reminded herself. *But none of them were quite so solid.*

She shook her head slowly as she made her way onwards, feeling oddly isolated even though the rest of the team was only a radio call away. They'd been told, at first, never to be alone on the alien structure, but they'd rapidly discovered that the more interesting events only took place when there were only one or two witnesses. It didn't help when they reported their findings back to Earth. Athena had a feeling, reading between the lines, that there were factions on the homeworld that thought the researchers were seeing things. There was no shortage of tales of weird sightings in the depths of space, of alien starships and entities that were—somehow—never captured by starship sensors. It was generally believed most of the stories were made up, and yet...

Her radio crackled, once. Athena keyed her wristcom, a shiver running down her spine. She'd been told to remain in touch and, if there was a hint she was losing contact with the rest of the team, to back out at once. The Sphere just wasn't *safe*. She thought she saw something at the corner of her eye, a flicker that was gone when she looked. Her radio crackled again. There was no reply. She swore under her breath as she made her way back to her hatch. Perhaps it was nothing, just a random burst of energy within the alien structure. Perhaps it was not...

Light flared, behind her. Athena spun around. The chamber had come to life, glowing energy flaring through the air. A wave of panic shot through her. She was alone and defenceless and utterly unaware of what was happening...she found it hard to believe, deep inside, that a super-advanced race would deliberately seek to harm her, but it was hard to be sure. How many insects were trodden on by humans, without any malicious intent? The light grew brighter. She hoped—prayed—that her recorders were still working. They were meant to record everything and yet, ever since they'd started exploring the Sphere, there'd been odd gaps. It was suddenly very easy to believe the Sphere was toying with them.

The glow sharpened, the lights becoming something oddly familiar and yet alien...it took her several seconds to realise she was looking at a holographic starchart. Humanity's holographic projects always had a faint sense of insubstantiality, a reminder they really were nothing more than illusions. The alien projections were so sharp, so perfect, it was hard to believe they weren't real. She reached forward, despite her training, and felt resistance as her fingers brushed against a holographic star. Solid-light projections? They'd always been theoretically possible, but no one had made them work. Not until now.

And then the hologram snapped out of existence.

Athena felt a sense of overwhelming *loss* as darkness crashed down on her. The starchart was gone, as if it had never been…her radio crackled, her team trying to contact her. She barely heard them, tears prickling in her eyes as she tried to come to terms with what she'd seen. Her CO was demanding she report immediately, that she make her way back to the starship, but she couldn't bring herself to reply. Would they believe her? Athena hadn't believed some of the stories she'd heard, from the first teams to explore the alien structure. It would be ironic, indeed, if *her* team refused to believe her.

"I…I think I found something," she said, checking the wristcom. The sensors insisted they'd recorded everything. She hoped, desperately, that they were correct. "I'm on my way."

Her heart started to pound, again, as she recalled what she'd seen. The sensors might not have recorded anything—there was no way to know, not until she got back to the ship—but *she* had. There were ways to get memories out of someone, even memories that they didn't consciously recall. She could be hypnotised and urged to draw out the starchart and then…

If that was a starchart, it might have shown me their homeworld, she told herself. *We can find them. And then, we can learn so much…*

PROLOGUE II: LONDON, UNITED KINGDOM

"THEY USED TO SAY MY ANCESTORS couldn't see the white man's ships on the horizon, so alien they were to their experience," Admiral Lady Susan Onarina said. "I think I understand how they felt."

The First Space Lord studied the report from the Sphere. Training and experience demanded she rebuke the xenospecialists for a decidedly careless approach to exploring the alien structure, although—going by the reports—it was clear they'd had little choice. The weirder manifestations never showed themselves to more than two humans and there was only *one* witness to the alien starchart. Susan didn't like the implications. The Sphere was clearly neither dead nor understood. It might be playing with the human explorers, it might just be letting off random bursts of energy, or it might be something in-between.

It was just too alien for anyone to be sure. Of anything.

"I always had the impression such stories were exaggerated," Admiral Paul Mason said, as he sipped his tea. Her old friend, and occasional lover, had been running the top-secret research program into the enigmatic aliens since the first traces of their existence had been discovered, back during the war. "They might not have been capable of building ocean-going ships, but they certainly understood the concept."

Susan nodded, although she wasn't so sure. Humanity had encountered two alien races—three, if one counted the Virus—that possessed more advanced technology, but it hadn't been *that* advanced. The tech had been understandable. Human scientists had been able to reverse-engineer captured alien technology or, knowing something was possible, simply figure out how it was done and produce their own version. It had never been easy—and she knew there'd been admirals who'd expected the scientists to simply wave a magic wand and put the new tech into production instantly—but it had been done. Here, though…the scientists didn't even know where to begin. The tech was just too different.

The RAF of the Second World War might not have been able to duplicate a jet fighter of the Troubles, she reflected. *But at least they'd understand the concept of a flying machine. Here…*

She shook her head, slowly. The Sphere didn't have *any* technology, at least as far as the explorers could determine. It was just an empty shell. And yet, it was clearly doing *something*. Susan had read the reports, each one little more than empty speculation that read like something out of a science-fantasy novel. The tech was welded into the bulkheads. The tech existed in some weird alternate dimension. There was no tech. Instead, there was an alien ghost playing games with humans unable to so much as detect, let alone deduce, its presence. They just didn't know.

"The starchart does match the local stellar environment," Mason said, quietly. "And, if the tramlines are as laid out on the map, we can get a ship to the alien homeworld."

"If it is their homeworld," Susan said. "And if they're not trying to lure us there…"

The thought chilled her. She was a student of history. She knew what happened when a primitive race met a more advanced one, even when there was no malice involved. The primitive race found it hard, almost impossible, to take the shock. How many human societies had collapsed, falling to pieces in the wake of contact? The Vesy really *hadn't* had an easy time of it, after they'd encountered humanity. The gulf between the two races was just too wide for them to catch up, at least quickly enough to matter. Susan had read those reports too. There was a very real chance the Vesy would lose what remained of their own culture, becoming little more than copies of humanity. And the hell of it was that copying humanity might be their only chance to survive.

Whoever built the Sphere might not mean to harm us, she thought. *But contact with them might be destructive, all the same.*

She sipped her tea, organising her thoughts. Humanity had been space-faring for nearly two hundred years when it had discovered, to its dismay, that it wasn't alone in the universe. The concept of aliens had been far from unknown. Indeed, it had preceded the first true offworld settlements. And while there had been a gulf between humans and Tadpoles, the gulf hadn't been insurmountable. There had been some culture shock—Susan could hardly deny it, given the number of humans trying to model themselves on the Tadpoles—but not as much as the politicians had feared. The Tadpoles had not been vastly superior. But whoever had built the Sphere was different.

Mason cleared his throat. "What are you going to advise the PM?"

Susan said nothing for a long moment. She was mildly surprised the government hadn't asked her to step down, or resign, after the murky end of the war. She'd already been in office longer than she'd expected. The government just had too many other problems to worry about her... she wondered, idly, if that was about to change. What *would* she advise the PM? There were risks, very real risks, in trying to make contact and yet, failing to make contact would have other risks. It was just a matter of time before someone else sent a ship to the alien homeworld themselves.

If it is their homeworld, she thought, numbly. *What happened to them?*

It was a worrying thought. The days when humanity had all of its eggs in one basket were long gone. Earth had been shipping out millions of colonists yearly, before the war, and the colonisation program was starting to pick up steam again. A race that had been in space for far longer should have filled up the entire galaxy by now, leaving no room for humanity and its peers. Where were they? The researchers speculated they'd drawn back, leaving room for the younger races, but Susan was too cynical to believe it. She knew from experience that principles often went by the wayside when they demanded sacrifice of any sort. Maybe they'd run into something even a super-powerful civilization couldn't handle.

"We need to know what happened to them," she said. "And we have to get a handle on their technology before we encounter someone far more advanced than ourselves."

"And promote British interests," Mason added, dryly.

"That goes without saying," Susan said, although she had her doubts. She knew how Britain would react if one of the other Great Powers suddenly gained access to super-technology and she was entirely sure they'd react the same way. "I'll discuss it with the PM, but the final call is a political one."

She rubbed her forehead. The war was over and yet…it wasn't. Not quite. The virus's power had been broken and yet, it was still out there. It might never be eradicated completely, no matter what they did. And humanity was too tired and divided to continue the fight. She had no idea if the plans for a united government would ever be put into practice or not—they were far from popular, now the war in space was over—but it might not be enough to save the day. Humanity needed to rest, not to find new challenges.

Mitch—Captain Campbell—would have been ideal for the mission, she thought. It would have gotten him away from Earth for months, if not years, allowing the post-war political chaos to settle without destroying his career. Her *protégé* had made a fool of himself—he'd said as much in his final message—and yet, he was still a good man. *If he'd survived…*

She put the thought aside. She had no time to indulge in wishful thinking. The future of the entire human race, and Britain's place in the stars, might be at risk. She needed to act fast.

We have no choice, she thought, tapping her console. Her aide would set up the meeting with the PM, as soon as possible. *If we don't go look to see what's there, who will?*

CHAPTER ONE:
LONDON, UNITED KINGDOM

COMMANDER STACI TEMPLETON awoke, drenched in sweat.

For a moment, she was unsure of where she was. The nightmare had been intense, a bitter reminder of HMS *Unicorn's* final moments before she'd rammed the alien brainship, blowing both starships into atoms and giving HMS *Lion* a chance to escape before it was too late. It had been a hard battle, and a costly one, but they'd won. Or had they? Her nightmare had been so intense, so *real*, that she honestly wasn't sure what *was* real. She'd seen the virus infecting the ship, the crew turning into monsters before her eyes...

She rubbed her forehead as she sat up. She'd declined the offer of a bed in the admiralty barracks, or a room at one of London's many clubs, and chosen a simple bedsit on the outskirts of the city, simply because she wanted to be alone. Her peers didn't know what to make of her. She'd been ordered to abandon ship, to abandon her commanding officer, and yet they judged her for leaving him behind. One did not abandon one's comrades, they said, even if one was ordered to do so. Staci knew she'd feel the same way, if she was in their shoes, although she knew it wouldn't make a difference. Captain Mitch Campbell, Staci's friend and mentor, had gone down with his ship. All she could have done, if she'd stayed, was add one more name to the final casualty list.

And he told me to go, she thought. She felt guilty, even though she *had* obeyed her commander's orders. She'd had commanders she hadn't really respected, men and women who had never inspired loyalty, but Captain Campbell had been a good man, even if he *had* been fucking a married woman. *I had to do as I was ordered.*

The thought hurt as she stared around the cramped room. She'd spent the last nine months, after her return to Earth, standing in front of a Board of Inquiry and answering their questions...the same questions, time and time again. It felt like torture, even though she understood the logic. It was supposed to be hard to maintain a consistent lie if one was constantly asked the same questions, slightly differently phrased every time. She suspected that wasn't the real reason. If the Board had thought she *was* lying, they had the right—and the duty—to pump her full of truth drugs and ask her questions while the tech monitored her brainwaves to make sure the drugs were working. No, she was sure they were drawing the inquiry out as long as possible, simply because of the political implications. Staci snorted at the thought as she clambered out of bed, feeling old despite her relative youth. If Captain Campbell had kept it in his pants, perhaps his death and his ship's destruction would have passed unremarked. Perhaps...

He told you to remain in the navy and, when you reached command, stay there as long as possible, she reminded herself. Her former CO's last message had been both affectionate and stern, telling her to put her own career first. *And never ever give up.*

She staggered into the tiny washroom and glared at herself in the mirror. The face looking back at her didn't feel like *hers*. Blonde hair, blue eyes, a trim yet muscular body...she'd put on a little weight, she noted sourly, because she hadn't kept herself in shape. She'd allowed her hair to grow out, when it had dawned on her she wasn't going to be reassigned to a new ship in a hurry...she ran her hand through her chin-length curls, wondering if it was worth getting it cropped short again. The navy didn't encourage long hairstyles. They got in the way when one had to throw on a spacesuit in a tearing hurry.

Her nightmare flickered at the back of her mind as she stepped into the shower, washed hurriedly and then clambered out before the water could shut off. London was still in lockdown, the water—and everything else—rationed to ensure everyone had enough to eat, drink, and wash. It didn't bother her that much—the navy rationed water even though there was no shortage of ice asteroids that could be mined—but she'd read endless complaints on the datanet. The civvies believed the war was over. Staci wished they were right. Sure, the virus's space fleet had been destroyed, but there were still hundreds of infections right across the Human Sphere and beyond.

They just want it to end, Staci told herself. *And who can blame them?*

She flicked the wall-mounted screen on as she returned to the bedroom and started to dress. The BBC was as bland and boring as ever, talking heads pontificating about politics and the endless debate in the House of Commons over who—if anyone—should succeed Prime Minister Harrison and lead Great Britain into the post-war world. Staci rolled her eyes as they brought on a series of academics, none of whom had any experience of the real world nor any awareness of just how unworkable their suggestions actually *were*. One might as well wave a magic wand, chant some bastardised Latin, and expect it to work. She dismissed the thought as she finished dressing, then forced herself to watch a mindless show about navy life, silently listing the many inaccuracies in the show. She'd reached fifty-seven when her wristcom bleeped, informing her she had an appointment with the First Space Lord in two hours. She sighed as she stood, keying her wristcom to call a taxi. The Board of Inquiry had probably reached its decision.

And that could be either good or bad, she thought. She'd had the feeling the verdict was already done and dusted, before the inquiry had started, but that hadn't stopped the assembled officers from giving her a very hard time. Bastards. They'd had plenty of time to review the records well before she'd returned to Earth. They had no real cause to give her a dishonourable discharge, or even a black mark in her file. *If the Admiral herself is speaking to me…*

She put the thought out of her mind as she checked she had her wristcom and pistol, then made her way downstairs. The bedsit appeared empty, no one manning the desk in the tiny lobby. She knew it was an illusion. The people who rented such rooms—often for little more than an hour or two—wanted privacy, without any real social interaction. Everything was electronic. There was no such thing as room service and she wouldn't have trusted it if there had. The rooms were so unclean she dreaded to think what might come out of their kitchens. The only upside was that reporters couldn't track her down.

The taxi was waiting. She climbed inside and forced herself to relax during the drive into London, passing through a handful of military and police checkpoints before finally reaching Whitehall. There were fewer with every passing month, she noted, although it hadn't stopped the civvies complaining. Staci understood their point. She was used to passing through endless checkpoints, when making her way from one posting to another, but it was irritating to have to show her papers time and time again. And yet, there was no choice. A single zombie could cause no end of havoc, if he got into Central London without being detected. Staci had seen the statistics. Better to endure some minor inconvenience than get infected and killed.

Perhaps on the streets, perhaps in a hospital bed, she thought, coldly. There were ways to purge the virus from a host's body, but they were sometimes fatal. *The civilians don't understand how hard it is, even with modern medicine, to cure the infection.*

She put the thought out of her mind as the taxi stopped outside the Admiralty Building to let her disembark. A uniformed aide saluted, then led her down a series of corridors—and two more checkpoints—into an antechamber. Staci had expected to be told to wait, to cool her heels to show her who was *really* in charge, but instead she was shown straight into the admiral's office. She stood to attention and saluted. Admiral Lady Susan Onarina was one of the few flag officers who'd enjoyed Captain Campbell's unstinting respect. Her record spoke for itself.

"Commander," Lady Susan said. "Thank you for coming. Tea? Coffee?"

Staci relaxed, slightly. The offer of a drink was a clear sign she wasn't in trouble, although she wasn't out of the woods yet. The admirals would be looking for *someone* to blame for *Unicorn's* destruction; and her commanding officer was dead, his body nothing more than atoms orbiting an alien star. Staci doubted they could make her a scapegoat, but they could make life very hard if they'd decided she'd been technically in command of the frigate during its final moments. She knew officers who'd landed in hot water because they'd been technically in command, but never been aware they were the senior survivor until it was too late.

The aide brought her a cup of tea, then withdrew silently. Staci studied the admiral thoughtfully, waiting for her to speak. Lady Susan was a dark-skinned woman, her hair slowly shading to grey. Staci felt a twinge of sympathy. Lady Susan had been a starship commander, but now she was flying a desk in London, the uniformed head of the Royal Navy who was permanently accountable to politicians who knew little about how the navy really worked. It couldn't be an easy position, no matter the honours regularly poured upon the incumbent. Staci wanted to climb the ladder, but perhaps not *that* high.

"The Board of Inquiry has finished its deliberations," Lady Susan informed her. "They have ruled that you are personally blameless in the loss of HMS *Unicorn* and, in fact, following the orders you were given by your CO was the right course of action. The tactical analysts will be debating the precise course of the final battle for many years to come, I fear, but their conclusions will not affect you personally. Captain Campbell's final report on you, filed before he departed on his final mission, included a recommendation for you to be promoted to captain as soon as possible and given your own ship. I have chosen to accept his recommendation."

Staci's breath caught in her throat. She'd known she was blameless, but…her career might have suffered, just for spending so much of the last couple of years as Captain Campbell's XO. The man had had powerful enemies. It would have been easy for one of them to insist his recommendations were worthless, that Staci might even have picked up bad habits from her former CO. Who knew? Some senior officers, no longer in touch with the realities of naval life, became political creatures, fighting bitter bureaucratic wars rather than concentrating on what was really important. And they might have casually destroyed her career in passing.

The admiral smiled. "You are being given HMS *Endeavour*," she added. "And we have a very specific mission for you."

Staci blinked. *Endeavour*? A deep-space survey ship, if she remembered correctly. Her class had never been particularly popular, not when they were intended to serve as both military and civilian vessels. The Royal Navy had done its best to keep survey ships and crews isolated from the rest of the fleet, although—with an increasing need to find newer tramlines -prospective admirals often served a term on a survey ship before they were promoted. And *she* was being given a survey ship? She wasn't sure if it was a sign the admirals thought she'd join them one day or a cunning plan to get her out of their hair. Before the war, it had been common for survey ships to spend years away from home.

"I...thank you," she managed. A survey ship...it would be something *different*. And yet, she was sure there were more qualified officers. She'd spent most of her career on frigates and gunboats, not capital ships. "What do you want me to do?"

Lady Susan smiled again, perhaps recognising the unspoken question. "Tell me...did you hear anything about the alien artefact discovered at Virus Prime?"

"Yes, Admiral." Staci had no trouble recalling the details. "I was told it would be studied properly after the war."

"Quite." Lady Susan leaned forward, slightly. "Unfortunately, too many people on both *Lion* and *Unicorn* were aware of the artefact's discovery. They certainly heard rumours, rumours that—as always—grew increasingly wild as they moved from mouth to mouth. We were careful, in line with protocols devised after the first hint there *was* an ancient and very powerful race out there, to try to limit word spreading from place to place, but we may have been unsuccessful. We don't know how many unfriendly powers may have heard the stories."

Staci frowned. "If the stories are *that* wild, Admiral, surely they won't be believed."

"We hope not, yet we don't know," Lady Susan said. "You can read the reports later—I've had you cleared for them—but right now, all you need to know is that an alien starchart was discovered within the artefact under odd and slightly unclear circumstances. If it is accurate, we may know where to find the alien homeworld. Your mission is to travel to the alien homeworld and, if possible, attempt to make contact. Your orders are a little vague, I'm afraid, because we don't know what you'll find. You'll have considerable freedom to proceed as you see fit."

Because I'll be travelling well outside the flicker network, Staci thought. *I'll have a truly independent command.*

She schooled her face into impassivity. It was hard not to feel a twinge of excitement, mingled with unease and fear. She knew the basic parameters of interstellar combat, as laid down by the known spacefaring races. There were few true surprises. But unknown tech, from an unknown race...who knew what it could do? Who knew what certainties would vanish, as if they'd never been, in the face of technology she didn't have the slightest idea was even possible? Her imagination provided quite a few possible answers. Who knew what was so far beyond her imagination that it would blindside her completely, if it was deployed against her?

"We don't know much of anything about the Builders," Lady Susan said. "We know they were watching the virus, Captain, and we know they had some means of keeping it in check, preventing it from trying to overwhelm their installations. We know they left a large artefact behind, something we cannot even begin to understand. Beyond that, all we really have is speculation. Did they create the virus? Did they let it go or...or did it break free of their control? Or...or what? We don't know. We dare not assume their motives are friendly."

"If they are unfriendly," Staci pointed out, "we may be...screwed."

"They may do us a great deal of harm, just by existing," Lady Susan said. "Our existence did the Vesy no favours, when they finally realised just how advanced we were. There have been hundreds of complications, from them trying to discard their old ways and embracing ours to demands for newer and better weapons, medical technology and everything else we can offer them. In a sense, their society may have hit a brick wall and stopped dead, the moment the Russians landed on their world. They are steadily losing the ability to innovate for themselves—and why should they, why should they even try, when we already have all the answers? The same could happen to us. It *has* happened, in the past."

"Not on such a big scale," Staci said.

"No," Lady Susan agreed. "But contact between two very unequal societies has always been painful, even when there is no hostile intent. We know a great deal about how the universe works, and we were capable of using what we knew to catch up with the first aliens we encountered. But what will happen to us when the gulf is so wide as to be beyond all hope of jumping across, before it is too late? That's another reason for sending you out alone, Captain. If you encounter something beyond our ability to accept, word will not spread beyond the handful of people already involved in the project."

"It seems unlikely," Staci said.

"We don't know," Lady Susan said. "What if we encounter an alien race so advanced they just need to snap their fingers to do anything? What if we encounter a race of pure telepaths, who can read our thoughts effortlessly? What happens if they know there's life after death, or think their religion is the one true faith, or something—anything—that will disrupt our society and damage it beyond all hope of repair? We have to plan for the worst, without even being sure our thinking *can* encompass the worst."

"I see your problem," Staci said. Her stomach churned. "How do we know they're not already watching us?"

"We don't," Lady Susan said, flatly. "And because we know nothing about them, we don't know what they'll find objectionable. Not yet."

Staci nodded, grimly. The idea of being watched by alien minds was unpleasant, even though she'd spent most of her life in the navy, where there was no such thing as privacy. It was rare for a pervert to take advantage of it and, if one did, she knew how to deal with it. But watching aliens? She hoped they were just being paranoid. They might never know for sure.

"I understand," she said. "I won't let you down."

"I'm sure of it," Lady Susan said, passing Staci a datachip. "Your orders. A shuttle flight has already been organised to get you to your new command. Once you assume command, prepare for departure. I want you ready to depart by the time the ambassadorial and xenospecialist staffs arrive."

"Understood," Staci said. She felt a thrill of excitement, even if they were plunging into the unknown. "We'll be ready."

CHAPTER TWO:
LONDON, UNITED KINGDOM

THE STATUE DIDN'T LOOK LIKE HIM.

Lady Charlotte Hammond stood under the column, wrapped in a scarf that protected her identity from prying eyes and studied the statue sourly. Mitch Campbell had never been a particularly handsome man, although he'd had a certain charm—and *liveliness*—about him that had more than made up for the deficiency. Charlotte had grown up amongst the aristocracy. She'd known hundreds of boys and girls who'd body-shaped themselves before even reaching puberty, making themselves so stunningly handsome or beautiful that it had been common, then creepy. Their adult selves had lacked for nothing but character. They'd been boring, so boring Charlotte had been reluctant to spend any time with them. Mitch, on the other hand…

He told me he regretted nothing, she thought. Mitch's last message to her had been short and surprisingly sweet, for a man who knew he was going into harm's way…she wondered, not for the first time, if he'd had a premonition of his own death. *And that I should live my life to the full.*

She sighed, as a wave of despondency overcame her. She'd had no illusions about herself. She'd spent too long running her husband's estates to let herself hide behind self-deception. She knew she'd set out to build something for herself, to make a career that would give her a chance to be someone in her own right, not just the daughter of one aristocrat and the wife of another. She knew she'd hurt her husband badly, along with her daughters, and yet…she'd spent so long submerging her own ambitions and carrying out her family duty that she found it hard to care. Didn't she deserve something of her own? When was it going to be *her* time to shine? And…she shook her head, trying to resist the urge to curse herself, or to blame everything on her lover. She'd known what she was doing. She couldn't hide anything from herself, no matter what she hid from others.

And if he hadn't died, she mused, *I could have built one hell of a career.*

She held the image in her mind for a long moment, considering it. She wouldn't have held any public post, nor would she have tried to win elections. Captain Campbell, war hero, would have been the public face, while she pulled the strings and quietly built up a reputation of her own. She would have held power, real power…she dismissed the tantalising image. Her lover had died, saving—irony of ironies—her husband's life. And she was alone.

Her datapad vibrated, once. She ignored it. She'd burnt her bridges, chopped off the branch before realising—too late—that she was sitting on the wrong side of the cut. Her husband would hardly take her back, not after his public humiliation. She didn't even *want* to go back. Her daughters might not disown her, but…they wouldn't understand. Not unless they went through the same experience themselves. And they might, if their marriages were arranged by their father. Lord Hammond was a good man—Charlotte conceded as much, at least in the privacy of her own thoughts—but he was a very *limited* man. Military men tended to be unwilling to bend, unwilling to think about conceding something in the short term to gain a long-term advantage. It was why she'd planned to ensure she held the reins, as Captain Campbell started his political career. She would have taken him right to the top.

She shook her head, feeling a glimmer of frustration. She'd trapped herself, as surely as Lady Hamilton had put herself outside the boundaries of polite society after Lord Nelson's death. There were no invitations waiting in her inbox, no parties or gatherings or even private chats. Once, there'd been so many she could pick and choose as she pleased, showing favour or withholding it at will. Now...she resisted the urge to check her bank balance again. She knew it was dangerously low. Her trust fund was almost exhausted. She had no other sources of income, not even alimony, now that the political edifice she'd built was crumbling in the wake of her figurehead's death. She scowled in annoyance. She'd thrilled to the idea of throwing together something fragile, yet daring. She'd liked the idea of having to constantly improvise to keep her ramshackle edifice together. In hindsight, it had been a mistake. She really should have considered the possibility her lover would never come home.

The thought mocked her. Affairs, private affairs, were a given in High Society. No one cared, as long as they stayed firmly out of the public eye. She could have had any pretty-boy she wanted, anyone who...she shook her head. They hadn't been exciting. The idea of going to bed with them was about as thrilling as the idea of scratching her head. Mitch...oh, there'd been one hell of a thrill in bedding him. She'd loved every minute of wantonness, every moment she'd thrown caution to the winds and fucked him. And yet...it had bitten her. Hard. She knew, now, there was no way home. The last of her influence was fading quickly. Once it was gone, it would be the end. She had nowhere to go.

And I'm probably about to get my marching orders, she thought, sourly. *The PM's message left no room for doubt.*

She straightened, reminding herself she came from a long line of aristocrats who'd survived for nearly a thousand years, and started to walk towards Whitehall. Hardly anyone paid any attention to her, something that amused and irritated her in equal measure. Charlotte knew she was notorious, yet...who cared? She was yesterday's news, her story little more than sensationalist drivel that had run its course. Mitch Campbell had been a great man in life, a war hero feted by all; now that he was gone, his lover was of little importance. It was just a matter of time until she vanished completely. Why *should* anyone pay attention to her, if they saw her on the streets? If they recognised her, they'd pretend otherwise. They wouldn't want to be accused of paying attention to a has-been. The world had moved on.

The thought mocked her as she turned the corner and approached the checkpoint. There'd been a time when she'd been driven through, without having to stop and show her papers. Those days were gone too. She pressed her fingers against the scanner, allowing it to take a droplet of blood to check for infection, then waited for the policemen to confirm she *had* been invited to Downing Street. It galled her to wait, as if she was a prospective governess presenting herself at the tradesman's entrance. She would have been happier, perversely, if she'd thought it was deliberate, that someone was making her wait to put her firmly in her place. But she knew she'd fallen too far for anyone to bother. It was a minor miracle the PM had even bothered to summon her.

He either got the hints I sowed, or he wants to tell me to step out of society personally, she thought. She doubted it was the latter, although the former had been one hell of a long shot. It wasn't uncommon for political undesirables to be reassigned somewhere that looked prestigious—in reality, an excuse to get them out of the country—but she had a lot of political enemies. The PM's position wasn't as solid as he would prefer. *If my enemies demanded that he tell me to leave personally...*

Her heart sank as she was shown through the gates, then up to Ten Downing Street and into the waiting room. She just wasn't that important. She'd made a fool of herself, fallen so far that there was no point in driving her any further out of society. She could barely sustain herself, let alone rebuild her position. Her enemies didn't need to burn up their political capital, just to kick her when she was down. All they had to do was wait and watch the world do it for them. She'd be begging in the gutters shortly, if she tried to stay in London. She wondered, idly, if it might not be time to run up the white flag and try to negotiate some kind of settlement with her husband. If she agreed to leave quietly...

The steward brought her a cup of tea, then retreated. Charlotte sipped it carefully, trying not to show her impatience. There were no visible cameras in the waiting room, but that didn't mean they weren't there. Just having to wait was a mocking reminder of just how far she'd fallen. A year ago, the PM would have seen her instantly. A year ago...she'd been a mover and shaker, spending money like water to build influence and power. Now...

Forget the past, she told herself, savagely. *Concentrate on the future.*

An aide, a young blonde woman, stepped into the room. "The Prime Minister will see you now."

Charlotte stood, putting the cup to one side. "Thank you."

The aide said nothing as she led Charlotte through the maze of corridors. Charlotte scowled inwardly. The young woman wouldn't have been there, in the very heart of government, if she wasn't clever and perceptive. She wasn't fawning on Charlotte, which boded ill for the future. And yet... Charlotte dismissed the thought with a flicker of irritation. The young woman was only a few years older than Charlotte's daughters. The idea she'd have any real say in national policy was thoroughly absurd.

She composed herself, standing proudly as she was shown into the PM's office. Arthur Harrison stood to greet her, holding out a hand for her to shake as though she was an honoured guest. Charlotte doubted it. If the PM had seen her as anything other than just another person he had to deal with, he would have had her shown to his private reception room, where they could have had a much less formal discussion. She supposed she should count herself lucky they were having any sort of meeting. She was in such bad odour it would have been easy for the PM to quietly ignore her until she ran out of money and went away.

"Lady Charlotte," the PM said. "Thank you for coming."

Charlotte nodded, studying him thoughtfully. Arthur Harrison looked tired, tired and worn. He'd led Britain through the war, but now the population wanted the peace dividend yesterday, if not the day before. And it was pretty much impossible. Charlotte knew the only reason the Leader of the Opposition hadn't pushed for a Vote of Confidence, which would have led quickly to a general election, was the fear of having to tell the public their demands simply couldn't be met. It had to be galling to know the only reason you were still in office was because no one wanted your job. Charlotte wondered, idly, if the PM was already lining up his replacement. The country would have to have an election in eighteen months anyway and it might be better if the party was led by a younger, more charismatic, leader.

But they don't want to be encumbered either, she told herself. *They'd sooner have him make all the unpopular decisions, then try to take his place.*

"I was very sorry to hear of Captain Campbell's death," the PM continued. "He was a good man."

"He was," Charlotte said, resisting the urge to point out that he'd been effectively sanctified in death. The PM and everyone else could deliver all the eulogies they wanted, talking about a saint rather than a living breathing man, warts and all. It wouldn't have been so easy if Captain Campbell had returned home. "The country owes him a vast debt."

"Yes." Arthur Harrison met her eyes, coldly. "I trust you'll understand if I speak bluntly?"

"Of course," Charlotte said. She'd never had much patience for the iron fist in the velvet glove. If one was going to crush someone's hopes and dreams, one could at least have the courtesy not to pretend they were doing one a favour. "I will understand."

The PM said nothing for a long moment, then spoke with quiet deliberateness. "You attempted to build up a political machine that would propel you, and your paramour, into the heights of power. You did, in fact, use the machine to convince the government to send reinforcements to Virus Prime, which played a major role in fighting the final battle of the war. However, with Captain Campbell's death, and your own disgrace, your machine is flailing itself to death. Your supporters are edging away and your future lies in ruins."

Charlotte nodded curtly, hiding a flicker of amusement. Her own assessment of the situation was considerably worse. Her supporters weren't edging away—they'd *edged* away. She supposed it was possible they wouldn't be too overt about it—no one liked a traitor, even if edging away was the poor bastard's best move—but she doubted they'd give her more than lip service, if she asked. She hadn't tried, not really. The quickest way to undermine one's position was to give an order you knew might not be obeyed.

"This gives us an interesting problem," the PM continued. "We are trying to rebuild after the war. We don't need political scandals or high-profile divorces, with everyone taking sides and political coalitions rupturing. Your husband's enemies are already licking their lips, considering the chaos that might follow in your wake. We don't need that either."

"No," Charlotte agreed.

"It is important, therefore, to get you out of the country," the PM said. "We are prepared to offer you a position as titular head of a diplomatic mission, with a salary to match. You will, of course, have a staff who will do most of the actual work."

Charlotte's eyes narrowed. Ambassadors were often chosen for domestic policy reasons, rather than practical or diplomatic ones. They were little more than the public face of the country they represented, while their staff—as the PM had said—did the work. It wasn't uncommon, too, for an ambassador to take the fall if something went spectacularly wrong, but even then the ambassador would be pensioned off rather than simply sacked. She knew at least two ambassadors who'd had to carry the can for failures of government policy, but allowed to go into paid retirement to keep them from making a fuss. It crossed her mind to wonder if she was being set up, but it was unlikely. The PM didn't have to go so far if he wanted her to wind up with egg on her face.

"A tempting offer," she said. Where did they want her to go? America? France? It was unlikely it would be any major power, let alone an alien homeworld. Perhaps it would be Argentina. It would be an uncomfortable posting even if she wasn't expected to do more than chat about nothing, every so often. "Where do you have in mind?"

"Deep space," the PM said. "We may have a lead on another spacefaring alien race."

"And you want to send *me* as ambassador," Charlotte said, in disbelief. "Me?"

The PM explained, quickly. Charlotte had to fight to keep her face expressionless. The mission was…she honestly didn't know if she wanted to laugh or cry. If the alien race was dead and gone, she'd be out of the system for months…if not years. The country would move on, forgetting her. And if the alien race was still around, trying to make contact would be extremely difficult. Her staff would do all the legwork and probably get all the credit.

And there aren't that many xeno-trained ambassadors, she mused. The Foreign Office had plenty of xenospecialists, but ambassadors rarely had a xenospecialist background. *The ones we have are needed on homeworlds we* know *are alive and kicking.*

Her thoughts churned. If she accepted the offer, she'd have a chance to rebuild her reputation…or, at least, give the country a chance to forget her. And she'd be paid a healthy salary. If she refused…she doubted there'd be a second opportunity. The PM clearly thought he could take the risk of sending her on the mission. Hell, it wasn't *that* big a risk. If the Builders were dead and gone, she'd just be dead weight. If they were still around, her staff would do the hard work while she just sat at the table and pretended to work. She wondered, idly, if the Builders would know or care she was in disgrace. Somehow, she doubted it. Human politics meant very little to its alien allies and vice versa.

"The mission is due to depart shortly," the PM said. "Certain classified files will only be made available to you once you have accepted the assignment, at which point you will be bound by the terms of the Official Secrets Act. I need an answer shortly, ideally by the end of the day. If you decline the assignment, I'll have to look for someone else."

If you can find someone, Charlotte thought, coldly. *The assignment is unlikely to win anyone any plaudits.*

She had to admire the PM's gall. None of her enemies could object to sending her hundreds of light-years away from Earth. Her friends, such as they were, would probably be relieved. He'd get rid of a tricky little problem...the only downside, for him, would be that he couldn't put one of his cronies in the post, but even that worked in his favour. Who *wanted* to be so far from the corridors of power? And with little chance of actually making contact...

Everyone would know I'd been sent into exile, she thought. *But it might just give me a chance to pause and reboot my career.*

"I accept," she said. "I'll have to talk to the lawyers, to finalise everything, but I am happy to take on the assignment."

"Good." The PM smiled. "My staff will make the arrangements. They'll see to your supplies and transport to the ship. You'll leave in two days."

Charlotte nodded. "You move fast."

"Yes," the PM said. "It's only a matter of time before someone else realises what we've found. We need to know what we're dealing with before the rest of the world gets involved."

CHAPTER THREE:
HMS ENDEAVOUR, SOL SYSTEM

"CAPTAIN?"

Staci jerked awake, shaking her head as the shuttle glided towards its destination. It had been a busy few hours, before her departure from Heathrow Spaceport. The promotion ceremony had been thrown together on short notice, giving her almost no time to call her parents before her new pips were pinned on her collar and she was rushed to the spaceport. She wasn't sure if she'd have time to write a message to her family, certainly not one that wouldn't pass through the censors before it was allowed onto the datanet. Thankfully, they knew—now—that the Board of Inquiry had declared her personally blameless. They wouldn't have to keep deflecting questions when people asked about their daughter's career.

She rubbed her forehead, forcing herself to sit up. The shipyard ahead of them was a blaze of lights, hanging in the inky darkness of interplanetary space. It felt like yesterday when it had been attacked, enemy ships trying to take out humanity's ability to produce ships, starfighters and missiles to fight its battles. There were hundreds of ships within sensor range, all hastily being refitted in preparation for the next war. Staci liked to think the human race had entered a time of peace and prosperity, but she doubted it. The virus was still out there, even though it was no longer spacefaring. Who knew what *else* was out there too?

"We are making our final approach to *Endeavour* now," the pilot informed her. "Do you want me to orbit the hull before we dock?"

"Please," Staci said.

She braced herself as one collection of running lights seemed to grow sharper. She had no idea when she'd have a chance to see her ship's exterior again. She'd never held command in her own right, not until now, but she knew how much work her former commanders had had to do. She was going to be very busy, just handling matters that couldn't be passed down to her XO. It was funny, she reflected, how the movies trying to convince youngsters to join the navy never showed the paperwork. It was all action and adventure, with laser blasts and starfighter battles and heroes so heroic they never so much as got their hair mussed. Staci supposed she couldn't blame the producers. If she'd known how much paperwork she'd have to do, as she climbed the ladder, she might have thought twice about a naval career too.

Or perhaps not, she thought, as HMS *Endeavour* came into view. *If I'd become an accountant, I wouldn't have a command of my own.*

The blaze of lights suddenly resolved into a starship, illuminated by spotlights mounted on remote work platforms. Staci leaned forward, drinking in the details. *Endeavour* was over three hundred meters long, her hull seemingly rough and crude compared to a cruiser or battleship. Most human ships were modular, but sheathed in armour; *Endeavour* seemed almost naked, as if her interior was exposed to enemy fire. Staci reminded herself, not for the first time, that it made a great deal of sense. *Endeavour* wasn't expected to stand in the line of battle. Instead, her crew needed access to carry out repairs hundreds of light-years from the nearest shipyard. The thought made her grimace. Mounting deep-strike missions into enemy territory had been hard enough, back during the war. Now, they were going to be travelling even further.

She smiled as her eyes picked out the shuttles and landers docked to the starship's hull. *Endeavour* wasn't that different from *Lion*, at least in some respects. The docking ring looked larger, more generalist than the battlecruiser's, but the basic principle was the same. She wondered, suddenly, which one had come first. The battlecruiser's design had had its weaknesses, back in the war, but…she shook her head. *Endeavour* wasn't a warship. She was designed to evade enemy contact, rather than snipe at enemy ships from long range.

And we want to make peaceful contact, if possible, she told herself. *We don't want to find ourselves at war with a super-race.*

The shuttle levelled out and glided towards the command hatch. Staci braced herself, feeling a thrill matched with an odd sense of trepidation. She'd always assumed her first command would be a frigate, a ship she knew from top to bottom. It was rare for a frigate officer to be promoted straight into a command post on a capital ship. She wondered, suddenly, if the survey crews would resent her. They might have preferred someone with experience in survey work, rather than a cross-promoted officer. She would have to work hard to earn their trust. It wouldn't be easy.

She waited for the gravity field to shiver and stabilise, then stood, picked up her knapsack and headed for the hatch. She'd always travelled light. There'd been little room for personal possessions on *Unicorn*, even for the ship's XO. She made a mental note to make sure she had everything she needed in the ship's stores, just in case. She'd been in the navy long enough to know better to than to assume the bureaucracy would take care of it. It wouldn't be the first time a transfer was organised so quickly the poor officer wound up without a spare uniform. She'd once had to share one of her spares with a lieutenant who hadn't brought a spare with him.

The hatch hissed open. Staci stepped through and pressed her hand against the bioscanner inside the airlock. There was a long pause—she was *sure* they'd made it longer than it needed to be—and then the inner hatch opened, allowing her to board her ship for the first time. A wave of warm air washed across her face, bringing the scent of too many humans in too close of a proximity. *Endeavour* wasn't a new-build ship, Staci recalled. Her refit hadn't been anything like as extensive as her previous CO would have preferred. She made a mental note to check the air scrubbers, as well as everything else. She was going to have to spend the next few days crawling over the entire ship, just to make sure she knew where everything was. A CO who didn't know her own ship was asking for trouble.

"Captain," a young man said. "I'm Commander Mike Jenner. Welcome onboard HMS *Endeavour*."

Staci nodded, then shook his hand. Commander Jenner was older than she'd expected, although—if she recalled correctly—promotion was *always* slower in survey. He was a light-skinned man with brown hair, slowly shading to grey, wearing a simple shipsuit and gloves. She made a mental note to read his file as quickly as possible, just in case there were any unexpected surprises waiting. It was unlikely Jenner would have been left in his post, if there were any suggestions he wasn't capable of handling the job, but it was important to be sure. She sighed, inwardly. Jenner would be more than human if he didn't feel a twinge of resentment at her being promoted over his head, not if he'd been in the navy longer than she. She'd have to keep an eye on that too.

"Thank you," she said. "It's good to be here."

Jenner nodded and led her along the corridor. "We've finished most of the refit," he explained, as they passed a series of open hatches and work gangs pulling old components out of the bulkheads and replacing them. "The finishing touches are being completed now, Captain, and we should be ready to depart as planned."

Staci nodded. "What were you doing during the war?"

"Probing possible tramlines leading into enemy space, mostly," Jenner explained. "We found a pair of dead worlds, and three more so heavily infected that there was no hope of saving the local population. The tramlines themselves were hardly worth exploiting, or so we thought. We never had the chance to find out."

"No," Staci agreed. "Did you encounter the enemy fleet?"

"No." Jenner shrugged. "We stayed well clear of anything that might detect us. We had a nasty moment in one system, where we thought they might have caught a sniff of us, but they never gave chase. We decided, after a series of evasive manoeuvres that were designed to force a cloaked opponent to reveal himself, that we'd either been wrong or they decided it wasn't worth coming after us. It was never easy to know which way they'd jump."

Staci couldn't disagree. The virus had been the most alien of humanity's alien enemies, its thinking—if indeed it thought at all—so inhuman there was no way its actions could be easily predicted. Staci had read the discussion papers, some arguing the virus's behaviour was entirely instinctive, others insisting it was a single vast entity and cared as little for billions of infected bodies as humans cared about their skin cells and nail clippings; she knew, from experience, it simply didn't matter. The war had been total, ruthless on a scale that dwarfed anything in human history. They'd had to win or lose everything. She wondered, as they boarded the intership car and headed to the bridge, how long it would be before people who'd never been at risk started insisting the virus was just misunderstood. Not long, if she was any judge.

The hatch opened, revealing the bridge. Staci stared. It was bigger than a frigate's bridge and more modular, with consoles scattered all over the compartment rather than carefully organised to allow the CO to sit in the middle and draw information from every station. That might have to change, she thought. The survey ship might have been put together by a military shipyard, but she'd clearly been designed by a civilian. If she couldn't get used to the layout, it *would* have to change. She dared not risk confusion when the shit hit the fan.

And we are going into the unknown, she thought, taking a long breath. The crew looked professional, but casual. *We might fly straight into an alien ambush and get fired upon before we know what is happening.*

Staci stepped forward, onto the bridge. Eyes followed her as she made her way to the command chair and sat. It felt…different. She'd sat in Captain Campbell's chair, when she'd taken command of his ship, but this was hers. She ran her hand along the console, silently noting how it had been customised for survey command. Whoever had done the layout had changed everything, to the point she knew she'd have to switch it back to the regular version. Customised console layouts were forbidden on warships. There was no way to guarantee the right officer would be at the right console when the shit hit the fan.

She looked up at Jenner, standing beside her chair. "I relieve you."

"I stand relieved," Jenner said, tonelessly.

Staci nodded. It was hard to tell if he was pleased or resentful or merely unbothered by the whole affair. Jenner probably wouldn't have stayed in survey if he'd wanted rapid promotion. The war had killed a *lot* of officers, leaving plenty of room for younger men to climb the ladder at a terrifying rate. Staci knew a dozen officers who'd jumped up so rapidly that, in peacetime, it would have been seen as a sign of rampant nepotism. Or worse. Now…she smiled, wondering how many of their comrades would see them as bad luck. Spacers were often more superstitious than groundpounders. They knew how easy it was for something to go spectacularly wrong.

She keyed her console, bringing up the status display. *Endeavour* wasn't ready to depart, not yet, but she was getting there. Her weapons and sensors were being checked and rechecked, her crew drilling endlessly to make sure they knew how to use the advanced technology at their fingertips. It was odd to realise that the survey ship's sensors were far superior to anything she'd used before, yet inferior to advanced alien tech. They might as well have been sticks and stones. Staci remembered what she'd been told about the risks of alien contact, and shivered. The last thing humanity needed was a racial inferiority complex.

"I have to explore the ship," she said, standing. "You have the bridge."

"Yes, Captain," Jenner said. "You also have some private messages in your ready room."

Staci nodded curtly, then stepped through the hatch. The ready room felt uncomfortably large, even though it was tiny compared to the admiral's office on Earth. She felt oddly guilty for having so much space devoted to her, after using her tiny cabin on *Unicorn* as an office. But then, *Unicorn* had been a frigate with hardly any space for the crew. *Endeavour* was large enough to ensure everyone had a proper cabin, although the junior crew would still be doubling up. Staci smiled, reflecting—not for the first time—that the bigger the ship, the smaller the space set aside for junior officers and crew. It was practically navy policy.

They don't want a young midshipman to have a big cabin on a battleship, then move to a hot bunk on a frigate, she thought. *That might cause discontent.*

She sat at the desk and pressed her hand against the terminal, allowing herself a moment of relief as the screen lit up. It was silly, but she hadn't felt like a commanding officer until she'd unlocked the terminal herself. The CO's terminal was strictly for the CO's use only, the regulation enforced so strictly that no one—not even the CO himself—could grant anyone else permission to use it. She understood the reasoning behind it—the CO was often the only person onboard cleared for certain files and messages—but it was still a potential headache if her XO had to take command in a hurry. They might *need* access to the former CO's private datacore.

The messages appeared in front of her, a handful of orders, reports from Virus Prime and a set of refit updates that had been copied to Commander Jenner. None were marked urgent, so Staci took a moment to read Jenner's file first. There was nothing particularly special inside it, no commendations or reprimands or anything else that might suggest he wasn't as good an officer as the file suggested. Staci had had plenty of experience in reading between the lines, of spotting reports that were carefully written to hint at dangers without ever coming out and saying them. There were no hints in Jenner's file. The only real oddity was that he'd spent most of his early career on a deep-space monitoring station, rather than starting his climb up the ranks. But then, it probably explained why he wasn't a captain by now.

She shrugged, then brought up her orders. They were vague, something that pleased and disturbed her in equal measure. Proceed to Virus

Prime. Pick up the xenospecialists from the Sphere. Proceed to the system indicated in the alien starchart. If possible, survey the system from a safe distance before making any attempt to open contact…she frowned, noting how many weasel words were written into *that* section of the orders. Standard procedure was to make sure Earth was alerted *first* if a new alien race was discovered, before the survey ship tried to open communications. She suspected, reading between the lines, that whoever had written the orders feared retreat might be impossible. A hyper-advanced race might be able to detect a cloaked starship from hundreds of light-years away.

"And if they're that advanced," she muttered to herself, "there's no point in trying to hide anyway."

Her lips thinned. Humanity had been pumping out radio messages for nearly three hundred years. There was no way, now, to jam those messages, let alone keep them from being detected. Anyone with the right equipment, within range, would be able to detect the messages, even if they couldn't understand them. They'd know the human race was there… Staci frowned. There were stars within a hundred light-years of Earth that were completely inaccessible, unless one used a catapult or tried to cross the interstellar gulf at sublight speeds. Who knew what might be waiting there? Or what they might think of humanity?

She put the thought aside as she scanned the next set of orders, her thoughts crashing to a halt as they penetrated her brain. She'd known they'd be taking a diplomatic mission, just in case they encountered live aliens, but one headed by Lady Charlotte Hammond? It was unthinkable. Staci knew what Lady Charlotte had done to Mitch Campbell, as well as her husband. Why was *she* in command of the ambassadorial team? It was absurd!

Perhaps it's a different person, Staci told herself. *Charlotte is hardly an uncommon name.*

She worked her way through the rest of the orders, her thoughts churning. It couldn't be the same person, could it? Perhaps not…but it did hint it *was*. Lady Charlotte had been trying to build up her position in London, screwing her lover in every sense of the word. Staci grimaced in disgust. She'd actually told her CO he was letting his little head get his bigger head in deep shit. If he'd survived the deployment, who knew what would have happened afterwards? Somehow, Staci doubted it would have gone very well. Society took a dim view of women who left their husbands, if those husbands were in the military and fighting to save the homeworld from death or infection. Lady Charlotte was probably already in deep shit.

And she's going to be on my ship, Staci thought. *Fuck.*

She scowled, then stood. She had work to do. She had to explore her ship from top to bottom, to meet her crew and learn the ropes before it was time to depart. Lady Charlotte could wait. If she was the same person…

Orders are orders, Staci told herself, firmly. There was no point in trying to complain about the ambassador. The First Space Lord would not be impressed. *Hopefully, she'll just stay in her cabin and you won't have to put up with her.*

CHAPTER FOUR:
HMS ENDEAVOUR, SOL SYSTEM

"LADY CHARLOTTE," Ambassador Humphrey Paris-Jackson said. "Is this your first time off-world?"

"Yes." Charlotte felt sick, her stomach in knots even though the shuttle was travelling in a straight line. "I never even went to the moon before."

"It does affect some people like that," Paris-Jackson told her. "Keep swallowing and it will get better."

Charlotte gritted her teeth. Paris-Jackson wasn't her equal, according to the official paperwork, but he was an experienced diplomat. She suspected he'd been given private orders to override her, if he thought it necessary. Or…she wondered, sardonically, if Paris-Jackson had been expecting a more prestigious posting before he'd been assigned to her and her staff as a minder. She could easily imagine him in an embassy, speaking to his counterparts over lunch and hammering out details while his nominal superiors distracted public attention from the *real* diplomats. Who knew? Perhaps his career would suffer, if it turned out the cruise was nothing more than an expensive holiday. Or if he overruled her, only to be overruled in turn by his *real* superiors. She would have felt sorry for him, if her stomach hadn't been churning so badly. She wished she'd thought to fast before boarding the shuttle only an hour or so ago.

As long as I'm not a natural-born groundhog, she thought, crossly. There were people who simply couldn't endure life in space, even in a habitat in orbit or a settlement on the moon. *If I'm going to be sick every day, this mission is going to be over before it even begins.*

She gritted her teeth, then forced herself to return to the datapad. The idea of appointing her a diplomat wasn't *that* crazy, she had to admit. She had a *lot* of experience in being diplomatic, when she'd been running her husband's estates. The stakes were different—and higher—but the principles were the same. If you understood your counterpart's point of view, and the limitations they faced, you could make a series of very good guesses about what they actually wanted and how far they'd be prepared to go to get it. It was never easy—the papers had reminded her, time and time again, that she was a *British* diplomat—but it was doable. She was almost hopeful there would be someone to talk to at the far end, although she didn't have the slightest idea what they'd want. It was hard to bargain when you had nothing to bargain *with*.

The shuttle shuddered slightly, the gravity field washing over her like a wave on a beach. She swallowed hard, looking up as the hatch hissed open. Paris-Jackson and the rest of his team—five professional diplomats-in-training—stood and made their way onto the ship. Charlotte forced herself to stand and follow them, her legs quivering uneasily as she passed through the hatch and pressed her hand against the bioscanner. Her estranged husband—the divorce was still being finalised—had told her starships could be claustrophobic, for someone used to the open air. She realised, as the inner hatch opened, that he was right. The interior of the survey ship felt like the bunker beneath the family mansion, the bomb shelter some distant ancestor had emplaced when the world trembled under the threat of nuclear destruction. The only real difference, she noted as a middle-aged man greeted them, was that the corridors were brightly lit.

Her stomach calmed, slowly, as they were shown to their quarters and cautioned to remain inside unless they were summoned. Charlotte looked around, keeping her feelings under tight control. A year ago, she would have thought the cabins far too small for a lady of her standing. They were barely large enough to swing a cat. Now, she knew she was lucky to have a private washroom. Hell, she was lucky they had a private compartment to study their papers and run through the scenarios the admiralty's brain trust had put together. She wasn't sure what they'd been drinking or smoking when they'd devised their list of possible encounters, but her team had to take them seriously. If nothing else, it would stretch their minds.

"This is it?" Kari Potter was a young woman, barely starting her career. "I thought we'd have a proper cabin."

Paris-Jackson laughed, humourlessly. "If you go down to the crew compartments, you'll discover you have a very *good* cabin," he said. "You may be cramped, but you don't have to share."

Kari looked as if she didn't believe him. "But the ship is huge!"

"Yes," Paris-Jackson agreed. "And much of that space is consumed by the drives, the stores, the weapons and everything else. The remaining space is relatively tiny. Our cabins are amongst the best on the ship. Believe me, there aren't many officers who'll have better quarters. Here, at least, we have space to work."

Charlotte nodded as she stepped into her cabin and looked around. She'd been in worse places. Really, she had. The air was clean, smelling faintly of air freshener rather than anything less pleasant. She recalled boarding school and shuddered, the memories reminding her of things she'd sooner forget. It was hard to believe her parents had spent nearly a million pounds on her education. She should have been paid to attend that boarding school of horrors.

She sat on the bunk and composed herself. She was getting better. She would be fine, by the time the ship left the shipyard and headed to the tramline. She'd have plenty of time to brainstorm, to consider how best to handle any alien contacts…and her political future, when she returned home. It was unlikely she'd stay for the rest of her life, even if she did so well no one could hope to match her. The government would send a proper ambassador, without the sharply circumscribed powers she'd been given. And yet, if she returned a heroine...she allowed herself the fantasy, just for a moment, before standing and heading back into the main compartment. There was nothing to be gained by putting the cart before the horse. If she did well, she could think about her future afterwards.

And if this is just a very expensive cruise, I can spend it preparing for a new career, she told herself. *Or even planning to emigrate somewhere I can start afresh.*

Paris-Jackson caught her eye. "The captain has requested the pleasure of your company, at 1800," he said, holding up a datapad. "Do you wish me to accompany you?"

"No, thank you," Charlotte said, checking her wristcom. It was 1740. "Have our bags arrived yet?"

"No," Paris-Jackson told her. "They'll be put through the security sensors first."

Charlotte grimaced—normally, she didn't have to worry about her bags being opened and her clothes pawed—but reminded herself, not for the first time, that she didn't have anything to hide. She'd packed one good outfit, something she could wear to a diplomatic meeting, then filled the remaining space with simple tunics and underwear. The days of being a clotheshorse were long gone too. She keyed her wristcom to pull up a starship diagram, then headed for the hatch. If she started now, she should be at the captain's cabin well before 1800.

"The captain will send an escort," Paris-Jackson said, without looking up. "I suggest you wait for him."

Oh, you do, do you? Charlotte flushed. *And if I choose not to take your suggestion?*

She bit down, hard, on the flash of irritation. "Why do I get an escort?"

"This isn't your home, back home," Paris-Jackson pointed out. "This is a starship. A very dangerous environment, if you don't know what you're doing. If you go through the wrong hatch, or push the wrong button, you might accidentally kill yourself."

Charlotte scowled, unwilling to admit he might have a point. "And does that ever happen?"

"It has," Paris-Jackson said. "There was a horror story, a couple of dozen years ago, about a trio of young groundhogs who were vented into space. No one wanted to believe they'd somehow bypassed the safety systems, and there was a big investigation on suspicion it had been murder, but finally everyone had to concede the idiots had rigged an airlock to open on both sides at once. I don't know what they were thinking. They said they were idiots, but—in truth—I think they were more ignorant of their own ignorance."

Kari cleared her throat. "Perhaps we should just stay in here."

"That would be a good idea," Paris-Jackson agreed. "Right now, the crew is very busy preparing for departure. They don't need distractions."

Charlotte nodded, stiffly. She'd never been in a really dangerous environment in her entire life, unless one counted boarding school. No, that hadn't been *really* dangerous…not unless you did something stupid like climbing on the roof in winter or swimming in the ocean where the currents would drive you onto the rocks. The worst that could happen was six of the best from the headmistress, or simply being expelled. She looked at the bulkhead, wondering if it was as strong as it looked. It seemed solid, but was it? A military weapon might be able to go through the hull like a knife through butter.

And we're dealing with the remains of a powerful alien race, she thought, numbly. *We might not even recognise a weapon until we pull the trigger.*

The hatch bleeped. Paris-Jackson opened it, revealing a young midshipman. "Captain Templeton's compliments, Madam Ambassador, and she'll be pleased to see you in her cabin."

"Thank you," Charlotte said. She glanced at herself in the mirror—she looked strikingly out of place—and then headed for the hatch. "I'm on my way."

The starship was a human ship, but—to her eyes—it was as alien as a truly alien ship. Crew hurried past her, speaking in incomprehensible tongues and carrying out tasks she couldn't even begin to comprehend. She almost doubted her grasp of English as a trio of spacers hurried by, snapping instructions as they shoved a loaded cart down the passageway. The chaos seemed never-ending, the madness gripping her mind...she felt her head start to pound as they walked through the nightmare, struggling desperately to understand what was going on. It felt like a complex dance, the kind that took days to learn and weeks of practice to perform flawlessly. She wondered, suddenly, if her husband had faced the same chaos on his ship. How had he coped?

And he had the nerve to say my life was boring, she thought, as she stepped aside to avoid another cart. *At least my people weren't running around like mad, shouting and swearing and trying to meet a deadline that could be moved at a moment's notice.*

Her escort led her through an open airlock, then stopped in front of a closed hatch and pressed his hand against a scanner. There was a pause, just long enough for Charlotte to wonder if the captain was even in, then the hatch hissed open. Her escort stepped aside and motioned for her to enter. Charlotte nodded her thanks—she wasn't sure if she should tip him—and then stepped inside. The hatch hissed closed behind her. She felt oddly uneasy as she looked around the tiny cabin. It was larger than hers, but still tiny compared to her bedroom back home. The young woman sitting at the fold-out table—she stood as Charlotte entered—looked surprisingly young to be in command of a starship.

Although everyone seems young to you these days, she reflected, sourly. It was hard to believe, sometimes, that she'd crossed forty a few years ago. Not that she'd ever admit it out loud. As far as she was concerned, she was still in her thirties and had been for over a decade. *You cannot hide from time for much longer.*

"Madam Ambassador," Captain Templeton said. There was a hint of deeply personal disdain in the captain's tone, although she hid it well. "Welcome onboard."

Charlotte shook her hand, studying her thoughtfully. The captain was a stranger, yet she clearly knew Charlotte. Charlotte had always been good at reading people and she was sure Captain Templeton's dislike really *was* personal. One of her husband's former officers? A young officer who owed her position to his patronage, someone who would take his side on instinct? Or…or what? Charlotte didn't know many naval officers, outside the aristocracy. The commoners had rarely been invited to her gatherings.

"Thank you," she said. She was tempted to engage in verbal fencing, but she had the feeling the naval officer in front of her would prefer directness. "It's good to be here."

Captain Templeton smiled. Her first command, Charlotte guessed. Given her relative youth—and Charlotte could spot someone who'd had cosmetic surgery a mile off—it almost certainly *was* her first command. Lord Hammond had spoken, often enough, of the freedom of being in command of a ship, of being the sole ruler of a realm. Charlotte had pointed out, at the time, that he was also supposed to be in command of his estates… she cut that thought off quickly, before it could lead her somewhere she didn't want to go. A starship wasn't anything like the estates. The latter needed far more tending from their master.

"We should be departing in two days, if all goes according to plan," Captain Templeton said, coolly. She made no attempt to serve tea or coffee. "The Admiralty is still debating if they should send a second ship with us, to watch from a safe distance."

"And we have no idea what *is* a safe distance," Charlotte pointed out. "If some of the more absurd possibilities are even remotely accurate, there might be no such thing."

"No," Captain Templeton agreed. She looked unsure of herself, just for a second. "But we will find out."

Charlotte understood. It was one thing to know the rules had changed. It was quite another to be unsure if they were changing or not. *Endeavour* had a cloaking device capable of hiding her from top-of-the-line sensors. *Human* sensors. Would they hide her from the mystery aliens? Or would trying to cloak look like a child's game of hide and seek?

She motioned for Charlotte to sit, then also sat. "This is your first offworld mission?"

"My first trip offworld," Charlotte confirmed. "It's different."

"Yes, it is," Captain Templeton said. "And I must speak bluntly."

She didn't wait for Charlotte to say anything, merely pushed on. "There are ground rules. I need you to follow them. If you don't, I'll put you in the brig until we return home. Are we clear on that point?"

"I read the briefing documents," Charlotte said. She'd also learnt a great deal just by listening to her husband. And Mitch. "I know the Captain is the sole commander of her ship."

"Yes," Captain Templeton said. "During transit, I need you and your team to remain in your quarters unless escorted outside, both to keep you out of my crew's way and for your own safety. You will be assigned hours in the gym and I suggest you make use of them. When we reach our destination, you will have full access to our sensor readings, but—again—you will remain in your quarters unless invited to leave. If we do make contact with an unknown race, you will be in charge of handling the negotiations, but you are not to make any agreements that might put the ship at risk. For example, you are not to promise we'll proceed to a destination they suggest without my prior agreement. The safety of this ship, and this crew, and the entire human race, is my first priority. Is that understood?"

"Yes, Captain," Charlotte said, tartly.

"Good." Captain Templeton met her eyes. "I expect, given time, that you and your team will forge friendships with my crewmembers. I don't object to that, and I can't forbid it, but those friendships are not to distract my crew from their duties. Once we take the xenospecialists onboard, you'll have more time to spend with them. You'll need to read their reports and ask questions about matters they didn't explain completely."

"Of course," Charlotte said.

"There will be some emergency drills," Captain Templeton added. "Ideally, if we run into hostile aliens, you'll remain in your cabins until we break contact and run. If we do suffer damage, you may be pressed into service to help treat the wounded. If we have to abandon ship, you'll have to make your way to the lifepods and get out. There are rules concerning what you can take with you and it is vitally important you don't break them. We do not want to give prospective alien captors a starchart leading directly to Earth."

"We were given a full briefing," Charlotte said. "We do understand the risks."

"If we have to abandon ship, this hull will be blown to atoms," Captain Templeton told her. "It isn't easy to make sure you're not carrying anything dangerous, before you get into the lifepods and out of the doomed hulk."

"No," Charlotte agreed. She made a mental note to download and read the captain's service record, very—very—carefully. It was clear they wouldn't be friends, but they'd have to work together or risk losing everything. "We understand what we need to do."

"I hope the mission will be relatively simple," Captain Templeton said. "But realistically, I doubt it."

"The Builders may be gone," Charlotte agreed. She wasn't blind to the underlying motive behind the mission. The Builders might be gone, but they'd left plenty of rubble behind. Who knew what discoveries were waiting to be made? "Or they might not."

Captain Templeton nodded. "They were an interstellar superpower, with technology beyond our comprehension," she said. "What could wipe them out?"

"I don't know," Charlotte said. The speculations had ranged from the possible to the unhinged. None of them had made comfortable reading. "But I think we have to find out."

CHAPTER FIVE:
HMS ENDEAVOUR, SOL SYSTEM

"CAPTAIN," LIEUTENANT ANDY MACPHEE SAID. The communications officer was older than most, a reflection of the far greater demands placed on survey personnel. He might have to do more than just open hailing frequencies and exchange pleasantries with humans and known alien races. "*Grantchester* is taking up escort position now."

"Good." Staci kept her voice under tight control. The idea of assigning a corvette to escort *Endeavour* wasn't a bad one, but the delays had nearly scuppered the plan twice. There were just too many demands on the navy's limited time and resources, from escorts for convoys heading to the border to patrolling the solar system in case the virus had a few ships left that might be sent to attack the homeworld. "Inform them we'll be leaving as planned."

She took a long breath. She'd spent the last few days walking her ship, crawling through the tubes and speaking to her officers in a bid to get to know them before she had to take the ship into unexplored space. The mission had been thrown together in a tearing hurry, something that bothered her more than she cared to admit. *Unicorn* had taken several weeks to get everything shipshape and *she'd* been a frigate, with a crew so small everyone knew everyone else. *Endeavour* was much bigger, with so many different departments that there were very few cross-departmental relationships. She hoped the cruise would break down some of the barriers—they'd be alone, the moment they left Virus Prime—but there was no way to be sure. The task ahead of her seemed daunting, yet...they had to be ready. There was just no way to *know* what they'd be facing once they reached their destination.

I suppose that's why so many people stay in survey, she mused. She'd eaten dinner several times with Jenner, in hopes of getting a feel for his personality. He'd admitted he loved the thought of being the first, or amongst the first, to see what lay beyond the borders of explored space. *They may be the ones to have their names written in the history books.*

Her lips twitched as she scanned the departmental reports. The thought was not displeasing. If she'd died on *Unicorn*, would anyone have known her name? There were very few people who'd remember the names of anyone below the vessel's commander, save for students of the battle or biographers of the officers involved. Who'd been Christopher Columbus's XO, when he'd sailed across the Atlantic and laid eyes on America for the first time? She didn't know. She wasn't even sure the name was recorded in the history books. The thought of doing something so spectacular people would *have* to remember her was very tempting. But the odds were not in her favour.

Except this time, we're following an alien starchart, she thought. *The odds might be better than we think.*

She frowned. The navy's analysts had put forward a host of theories and scenarios, ranging from the plausible to the downright insane. The researcher had been hallucinating. The researcher had misremembered something. The researcher...had been misled. The starchart didn't lead to the alien homeworld, or even a settled system, but a black hole. Or a minefield. Or...she shook her head. It was hard to believe a hyper-advanced race would deliberately set out to torment a primitive one, but who knew? There was no reason to think they shared humanity's concept of morality. The aliens humanity had met, over the years, certainly didn't.

"Captain," Jenner said, from his station. "All departments have reported. We are ready for departure."

Staci nodded, reminding herself that *Endeavour* wasn't a new-built starship. She'd left the slip years ago, all the kinks worked out well before she'd set off on her first mission. The refit hadn't been *that* extensive, she told herself, and all the new sensors and weapons and other pieces of technology were well understood. And they'd been tested, extensively, over the past few days. There was no reason to think the ship would suffer a catastrophic failure the moment she powered up her drives and headed for deep space.

But it would be embarrassing as hell if we did, Staci thought. *We'd never live it down.*

She pushed the thought aside. "Helm, bring the drives online," she said. "Communications, inform System Command that we are ready to depart."

"Aye, Captain," Lieutenant-Commander David Atkinson said. The helmsman was older than the average pilot, but his reflexes were still in good shape. Staci had insisted on putting him through his paces before allowing him to retain his post. There was no way to know what the ship might encounter, or what it might need to evade. "Drives coming online...now."

Staci took a breath as a low thrumming echoed through the ship. It felt oddly unnatural. *Endeavour* was quieter than a warship—the designers had included engine baffles, for reasons that escaped her—and her experience told her the ship wasn't powering up, even though the displays insisted it was. She scowled as she studied the power curves, silently comparing them to *Unicorn*. *Endeavour* was hardly as slow and cumbersome as the legendary *Ark Royal*—the ancient carrier had handled like a wallowing sow, if the reports were to be believed—but she still lacked the agility of a frigate or the heavy armour of a modern battleship. If they ran into hostile aliens, even with technology a decade or so behind hers, they'd find themselves in hot water very quickly. She would have to deploy decoys, try to break contact and hope they could escape before it was too late. And if they were wrong...

I'm not in command of a warship, she thought, waspishly. *I'm in command of a bloody cruise liner.*

She felt a twinge of pity for her civilian counterparts. In theory, a civilian commander was master of his own ship, the final authority as long as his vessel was underway. In practice, it wasn't anything like so simple. A cruise liner for the rich and powerful was far from an easy command. Say the wrong thing, to the wrong person, and one's career might come to a screeching halt, even if one was in the right. The same was true in the military, she supposed, but she at least had the comfort of knowing her fellow captains would back her if she gave commands to an admiral. The civilian spacers had to answer to men who might never have even left Earth, let alone travelled the known universe. Their grasp of the realities of interstellar traffic might be very limited.

"Communications," she said, putting the thought aside. "Are we cleared for departure?"

"Yes, Captain," MacPhee said. "*Grantchester* is standing ready to escort us."

Staci nodded. "Helm, take us out."

Endeavour quivered slightly, very slightly, as she glided out of the shipyard, passing a swarm of automated weapons platforms. Staci frowned as she studied the displays. It still felt odd, as if they were in a simulator rather than a real starship. Perhaps she'd have a word with the engineers, see if the baffles could be removed. She found it hard to believe anyone, baffles or no, could actually forget they were on a starship. The background hum was just part of the experience. Given time, they'd stop noticing it was even there.

"Power curves are nominal," Jenner reported. "All systems go."

"Bring all the sensors online," Staci ordered, "and put the results on the main display."

She leaned forward as the display started to fill with red icons, switching rapidly to green, blue and yellow as the datacores confirmed the prospective targets weren't hostile. The Sol System swarmed with activity, starships making their way to and from the tramlines while smaller interplanetary ships glided between the settled planets, moons and asteroids. She spotted a pair of colony ships making their way to the tramline, crammed with settlers hoping to make a better life away from Earth. It made her heart sink. Humanity's homeworld had taken one hell of a beating, over the last few decades. There were people who thought the planet was doomed, doomed beyond all hope of recovery. Personally, Staci thought they were being idiotic. Given time, the planet could and would recover.

It isn't as if the virus ever managed to infect the atmosphere itself, she thought, curtly. *And now we know what to look for, and how to counter it, it never will.*

The display updated, again. Staci was impressed. *Unicorn's* sensors had been good, but *Endeavour's* were better. If something was radiating emissions, they could see it. If something was cloaked...her eyes lingered on the passive displays, cataloguing flickers of energy right across the system. It was hard to be sure, but she was fairly certain a modern cloaked ship wouldn't be able to sneak up on them. She told herself, sharply, not to get overconfident. They couldn't take anything for granted. As technology advanced, the technology to fool it advanced too.

She felt a flicker of excitement as she braced herself, preparing to issue the next set of orders. She was the captain. *Endeavour* was *her* ship. And the moment she passed beyond the tramline, she would be sole mistress of her vessel...her lips twisted as she remembered the flicker network, a line of relay stations extending all the way to Virus Prime. The Admiralty *could* look over her shoulder, at least until she headed into truly unexplored space. She wondered, grimly, just how badly it would change things. The navy had trained its commanders to act on their own, to be aware it would be weeks—if not longer—before they could get updated orders from home. Now, they could get the orders very quickly. What would it do to their initiative?

A problem for another time, she thought. *Right now, we are going well beyond the network's reach.*

"Helm," she said. Her mouth was suddenly dry. Her heart was pounding like a drum. "Helm, set course for the tramline."

"Aye, Captain," Atkinson said. He'd already plotted out the course, or she was a civilian with as much military experience as an actor who played a movie star captain. All he'd have to do was bring up the one he'd plotted earlier and load it into his console. "Course laid in."

Staci smiled. "Take us out. Best possible speed."

Endeavour quivered, again, as she picked up speed. Staci watched, keeping a wary eye on the power curves. If there were going to be problems, perhaps something that would necessitate an immediate return to the shipyard, they would occur when the vessel brought all of her drive nodes online. Staci didn't expect any—*Endeavour* had been deployed a dozen times before she'd assumed command, plenty of time for any problems to make themselves apparent—but she was still careful. The navy had taught her to check and recheck everything before she found herself isolated, light-years from any possible help. *Grantchester* would do everything in her power, if *Endeavour* needed help, but there were limits. There was no way the corvette could take off more than a handful of the survey ship's crew.

Perhaps we should assign two survey ships to the mission, she thought. *Or a small fleet of military transports.*

She shook her head, crossly. There were so many demands on interstellar shipping, now, that the navy hadn't been able to assign her a single transport, let alone a small fleet. The shipyards were churning out liberty freighters as fast as they could, but there were never enough to meet *all* the demand. She was lucky she'd be able to draw on stores, when they reached Virus Prime. Her skin crawled at the thought. If there was one system she'd be content never to visit again, it was Virus Prime. Even now, there were still pockets of infection within the system. A careless man might lose everything in the blink of an eye.

"Captain," Atkinson said. "We will cross the tramline in two hours, forty minutes."

"Good," Staci said. "Mr. XO, inform the crew they have two hours to write any final messages, then upload them for transmission."

"Aye, Captain."

Staci nodded. The old tradition had weakened, now FTL signalling was more than just an unattainable dream, but the navy had always been slow to change its traditions. Besides, any personal message uploaded to the flicker network would always be right at the bottom of the priority list. The bandwidth was so low that it was difficult to send anything more advanced than a basic text message. She'd heard horror stories of messages only being delivered *after* the sender had returned to Earth himself. They were exaggerated, but not by much.

She glanced at her console, then shook her head. She'd already sent her final messages. Her family would be disappointed she hadn't had a chance to visit, between returning to Earth to face the Board of Inquiry and being assigned to *Endeavour*, but they'd survive. She'd never been *that* close to her parents, not after she'd reached adulthood. They had never really approved of her decision to join the navy, not when they would have preferred her getting married and churning out grandchildren. She scowled at the thought. She liked children, and she wanted kids one day, but she also wanted a career. She wanted to do something for herself.

And that might have been what Lady Charlotte was thinking, she reflected. *What might she have become, if she'd started her career instead of becoming a homemaker?*

She shook her head. The aristocracy was…*different*. Their thinking was as alien as any alien, without the excuse of being alien. She didn't pretend to understand how they could act like people out of a bad romance sim, claiming that honour and dignity and reputation were important while, at the same time, proving through their deeds that they didn't really care. It was hard to feel sorry for someone who'd been born to wealth and luxury beyond imagination, even if it was a gilded cage. They certainly had no shortage of diversions to keep them occupied. The poor bastards banged up in Colchester were lucky if they had books to read. There were certainly no luxuries.

Endeavour maintained her course, the display updating time and time again as she was put through her paces. Staci allowed herself to relax, slightly, as no problems became apparent. It was a relief. The crew knew how to repair their ship while underway, and *Endeavour* had been designed to make it as easy as possible, but she didn't want to test the theory when they were a long way from Earth. A dozen survey ships had vanished over the years, vanished so completely no one had the slightest idea what had happened to them. Staci had heard all the theories, from catastrophic drive failures to hostile aliens or tramlines that led straight into black holes, but she suspected the real explanations were a great deal more prosaic. So far from home, even a minor problem could easily cascade into something catastrophic. In theory, *Endeavour's* crew could set up a colony and wait for rescue. It wasn't something she was eager to test.

"Captain," MacPhee said. "We are approaching the tramline relay station."

"Upload the messages, then copy our final status report to System Command," Staci ordered, calmly. "Helm, take us across the tramline."

"Aye, Captain."

Jenner keyed his console. "All hands, prepare for jump. I say again, prepare for jump."

Staci smiled, keeping her eyes on the display as a timer popped up and started to count down to zero. There were no virgins in her crew, no youngsters so fresh out of the academy they'd never crossed the tramlines…she frowned, suddenly, as she recalled Lady Charlotte had never even left Earth. It struck her as absurd to put a novice in command of a diplomatic team, certainly one handling such a mission, although she suspected her team had orders to quietly sideline her if she proved she couldn't handle it. It was one thing to handle an estate's affairs, quite another to open communications with an alien race of unknown power and intentions. Unless someone was entirely sure the mission would only find alien ruins...

The countdown reached zero. The display blanked. Staci's stomach twisted, unpleasantly, as the ship crossed the tramline. The display rebooted, icons flashing back into existence as new data poured into the sensors. Terra Nova system was as screwed up as ever, she noted sourly. Between the virus, the various human powers and countless little warlords fighting over their patches of land, the system was one hell of a mess. She noted the number of ships fleeing the planet and scowled. No one really wanted to stay, save for the warlords and their armed forces. Why bother, when the planet was so unstable?

And why bother to try to fight, when your efforts will be for naught, she reflected. There were just too many factions that preferred anarchy to effective government, for one reason or another. The warlords didn't want anyone ordering them to give up their armies, the religious fanatics wanted to impose their beliefs on everyone else, the asteroid dwellers didn't want a powerful government trying to tell them what to do... *If someone put together a working government, someone else would knock it down before it could get control of the entire system.*

"Jump completed, Captain," Atkinson said. "No system abnormalities detected."

"Good." Staci let out a breath she hadn't realised she'd been holding. She'd feared, at some level, that something would happen before they could make the jump. "Set course for Virus Prime, best possible speed."

"Aye, Captain."

Staci stood. "I'll be in my ready room," she said, brushing down her shipsuit. She needed to go through all the reports, then write one of her own. "Mr. XO, you have the bridge."

CHAPTER SIX:
HMS ENDEAVOUR, IN TRANSIT

"ALL HANDS, PREPARE FOR EMERGENCY EVACUATION," the intercom boomed. "I say again, all hands prepare for emergency evacuation."

Charlotte swore as the alarms howled. The emergency drills had been exciting, at first, but they'd long since lost their lustre. Grab one's mask and put it into place, grab one's helmet, grab one's emergency kit...then wait, bracing oneself for the order to make their way into the corridor and down to the lifepods. Charlotte hadn't needed to read all the horror stories to know their odds of survival were not high, if they actually *had* to eject themselves into space and wait for rescue. In theory, they could deorbit and land on a planet. In practice, there might not even *be* a planet for them to land on.

She glanced from face to face as they waited, noting how her entire team looked as irritated as she felt. The naval officers seemed determined to ensure no one had a quiet night. They'd been woken up, day after day, to get ready for an evacuation that never took place...she scowled, reminding herself that emergency drills were necessary. They had to know what to do, if the next emergency happened to be real. And if that meant being woken in the middle of the night...she wondered how the crew coped, then remembered they'd been drilling ever since they started their careers. They were probably used to being woken and put through their paces, then ordered straight back into their bunks.

The alarms died away, the all-clear sounding moments later. Charlotte glanced at the clock, cursing under her breath. It was too late to go back to bed, yet too early for her peace of mind. If the bunk had been more comfortable, she might have considered going back to it anyway. Instead, she dismissed her team with a wave of her hand and headed over to get a cup of coffee. She'd taken a liking to navy coffee, even though it was nothing like the coffee she'd had back home. She was tempted to wonder what would happen, if she served it at a gathering, before remembering it was unlikely she'd host a gathering ever again. That part of her life was over.

She poured herself a mug, then settled down on the sofa with her datapad. The common room—she couldn't help thinking of it as a common room—might be large by navy standards, but it was tiny by *her* standards. Back home, she could have taken a horse or pony out of the stable and galloped around the estate; here, onboard ship, she was effectively trapped in a small compartment, barely large enough to swing a cat. She'd been cautioned not to leave the ambassadorial section without an escort and yet, even if she had been allowed to roam freely, there was nowhere to go. The ship was a maze of corridors and compartments, each one in constant use. She'd been to the gym a few times, under escort, but it had been boring. She would have sooner walked around the mansion or explored the streets of London and…

It struck her, suddenly, that she was trapped, that she would be trapped for months—perhaps years—on the ship. She lifted her head, staring at the bulkhead. The walls were closing in…she cursed under her breath, telling herself not to be silly. The walls hadn't moved one jot. It was just her awareness that she was trapped, that she couldn't leave the ship…that, in fact if not in name, she was a prisoner. The world she'd left would go on without her…she remembered, suddenly, a schoolmate who'd believed everyone missed her when she'd had to leave for a term, who'd seemed to think everyone had spent the entire term talking about her, who'd expected a heroine's welcome when she'd returned the following term. No one had called, Charlotte recalled. The girl hadn't been anyone *important*, not to them. Her absence had barely been noted. And the same was going to happen to her...

Unless you come home covered in glory, she told herself, sharply. *And what are the odds of that?*

She sighed, returning her gaze to her datapad. Her sealed orders had unlocked the moment the ship had passed through the tramline, outlining a handful of scenarios and detailing what she should do if any of them came to pass. Charlotte had read enough, over the past few weeks, to know the government was taking the matter very seriously, but she honestly wasn't sure what to make of some of the stranger scenarios. She would almost have preferred to believe the government was being taken for a ride, by contractors who thought they could get away with it. The thought of some of the scenarios being real was terrifying.

They're just trying to cover all the bases, she thought. *And they know better than to expect all of the listed possibilities to be true.*

Her head started to ache as she dug through the files. She wanted—she needed—to understand what was expected of her, rather than doing little more than putting a face on the negotiations while her team did the work. It galled her she didn't know if there *would* be any negotiations, if there would be anyone—anyone at all—interested in talking to the human race. If there was...she intended to play a major role in the discussions, to lead rather than have her strings pulled by her team. She would listen to their advice, and take it if necessary, but she wouldn't let them sideline her. It would be risky—she'd get the blame if something went wrong—yet she found it hard to care. She wasn't blind to the real reasons she'd been offered the assignment. If there was a major screw up, she'd be the one carrying the blame.

She took another sip of her coffee, then stood and started to pace. The cabin felt even smaller somehow, her mind insisting the bulkheads really *were* closing in even though she knew they couldn't move. She scowled as she remembered the reports from the Sphere, the strange tales that insisted the interior changed randomly...it was hard to believe, yet she knew from grim experience there was no smoke without fire. And when there were so many people making similar reports, she had to take them seriously.

The buzzer rang. She looked up, half-expecting someone to get the hatch before remembering the rest of her team had gone back to their bunks. She laughed at herself, humourlessly, as she walked over to the hatch and keyed the switch. The butler was back home...no, it wasn't *her* home. Not any longer. She didn't even have a personal maid now, let alone a household staff. The thought mocked her. She was hardly useless without servants, but...how much would she have to get used to doing for herself?

You spent nine months alone in London, she told herself, sternly. *You don't need a maid.*

The hatch opened, revealing a young midshipman. "Madam Ambassador," he said. If he was surprised she'd opened the hatch personally, he showed no sign of it. "The captain would like to see you in her cabin."

Charlotte frowned. She'd barely seen Captain Templeton since their brief interview when she'd boarded the ship. The captain's file, however, had made illuminating reading. She'd been Mitch Campbell's XO, back when he'd fought his final battle. And that meant...Charlotte didn't know. Would she be a friend? Or an enemy? She hadn't seemed very friendly when they'd met, although both Charlotte's husband and her lover had told her military personnel didn't always think much of civilians. The civilians could afford to hold delusions about how the world worked. Soldiers and spacers couldn't allow themselves that luxury.

"It will be my pleasure," she said. She wondered if she should change into something a little more comfortable, then shook her head. Her shipsuit would suffice. "Lead on, MacDuff."

The midshipman nodded, then turned to lead her down the corridor. Charlotte followed, feeling almost as if she'd been let out of gaol. She understood the ship was a dangerous environment, a place that could easily hurt or kill her if she touched the wrong thing, but wandering the corridors was still better than staying in the suite. The corridors didn't seem to be so busy, now the ship was underway. They only passed a handful of crewmen, none of whom paid any attention to her. Charlotte glanced down at herself and snorted. The shipsuit was comfortable, and disturbingly clingy in certain places, but it wasn't the sort of thing she was used to wearing. It certainly didn't mark her out as an aristocrat. The only sign she wasn't a military officer or crewman was the lack of any rank badges.

She eyed the midshipman thoughtfully as they entered Officer Country and made their way to the captain's cabin. Should she try to befriend him? Or would he be unsure of himself, if she tried? She didn't want to push him to talk to her. It could make things awkward if someone felt pushed, even if they weren't. Charlotte was old enough to know how to read a situation. A young man, easily young enough to be her son, might not have those insights. She sighed inwardly. She knew how to comport herself, in the halls of power. Here, on a starship, she felt utterly unsure.

The hatch hissed open. Charlotte thanked her escort and stepped into the cabin, noting—ruefully—that the captain's cabin wasn't that much larger than her own. Captain Templeton looked disgustingly fresh for someone who couldn't have much more sleep, if any, than Charlotte. Charlotte reflected the captain was younger as well as more experienced in shipboard life. Captain Templeton's file stated she was in her late twenties, which made her at least fifteen years younger than Charlotte. She felt a sudden stab of pain. Her daughters weren't *that* much younger than the captain.

"Madam Ambassador," the captain said. The hint of subtle dislike in her voice was all too easy to hear. "Thank you for coming."

Charlotte knew she should be diplomatic. But she was too tired to care. "Why don't you like me?"

Captain Templeton blinked. She hid her surprise well, Charlotte noted, but not well enough to hide it from *her*.

"You can speak freely," Charlotte added, a moment later. "It's your ship."

"You seduced my previous commander, who was a friend as well as a commander," Captain Templeton said, flatly. "And you landed him in hot water."

Charlotte felt a hot flash of anger. "Do you think I dragged him to the bed and had my way with him?"

Captain Templeton reddened. Charlotte hid her amusement. Mitch Campbell had hardly been a bodybuilder with enhanced muscles, but he'd been strong and a martial arts artist to boot. The idea she could have dragged him into her bed, if he hadn't wanted to go, was thoroughly absurd. She had made the first move, in a manner no one could ignore, but he could have easily said no. What could she have done about it? Sued him? It would have been so utterly laughable no one would ever have taken her seriously.

"No," Captain Templeton said, finally. "But you didn't have to make a spectacle of it either."

Charlotte gritted her teeth. *That* had hit a little too close to home. No one would have cared, much, if she'd had a very private and discreet affair. There was no shortage of hotels...hell, she could have taken her lover to one of the family's smaller properties and slept with him there, well away from anyone who might have made a fuss. She knew she'd used him for more than sex. She knew...

"I never intended to hurt him," she said, finally.

"You put him in an untenable position," Captain Templeton told her, bluntly. "He was fucking his commanding officer's wife, for crying out loud!"

"I know." Charlotte tried not to flinch. "I was there."

Captain Templeton gave her a sharp look. "What did you expect to happen if you were caught? Did you think your husband would overlook it? That he would be *happy* working with a man who'd cuckolded him? That he wouldn't try to ruin your lover's career in retaliation? That... fuck it! You put them both in the worst possible position, where your husband's reputation would be smashed flat if he *didn't* retaliate. You're damn lucky Admiral Onarina laid down the law before things *really* got out of hand."

Charlotte kept her voice under tight control. "I am aware of my own role in the whole affair."

"And do you expect people to trust you?" Captain Templeton scowled at the table. "You made a series of very bad decisions, which were made worse by the fact no one could handle it quietly. And then you took to the media and dragged everyone through the mud."

"I had no choice," Charlotte said. She couldn't escape the sense Captain Templeton was right. "It seemed the right thing to do at the time."

"If you were that unhappy in your marriage," Captain Templeton pointed out, "you could have just left."

"It isn't that easy," Charlotte said. "And if I'd planned it better…"

She sighed, the anger draining out of her. She hadn't planned it, not really. Sure, she'd had vague concepts of what she might do if the truth came out, but she hadn't intended for them to be discovered. And yet, she feared part of her had *wanted* to get it over and done before it was too late. She hadn't *had* to lure Mitch Campbell into her bed in the middle of a gathering, at an event it was all too likely someone would ask where she'd gone. She could have waited a day or two, then arranged a seduction somewhere a little more private.

"You don't know what it's like," she said, finally. "I had to burn my bridges behind me."

"And you burnt the one someone was standing on," Captain Templeton said. "And now you have to live with the consequences."

Charlotte said nothing for a long moment, then leaned forward. "Yes, I do. And I will."

"I knew someone, once, who was in a bad situation," Captain Templeton said, quietly. "She made a very bad decision, because she was so desperate to get out she wasn't thinking clearly, and that decision hurt other people. And no matter what she did, afterwards, she couldn't make it better. Her desperation does not excuse the decisions she made or the harm she caused."

"No," Charlotte agreed. "But it is easy to say that, when one is looking back from a position of safety. It is harder to pick the optimum course of action when you are drowning in your own desperation."

She met the captain's eyes. "If Mitch had survived, I would have married him and we would have built a life together," she said, ignoring the glint of disbelief she saw on the younger woman's face. "If…"

Her heart sank. "I am aware of my own role in the affair. I will face the consequences, as they come to me, and deal with them as best as I can. But I was not the only person involved and I will not pretend otherwise, not even now. We both made mistakes."

"You used him," Captain Templeton said.

"I am not the innocent here," Charlotte said, "but neither was he."

She took a breath. "I will do this job to the best of my ability and I expect the same from you," she added. "I don't expect you to like me. I've dealt with plenty of people who didn't. But I do expect you to be professional."

"Duly noted," Captain Templeton said. She stood and poured two mugs of coffee. "Tell me, what do you think of the scenarios the researchers outlined for us?"

"They may be too wild, or not wild enough," Charlotte said. She took a mug of coffee, recognising it as a peace offering of sorts. "We just don't know. The Builders may be dead and gone, or so far advanced that communication of any sort is impossible. Or that direct contact will destroy us, directly or indirectly."

"Yeah." Captain Templeton sipped her coffee. "Normally, the survey crews would have orders to avoid contact. Here, we don't know if it's possible."

Charlotte leaned forward. "How so?"

"Fifty years ago, the best cloaking devices we had would render a ship more or less invisible until it got to point blank range," Captain Templeton explained. "Now, that same cloaking device would be laughable. The user wouldn't be able to get within weapons range without being detected and tracked. Fifty years in the future, they may be saying the same about *our* cloaking device. Who knows what the Builders can do? For all we know, their sensors may be capable of detecting even the faintest gravitational twinge in the fabric of space-time, allowing them to detect us from light-years away. We just don't know."

Charlotte felt cold. She'd read the briefing notes, but hearing Captain Templeton say the words somehow made it *real*. "They might spot us the moment we arrive."

"Yes," Captain Templeton agreed. "And who knows how they'll react, if they think we're sneaking around their system?"

"Poorly." Charlotte shivered. "Shit."

CHAPTER SEVEN: HMS ENDEAVOUR, VIRUS PRIME

STACI HAD NEVER EXPECTED to *like* Charlotte Hammond. The aristocratic woman had made a fool of her mentor, something that bothered Staci even though she knew Captain Campbell deserved a share of the blame for the whole affair. Staci was quite familiar with men who wouldn't take *no* for an answer, but she was also aware that her former CO would have had *no* trouble escaping if Lady Hammond tried to push matters. She wondered, rather sourly, what he'd even *seen* in her. There was no shortage of brothels, high-class escorts and even women looking for a naval husband. He hadn't been short of options. There'd been no reason to let himself fall for a middle-aged woman well past her prime.

And yet, she had to admit there was *something* about Lady Charlotte. She couldn't put her finger on it, but it was there. It wasn't her looks so much as her charm, her ability to make herself appear to be a good listener. She made the people who talked to her feel *important*, Staci decided, something that didn't make Staci herself feel better. Captain Campbell might have felt drawn to Lady Charlotte because she made him feel good about himself, but he also might have seen himself as her knight in shining armour...Staci shook her head in irritation. She'd liked and respected and even admired her former CO, but she had to admit he'd never been a long-term thinker. He would have made a good starfighter pilot, she supposed. Their unofficial motto—*live fast, die young, leave a cloud of atoms behind*—suited him perfectly. She wondered, not for the first time, if her CO had known, on some level, that he was fighting the last battle of the war. There would have been nothing for him, back on Earth. Better to die in fire than spend the rest of his life looking back at past glories...

He thought it was a full-fledged relationship, she reminded herself. *And maybe it was.*

It had been a long trip, too long. She would have preferred to stop, to give her crew some shore leave, but the formerly infected sector had nowhere safe for them to take a break. The virus had devasted the region, turning entire biospheres into infected nightmares. She'd been told the BioBombs would wipe out the virus, but it seemed determined to take the rest of the infected planets with it. The human race would probably have to terraform the planets from scratch, if they wanted to settle them. She doubted it would be done in a hurry. There were too many other worlds that had barely been touched by the virus. And few people would really believe the virus was gone for good.

"Captain," Atkinson said. "We are ready to make transit."

Staci studied the display for a long moment, bracing herself. She knew there was no real danger, not as long as they didn't risk landing on any of the infected worlds beyond the tramline, but her skin still crawled. She told herself, firmly, that it was just her imagination. The virus might not be gone completely, but it was no longer capable of mounting a deep space offensive. There were no enemy starships left, as far as they knew. If there were...she wondered if they'd headed into unexplored space too, hoping to survive and prosper somewhere far from the human race. It wasn't a pleasant thought. The virus might pop up again, years after it had been defeated and thought to be gone for good.

"Jump," she ordered, quietly.

The display blanked, then rebooted. Virus Prime had been a cluttered system when she'd first made transit, over a year ago, and very little seemed to have changed. The occupation force had been sweeping the system, picking off asteroid mining stations or dropping rocks on planet-based installations, but there was no way to be sure they'd got everything. The system would probably be monitored for years, the slightest hint of industrial activity summoning a fleet to wipe it out. She wondered, sourly, if Virus Prime truly was the alien homeworld, or if it had belonged to another race that had been infected and overwhelmed before realising it was under attack. She suspected no one would ever know. The planetary surface had been utterly devastated. It would be decades, if not longer, before anyone could land and start looking for surviving records.

If the virus bothered to keep records, she reflected. *It didn't need to store anything in external databases.*

"Captain," MacPhee said. "We are picking up a challenge from a guardship."

"Send them our ID and transit clearance, then request permission to proceed," Staci said, her eyes never leaving the display. "And then inform Admiral Summerfield that we're inbound."

"Aye, Captain," MacPhee said.

"It's a real needle in a haystack situation," Jenner said, quietly. "How many other alien structures are hidden in the asteroid fields?"

Staci shrugged. There was some suggestion in the files that Virus Prime had once had significantly *more* planets, planets that had been blown to rocky chunks to produce the clouds of asteroids orbiting the primary star. She didn't believe it—the virus had certainly never demonstrated the ability to blow up a whole *planet*—but she had to admit it was possible, if pointless. There'd been so much raw material in the system that it was hard to believe a spacefaring civilisation could run out, certainly not before they discovered the tramlines. But then, who knew how aliens thought? She'd read human plans to blow up Mercury. It wasn't that hard to believe someone might have tried to go through with them.

Particularly if they're not sentimental about their worlds, she mused. Pluto had been classed as a planet, then an asteroid, then a planet again. *They might have seen them as nothing more than raw material.*

"We may never know," she said, quietly. "We only stumbled across the Sphere through sheer luck."

She forced herself to wait as they made their way across the system. The Sphere was hidden within a cluster of asteroids, a cluster that the virus had never touched...there were people, Staci knew, who suspected the Sphere had protected itself from possible infection. It was certainly true other alien artefacts had dulled the virus, ensuring they remained safe from its interference. No one knew how the trick was done, but they wanted to. Desperately. If the human race could put the virus to sleep permanently, the threat would be gone for good.

"Captain," MacPhee said. "Admiral Summerfield's compliments, and he'd like you to join him for dinner when we reach the Sphere."

"Signal the admiral and inform him I would be delighted to accept," Staci said, trying not to feel a twinge of guilt. It wasn't shore leave—visiting the port admiral was hardly *relaxing*—but she still felt as though she was putting herself first. "And then request permission for some of my teams to visit the Sphere."

"Aye, Captain."

Staci glanced at Jenner. "Make the arrangements to bring his men onboard, as soon as they're ready," she said. "We don't want to stay here any longer than strictly necessary."

"Aye, Captain."

Endeavour slowed as she reached the edge of the asteroid cluster. There was no real danger, not when the gap between the two closest asteroids was still wide enough to fly an entire fleet through without risk of disaster, but it was well to be careful. The asteroid pattern didn't *feel* random. It looked as if someone had carefully orbited the asteroids around the Sphere, hiding it from prying eyes. Staci had no idea if she was imagining it or not. The researchers seemed divided. Half of them were sure the

Sphere had been deliberately hidden, the other half thought it completely pointless. The asteroid cluster alone, they'd argued, was enough to draw spacefaring visitors like moths to flames.

She sucked in her breath as the Sphere appeared on the display. It wasn't the largest structure she'd ever seen—she'd seen industrial nodes and asteroid settlements that were considerably bigger—but it was the largest that gave the impression of being a single solid object. There was no sense it had been put together piece by piece. Rather, it looked as if the makers had taken an asteroid—as one might take a diamond in the rough—and sanded it down until it became a perfect sphere. The only blemish on the hull was the entrance, a black hole leading into the interior. A shiver of unreality ran down her spine. The Sphere was just too perfect. It had drifted in space for centuries, perhaps even longer, and yet it remained unmarred by the passage of time.

"Mr. XO, you have the bridge," Staci said. "I'll be back as soon as possible."

"Aye, Captain," Jenner said.

Staci nodded, then stepped into her ready room and hastily changed into her dress uniform before making her way down to the shuttle hatch. The pilot disengaged from the starship and took his craft towards the research station, orbiting the Sphere at what was devoutly hoped to be a safe distance. Staci suspected no one, not even the more optimistic members of the team, really believed it. If the Sphere turned nasty, the research station was doomed. Even merely *human* tech would have no trouble blowing it into atoms.

And the most worrying thing about the station is that no one has set it up on the Sphere itself, she thought, coldly. *They're reluctant to risk sleeping on the Sphere.*

The research station was typical—a collection of modules, linked together by a network of airlocks and cables—but it looked crude compared to the alien structure. Staci couldn't help feeling a twinge of disappointment, even though she *knew* the research station was extremely efficient. It just looked like a child's drawing, an attempt to emulate the adults who'd been doing it longer than the poor kid had been alive. She bit her lip, suddenly feeling like a child again herself. It was rare to feel inherently inferior to anyone, let alone *anything*. And yet the Sphere, just by existing, mocked humanity's pretensions to technological greatness.

We think of ourselves as an advanced race, she thought, as the shuttle docked at the station. *But, compared to the Builders, we're just playing with sticks and stones.*

The airlock hissed open. She barely heard it. She'd been told that a society could be destroyed by a cultural inferiority complex, but she'd never believed it. Not until now. The Sphere was…she shook her head as she stepped through the outer hatch, pressed her hand against the bioscanner and then entered the station itself. The officer who met her looked…jumpy, as if she expected to be attacked at any moment. Staci didn't like the look of it as she followed the young woman through a maze of corridors. The rest of the team didn't look much better.

"Ah, Captain Templeton," Admiral Summerfield said. He was a beefy man, with dark hair and a beard that was decidedly non-regulation. He'd traded in his uniform for a shipsuit with ADMIRAL written across the front. "Congratulations on your promotion."

"Thank you, sir," Staci said. She told herself not to feel overdressed. The admiral would have been well within his rights to take offense, if she'd turned up in a shipsuit. "It's been an interesting few weeks."

"I bet it has," Summerfield said. He motioned for her to enter his cabin, then nodded to the table. "I'm afraid we don't have much in the way of fancy food, and I'm pretty sure the cook hates his life, but we've done what we can."

"I'm sure it will be fine," Staci said, taking the proffered chair. The admiral poured her a glass of clear liquid—shipboard rotgut, judging by the smell—and then sat facing her. "This is a fascinating place."

"It's a downright worrying one," Summerfield said. He took a sip of his drink and made a face. "Do you realise, most of what we know about the Sphere is little better than guesswork? We don't know what it's made of, we don't know how long it's been here and we don't have the slightest idea what it actually *does*. Our equipment is dangerously unreliable within the Sphere. We tried to measure the inner chambers and got a whole string of different results. One even insisted the chamber was *light-years* in diameter."

Staci blinked. "That's impossible."

"Or so we thought," Summerfield said. "And yet it happened."

He shook his head. "The general theory is that the Sphere is protecting its secrets," he added, taking another sip of his drink. "Recording and communications equipment fails at the worst possible times. We started laying down cables to carry messages through the Sphere, very primitive pieces of junk, and they started to fail too. Then…some of the weirder sightings only occur when there's no more than one or two witnesses. I thought, at first, that people were playing jokes, the sort of thing you get on distant stations when there isn't enough to do. But there were too many odd reports…"

Staci tried her drink. It tasted foul, worse than she'd dared fear. "You've been sending people into the Sphere alone?"

"It seems the only way to provoke a reaction," Summerfield said. "And no, we don't know how it works. When there's more than three people, the Sphere seems completely inert. A couple of my researchers think the Sphere is really an intelligence test and we're failing it. We still know very little about it. For all we know, it's haunted."

"I see, I think," Staci said. "Why did it show your researcher the starchart?"

"We don't know." Summerfield stared into his glass, his eyes a long way away. "There are a bunch of theories. The entire system could still be in place, with us blundering around like a mouse in a computer lab and hitting random buttons that sometimes do something. There's a possibility their eyes are different from ours, that they can see controls we cannot… that, in short, we simply don't know how to turn it on. Or…like I said, the whole thing could be an intelligence test. Or it's playing with us, toying with us as a cat might play with a mouse. It certainly made sure we didn't get a proper recording of the starchart before it vanished again."

Staci frowned. The reports she'd read had sounded a great deal more certain. "Are you sure it *was* a starchart?"

"The researcher—she'll be going with you, when you depart—was hypnotised and regressed to the moment she saw the chart," Summerfield said. "She drew it out for us while she was in a trance. At that point, we compared it to the starcharts within our datacores and found a match. Obviously, we cannot confirm the existence of the tramlines shown on the chart, at least the ones outside explored space, but we know they *could* exist."

"And leading us to a point well beyond explored space," Staci mused. It was hard not to feel excited and yet fearful. She hadn't felt that way since she'd lost her virginity. "Why do they want us to go there?"

"We don't know," Summerfield said. "One school of thought is that the starchart was activated accidentally. Another thinks it's an invitation. A third thinks it's a trap. And a fourth thinks we've misunderstood what she saw, although the odds of it being a coincidence are very low. There is no way the starchart could have matched so perfectly if it was a coincidence."

"No," Staci agreed. She let out a breath as the cook arrived with dinner. It smelled appetising, despite the warnings. "How do your researchers cope with…with everything?"

"Poorly," Summerfield admitted, motioning for her to dig in. "The first bunch were a combination of specialists in xeno-culture and xeno-tech. The former found nothing, no clues about the alien culture or anything else. The latter rapidly discovered it was completely mystified. There has to be something within the Sphere, something that messed with our gear, but they found nothing. The best theory they have is that the entire structure is a singular piece of technology…something they haven't been able to prove. And…"

He shrugged. "Some have been enthused. Some think the interior is shifting rapidly and, if we keep looking, we'll eventually be shown into the control room. Others…have started to give up. Back on Ganymede…you've heard of the Jovian Effect?"

Staci nodded. "That happens here?"

"The colonists on Ganymede see Jupiter looking down on them and… it starts to get to them," Summerfield said. "Most get used to it, but some can't and have to leave permanently. Here…we have people looking at the Sphere and finding themselves overwhelmed by its mere existence. Some go into shock. Others just start drinking."

His lips twitched. "There's a theory the Sphere is screwing with our minds, just as it messes with our tech," he added. "They think it's trying to drive us away. Others think the effect is accidental, that the Sphere simply doesn't know we exist. And still others think it is purely psychological. Again, we just don't know."

"The Sphere is a very daunting artefact," Staci said.

"And one that is only *really* daunting to someone who can appreciate how tricky it would be to produce," Summerfield said. "There are times, I admit, that I believe it really is an intelligence test. And then I think the Builders simply didn't realise what their tech would do to us."

"If they knew we'd be coming," Staci said. "For all we know, the Sphere predates every other known spacefaring race."

"It does, or so we think," Summerfield said. "But we know so little, Captain, that we cannot be sure of anything."

He smiled, rather dryly. "Now, what news from Earth?"

Staci hesitated, then started to answer.

CHAPTER EIGHT:
THE SPHERE, VIRUS PRIME

"KEEP YOUR TETHER ATTACHED AT ALL TIMES," the young midshipman ordered. "If you feel uneasy or unwell at any point, please inform me at once."

I feel uneasy now, Charlotte thought. The spacesuit was thoroughly uncomfortable. It felt as if she was wearing a suit of armour, or flying a one-person spacecraft, and the less said about the tubes hooked up to her genitals the better. The training officers had gone into great detail about *precisely* what would happen if the tubes came loose, leaving her afraid to even think about putting them to the test. *If I didn't have to see the alien structure for myself...*

She staggered into the airlock, the rest of her team behind her. The spacers hooked up the tethers, like a fish caught on a line, then deactivated the gravity field. The airlock went dark the moment her feet drifted off the ground. Charlotte felt a moment of panic—surely, something had gone wrong—before the hatch opened to reveal a field of burning lights, set in endless darkness. Stars, she realised numbly. They weren't twinkling...the briefing notes had said as much, pointing out there was no atmosphere in space, but it still looked *wrong*. The radio crackled, spacers checking in with the guests one by one. Charlotte answered when her name was called, but otherwise kept her mouth shut. She'd been cautioned that the radio channels were for emergencies only.

The tether tightened, yanking them out the airlock. Charlotte felt another flash of panic as the deck vanished, an inescapable sense she was falling to her doom threatening to overwhelm her before she told herself—quite firmly—that she was floating, safely, in the middle of an endless sea of stars. The helmet wouldn't let her see the ship behind her, but she could see the research station—surrounded by moving lights—and the Sphere beyond, glowing faintly under powerful floodlights. The spacers led them forward, the Sphere growing rapidly until it dominated the horizon. Up close, it felt subtly *wrong*.

Charlotte took a long breath as they fell—flew—towards the entrance. The Sphere looked as if it were made of bronze, although the files stated the research team hadn't been so much as able to take a scratch from the surface for analysis. Charlotte didn't pretend to understand the technobabble, the endless gibberish that seemed written to confuse rather than educate, but the summaries had been relatively clear. They knew very little about the alien structure. Origin? Unknown. Purpose? Unknown. Current status? Unknown. Charlotte wondered, suddenly, if she'd bitten off more than she could chew. The aliens who'd built the Sphere were incomprehensible.

And if we were advanced enough to turn our starships and structures into works of art, she asked herself, *wouldn't we do it?*

It was a surprisingly reassuring thought. The team had tried to relax by watching movies and television programs from the pre-space days. Some of them had been thoroughly absurd, by modern standards; others had thought things about the universe, and the pace of technological development, that just weren't so. And their starships had been works of art. She smiled as she contemplated the question. *Endeavour* wouldn't win any design awards. Even cruise liners looked blocky and crude, compared to fictional starships. If human tech reached the point where starships could become works of art, wouldn't they? It was what *she'd* do. She knew from experience that making things look good would make it easier for people to accept.

The thought distracted her just long enough for the tether to pull her inside the Sphere. Darkness fell like a physical blow, then parted as the spotlights came online. Charlotte stared around the alien structure, feeling as if she were an insect crawling over something vast and incomprehensible. The chamber was spherical too, the perfection broken only by gaps in the walls that led into other—deeper—chambers. She frowned as she spun her spacesuit around, wondering if the designers had preferred to live in zero-g. The structure made no sense otherwise. There was no distinct floor or ceiling. She reminded herself, sharply, that this particular chamber was open to space. For all she knew, it was nothing more than a shuttlecraft hangar. It was certainly large enough to take a good-sized shuttle without a qualm.

But surely they should have airlocks, she thought. *What sort of idiot designs a shuttlebay that cannot be sealed and pressurised?*

She frowned as they glided towards the next chamber. She'd seen images of yarddogs working in orbital shipyards, where large sections of the complex were completely unpressurized. Perhaps the Sphere was really an alien shipyard, or a shell of an industrial node that had had most of the equipment torn out and taken elsewhere years ago. Or perhaps she was missing something. The movies she'd watched had included such technological impossibilities as forcefields, something the navy had been researching for years. As far as she knew, they'd never come close to producing workable hardware. The Builders might have succeeded. They might have thought they didn't *need* to seal their hull completely. It struck her as dangerously complacent—even the most advanced human technology was prone to failure, often at the most dangerous time—but they *had* been a very advanced race. Their technology might have been too advanced to fail.

And then they pulled it out of the shell when they left, she mused. *There might be nothing left for us to find.*

The sense of alienness grew stronger as they glided into the next section. It was as perfectly spherical as the first, the walls so completely unmarked she couldn't help thinking of a newly built house, just waiting for the first family to move into their new home. And yet...she remembered some of the old houses on the estate, abandoned for years and yet bearing signs of their previous occupants. Where was the stuff they hadn't thought worth taking with them? The old tables, chairs, cupboards and other junk not even worth being given to the local charity shops? Or...what about the bookcases built into the walls, or wiring running *through* the walls? The Builders had clearly not been pressed for time, when they'd abandoned the structure. Or maybe some of the more exotic theories were right and it had never been intended as anything other than an intelligence test, for any wandering spacefarers who happened to notice it.

There isn't even any graffiti on the walls, she thought, wryly. Her daughters had drawn on the walls when they'd been toddlers, leaving marks that had eventually been painted over when they'd moved out of the nursery. The poor nannies had never been able to stop them, not completely. *Where is the alien 'KILROY WOZ HERE?'*

She felt her head start to hurt as she glided from chamber to chamber, pulled along like a duckling following her mother. The Sphere just felt *wrong*. The endless series of interior chambers, each one a perfect sphere, was getting to her. She kept trying to think of it as a human building, but it only made her headache worse. The chambers were just *too* perfect. There were no little imperfections, no compromises where the designer's ambitions had clashed with the builder's realities...no sense, she reflected numbly, that they'd ever had any limitations at all. She couldn't help thinking of bubbles in a bubble bath, pressing against each other, but...what lay *between* the bubbles? It was impossible to tell. The reports had stated that the interior of the structure was as invulnerable as the exterior. No matter what tools—or weapons—were used, the bulkheads remained untouched. One could detonate a nuke inside the chambers, one report had stated, and there'd be no damage. At all.

Which is hard to believe, Charlotte thought. *Has anyone ever tried?*

The radio crackled. "Check in," the spacer said. "Does anyone want to go home?"

Charlotte said nothing. She owed it to herself to stick with the team. The thought of just going back to the ship was appalling. And yet, half of her people seemed to think it would be a very good idea. Charlotte understood, even though she had no intention of saying so anywhere other than her report to the PM. It wasn't uncommon for humans to feel uncomfortable in alien environments and the Sphere was very alien indeed. Charlotte had used VR tools to explore Tadpole starships and yet, they'd practically been *human* compared to this.

A thought struck her as she looked around. Tadpole starships had no discernible sense of up or down either. They were water-dwellers, uncomfortable spending almost *any* time on the surface even with proper protection. Was the Sphere designed to be filled with liquid, too? It was possible. They had no trouble making their way around because of the lack of gravity, but it would be just as easy if they were swimming instead. It was an odd insight. She'd always thought the Tadpoles had been very lucky, to develop technology without abandoning the waters for good. Could it be the Builders were the same?

It isn't as if we've met many aliens, she reflected. Humanity had only encountered nine intelligent races, if one included the virus and the races it had turned into zombies. The latter were still very much a mystery, their original cultures erased beyond all hope of repair or recovery. *For all we know, land-dwellers might actually be in the minority.*

She filed the insight around for later consideration as they glided further into the Sphere. It felt like a tour of a stately home, the guide blathering on about history that meant nothing to most of his charges, but there was something about the alien structure that kept it from becoming monotonous. It nagged at her, a faint sense of *something* lurking at the back of her awareness, as if she were being watched. She was used to people keeping a covert eye on her—it hadn't been *that* long since she'd been surrounded by servants, people whose livelihoods depended on recognising and adapting to her moods—and yet, this felt different, almost unnatural. She found herself looking for watching eyes or hidden cameras, even though they were probably designed to be impossible to spot. Sure, her estate—her *husband's* estate—had been lined with very visible cameras, but they'd been designed as a deterrent rather than anything else. There'd been others concealed in places that would be very difficult to find without climbing over the walls.

The sense of watching eyes only grew stronger as they probed deeper into the structure. She found it hard to tell how far they'd gone, let alone find their way back to the entrance. It should have been easy to map the structure, to figure out where all the chambers were in relation to one another, but the reports had made it clear the researchers hadn't been able to do anything of the sort. Charlotte had been scornful, when she'd read their reports. She wasn't now. It was suddenly very easy to believe the chambers were changing position when the research teams weren't looking.

It would be easier if we knew, one way or the other, she mused. *But the Sphere seems designed to keep us guessing.*

She took a sip of juice from the nipple in her helmet—the jokes had stopped being funny long ago—and forced herself to keep going. The sense they were being watched grew stronger and stronger, to the point she half-expected to feel breathing on the back of her neck. She hadn't felt so crowded since she'd attended a ball where the organisers had grossly underestimated the number of attendees…and even then, no one had stood *that* close to her. She felt as though her personal space was being violated, as if someone was in the spacesuit with her…

The chamber went dark. Charlotte gasped—she wasn't the only one—as the floodlights clicked off. She thought she saw lights on the walls, just for a moment, before the radio crackled loudly, then failed. A wash of panic ran through her. If everything had failed…did that include the radio and the life support and everything else? The spacesuits were as safe as human ingenuity could make them, with multiple redundancies worked into their systems, but…no one knew what would happen if they lost power. She started to hyperventilate. If the life support failed, she would quickly run through the air in the suit and find herself breathing her own fumes. She'd suffocate.

She heard another crackle. The lights came back on a moment later. The chamber looked unchanged and yet, she sensed something *different* about it. She tried to put it into words, narrowing the feeling down so she could add it to her report, but it was impossible. She couldn't see any change and yet…she was sure *something* had. It was…

"We'll make our way back to the exit," the spacer said. "If you'll follow me…"

We don't have a choice, Charlotte thought. She'd been annoyed, when she'd been told they'd all be on tethers, but she could see the sense of it now. It would be terrifyingly easy to get lost within the Sphere, to find oneself walking in circles until the life support ran out and you died. *If the Sphere starts cutting the tethers…*

She shook her head as they started to retrace their path through the structure. The researchers had worked their asses off, according to the reports, trying to find ways to identify the different chambers. Nothing had worked, from writing on the bulkheads to leaving beacons within the separate chambers. She thought she understood, now, why so many researchers believed the Sphere was toying with them. It might not be intentionally screwing with their minds, but it was just too alien to have any other effect. She scowled as she recalled some of the more exotic theories about the alien structure. The Builders might be just *too* alien for any sort of meaningful contact.

And that would be ironic, she thought. She'd thought she was prepared for anything, from hyper-advanced aliens who looked down on her to the ruins of a long-gone race, but the thought of simply being unable to talk was oddly galling. *We might never be able to ask them what they had in mind when they built the Sphere.*

The radio crackled again, then fell silent. Charlotte winced. The team kept moving, hurrying through the eerie doors—if they were doors- until they reached the first chamber. It was as empty as ever, but a shuttle held station on the far side, waiting. Charlotte wondered, idly, why the pilot didn't take his craft into the Sphere. It wasn't as if it would pose any real challenge. A dozen shuttles could enter and leave the shuttlebay, if it was a shuttlebay, without any risk of collision.

She didn't relax, not completely, until she was on the shuttle. The gravity was a surprise—she told herself, sternly, she should have expected it—and she had to wait to remove the spacesuit, but at least the shuttle was *human*. The interior might be crude—half the passenger seats had been torn out, to make room for crewmen in spacesuits—yet it was simple and easy to understand. Charlotte had never had dreams of becoming a spacer, she'd never seen it as her duty, but...she *understood* the shuttle.

I don't need to know how an aircraft flies to recognise it as an aircraft, she thought. *But the Sphere is just too alien to understand.*

She sipped more juice and waited for the shuttle to make its way back to the mothership, her mind running in circles. The Sphere really *was* alien. The reports had harped on it time and time again, but...she hadn't understood, not really, until she'd seen it for herself. There was no way to know what the Sphere was meant to do, when it had been built. She'd expected clues scattered throughout the structure and yet there were none. Perhaps it was just an alien orbital dorm, like the ones asteroid development crews used when they were hollowing out asteroids to turn them into orbital settlements. It would be a decidedly mundane answer, and she'd be disappointed if it *was* the answer, but she had to admit it was possible.

The gravity field seemed to flicker as the shuttle docked with *Endeavour*. Charlotte breathed a sigh of relief as she stumbled through the hatch—the spacesuit made walking tricky, at best—and then relaxed, slightly, as the crew helped her clamber out of the suit. Her tunic felt hot and sweaty, and she tried not to flush as she was unhooked from the tubes and pointed towards the shower. No one had said anything, but she was sure she stank. The timer insisted they'd been gone for only three hours. It felt longer. She felt a twinge of pity for anyone who had to work all day in a spacesuit. No matter how much they were paid, it wasn't enough.

Paris-Jackson caught her eye as they stumbled into the washroom. "The admiral has requested the pleasure of our company tomorrow evening, before we depart," he said. "I took the liberty of accepting on your behalf."

He may regret that, Charlotte thought. Her tainted reputation had clearly not reached Virus Prime. Someone would give the admiral a hard time for inviting her or her name wasn't Charlotte. *But at least it's something normal.*

She nodded, curtly. Right now, she *needed* something normal. And the admiral could take care of himself.

CHAPTER NINE: RESEARCH STATION, VIRUS PRIME

"DON'T FORGET TO PACK EVERYTHING, and I mean everything," Lieutenant Colin Lancaster said, as he popped his head into the compartment. "There's no guarantee we'll be coming back here."

Richard Tobias Gurnard—Tobias to his friends—nodded without looking up. The navy had never seemed quite sure what to do with him and the rest of his unit. Some of them had gone back to Earth on HMS *Lion*, to be demobilised as the war was over, but a handful had remained in the system as shuttle pilots. Tobias was mildly surprised he hadn't been ordered back home long ago, given how he'd entered the navy in the first place. There wasn't much call for gunboat pilots now, while there were more shuttle pilots than shuttles. The only reason he'd been left in place, he suspected, was that it was cheaper than sending a new pilot or two from Earth.

He shook his head as he dropped the last of the datachips into his carryall and stood. If someone had told him, two years ago, that he and Colin Lancaster would wind up friends, of a sort, he would have thought the idiot was taking the piss. And if that idiot had told him he'd also have a long-term girlfriend…he snorted, inwardly, at the sheer absurdity. Boys like him didn't *get* friends, let alone girlfriends. And yet, he had. It was hard to understand how it had happened—he looked back at the past and found it impossible to believe—but it had. He didn't *want* to go back to Earth. He was sure, deep inside, that reality would reassert itself with a vengeance.

"I have everything I need," he said. He'd never had *that* much with him since joining the navy, even after beginning a long-term assignment to the research station. The navy had taught him to be careful what he brought, if only because he might not be able to take it home with him afterwards. His datapad and collection of datachips was about the only thing he didn't want to lose and they barely took up any space. "You?"

Colin shrugged. "I think so," he said. "The platoon can draw most of what it needs from onboard stores."

Tobias shrugged. He'd never been clear on precisely why *Colin* and his platoon had been assigned to the research station either, although he could hazard a guess. The Sphere *might* turn nasty and, if it did, the Royal Marines might be required to extract the researchers and run before it was too late. Tobias suspected that was stupid—the Sphere was just too advanced to think the Marines would stand a chance—but no one had asked his opinion. Perhaps there were other considerations. It was just a matter of time before the news leaked and someone realised there was a massive alien artefact within the infected system. And then all hell would break loose.

Not that anyone has expressed much interest in the system, he thought. *They were content to leave us with the task of finishing the job.*

He shuddered. He'd spent the first four months of the deployment pushing asteroids into impact trajectories, steadily wiping out the remains of the infected population. He tried not to think about how many host bodies he'd condemned to death—the days when he could pretend it was just another online computer game were long gone—and it still bugged him, even though he knew there was no choice. The infected were lost beyond all hope of recovery. He wondered, at times, how Colin and his peers coped. Starfighter and gunboat pilots engaged icons on their displays. It was easy to pretend they weren't firing on living people. The Marines, however, got

ENDEAVOUR

up close and personal with their targets. They couldn't avoid *knowing* they were killing intelligent beings.

Although no one knows for sure if the virus is actually intelligent, he reminded himself. *It certainly doesn't always show intelligence.*

He nodded as he glanced at his wristcom. One thing he'd learnt very quickly was that navy bureaucracy was very poor at finding round pegs and slotting them into round holes. His old CO had told him the bureaucrats read the reports, and the reports were accurate, but they didn't have any feel for the realities behind the words. There were times when he'd wondered if his presence in the system had simply been overlooked, if the bureaucrats would one day realise he was there and hastily call him home for discharge before anyone noticed. Now...he had to admit they'd made a good call. No one got *used* to the Sphere—one of the reasons the station was surprisingly luxurious was to help the researchers cope with the sheer alienness of the Sphere—but he didn't let it affect his piloting. If the rumours were true, and they were going to look for whoever had built the Sphere...

They might need me, he told himself. *I wouldn't have an adverse reaction to a second Sphere.*

"It's a survey ship," he said. "You'd better make sure they *do* have everything."

"I did," Colin assured him. He made a show of looking around the cabin. "I'm afraid our quarters will be much smaller, once we're on the ship."

Tobias winced. He'd grown used to sharing a bunkroom on HMS *Lion*. The cabin on the research station, which he'd been allowed to share with his girlfriend and fellow naval pilot, Marigold Harkness, was a palace compared to the bunkroom. *Endeavour* was a big ship and yet, she probably wouldn't have much room for a pair of new pilots. He cursed under his breath. It would be hard to get used to sharing another bunkroom with a dozen strangers, most of whom would probably look down on him for not being a career shuttlecraft pilot. And there'd be no privacy, again...

We'll just have to book the privacy tubes, again, he thought, crossly. *And that will be a great deal less spontaneous.*

"We'll cope, somehow," he said. He *had* been in worse places, back on Earth. The last email from his mother suggested finances were tightening, once again. The government had done what it could to keep the population from starving, and to keep millions of families from being evicted, but now that the war was over the ministers were under immense pressure to dismantle the social security network. "Don't you get a special cabin to yourself?"

"Not a chance." Colin shook his head. "Marine Country is pretty damn small. There's ten of us, fifteen if you count our attached staff, and we're going to be crammed together like...fifteen people crammed together. If we had more time to prepare..."

The hatch hissed open. Colin stepped aside to let Marigold—Tobias's girlfriend—step into the cabin. Tobias smiled, then picked up his carryall. Marigold picked up her own and checked it, just to make sure she had everything, then nodded. They'd been ordered to report to the shuttle hatch at 1700, but their orders had changed so often Colin was starting to wonder if the admiral was making it up as he went along. Or perhaps there were other considerations. The briefing he'd been given, when he'd been told he was being assigned to *Endeavour*, had been grim. If they fell into alien hands, they might be forced to talk. The only way to keep from surrendering intelligence to the enemy was not to have anything to surrender.

And that includes starcharts and tramline diagrams, he thought, sourly. *But we don't even know for sure the Builders are hostile.*

The thought mocked him as they made their way down to the shuttle hatch. He'd taken the time to read the files, the ones he was allowed to read, and they'd agreed that most survey missions were uneventful. The long-range ships swept through a dozen systems, noted tramlines, planets and natural resources, then returned home to arrange for other ships to follow up on their findings. It was vanishingly rare for a survey ship to discover an alien race and, so far, none of those encounters had turned violent. But this time...he shook his head. They were following an alien starchart, one leading them to a system they'd picked...who knew what they'd find? Or what might be lurking in the rubble, waiting?

There could be anything, anything at all, he told himself. *And if they really are hostile, a race so powerful could turn the sun nova.*

He shuddered. He'd always been a science-fantasy fan. He'd thrilled to impossible starships doing impossible things, to strong-jawed heroes and heroines fighting fantastical monsters and winning hopeless wars, time and time again. And yet...the prospect of fighting such a war chilled him to the bone. Could the human race hope to defeat a super-advanced race, if it turned out to be hostile? Or would their certain destruction be very... *certain*? The gap between Earth and the Tadpoles hadn't been *that* wide, but the Tadpoles had still come very close to winning the war outright. If *Ark Royal* had been scrapped...

Marigold nudged him. "You're being quiet."

"Everything is changing, again," Tobias said. "And the ground is shifting beneath our feet."

"I think that might be the cheese toast you had for supper last night," Colin teased. "I'm pretty sure they don't bother to preserve it properly."

"You know what I mean," Tobias said. "We're being transferred to another ship and heading off into the unknown..."

"It could be worse," Colin said. "You have to roll with the punches as they come."

He grinned. "Hey, you want to know what happened to me during Basic?"

Tobias didn't, but there was no point in saying so.

"There's a test," Colin said. "You have to beat this guy in unarmed combat. You get told the guy's feet are chained to the floor, so as long as you keep your distance he can't get you. Easy, right? And then you go into the chamber and you have a few seconds to realise they lied to you, that his feet aren't chained down, and you're *this* close to getting a fist in the jaw. And if you don't get out the way fast, you're fucked. You're going to be the one buying the drinks after the sergeants have finished scolding you."

Marigold gave him a sharp look. "But they told you his feet were chained, right?"

"Not quite," Colin said. "If you go back over what you were told, afterwards, you realise you didn't quite hear what you thought you heard. But by then it's too late."

Tobias wasn't sure he believed the story, although—compared to some of Colin's wilder stories—it was quite tame. His own instructors had loved throwing curveballs at them during basic training, using the simulators to let the trainees get their mistakes out of their systems without expending vast numbers of gunboats and shuttlecraft. And yet...he couldn't recall any of them lying, directly or indirectly. Perhaps it was because he hadn't precisely volunteered for the program. Or perhaps Colin was just trying to make them smile.

He put the thought aside as they reached the shuttle hatch and joined the line of researchers and support staff making their way past the guards. The admiral hadn't been happy to be ordered to send half of his research team to *Endeavour*, even though they were the closest thing anyone had to experts on Builder tech. Tobias recalled the briefing and scowled. It was quite possible some of the researchers knew enough to be dangerous, if they fell into enemy hands. A lone astronomer who knew the coordinates of each and every one of humanity's stars would be enough to let the aliens sneak all the way to Earth, then open fire, without being detected.

Tobias shivered. As if things weren't bad enough already.

The guard held out a bioscanner. Tobias pressed his hand against the sensor and waited for the ping. They'd learnt the hard way just how dangerous the virus could be, even if it wasn't *really* intelligent. It had come very close to infecting the research station itself and that should have been impossible. Tobias was inclined to wonder if the virus could survive in interplanetary space. The biomatter would have frozen, surely, except that would only have put the virus in stasis. If it reached somewhere warm and started to thaw...

He relaxed, slightly, as he heard the ping. The guard motioned him into the shuttlecraft, where a steward pointed him to a seat. Tobias breathed a sigh of relief as he sat and waited for Marigold to join him. He'd had no reason to think he might be infected, but—as he'd been cautioned often enough—there was no way to be *sure*. The virus had evolved with terrifying speed. The days the victim had felt ill before it was too late to save them were gone. If he'd been infected...

The shuttle rocked, then undocked and headed away from the station. Tobias gritted his teeth as he felt the gravity field vibrate slightly, as if the drive harmonics were very slightly out of phase. He made a mental note to report it. He'd flown enough shuttles to develop an instinct for when something was wrong, although it would be a while before the mismatched harmonics did anything more dangerous than putting additional wear and tear on the equipment. And...he sighed inwardly. He would have preferred to fly the shuttle himself. It was funny how hard it was to relax when someone else, even Marigold, had their hands on the controls. He wanted to be in control of his flight.

And you know better, he told himself. *You can't fly every last flight.*

The shuttle vibrated, the gravity field flickering as it merged with the starship's field. A low *thump* echoed through the tiny ship. Tobias smiled, weakly. There were no portholes within sight. It was hard to believe, somehow, that they'd just flown nearly a thousand kilometres in a few short minutes. There were civilians, he'd heard, who honestly refused to believe it. They didn't know how to read the flickers passing through the shuttle. A handful of researchers started to unbuckle, only to be told off by the stewards. Tobias hid his amusement with an effort. He'd made the same mistake himself, when he'd been a new trainee. The passengers had to remain seated until their names were called.

"Good luck," Colin muttered, when his name was called. "See you on the far side."

Tobias watched him go, then leaned back in his seat and waited. The shuttle was starting to feel claustrophobic, even though it was hardly his first shuttle. There was more room on the flight deck, he reflected. He closed his eyes and tried to concentrate, to recollect the book he'd been reading when he'd been on duty, waiting for something to happen. It had been a science-fantasy that had been good and funny, good because he'd enjoyed the story and funny because none of the tech was even remotely plausible. And...

"Richard Gurnard," the steward called. "Marigold Harkness."

Tobias opened his eyes and forced himself to stand, then walk into the hatch and through the airlock. The bioscanner reported he was clean. Again. He felt a flicker of irritation, despite knowing they *had* to test and retest everyone to be *sure* they weren't infected. It was hard not to feel as though they were wasting their time. And yet...he pushed the thought out of his mind as they stepped onto the starship itself. The air didn't smell *clean*. It took him a moment to recall *Lion* had been fresh off the production line, while *Endeavour* had been in service for over a decade. He hoped she was still up to the job.

"Welcome onboard," a dark-skinned man said. He was at least five years older than Tobias, although it was hard to be sure. "I'm Chief Harrington, Shuttle Ops."

"Tobias Gurnard," Tobias introduced himself. "And this is Marigold Harkness."

"Pleased to meet you," Harrington said. Tobias doubted he needed the introductions. "If you'll come with me..."

Tobias glanced at Marigold, then followed Harrington down the corridor. *Endeavour* didn't have the same *feel* as *Lion*, although he couldn't put his finger on precisely how. The crew was hurrying, readying the ship for departure. They looked as calm and professional as the battlecruiser's crew, without the sloppiness that had settled—unfortunately—into the research station's staff. The admiral had done what he could, so Tobias had been told, but there were limits. The combination of civilian staff and the sheer *presence* of the Sphere had done immense damage to military discipline.

Although we didn't have a real breakdown, Tobias thought. *Perhaps that was why Colin and his men were really assigned to the station, to keep us in line if things went wrong.*

"Your berths are in here," Harrington said. "There are six other pilots on the ship. I expect you to get along or else. Don't worry about pecking order here, just do your duty and the rest will take care of itself."

"Got it." Tobias wasn't reassured. The berth—the bunkroom—wasn't that big and adding two more people would make it seem even smaller. The others wouldn't be pleased to have more pilots, even if they didn't have other reasons to be unhappy. "Do you have an updated mission brief?"

"Nothing you won't already have," Harrington said. He lowered his voice. "But we do have a betting pool, if you're interested."

"No, thank you," Tobias said, quickly. "I'm saving my money for old age."

Harrington laughed. "Good luck," he said, clapping Tobias on the shoulder. "I'll see you both in the simulators, when we get underway."

Tobias nodded. "Got it."

CHAPTER TEN:
HMS ENDEAVOUR, VIRUS PRIME

"SO," STACI SAID. "What do you make of our new guests? Any problem children?"

Jenner took a moment to sip his tea before answering. "They are either military personnel or have spent a goodly amount of time on a military installation," he said. "I don't think any of them are going to give us any real trouble, not once we're underway. They volunteered for this mission."

Staci nodded. Admiral Summerfield had told her practically the entire research team, military or civilian, had requested permission to transfer to the survey ship when it headed into unexplored space. She understood, although she doubted the civilians grasped the risks. The chance to be the first to lay eyes on an alien system, one crammed with hyper-advanced tech, was hardly to be missed. And yet...she hoped, grimly, that they wouldn't run into trouble. The last thing they needed was civilians getting underfoot while they were trying to run from a new and terrifying threat.

"Keep an eye on them," she said. "It won't take them long to realise we don't have as many amenities as the station, let alone a cruise liner."

She scowled at the thought. *Endeavour*, compared to *Lion* or *Unicorn*, practically *was* a cruise liner. She was designed to travel hundreds of light-years into the unknown and no expense had been spared to make sure the crew were comfortable, even though they were a long way from their friends and families. Staci knew she would have been delighted with the gear onboard, from entire libraries of entertainment to gyms and playrooms, but someone used to Earth might disagree. They might even feel they'd gone down in the world. And then cabin fever would start to bite.

"I will," Jenner promised. "I don't see any reason to be concerned, but I'll make sure to nip any trouble in the bud."

"And they know the Sphere," Staci added. "They should have at least an *idea* of what we might encounter."

Her hands tightened, almost of their own accord. She would never admit it, certainly not unless she had no choice, but the Sphere had frightened her at a very primal level. The reports hadn't even *begun* to convey how alien it was, how badly its mere existence screwed up the human mind. Lady Charlotte had noted it too, judging from her painfully detailed report. Staci had been taught to be as blunt and precise as possible; Lady Charlotte, it seemed, preferred purple prose to detail her feelings. And she'd done a good job. It made Staci wonder what the older woman would have become, if she hadn't been trapped by family obligation. Perhaps she would have made something of herself.

"Their reports keep disagreeing on that point," Jenner cautioned. "There won't be any agreements on anything until we actually reach our destination."

"No," Staci agreed. "But their theories are at least interesting."

She sipped her own tea and waited to see if her XO had anything else to say. It was galling to admit that being XO on a frigate had not prepared her for having an XO of her own, certainly not one on a bigger ship. They'd spent the voyage sorting out their areas of responsibility, and keeping each other informed of their respective blind spots, but…in hindsight, it was the sort of problem that should have been obvious well before they took up their positions. She'd have to be careful. Jenner might assume she already knew something and not tell her, unaware she *didn't* know. Better to have him bombard her with detail than miss something important. She could cope.

"I think we should be ready to depart as planned," Jenner said, finishing his tea. "And then head into the unknown."

Staci keyed her terminal, displaying a holographic starchart. The human race had explored many of the tramlines around Virus Prime, dropping BioBombs on every infected planet within the region, but too many of the tramlines had never been given more than cursory attention. The starchart discovered on the Sphere led *far* into the unknown, their flight plan leading down tramlines that had just been logged and tramlines no one was even sure existed. A handful of researchers had even speculated they *didn't*. If humanity could build catapults to toss ships across a dozen light-years in the blink of an eye, why couldn't the Builders?

"We should be fine," she said. "*Grantchester* will keep an eye on us, from a distance."

"Yes, Captain," Jenner said. "With your permission, I'll prepare the bridge for departure."

"I'll join you shortly," Staci said. "Have fun."

Jenner smiled—it was one of the few hints of his sense of humour—and left the compartment. Staci looked back at the starchart. It had been easy enough to take *Endeavour* out of the shipyard, with hundreds of starships and shuttlecraft well within range to lend assistance if something went wrong but going into the unknown was different. She'd done it before, on *Unicorn*, yet they'd been part of a big fleet. Now…she knew better than to think *Grantchester* would be able to help them if they ran into something the survey ship couldn't handle. The corvette didn't have the life support to evacuate more than a fraction of her crew. The thought of being trapped light years from home worried her. It was far worse than leaving the shipyard.

Her lips twitched. *And if I'd refused to leave the shipyard, I'd have been relieved of command so quickly I'd set a new record.*

She snorted, then checked her terminal for the final updates from

Admiral Summerfield before heading onto the bridge and taking command. There was no proper authority covering the system, not yet, but it was polite to inform the admiral that *Endeavour* was about to get underway. She wondered, idly, if anyone would ever try to settle the system or if it would just be abandoned, a grim reminder of a repulsive historical nightmare. The system wasn't short of raw materials—there were enough asteroids and gas giants to support a major population even with the planets remaining firmly off limits—but it was hardly unique. She had a feeling it would be a long time before anyone tried, unless they were desperate. And desperate settlers rarely risked establishing colonies in places that were regularly patrolled by space navies.

Jenner stood. "Captain," he said. "We are ready to depart."

"Thank you, Mr. XO." Staci took her chair and checked the status displays. Everything was nominal. There'd been a handful of minor glitches during the voyage, but they'd been fixed before they'd become serious problems. "Communications, inform the research station that we will be departing shortly."

"Aye, Captain."

Staci took a breath, studying the displays. The system was decidedly odd. It was hard to tell if there were any human eyes watching them, let alone alien. The Sphere wasn't *precisely* a secret, but no one had gone out of their way to draw the galaxy's attention to it either. And yet...she frowned as the long-range sensors spotted hints of distant activity. The last traces of the enemy colonies? Admiral Summerfield's teams, looking for alien bases and raw materials? Something more sinister? Less? Virus Prime had been shattered. The traces could be nothing more than an enemy installation breathing its last, making one final cry for help before it died. She might never know.

"Helm," she said. "Take us out."

A low quiver ran through the starship as her drives came online, propelling her away from the research station. The Sphere vanished, lost amongst the cluster of asteroids. It had been sheer dumb luck it had been found in the first place. A couple of different choices and the final campaign might have been lost, with no one having the slightest idea of how close they'd come to proof of super-advanced alien life. It was, in her private thoughts, a sign that the Sphere wasn't *really* an intelligence test. Why stake everything on sheer random chance?

Unless they intended to draw us to it later, she thought. *Or is that just naked paranoia?*

"Captain," Atkinson said. "We will cross the tramline and jump in ninety minutes."

Staci nodded. "Keep us on course."

She leaned back in her chair. "Mr. XO, implement the Silent Running protocol as soon as we cross the tramline. We'll proceed on an evasive course until we reach our final destination."

"Aye, Captain," Jenner said.

Staci sighed inwardly. Silent Running was neither fish nor fowl nor good red hen, a government-mandated compromise that would—at best—wind up making them look like fools. They would keep all power and sensor emissions stepped down, in hopes of avoiding notice, without using the cloaking device to ensure they wouldn't be spotted…at least by human tech. Staci found it hard to follow the logic. They didn't want to look as if they were sneaking up on an advanced alien society, particularly if that society had no trouble tracking them even if they were cloaked, but—at the same time—they didn't want to advertise their presence. Personally, Staci would have made a show of openness. The last thing they wanted was to look shifty, not when there might be no time to make a better impression. And yet, her orders offered little room for manoeuvre. She wasn't allowed to make a show of openness until it was clear they'd been detected.

When we get back, we're going to have to take a long hard look at our policies, she thought, crossly. The Royal Navy had been meaning to do so for years, but they'd been born out of political compromises that had been made before alien life had been anything more than something out of science-fantasy. *What do we do, when we run into someone more advanced than ourselves?*

The original regulations had assumed, with a dangerous amount of arrogance, that humanity would *never* encounter anyone more advanced than themselves. It had fallen by the wayside on the first hurdle, when the Tadpoles had proven themselves more advanced—at least in some areas—than their human enemies. And yet, they hadn't been *that* advanced over the human race. The Vesy, by contrast, had been so primitive they should have been left strictly alone. If the Russian renegades hadn't broken all the rules and made contact, they would have remained in blissful ignorance of the universe beyond their atmosphere.

And yet, what would it have done to them, she asked herself, *if they'd made it into space only to discover the galaxy was taken?*

The thought nagged at her mind as she read the departmental reports, one by one. It wouldn't have been fun, not for them. Humanity and its peers would hardly have stepped aside to let the Vesy claim a seat at the table. Why should they? Staci was too realistic a person to believe, even for a moment, that idealism would trump sheer self-interest. Unless, of course, the human race had evolved into beings of pure energy by that point. She supposed it wasn't impossible. Just very unlikely.

She stood. "Mr. XO, you have the bridge," she said. She had departments to inspect, which would keep her from brooding and keep her crew on their toes. And she needed to get to know the newcomers under her command. "Alert me when we're about to make transit."

"Aye, Captain."

Staci stepped through the hatch and made her way down to Marine Country. It was tiny, barely large enough for a lone platoon. *Unicorn* hadn't had any Marines, she reflected, but *Unicorn* had been a frigate, not a deep-space explorer. *Endeavour* should have had room for more, perhaps bringing the bootnecks all the way from Earth rather than borrowing—stealing—them from Admiral Summerfield. But then, Staci had *seen* the Sphere. She needed men who were used to the alien structure…

Her lips twitched as she stepped through the hatch and saw the Marines performing their exercises. Marine Country had always been a world unto itself, a place where the normal spacefaring rules didn't quite apply. Indeed, normally, the starship captain would issue orders to the bootneck commander and rely on him to pass them down to his men, rather than ordering the bootnecks around personally. But now...Staci straightened as a young man in a tunic snapped to attention. It was clear he was in command, even though his jacket was missing. And yet, he was a little too junior.

They should have sent out more bootnecks, Staci reflected, as she returned his salute. *There just aren't enough men who spent enough time in the Sphere.*

"Captain," the Royal Marine said. There was a hint of an edge in his voice, a sense he felt caught between two fires. He was dangerously junior for his post, a position that needed an experienced colonel or perhaps someone even higher. "I'm Lieutenant Colin Lancaster."

"Welcome onboard," Staci said. Colin Lancaster was from Birmingham, judging by his accent, and probably from the very lowest classes. She felt a flash of kinship. She'd grown up in the lower classes, too. "How are you finding the ship?"

Lieutenant Lancaster dismissed his men to the showers with a single hand motion. "Space is tight, but we've been in worse," he said. It was unlikely he'd bring any complaints to her, unless conditions really *were* intolerable. "We have the gear we need to keep up with training, although I would prefer more live-fire exercises and suchlike. We did what we could, on the station, but we didn't have the facilities to keep ourselves in tip-top shape."

"I'll see what I can do," Staci said. "We do have a shooting range, but it isn't configured for anything more than pistols and rifles."

"I think anything would be helpful right now," Lancaster admitted. "There's a lot of work to do."

Staci nodded, curtly. "Ideally, we would have a full company onboard," she said. "But we needed people who'd been on the Sphere. What's *your* impression of the artefact?"

"I think we have been pushing buttons at random, without having the slightest idea what the buttons actually do," Lancaster said, bluntly. "And I'm not too impressed by people who suggest otherwise."

"Interesting," Staci said. "Why do you feel that way?"

Lancaster, she noted, had the confidence to continue. "Take…a simple car. It's a very basic vehicle, compared to a shuttle or a starship, and most people can drive one…if they have the keys. Or the keycards. Or their biometrics are loaded onto the car's datacores as an authorised user. But what happens if they don't? They can still use some of the car's gear, because it isn't linked to the datacores, but not everything. And it takes specialised knowledge to either hack the datacores or bypass them, if they want to take the car without permission."

He paused. "That's a very simple example. A shuttlecraft is a great deal more complex. If you didn't know what it was or what you were doing, how could you hope to fly it? You could push buttons at random, like kids do at air shows, and nothing will actually happen because the control keys have been removed. The Sphere could easily be something along the same lines. We can't see the controls, so we're touching them accidentally and some of them do something without us being quite aware of *what*."

"The researchers say they haven't found any controls," Staci pointed out.

"That they've recognized," Colin Lancaster countered. "Back in the early days of flying, everything was mechanical. Now, we have computers to do all the hard work for us. The flyers who fought the Battle of Britain wouldn't understand a starfighter, even if they figured out what it was. For all we know, the Sphere is controlled by motion sensors and the key to making it work is to do a very specific set of hand movements."

"Good thought," Staci said. "Did you put it in a report?"

"The researchers weren't too interested," Colin Lancaster said. "They're obsessed with the concept of the Sphere being an intelligence test, rather than a hunk of abandoned technology lacking the command codes it needs to function. They refused to think the Sphere might be based on the KISS principle, or that it might not match their preconceptions. It's like…"

He paused, considering his next words carefully. "A very long time ago, a Roman soldier in Britain buries his stash of coins somewhere he thinks they won't be found, then marches off and gets himself killed in battle against the Celts. A couple of thousand years later, someone stumbles across the coins, claims them for himself and uses them to make his family very rich indeed. He may think the Roman left the coins for him, that he is in fact that Roman's distant descendant, but the truth is very different. The Roman had nothing to do with him and never did. The discovery is just a coincidence, a stroke of wild luck. There's no deeper meaning behind it."

Staci asked, "And you think the Sphere is the same?"

"Just because it was left here, doesn't mean it was left here for *us*," Lancaster said. "The Builders didn't know who, if anyone, would find the Sphere. Why should they care about us?"

"That's something that should be mentioned," Staci said. "Good thinking."

Colin grinned. "Some of us *can* count past ten without taking off our shoes."

He flushed, realizing—a moment too late—that he was being familiar. Staci hid her amusement. It was traditional for the starship captain to talk to the marine CO and use him as a prospective sounding board, although…

She nodded, instead. "I'll add that to my report," she said, as her wristcom bleeped. "And keep me informed of your progress."

"Aye, Captain."

CHAPTER ELEVEN:
HMS ENDEAVOUR, IN TRANSIT

"IT WAS GOOD OF YOU TO INVITE us to dinner," Charlotte said. "And it was a very good meal."

Captain Templeton nodded, politely. The dinner had been surprisingly informal. Charlotte had attended navy dinners which had been a great deal more formal, with everything moving in perfect synchronisation and endless toasts to the monarch, the country and the navy itself. She rather preferred the informal setting, at least for a small number of guests. It was easier to let the conversation flow without worrying about performing one's piece in the great dinner dance. She couldn't help reflecting that some of the dinners she'd hosted might have been more interesting if everyone *hadn't* had to follow the rules.

But then, the etiquette guidelines do have the advantage of letting everyone know what is expected of them, she mused. *And no one needs to be surprised by anything.*

"It was certainly good to see new faces," Doctor Athena Gaurs agreed. "There were never many newcomers on the research station."

Charlotte studied the doctor thoughtfully. Doctor Gaurs was younger than the average xenospecialist, although—as the files had pointed out—being an expert in one race didn't always make one an expert in another.

Xenospecialists tended to specialise in a particular race, with only a handful of generalists on standby to study a new race when it was discovered in the inky darkness of space. Athena was young enough not to be bound by preconceptions, nor to think humanity was at the peak of technological development. Some of her older colleagues were still in deep denial. Charlotte understood, all too well. The files had failed to convey the sheer alienness of the Sphere.

"I was surprised the research station wasn't bigger," Charlotte said. "Aren't there others who want a look at the Sphere?"

Athena shrugged. "I think many of the up-and-coming researchers think it will be a long time before we learn anything from the Sphere, certainly anything we can duplicate and put into production ourselves," she said. "There's no writing we can decrypt, nothing we can use to determine anything about the people who built it. Every conclusion we've drawn is little more than guesswork, at best. There are researchers who think it's designed for an amphibious race, like the Tadpoles, and others who think the occupants simply preferred to live in Zero-G. We simply don't know."

"And none of the chambers are marked or anything," Captain Templeton mused. "Or are they marked in a way we can't see?"

"We don't know," Athena said. "In theory, our sensors should have been able to detect writing even if it was somehow outside the visible spectrum. The Tadpoles, for example, have better eyes than us and some of *their* works are practically invisible to our sight, unless we wear specialised goggles. In practice, we don't know. There's a school of thought that insists the Sphere was simply stripped bare, then abandoned. If I hadn't seen the starchart, the one that started this adventure, I would have wondered if the Sphere had been abandoned centuries ago too."

Charlotte's lips twitched. "How *old* is the Sphere?"

"Impossible to say," Athena said.

"I thought it was possible to carbon date alien artefacts," Paris-Jackson said, taking a sip of his wine. "Can't you use it to determine when the Sphere was actually built?"

"No," Athena said. She hesitated, clearly trying to figure out how to explain a scientific concept to a layman. "Carbon dating—the process we use on Earth—can only be applied to living tissue and is based on the assumption the level of carbon within the atmosphere remains roughly consistent at all times, or at least between the artefact getting buried and being dug up. We could probably use it to date a set of ruins on Earth, if there was some preserved tissue within the remains, but not on another world because we wouldn't have a baseline for carbon levels and our results might be completely misleading. The Sphere does not appear to be organic, as far as we can tell, and we didn't find anything resembling living tissue within the chambers."

She stared down at her fingers. "The Sphere might be a billion years old. It might also have come into existence last year. We simply don't know."

"You'd think the virus would have noticed someone setting up shop within the system," Lieutenant Lancaster pointed out. "The Sphere is hardly *small*."

"*Lion* and *Unicorn* entered the system without being noticed," Captain Templeton countered, dryly. "And the virus didn't react to our presence until we started raining rocks on them."

"We don't know," Athena said. "The Sphere doesn't emit any betraying emissions. And it is quite some distance from Virus Prime. For all we know, it really *was* pushed into place last year. There is no way to tell."

"You don't know," Charlotte said. "Is there anything you *do* know?"

"The limits of our ignorance, at least where the Sphere and the Builders are concerned," Athena said. "We don't know who they were, or what they wanted, or what they were doing, skulking around the infected system."

"They might have reached the system before the virus," Captain Templeton said. "We still don't know where the virus actually came from. Which world is its *real* homeworld?"

Charlotte shivered. The reports had been grim. The virus *might* be a natural development, a microscopic life form that had somehow evolved into something that resembled an intelligent species, one capable of infecting humans and other races and bending them to its will. Or it might be something altogether different, a weapon designed by a long-lost race that had gotten out of control—or, worse, had been doing precisely what its makers intended, effectively wiping out every race it encountered. There was no way to know. The virus was so complex, the specialists had noted, that it might have evolved past a kill-switch worked into its genetic makeup. Or it might be something so subtle they simply hadn't been able to locate it. Not yet.

"They were capable of protecting their installations from infection," Lancaster said. "Why would they bother doing that, unless they knew their installations needed protection?"

Charlotte nodded, despite a twinge of discomfort. Colin Lancaster reminded her of Mitch. He might be the junior man in the room, at least as far as the naval officers were concerned, but he wasn't afraid to argue. It didn't mean he was right, of course...she made a mental note to check his file, to perhaps smooth his career if she came home covered in glory. If she didn't, the best thing she could do for him was pretend she'd never even *heard* of him. It wouldn't be hard. No one would expect someone like *her* to pay attention to anyone below command rank.

"Good point," Athena said. "There's a theory the Builders were simply studying the virus from a safe distance."

"And yet, they did nothing to stop it, beyond protecting themselves," Captain Templeton said. "Why not?"

"They might not have felt threatened," Athena said. "Or they might have felt they had no right to intervene."

"This isn't a minor skirmish on Vesy," Captain Templeton said. "This isn't a petty little dispute between two sides, one that will be completely meaningless in the long run. This is"—she paused, grasping for words—"this is more akin to an asteroid heading straight towards the planet, something the locals can't hope to stop even if they realise their days have suddenly become numbered. If we saw it about to happen, surely we'd do something about it."

"Perhaps," Charlotte murmured. She wasn't so sure. She'd known enough politicians to be sure *some* of them would have their doubts, perhaps even veto any attempt to save the primitive race. Their opponents certainly wouldn't hesitate to give them a hard time over the affair. It was easy to believe *someone* would try to argue that, one day, the aliens would become a potential threat. "Or they might have considered themselves so far above us that they didn't think we mattered."

"That's impossible," Athena said. "Surely, an advanced race would be capable of empathy. *We* are."

"We don't always act on that empathy," Lancaster said. "Humans have done truly horrific things to each other."

"In the past," Athena said. "Yes, we have. But we've grown up. Matured."

"I doubt we've matured as much as we would like to think," Captain Templeton said. "We are still a very self-interested race."

"We didn't try to invade Vesy," Athena said. "Or even crush the Foxes and Cows into the ground."

"There's little to gain from taking Vesy," Captain Templeton said. "We don't need living space. We don't need technology or raw materials or *anything* on the surface. Why bother?"

She shook her head. "But if that planet was the only place in the known galaxy we could find unobtanium, we'd invade and take over without a second thought."

"I think you're wrong," Athena said. "We'd try to trade with the locals."

"And if they said no?" Captain Templeton looked grim. "We'd take it anyway, because we needed it. Or at least we'd *tell* ourselves we needed it."

"And they are aliens," Lancaster said. "I did a few months stationed in the Security Zone. I saw horrors…"

He seemed to stare into the past for a long, chilling moment. "People murdered, tortured to death for following the wrong religion. Women raped, then cut open so their bowels spilled on the land. Children brutalised, then gunned down for shits and giggles. Wounded being used to conceal bombs, in hopes of killing or maiming a patrolling soldier. White flags being used to sneak up on our lines, to the point no one dared let anyone close with the lines if they were carrying a flag. It was a nightmare. The atrocities...they were so far beyond reason they served no purpose, not even terrifying the population into submission. They were so lost to themselves that they just committed horror after horror, purely for the sake of horror. And all those crimes were perpetrated on people who looked no different from them."

Athena looked as if she didn't believe him. "It can't be that bad."

"It is," Captain Templeton said, flatly. "If anything, it is an understatement."

"Surely, someone should do something," Athena said.

"Like what?" Lancaster looked up. "Send in the troops, guns blazing?"

Charlotte winced, inwardly. She'd lived a very sheltered life. She'd been safe and warm and secure. It was hard to believe, at times, that people really *would* do horrific things. Her peers might cut her dead, but they wouldn't *cut* her. She knew, intellectually, that not everyone was so lucky, yet it was hard to believe. A young person in Britain, even born to the very lowest classes, was infinitely luckier than someone born on the wrong side of the Security Zone. And yet, few of them would understand their good fortune until they came face to face with the realities of the world.

"There is no reason to assume the Builders will be hostile," Paris-Jackson offered, changing the subject deftly. "They might not see us as equals, but they might not see us as insects either."

"They might not mean to harm us, but that doesn't mean they *won't*," Captain Templeton said. "The Europeans didn't *mean* to introduce disease to the Native Americans. They didn't know, back then, how diseases spread, or what would happen if a particularly nasty disease entered a population that had absolutely no defences against it. And yet, it happened. The diseases ran up and down the continent, killing millions and leaving shattered civilisations in their wake."

"The Europeans wanted gold and slaves," Athena said. "What would an advanced race want with us?"

"It isn't as if we can offer them anything," Paris-Jackson agreed. "The Sphere is *light-years* ahead of anything we can build, isn't it?"

"We humans are kindred, we share the same genetic makeup," Lancaster said. "And yet we find it hard to predict the behaviour of our fellow humans. It would be inadvisable to assume their sense of morality or ethics has anything in common with ours."

"And yet, most of our major advances came from freethinking societies with strong adherence to the rule of law," Athena countered. "Fascistic and communist societies hit their social and technological peak very quickly, then ate their seed corn until they ran out and starved. They had to steal tech from the rest of the world, yet it was never enough to give them an edge. Surely, the Builders would have followed the same route."

"We can't take that for granted," Captain Templeton pointed out. "There's no guarantee they followed the same social development path as ourselves. They might easily have reached their peak, then devolved like the Roman Empire or the European Union. Or they might"—her lips thinned—"have the same attitude *we* do, towards the Security Zone. Let the barbarians kill each other, as much as they like. If they try to cross the border, we drop rocks on them."

"We should be able to do something about it," Athena said.

"It would be politically impossible," Charlotte said. "There's no way you'd convince Parliament to launch a major peacekeeping mission."

Captain Templeton nodded, curtly. "It would be hugely unpopular."

Athena looked irked. "You think a super-advanced race would set out to destroy us?"

"We fire on migrant boats crossing the Mediterranean," Lancaster pointed out. "We don't have a leg to stand on if they feel the same way, when they see us coming."

"We may have nothing in common with them," Captain Templeton said. "They may harm us unintentionally. Or they may not talk to us at all. Or they might think, in a few million years, we will be a threat, so better to swat us now. Or they might have vanished long ago, leaving us to pick through the ruins. For all we know, they created the virus and ended up as its first victims."

"It seems unlikely," Athena said. "If there's nothing to fight over, why bother to fight?"

"They seem to be a very advanced race," Lancaster said. "They might decide the galaxy isn't big enough for both of us."

Athena snorted. "The galaxy is *big*," she said. "There's room for hundreds of races."

"Maybe on our scale," Lancaster agreed. "But what about theirs?"

Charlotte frowned. "What do you mean?"

"In the old days, there were hundreds of small kingdoms and tribes and whatever scattered over the world," Lancaster pointed out. "The tech to hold a bigger kingdom together simply didn't exist. The larger empires still granted a great deal of autonomy to its districts, because they had no choice. As tech advanced, the smaller kingdoms coalesced into bigger ones because they could be held together now. For all we know, the Builders are so advanced that—to them—the galaxy is a small place. And one that isn't big enough for both of us."

Charlotte considered it for a long moment. She didn't want to think about the prospect, although she'd seen and done enough to know people could be dangerously irrational when they saw their self-interest at stake. The idea of people being *rational* depended on a shared understanding of rationality, and on a willingness to understand and accommodate the other side's point of view. But when one side regarded the other as the epitome of irrationality and selfishness...

"I don't believe they'd be openly hostile," Athena said. "Just think what we could learn from them."

"There's no guarantee they'd share their technology," Paris-Jackson said. "I'd be surprised if they offered us anything, even something simple by their standards."

"No," Charlotte agreed. "And what would it do to us if we couldn't match them?"

Captain Templeton tapped her glass. "It has been an interesting dinner, and conversation," she said, seriously. "But the debate is not one we will settle in the absence of facts. We don't know"—she smiled—"anything like enough to draw any real conclusions, not yet. We will reach our destination shortly and there, hopefully, we will find some answers."

Charlotte nodded. She told herself, sharply, not to let her preconceptions blind her when the facts started to arrive. They might be about to meet a hyper-advanced race, or locate the remains of a long-dead race, or simply discover—too late—that they were on a wild goose chase. She feared the Builders were gone. If they'd been around millions of years ago, and they'd been anything like humanity, they would have settled Earth well before humanity's ancestors crawled onto the land for the very first time. Humanity would never have existed at all.

Unless they decided it was better to leave the planet alone, she thought. *Or they'd reached a point where they no longer needed planets...*

"Until then, we will do our best to prepare for anything," Captain Templeton continued. "And now, I need to head to my cabin and get some rest. So do all of you."

And so you're kicking us out, Charlotte thought, wryly. She felt a flicker of sympathy. It was astonishing how many guests outstayed their welcome, whatever the etiquette books might say. She'd had guests stay so long she had to feed them breakfast as well. *I can't really blame you, can I?*

She stood. "Thank you for the dinner, Captain," she said. "I enjoyed it."

"So did I," Athena said. "And the discussion, too."

Charlotte nodded. "I'll see you all tomorrow," she said. "How long until we reach our destination?"

"Six weeks, assuming we maintain our current speed," Captain Templeton said. "We're already beyond the edge of explored space."

"Six weeks." Charlotte felt a twinge of dismay. She'd seen the mission timetable, but it hadn't really felt *real* to her. Not until they'd departed Virus Prime. "And then, we'll see what we see."

"Yes," Captain Templeton agreed. "We will."

CHAPTER TWELVE: HMS ENDEAVOUR, IN TRANSIT

IT WAS HARD NOT TO FEEL UTTERLY ALONE.

The days started to blur together as *Endeavour* jumped through unexplored tramline after tramline, waited long enough to see if anything reacted to their arrival, then made their way to the next unexplored tramline. It was difficult for anyone, even Staci, to believe there was a corvette following them, keeping the survey ship under observation from a safe distance. She even feared, at times, that they'd accidentally given their shadow the slip. It wasn't impossible. *Grantchester* had strict orders not to communicate unless the situation was dire.

She went through her daily routine, trying not to think about how far they were from explored space, from anyone who could help if they ran into trouble. Civilians never understood the sheer vastness of interstellar space, or just how long it could take to get from one point to another even at breakneck speeds. The maps lied, hiding the sheer distance from casual observers. Even a courier boat would take weeks to get from Earth to Virus Prime.

It wore on her crew, and the civilians. The former, at least, had their duties to keep them busy, although there was a steady series of minor incidents that might become serious if she left them to fester. The civilians took it harder, slowly losing their focus and spending more and more time in the entertainment compartments or privacy tubes. She was lucky, she told herself, there hadn't been clashes between civilians and her crew. They never ended well.

She sat in her ready room, reminding herself—not for the first time—that naval service was ninety-nine percent boredom combined with one percent screaming terror.

She wished the boffins had managed to iron the kinks out of their jump-capable probes, allowing her to peek through the tramline without risking the entire ship, or that she'd asked the admiral for a second corvette under her command. She found herself sketching out a concept for an upgraded *Lion*-class starship, a supercarrier carrying corvettes instead of starfighters and gunboats, then shook her head. The design didn't make sense, not even on paper.

Maybe they'll come up with a gunboat that can make transit instead, she thought. *That would work just as well.*

Her eyes lingered on the starchart, and the tramlines leading from star to star. She'd been in the navy long enough to know that the odds of being detected, let alone intercepted, during transit were incredibly low. It hadn't happened very often and it had only worked, a very few times, because the ambusher had had enough warning to get into position before the victim jumped through the tramline. And yet...her head pounded as she studied the starchart. The alien technology wasn't just advanced, it was largely a complete unknown. She couldn't even begin to guess at what it could do.

Perhaps it was a mistake to read all those speculative papers, she reflected, ruefully. *It just made me paranoid for nothing.*

The buzzer rang. Staci looked up, surprised. She didn't have any appointments. Hell, she'd run out of excuses not to read the departmental reports and had written a few of her own, even though no one would see them for months. Jenner would have alerted her if something had changed...she shrugged and keyed the terminal. The hatch hissed open, revealing Jenner and a young woman wearing a science-track uniform.

Staci lifted her eyebrows. Jenner wouldn't have brought the woman to his captain unless it was important, yet...

I should have spent more time as XO on a bigger ship, she reflected. *It might have given me a better idea of his role.*

"Captain," Jenner said. "This is Specialist Sasha Wu. She brought something to my attention and I thought you needed to hear it, too."

Staci nodded. The young woman looked absurdly young—Staci wasn't sure she was even out of her teens—but she wouldn't have been assigned to a survey ship unless she was very good at her job. That she'd been the one to make the report, rather than her superior...Staci wasn't sure that was a good sign. Her departmental head might have rubbished whatever she'd found, if she'd found anything. Or she might have gone over his head...

"Please, take a seat," she said, calmly. She welcomed the distraction. The paperwork could wait. "What have you found?"

Sasha hesitated, her eyes flickering from side to side as if she was no longer sure of her own conclusions. Staci waited, reminding herself she'd been young once, too. She'd spent enough time being the stupid greenie midshipwoman to know it was awkward, no matter how well one had done at the academy. The instructors had always left out the emergencies, insisting that everything be done by the book even when the book didn't apply. Sasha might have made a mistake, and then compounded it by bringing her mistake to her captain's attention, but Staci didn't want to discourage her. Better that Sasha wasted her time than missed something important.

"Captain," Sasha said. "As you know, we have jumped through five alien-grade tramlines in the last four weeks and we have four more jumps to go before we reach our final destination."

"I do," Staci said, keeping her voice even. If she *hadn't* known that... her court-martial for gross incompetence would have been the shortest formality on record. "I have been keeping count."

Sasha flushed. "We launched stealth probes in each of the systems," she continued. "I...I've been compiling their findings and my results... ah, they don't make sense."

"They don't?" Staci cocked her head. "In what way?"

"I…" Sasha paused and started again. "Captain, the stealthed probes carry some of the most advanced passive sensors in existence, from simple optical devices to gravimetric scanners. They are capable of sweeping entire systems relatively quickly and they should be able to find anything, provided it isn't trying to hide."

"Perhaps," Staci said, resisting the urge to point out she already *knew* how probes worked. "A star system is a very big place to hide something."

"That's the point," Sasha said. "Captain, they're not star systems. They're just stars."

Staci blinked. "What?"

"I checked the records, again and again," Sasha said. "Three of the systems we passed through are completely empty. No planets. No asteroids. No comets. I think the largest thing we noted was a cloud of dust, probably drifting in from interstellar space. Beyond that…there was nothing. This one"—she waved a hand at the bulkhead—"is just the same."

"Interesting," Staci mused. She met the younger woman's eyes. "It isn't unknown for a star not to have planets."

"Yes, Captain," Sasha said. "But statistically, the odds against them *all* lacking planets—and everything else—are very high. I checked the records. G2 stars, like Sol, always have asteroids and comets even if they don't have planets. The stars we passed are the first of their type, at least going by earlier discoveries, to be alone in the dark."

Staci said nothing for a long moment. She knew better than to think the passive sensors were perfect. It was easy to hide a starship from them, if one knew powered down everything that radiated a betraying emission. But it was impossible to believe someone could hide an entire planet. There was no cloaking system in existence that could compensate for a planet-sized gravity well. The planets might have been on the wrong side of the primary star, hidden from visual sensors, but the gravimetric sensors would still detect them. Sasha had a point. A lone system without planets wasn't that uncommon. An entire series of them was statistically impossible.

Although we have only explored a tiny fraction of the galaxy, she thought. *For all we know, we live in a uniquely populated section and the rest of the galaxy is uninhabited.*

"I take your point," she said, finally. "What do you think it means?"

"It's hard to say," Sasha said. "The idea of someone just *stealing* the planets..."

Staci shook her head slowly. The largest starship in the known universe was tiny compared to the planet. She'd heard of schemes to outfit a planet with drive fields and turn it into a massive starship, but they'd been little more than vague concepts, the stuff of science-fantasy or just plain fantasy. And yet, she couldn't come up with any other explanation. It couldn't be natural. Surely.

She took a breath. "Do you have any proof the planets existed in the first place?"

"It's hard to say," Sasha said, again. "But...there are traces within the stellar dust that suggest there was a time when this system had a number of planets, although it was a very long time ago. We don't have telescopic data on file for this system. I can file a request to go back to Earth, when we send a message home, to see if anything got recorded, but I doubt it. The planet-searching telescopes were never pointed this far from Earth."

"And if it happened over a thousand years ago," Jenner said, "the records will be useless anyway."

Staci tapped her console, switching the starchart to an in-system display. Sasha had a point. The G2 primary star really *was* oddly alone. And that meant...what? She didn't recall hearing anything from the files, when they were checked to see if the ancient telescopes had spotted anything unusual about their target system. That might well be meaningless. If the planets had been stolen thousands of years ago, the light from their capture would have swept past Earth well before the human race started launching telescopic platforms into orbit. It was vaguely possible someone on the far side of explored space would have spotted something, but she doubted it. The planets had vanished thousands of years ago.

"Interesting," she said, finally. "There's nothing we can do about it now, though."

She looked at her hands thoughtfully. "Keep monitoring the system," she ordered. "And inform me if anything changes."

"Yes, Captain," Sasha said. "And thank you for listening."

Staci dismissed her with a nod, then looked at Jenner. "What do you make of it?"

"A single empty star system might be statistically possible, if unlikely," Jenner said. "An entire collection of them...? I doubt it. And yet...it isn't just planets. The asteroids are missing, too. That's even more statistically unlikely."

He met her eyes. "I don't like the implications."

Staci nodded. The idea of someone just *taking* the planets was too big for her to believe it emotionally, even though it seems the most logical answer. Who could do that? And how? She couldn't wrap her head around it. She'd never heard of anyone taking an asteroid through a tramline, even though asteroids were a great deal smaller than planets. Why would anyone bother? The only answer that came to mind was raw materials and yet...anyone who could do that wouldn't have a shortage, would they? She didn't know.

A thought struck her. "Was there intelligent life on those planets?"

Jenner shrugged.

Staci nodded in irritation. There was no way to know and yet...if someone could move an entire planet, would they bother to check it was uninhabited first? Or would they care as little for the inhabitants as humans cared for insects? Or...moving a planet would make one hell of a weapon. She'd once read an old story in which entire planets had been tossed around like rocks and thrown straight at their targets. It seemed impossible to fight a war on such a scale and yet...she knew it was possible. The proof was right in front of her.

"Inform the diplomatic staff and the xenospecialists," Staci ordered. "What else can we do?"

"I haven't been able to think of anything, Captain," Jenner said. "They did more than just take the planets. They took *everything*."

Staci winced. The sheer *completeness* of the alien effort, if indeed it wasn't pure coincidence, was terrifying. How had they swept an entire star system clear of raw material? It was impossible…she wanted to believe Sasha was mad, that someone had spoofed her sensors, rather than concede it was possible for someone to find and remove every last chunk of raw matter within a star system. Her mind threatened to overload. It was impossible…

"Asteroids don't cast much of a gravity shadow," she said, hearing her voice shake. It was lucky they were alone. "How did they even find them?"

"Their sensors might be sharp enough to pick up anything larger than a dust mote, Captain," Jenner suggested. "And if that's true, they might be able to track us too."

"I have no doubt of it," Staci said. The thought had already occurred to her. "What the fuck are we dealing with?"

"Captain, there's no evidence the Builders are still around," Jenner said, calmly. "There's no reason to think we're in immediate danger. We'll have to see the records from Earth, but I think whatever happened here happened a very long time ago. If there was intelligent life on the stolen planets…we don't know. We may never know."

"No," Staci agreed. "And what'll we do if they *are* still around?"

She stared at the display for a long moment. "If we go back to Virus Prime and report to the admiral…"

Her heart sank, torn between two separate priorities. She had to report the discovery of advanced technology…except they hadn't found the technology itself, just hints of its existence. She also needed to make her way to the alien system and then…and then *what?* Her contingency plans suddenly seemed dull and futile, a child's attempt to impress jaded adults who didn't care. She swallowed, hard. There were times when she was authorised, indeed expected, to abort the mission and retreat into the shadows. This wasn't one of those times.

Except it might be, she thought. *And if I make the wrong call…*

Her instructors had discussed, once upon a time, a fictional situation involving an equally fictional FTL drive. The test pilots had discovered, the hard way, that the drive was nowhere near as accurate as the designers thought. They'd also figured out how to fix it. And *then*, instead of going home to report to their superiors, they'd continued with their mission. The book had presented it as the right thing to do. Staci's instructors had disagreed. They'd pointed out the test ship could have been lost with all hands, taking their discovery with them and ensuring no one would ever know what had happened to them. Their duty was to go home, report in, and *then* carry out their mission. The instructors had been very clear on that point. There were times when reporting home was more important than anything else.

And now she was in the same boat. Should she take *Endeavour* back to Virus Prime? Or order the corvette to go?

She cursed under her breath. She knew what to do if the ship came under attack. She knew how to handle everything from terrorists holding her crew hostage to an alien fleet thundering towards her. She knew how to react to clear and present dangers, natural or manmade. She wouldn't say she was fearless—only idiots were truly fearless—but she never let her fear interfere with her duty. She had been trained to handle anything. But the unknown worried her. She didn't know anything like enough to judge the situation properly.

And if I keep second-guessing myself, she told herself, *I'll drive myself mad.*

"No." Staci switched the display back to the starchart. "We will proceed as planned, keeping a wary eye out for any further signs of supertechnology. When we reach the last transit, we will take every precaution. If there are signs of an alien presence…we will do as we see fit."

"Aye, Captain," Jenner said. He smiled, suddenly. "For what it's worth, I'm betting we'll find nothing but ruins."

"I hope you're not putting money in the pot," Staci said, with mock severity. There was no way to keep the crew from placing bets, and gambling with their paychecks, but officers were forbidden to take part. The last thing anyone needed was an officer on the command track owing money to a junior crewman. That never ended well.

"No, Captain," Jenner said. "But really, if they were still around, I think we would have noticed. The Sphere was discovered through sheer luck. So were the other artefacts. I think, if they were active, we would have seen something."

"Point," Staci agreed. She recalled her earlier thoughts and nodded to herself. The Builders should have settled Earth and precluded human evolution a long time ago. "But even ruins could be disconcerting, if they're as eerie as the Sphere."

"True," Jenner said. His lips twitched. "Do you know, there was a cult on Earth that believed aliens came to us, when we were young, and helped us build society?"

"No," Staci said. "And did they have proof?"

"Proof? We don't need no stinking proof." Jenner smiled. "No, there was no actual proof of anything. But that didn't stop them claiming the pyramids were built with alien technology because they thought our ancestors couldn't have built them for themselves. They insisted the similarities between buildings on opposite sides of the planet was proof aliens had been involved."

Staci cocked her head. "And your point?"

"If you look at the problems the locals faced, the pyramids are pretty good solutions," Jenner said, simply. "And we can see why they were built that way. We can unlock the mysteries of the Sphere too. Given time, we can solve everything. And we will."

"I hope you're right," Staci said. "I really do."

CHAPTER THIRTEEN: HMS ENDEAVOUR, IN TRANSIT

THE BRIDGE CREW FELT...ALIVE.

Staci took her seat and checked the console, bracing herself as the survey ship glided towards the tramline. It was unusually faint, the strand of gravimetric force linking the two stars oddly weak, to the point they'd had to reprogram the drive to be sure they could jump to the next system. Staci eyed it warily, unsure if it could be trusted. The tramline seemed to be fluctuating in a manner that made no sense to her, or the researchers below decks. If it was too weak to ride...

We might be about to find out, she thought, grimly. The alien starchart had implied the tramline was usable, but it was impossible to be sure. *And if we can't make transit, we'll have to see if we can find another way to our destination.*

She glanced at Jenner. "Status report?"

Jenner sounded calm, reassuringly. "Condition One has been set throughout the ship. All departments have reported ready. All sensors and weapons are on standby, the latter locked to be unable to fire without direct orders from the bridge. The research crews and diplomats are in their quarters, watching proceedings."

Locked in their quarters, Staci translated, dryly. The official report would be a little more diplomatic, but everyone would know the truth. The last thing she needed, if the shit hit the fan when they jumped into the alien system, was the diplomats trying to throw their weight around. Lady Charlotte had more common sense than Staci had assumed, but the rest of her team was composed of career diplomats. *They can do their job once we're sure we're not in immediate danger.*

"Communications, bring up the first contact package," she ordered, as if the communications officer wouldn't have already done it. "Prepare to transmit, but do not unless I give the order."

"Aye, Captain," MacPhee said.

Staci nodded. The first contact package was supposed to be universal, although—from reading between the lines—she had a feeling it was nowhere near as universal as the xenospecialists claimed. None of humanity's alien allies had been particularly impressed, while the virus had completely ignored all attempts to make contact. Staci suspected there were too many hidden assumptions worked into the package, despite the involvement of non-human researchers. But then, the package had only ever been deployed during combat. It would be odd for anyone to pause long enough to decipher the message, then put together a reply.

They kept saying we needed to give the new aliens a chance to work out how to use the package, she reflected. *And none of them ever had the time they needed to do it.*

She leaned back in her chair, trying to project a calm image to her crew. The final series of transits had been stressful, as they'd passed through four star systems that had been swept clean of everything from comets to gas giants. The crew had found it difficult to take. The civilians, oddly, had seemed to take it in their stride, but then they didn't grasp how impossible it was. How could they? To them, it was just something that had happened. The spacers, by contrast, saw the devil in the details. It was impossible, with modern technology, to pulverize an entire star system, let alone steal its planets and asteroids. What sort of tech did you need to do it?

"Helm," she ordered. "Start the countdown."

"Aye, Captain."

Staci watched the seconds tick down to zero, her heart pounding so loudly she feared her crew could hear. She'd done nearly a dozen blind jumps during the mission, but this...this time, the Builders might be waiting on the other side. Did they know *Endeavour* was coming? The sensors had picked up no trace of installations on the near side of the tramline, but that was meaningless. Stealthed platforms would be missed, as long as they kept their active sensors powered down. God alone knew how the Builders might monitor the stars around their homeworld. She'd heard the crew's speculations. They'd veered between technology that was plausible, if beyond anything the human race had developed, to tech that might as well be magic. She hadn't tried to stop them thinking about it. One of them might even come up with the right answer.

"Ten seconds," Atkinson said. "Nine...eight..."

Here we go, Staci thought. Nervousness gripped her heart. She hadn't been so nervous since she'd entered the academy, since she'd lost her virginity. Back then, she'd charged right at it, overriding her nerves through sheer force of will. Now...that wasn't an option. *Ready or not.*

She had a sudden overpowering sense of a gulf opening in front of her, as if the starship was precariously balanced on the edge of a cliff, about to plunge into the unknown...before her vision seemed to dim. A flash of panic shot through her. She'd read the report from HMS *Warspite's* first transit, when the meld of human and alien technologies had caused a catastrophic power failure, and *that* had been very close to Sol. Here...the darkness seemed to linger, resting on her vision like an unwelcome touch, before snapping out of existence. She heard someone being sick behind her as the display blanked and carefully didn't look around. Jenner would see to their relief, if they were unable to continue at their post. Staci didn't like the implications. There were twelve people on the bridge. If one in twelve had been sick, what was it like below decks? How many...?

Alarms howled. The display blazed with red lights. Staci felt her thoughts freeze, just for a seconds, as the icons cycled rapidly. They were under attack! No, they were caught in a meteor storm. No...

"Evasive action," she snapped. Her mind raced, trying to find an explanation. Had someone emplaced junk along the tramline, in hopes any unwelcome guests would crash right into it before they had a chance to react? It was theoretically possible, but the logistics would be appalling. "Stand by all weapons!"

Endeavour lurched, violently. Staci wished she had a proper warship under her command. *Endeavour's* drives were cycling as quickly as possible, but she didn't have the weapons or armour to protect herself for long. The enemy seemed to have them at point-blank range. Or...the display quietened, slightly, as the tactical officers downgraded the threat. The wall of icons—Staci couldn't think of it as anything else—wasn't getting any closer.

She found her voice. "Report!"

"Captain." Lieutenant Helen Yang sounded poleaxed, as if someone had hit her over the head with a brick. The sensor officer had never lost her cool before. "Captain, I think you should see this."

Staci gritted her teeth as the display updated rapidly. Her mind refused to accept what she saw. A wall of debris...her thoughts spun in circles, trying to grasp the sheer impossibility in front of her. There was no such thing as an asteroid field so dense one couldn't fly an entire fleet of carriers and battleships through it, not until now. It was...it was too big. The display kept pulling back, revealing more and more pieces of debris orbiting the distant star...no, not *that* distant. She couldn't believe her eyes. The sight was just...

"Impossible," Jenner breathed. "Captain, it's a Dyson Sphere."

"It was," Staci managed. The sphere had been shattered beyond repair, the chunks of debris—some larger than an entire planet—drifting in their old orbit. She could see the star peeking out behind the wreckage. "Why didn't we *see* this?"

"I don't know, Captain," Helen said. "I...it's possible the destruction only occurred a few short years ago."

She shook her head. "No, because we saw a star..."

"Captain," Atkinson said. "We're not where we should be."

Staci stared at him. "What do you mean?"

"The tramline was projected to take us to a G2 star ten light-years from our location," Atkinson said, in the tone of a man who knows he had to tell his superiors something they wouldn't believe. "Instead, it took us here"—he brought up the starchart—"and...and we crossed thirty-seven light-years in a single bound."

"Oh." Staci kept her voice under tight control. It would be a record, if they could get home. The longest jump ever recorded was fifteen light-years and that had been under very specific circumstances. "Can we get back?"

"Unknown," Atkinson said. "The tramline is still there, but..."

But we have no way to know where it'll take us the next time, Staci finished. *We don't even know how it brought us here.*

She stared down at the display. It was incredible. There was so much wreckage in the system that...that it was impossible. She thought she knew, now, where all the missing planets had gone. The evidence was right in front of her. She tried to calculate, mentally, just how much raw material it would take to wrap a shell around a star and drew a blank. Her mind was too stunned to work it out. She'd need to toss the question to the analysts, along with everything else. Her earlier thoughts came back to haunt her. There was a very real risk they'd never be able to go home.

"Tactical," she said, carefully. "Are we in any immediate danger?"

"I don't think so, Captain," Lieutenant Commander Philip McDougall said. He was an older man, a reassuring presence on the bridge. It helped that he'd fought in many of the later battles during the war. "The wreckage appears to be in a stable orbit. I suspect the pieces that wound up in unstable orbits either plunged into the star or interstellar space a long time ago. The long-range sensors aren't picking up anything hostile, at least as far as we can tell. If there's anyone still alive within the system, they're keeping their heads down."

Staci nodded. They'd been lucky. She'd made the jump a goodly distance from the primary star, or so she'd thought, but whatever force had yanked them to the rubble had dropped them far too close to the shell for comfort. A few thousand kilometers closer to the star and they'd have flown right *into* the wreckage. *Endeavour* would've become the first starship to fly right into an asteroid field and crash. And no one would ever know what had happened.

Her eyes narrowed. "Sensors, is there any sign of *Grantchester*?"

"No, Captain," Helen said.

"Helm, take us away from the tramline, then hold us on station," Staci ordered. Her mind raced, tossing up possibilities she didn't care to think about. What if *Grantchester* jumped to the original target star? Or what if she materialised right on top of *Endeavour*? It was impossible, but...what was one more impossible thing before breakfast? "Tactical, continue to sweep the system for possible threats."

"Aye, Captain."

Staci glanced at Jenner. "Status report?"

Jenner looked grim. "It was a rough transit," he said. "Nineteen injured, three seriously."

"Shit." Staci closed her eyes for a long moment. She wanted to go down to sickbay to check on the wounded, but she couldn't leave the bridge. "And the ship itself?"

"Minor damage to the drives, and power surges in the network, but nothing major," Jenner assured her. "We have enough redundancies built into the system to handle it."

Staci allowed herself a moment of relief. They could jump...although she had no idea where they'd find themselves. If they tried to get back to their start point...she shivered helplessly. How the hell had they even gotten here? The tramline couldn't have been that long and, even if it had, it hadn't pointed at the wreckage. They shouldn't have gotten anywhere near the ruined sphere.

"Get repairs started," she ordered. "I want to be ready to leave in a hurry if necessary."

"Aye, Captain."

"Captain," Helen said. "I...I think this is a binary star system."

"What do you mean, you *think*?" Staci put firm controls on her temper. She needed to set a good example, even though she felt as though everything she knew about the universe had suddenly become as insubstantial as a ghost, as if the laws of nature were being rewritten on the fly. "It is or it isn't?"

Helen tapped her console, altering the display. Staci's mind froze in utter disbelief. It was impossible. It was...

Her mouth was dry. "A second sphere," she managed. "They built two."

"I think so, Captain," Helen said. "And this one is intact."

Staci forced herself to take a breath. "Are you sure?"

"As far as I can tell, from this distance, the shell is intact," Helen reported. "The optical sensors cannot pick up any hints of sunlight. It's possible the pieces are closer together, to the point they're blocking the sunlight, but I don't think so. The shell appears to be intact."

"Incredible," Staci muttered. "Any energy emissions? Communications? Any hint the sphere is inhabited?"

"No, Captain," Helen said. "If there's anyone inside, they either don't know we're here or simply aren't interested in talking to us."

Staci's mind churned as she took a seat. The sphere—the *spheres*—were construction projects on a scale that dwarfed anything humanity had ever built. They were huge beyond words, trapping two entire stars so their entire energy output could be put to use. She couldn't imagine what it would be like to live in the interior, to have all that land for herself...the entire human race, all twenty billion, would have all the living space they wanted. It was...she took a long breath as she considered the implications. It was possible the sphere was dead, that the occupants had died out years ago. But it was also possible the occupants were watching and waiting...

"Captain, I'd like to direct a pair of probes towards the second sphere," Helen said, looking up from her console. Her eyes were bright with enthusiasm. "There are limits to what we can determine from this distance. We might be able to find a way inside, or find a control centre, or…"

"Wait," Staci ordered. If there were occupants watching and waiting, they might take the probes as a hostile act. *Endeavour* was tiny, compared to the sphere, but she dared not assume their arrival hadn't been noticed. She remembered just where the starchart they'd followed had come from and scowled. The paranoid part of her mind was starting to wonder if they'd been lured into a trap. "If we…"

Her mind raced. They had to try to make contact. If there was someone watching them, they needed to convince them of their good intentions before it was too late. The probes weren't dangerous—they were too expensive to turn into ballistic missiles—but the aliens wouldn't know. If there were aliens…it had been easier, she reflected darkly, during the war. At least they'd known what they had to do.

"Communications," she said, keeping her voice steady. It wasn't easy. She'd thought herself used to it, to seeing clear proof of alien super-technology, but she'd been wrong. "Transmit the first contact package."

"Aye, Captain."

Staci forced herself to wait, her mind churning. It would be hours, at least, before the aliens got the message, decrypted it and came up with a response. Assuming, of course, they could understand the message. She tried not to consider the possibility they might have an FTL communications technology that made the flicker network look like signal fires or telegraph systems. If they did…*Endeavour* might get an answer a *lot* sooner than she expected.

She glanced at Jenner. "We'll hold position here, for the moment," she said. "If we don't get a response, we may have to risk sending the probes anyway."

"Understood," Jenner said. He sounded like someone desperately trying to look on the bright side and failing, miserably. The rest of the crew were concentrating on their duties in a manner that suggested they were trying not to think about the scene on the display. "If nothing else, there should be plenty of living tissue in the debris. We can finally determine just how old their civilisation was. Is."

"Good thinking," Staci said. "But we'd better wait to see if we get a reply before we start poking through the debris. We don't want to offend anyone."

And it doesn't matter if we didn't mean to offend anyone, her thoughts added, numbly. *They have the bigger guns. It is their opinion that counts.*

"I need a drink," someone muttered behind her.

"That will do," Jenner snapped.

Staci said nothing as she sat in her chair and watched more and more debris appear on the display. It was incredible. She'd seen the debris left behind by full-scale fleet engagements, but...this was so far beyond them that her mind had problems coping with what she was seeing. There was enough raw matter drifting in front of her to produce hundreds of thousands of starships...she forced herself to consider the implications as she waited. The first sphere was nothing more than ruins. She found it hard to believe a race that could build something like that would make a simple mistake, something that would set off a chain of disasters that would eventually destroy the sphere. No, they'd know what to expect and compensate for everything that could go wrong. And that raised an obvious question, one she needed to answer.

We need to know, and quickly, she thought. *Who, or what, destroyed one of the spheres?*

Her blood ran cold. *And if it was destroyed by hostile action*, her thoughts added, *is whoever did it still around?*

CHAPTER FOURTEEN: HMS ENDEAVOUR, DYSON SYSTEM

"THEY DIDN'T REPLY?" Charlotte wasn't sure what to make of it. "No answer at all?"

She stood in the science compartment, watching as the holographic display updated time and time again as the sensors noted and logged debris orbiting the primary star. It was hard to grasp the sheer scale of what she saw, to believe that some of the pieces of debris—the wreckage of a star-encasing sphere—were actually larger than a life-bearing world. Part of her mind wondered if they could truly apply the word *debris* to something bigger than Earth, part of her—looking from a vantage point well clear of the debris field—agreed that debris was what it truly was. The catastrophe had been so big, so all-encompassing, that mere words could not describe it. There was nothing in human history to compare.

"No, My Lady," Doctor Athena Gaurs said. She sounded as stunned as Charlotte, even though she'd spent the last nine months exploring an inexplicable alien artefact. "If there's anyone in Dyson Two, they either can't hear us or they're not replying."

Charlotte shot her a sharp look. "They have to be able to hear us, right?"

"It's hard to say." Athena's lips quirked. "In theory, we could read smoke signals and semaphore messages. In practice, we might have trouble recognising they were even there, let alone read them. The inhabitants might be so far beyond using radio waves for communications that they don't even bother to monitor the channels for messages."

"I doubt it," a naval scientist said. "One can use radio waves for a great deal more than simple communication."

Charlotte nodded, taking a seat and watching the display update again. The briefing notes had raised the suggestion they'd find nothing but ruins, the remains of a long-gone alien civilisation, yet...the scene in front of her boggled the mind. She'd seen the speculations offered by the science department, as they started to parse the sensor readings; she'd read their outlines of how the sphere had been constructed, noted their estimates of how many people had lived in the interior. The figures were so high they were just...*numbers*. There had been enough space, inside the ruined sphere, for every living human to have an entire estate of their own.

And the second sphere is intact, she thought, numbly. *Who knows how many people are living inside, waiting for us?*

She felt her heart sink. Captain Templeton had, so far, refused to dispatch any probes towards the second sphere. They were relying on long-range observation, which made it harder to be *sure* of what they saw. Not, she supposed, that it mattered. The exterior of the sphere was unbroken, as far as they could tell. There didn't seem to be any way in or out. She wondered, idly, if the Builders had known how to teleport, or open wormholes, or simply decided to turn their backs on the outside universe. Hell, perhaps they'd forgotten to include a way out, when they'd built the sphere. Her lips twitched at the thought, although she knew it was unlikely. There were old jokes about builders accidentally trapping themselves inside the houses they were building, because they forgot the doors. They didn't seem so funny now.

The display updated, *again*. Charlotte glanced at the debris counter, feeling decidedly superfluous. The sensors had logged hundreds of thousands of pieces and the counter was *still* going up, as long-range sensor pulses bounced off the debris and returned to the ship. It was...it was just too *big*. She felt an urge to close her eyes and pretend it wasn't there, even though there was no point. Reality didn't go away when people closed their eyes. The debris field had to be searched...

She smiled, rather sourly. She was no expert, but even *she* could tell it would take centuries to search the entire field. They could send the entire crew and spend weeks exploring the nearest pieces of debris and they'd barely scratch the surface. Hell, they wouldn't even do *that*. The debris field was just too big. She wondered, idly, if there would be people trying to turn it into a settlement, perhaps mining it for raw materials. Or if the government would manage to declare the entire system off-limits, at least until they determined if the second sphere was inhabited. The alien contact regulations were clear. There were strict limitations to how far investigations could go until humanity knew *precisely* what it was dealing with.

But that's to keep us from cutting open alien bodies before we know how they treat their dead, she reflected. *It doesn't cover picking up debris and turning it into raw materials for habitats.*

She shook her head, a moment later, as one of the scientists started to speculate on the possibilities. There was a case to be made, under interstellar law, that the shattered sphere was nothing more than space junk, rubble that could be swept up and converted into something useful by the first person who came along. Hell, if one squinted just right, the prospector could lay claim to the entire system and everything inside it. But practically, it didn't matter. The Builders had never signed the interstellar treaties that made up the framework of interstellar law. And if they still had the tech to build a sphere, they probably had the tools to make human law irrelevant.

Their interpretation of the laws may be different from ours, she mused. *And if they have the bigger guns, their interpretation will be the one that stands.*

It wasn't a pleasant thought. She'd spent much of her time, during the voyage, studying the history of diplomacy. Humanity had moved from the strong dominating the weak to a pretence that all states were equal and then back again, as greed and ambition was overcome by idealism, which in turn gave way to cold realism. There was no way any country would honour paper promises, when its interests were at stake. The Builders might feel the same way. Charlotte understood Captain Templeton's reluctance to do anything that might be construed as a hostile act. It was hard to say what might offend the Builders. And if they took offence, they might blow up the sun.

She leaned back in her chair, feeling the seconds ticking by as the scientists argued. There was nothing for her to do, but wait. Either they'd get a response to their signals or…or what? Charlotte wondered, idly, how long she'd be expected to remain on the ship, if the system was completely dead. Would she be allowed to go home early or…or what? How long would she be expected to stay in the system?

"We're not picking up any artificial energy sources," one scientist said. "There's no hint anything survived the cold soak."

"Their systems may be radiating emissions we can't detect," another said. "How did they even build the sphere? We couldn't do it even if we had the raw materials on hand."

Charlotte leaned forward. "How much would one *need* to build a Dyson Sphere?"

"A lot," Athena said, quietly. "The shell alone would require"—she waved her hands helplessly—"a lot of raw material, even if it was little more than an inch thick. And it wouldn't be. I'd expect them to want the shell to be thick enough to survive an asteroid striking the outer surface, for fear the whole structure would be popped like a balloon and the atmosphere vent into space."

"One of the spheres *was* destroyed," Charlotte reminded her. "Was it…was it struck by a piece of space debris, setting off a chain reaction?"

"I can't imagine so, unless the Builders were truly incompetent," Athena told her. "They *must* have considered the possibility and taken steps to avert it."

"Maybe not," an older scientist said. "Earth knew about the risk of asteroid impacts for decades, and the technology existed to protect the planet, but it was still a great many years before we put a simple asteroid deflection system into operation. Sure, the odds of an asteroid striking the planet were very low, yet…one impact would be enough to send the human race back to the Stone Age, if it didn't wipe us out completely. The Builders might have had their own reasons not to set up a defensive grid around the spheres."

"But the sphere literally encases—encased—the star," Athena countered. "If a piece of passing space junk was caught by the star's gravity well and pulled inwards, it *would* eventually slam into the sphere. There's no way they could think the odds of impact would be vanishingly low. They'd *have* to do something about it."

"Unless they were confident their armour would keep them safe," the scientist said. "We were never able to make an impression on the Sphere's hull, were we?"

Charlotte cleared her throat. "What would it take to destroy a sphere?"

Athena said nothing for a long moment. "We're still trying to work out just how long ago it happened," she said, finally. "It's possible there was an impact that set off a chain reaction, as you said. If the impact was too great for them to patch the hole or compensate before it was too late, it's possible the sphere was eventually torn apart. Given the sheer scale of the thing, even an incredibly fast process would still have looked quite slow. But in truth, we may never know."

"And it could have been deliberate," Charlotte said. "For all we know, the two spheres went to war."

"It would be unwise," Athena said. "Mutual destruction would be a likely outcome."

"Perhaps, but that never stopped pointless rock wars," another scientist said. "Two idiot miners, banging at each other with pop guns when there's an entire *system* of unexploited rocks to mine."

"Or terrorists," Charlotte said. She wanted to believe an advanced race wouldn't *have* terrorists, but human history suggested otherwise. It hadn't been *that* long since the Troubles. Or when an asteroid independence faction had launched a rock at the homeworld in hopes of separating the settlements from Earth. "If there was a terrorist group that somehow got control of something very nasty…"

She let the words hang in the air for a long moment. "We need to know."

"Yes," Athena agreed. "But scientific discoveries simply cannot be made on a timetable. We may find out tomorrow. Or we may never know."

Charlotte nodded, reluctantly. There was no point in arguing. Athena was right. The answers might be waiting for them in an alien library, with all the books and datacores intact and waiting to be read, but they'd have to *find* the library first. The biggest library Charlotte knew was the British Library in London, a massive collection of buildings crammed with millions of books, and it was tiny compared to the debris field. She wondered, sourly, what would happen if the answer was *never* found. Would the human race learn something from the disaster? Or would they assume a long-dead race had nothing to teach humanity?

They built a pair of Dyson Spheres, Charlotte told herself. *Dead or not, they certainly have something to teach us.*

• • •

It was a commanding officer's duty, Staci knew, to visit the wounded in sickbay when she had finished dealing with the crisis and had a few moments. It wasn't something Captain Campbell had done often, but it had been rare for crewmen to be wounded on *Unicorn*. The frigate had been so small, by naval standards, that a direct hit was likely to blow the entire ship to atoms. She felt a pang of guilt as she moved from bed to bed, annoyed that she didn't know the wounded men's names. The ship was just too big for her to know *everyone*.

Which doesn't absolve you of the duty of visiting them, she told herself, sharply. *You should be grateful no one is dead.*

She kept the thought to herself as she spoke briefly to each of the wounded, trying to assure them their injuries had not been unnoticed. *Endeavour* had been lucky, given the rough transit and their arrival within a debris field, but she doubted any of the wounded felt that way. Modern medicine could handle almost anything, provided it wasn't immediately lethal, yet they'd still need weeks or months to recover. Normally, they'd be transferred to a proper hospital and recuperation centre as quickly as possible. Here...they'd just have to stay in sickbay, at least until they were cleared to return to duty.

"Captain," Doctor Jim Carnell said, when she'd finished her brief sweep through sickbay. "A word?"

Staci nodded and allowed the doctor to show her into his office. Jim Carnell was a very experienced medical professional, with a background that covered both human and alien medicine. He'd been very open with her about the limits of xenomedicine—each race was different, to the point that a cure for one race could easily be lethal to another—but he was one of the best in the business. If someone had to come up with a cure for an alien disease in a hurry, he would have the best chance of success.

And the prospect of a cross-species infection is now a great deal more likely, she reflected, grimly. *The virus had no trouble moving from the original host-bodies to us.*

"The physical damage will pose no problems," Carnell said, waving her to a chair. "The worst is a series of broken bones, all of which can be fixed with a combination of surgery and medical regeneration. I dare say most of the wounded will be ready for physical therapy within the week, then fit to return to duty within the month. There may be unexpected complications, but we should be able to handle them."

Staci nodded, curtly. "Do you think there'll be any long-term effects?"

"Physically, *no*," Carnell said. "Mentally...serious injuries always leave scars, mental scars, although in most cases the simple fact recovery is quick and pretty much complete tends to minimise the damage. This was not a brutal assault or something else that will leave long-term scars, ones that cannot be handled quickly. My professional opinion is that the wounded will recover quickly and be fit to return to duty, like I said, within the month."

"Good," Staci said. "Or is there a *but*?"

Carnell jabbed a finger at the bulkhead. "It's never easy to tell how people will react to alien contact," he said. "The idea humans and aliens would integrate more or less completely has been proven wrong. We and they are simply too different. Alien shock is not uncommon even when dealing with the Vesy, who are close enough to us for one of them to serve on a human starship. And now…I don't know how the crew will react to the Dyson Spheres."

Staci frowned. "Do you think there'll be any serious problems?"

"It's hard to say," Carnell said. "The Tadpoles introduced themselves to us by opening fire. The demands of war kept us from thinking about the long-term implications of alien contact and by the time the war ended, we were used to them. The same can be said for the other races, although the Vesy had their own form of alien shock when they realised just how powerful we were. Here…our crew will have too much time to brood."

"And you think the sphere will mess with their minds," Staci finished.

"I think that looking at clear proof of a more advanced race will mess with us, yes," the doctor said. "And we're not even sure how we got here."

Staci nodded, curtly. "I think we'll just have to monitor the situation," she said. The navy took mental health seriously, but it was never easy to convince officers and crew to trust the headshrinkers even if they were military personnel who understood the realities of military life. Civilian psychologists were worse than useless for military personnel. "Alert me if there are signs of real trouble…"

Her wristcom bleeped. She touched the keypad lightly. "Go ahead."

"Captain, this is Jenner," her XO said. "*Grantchester* just jumped through the tramline. They're a little bit surprised."

Staci nodded, torn between relief and apprehension. "Inform her CO I'll speak to him shortly," she said, standing. The news was either good or bad. If *Grantchester* couldn't jump back to human space, both ships might be trapped until they could find a new route back home. "And then, we need to decide how to proceed."

"Aye, Captain."

"I'll keep an eye on things," Carnell promised. "But they may get out of hand before we notice something is wrong."

"Monitor the stills," Staci ordered. There was a long-standing tradition of naval crewmen brewing their own booze, which officers tended to ignore as long as the brewers were careful to ensure no one showed up for their shift drunk and stinking of alcohol. If there was a sudden demand for more booze, it would be a good sign of trouble brewing. "I'll speak to you later."

She made her way out of sickbay and back to the bridge, thoughts churning. They could easily spend years cataloguing the entire debris field, learning little beyond the locations of countless pieces of junk. The scientists were already pressing for more intrusive examinations, for sampling missions and dozens of other things that might—might—provoke a reaction from the other sphere. Staci had no idea if they were being watched, or how the occupants might react if *Endeavour* did something they didn't like. And yet, she knew there was a limit to what they could learn through passive observation. Sooner or later, they would need to be a little more proactive.

We can spend a week or two collecting passive data, she told herself. *And if we don't get anywhere doing that, we can start probing the wreckage a little more openly.*

CHAPTER FIFTEEN: DYSON ONE, DYSON SYSTEM

"MY GOD."

Tobias was barely aware of his own voice as the shuttle glided away from *Endeavour* and headed towards the shattered sphere. The ruins were simply too *big*. It wasn't *right* that they could see pieces of debris with the naked eye, let alone that such pieces of debris were so large they could reasonably be counted as planets. He thought he saw the star, twinkling absurdly as pieces of debris orbited so rapidly that the star came in and out of view…it was an optical illusion, he told himself, but it still felt real. And unnatural. It was all he could do not to cower in front of the sheer immensity of the alien structure.

He bit his lip. He'd played countless games, years ago, when he'd had to fly a starfighter through a thick asteroid belt, something that simply didn't exist in the real world. One could pick a course at random, aiming right into the field, yet the odds of hitting something would still be impossibly low. Here…he had the feeling he'd have to be careful as they glided towards the debris. The debris field was so big the odds of hitting something were far higher than he would have preferred.

And if we hit something at interplanetary speeds, his mind insisted on pointing out, *the damage will be catastrophic.*

He checked his mask was within reach, although he was fairly sure he wouldn't have time to grab it if they really *did* hit something. His instructors had drilled him on emergency procedures time and time again and they'd made it clear that seconds counted, that if he failed to take action quickly enough he'd be dead. The procedures had struck him as odd, at first, until they'd pointed out that they all relied on life support gear being within reach. If it wasn't, they'd said, the only thing you could do as the air ran out was bend over and kiss your ass goodbye. They'd been right too. The random drills had proved it beyond all doubt.

Marigold muttered something under her breath—an oath of her own, no doubt—as they picked up speed. The debris field glittered in front of them, some of the pieces big enough for him to see without sensor enhancement. He tried to calculate how long it had been since the disaster and drew a complete blank. The orbits appeared to be relatively stable—anything falling towards the sun or out into interstellar space would have done it a very long time ago—which made it harder to deduce the timescale. It could have been before humanity crawled out of the ocean or only a *mere* thousand years ago. The time abyss gaped open in front of him. For all he knew, the spheres were so old entire civilisations had risen and fallen between their destruction and the present day. They were just too big.

"It doesn't feel like *the* Sphere," he said, at least partly to distract himself. "Could there be *two* super-races?"

"The Sphere is intact," Marigold pointed out. "This...this *thing* is in ruins."

Tobias nodded, slowly, as they picked up speed. They'd have to be careful. Some of the larger chunks of debris were big enough to have gravity fields, which would play merry hell with the shuttle if it got too close. Normally, it wouldn't be a problem, but with so many gravity wells in the same general area...it felt like an absurd game, with starships battling it out as black holes appeared randomly, tearing up the region and swallowing anyone unlucky enough to run into one. He told himself, firmly, it wouldn't be anything like as bad. The shuttle was perfectly capable of climbing out of a gravity well or landing on a piece of debris if it was caught and found itself unable to escape.

He heard rustling behind him as the Marines shifted uncomfortably. He wasn't sure why they'd been landed with the sampling mission, not when there was no hint of hostile aliens, but he suspected the captain hadn't wanted the scientists anywhere near the debris. They might do something stupid, purely in the interests of scientific enquiry. Or something…Tobias didn't know. He was glad to have them, knowing they'd have the sense to drop tools and run if they encountered something they couldn't handle. The scientists would be more likely to push buttons, just to see what they did.

Assuming we find any buttons, he mused. *We never did on the Sphere.*

The chunks of debris grew larger until they blotted out the horizon. It was impossible to believe, yet impossible to deny, that the flat plate in front of them was bigger than Britain itself. He peered at it through the optical sensors and saw jagged scars on the edges, the sort of damage a ship might take in battle if the enemy got a clear shot at her hull, but incredibly—impossibly—large. If it had been in combat, it would have been combat on a scale that would make the Death Star look puny. It was hard to believe it was just the remnants of a disaster that had taken place hundreds of thousands of years ago.

He frowned as he slowly orbited the debris, peering down through the shuttle's sensors. The outer exterior of the plate had been bare—he'd expected as much—but the sun-facing exterior was just as barren. The plate looked like stripped metal. There were no traces of water or soil, let alone anything one might need to turn the interior into something livable. It would have been vast beyond words and yet…there wasn't even a single house, no hint someone had ever lived there. He swallowed, ice running down his spine as he realised—again—just how huge the sphere had been, before its demise. There was no guarantee they'd find any traces of the aliens in a hurry. They could have built cities a hundred times the size of

London, the biggest city in England, and they'd vanish without trace in the sheer immensity of the sphere.

Marigold cleared her throat. "Do you want to land here?"

"I don't know." Tobias raised his voice. "I can't see any traces of anything, but bare metal. Do you want me to find another landing zone?"

Colin Lancaster scrambled forward. He didn't seem as awed by the ruins as either of the spacers. Tobias—uncharitably—attributed it to a more limited mindset. Colin wasn't stupid, but he wasn't that well-read either. The philosophical implications of the alien wreckage, and the clear proof of advanced alien technology, were beyond him. Tobias wasn't sure if he should pity or envy the other man. It was easier to get things done if one wasn't overawed by one's surroundings.

"If you can find one you think might be better, then yes," Colin said, finally. "If not, we have time."

Tobias doubted it. The survey ship would have to return home eventually. God alone knew what sort of response they'd get. The shattered sphere would draw attention from the rest of the world, even if there *wasn't* a second—seemingly intact—sphere right next door. Tobias looked up, towards where he knew the second sphere had to be. There was no way to tell if it was occupied, or if the population had died out long ago…hell, for all he knew, the far side of the sphere was as cracked and broken as the one in front of him. Captain Templeton was still refusing to dispatch probes to the second sphere.

"There's a smaller chunk of debris there," Tobias said. *Small*. It was about the size of Belgium. "It's hard to be sure, but there might be more than just metal on the surface."

Colin nodded. "I'll get my suit on," he said. "You take up station…"

He paused and corrected himself. "You put us down on the ground."

Tobias nodded in understanding. Normally, the shuttle would hold station near the asteroid or whatever, allowing the marines to make the jump to the surface. Here…they'd pretty much have to land on the debris, as if they really were landing on a planetary surface. A thought struck him and he keyed a search request into the console, sending it back to *Endeavour*. Some of the pieces of debris were large enough to have whisper-thin atmospheres of their own. If they could find one, they might be able to determine what sort of atmosphere the Builders had considered breathable.

Although the destruction might have wiped out what remains of the sphere's atmosphere, he thought. *Or simply contaminated it beyond all hope of proper analysis.*

The shuttle rocked, slightly, as it closed on the debris. Tobias rested his hands on the console, orientating the shuttle carefully. It was strange, a routine manoeuvre that was nothing of the sort. Logically, the gravity field shouldn't flicker unpredictably and yet…he shook his head, grimly, as the shuttle adjusted its heading. The last thing he needed was to fall into the trap of thinking the plate was just a space station and actually plough the shuttle straight into it. They wouldn't live long enough to be rescued.

"Ten seconds," he said, keying his console. "The ground is about to hit us."

A dull thud echoed through the shuttle. Tobias braced himself. He'd never had to land in the middle of a hot zone, but…he'd played too many games to be entirely sanguine about what might be awaiting them. The plate might not be as solid as he'd thought, the ground beneath the shuttle something alien…he waited, one hand hovering over the emergency boost, then relaxed slightly as nothing happened. The landscape beyond looked as dark and silent as the grave.

He shivered. *It is a grave*, he thought. *This entire star system is a tomb.*

Marigold caught his eye. "No obvious threats on the external monitors," she said. "I'm cycling the airlock now."

• • •

Colin took a long breath as the outer hatch started to open, revealing a desolate landscape that could have easily passed for the surface of the moon. His heart raced as he took a step forward, wishing he had a rifle in his arms even though he knew it would be worse than useless. A weapon would give him a sense of false superiority, perhaps even lead to a dangerous incident...he shook his head, slowly, as he reached the airlock and peered outside. Nothing moved. It was as cold and silent as the desert at midnight. The sun was a tiny penny, a pinprick of light that barely provided any real illumination. If the shuttle's spotlights weren't sweeping the landscape, the land before him would have been shrouded in darkness.

The gravity field faded as he stepped onto the debris. It was big, impossibly big. It looked flat, as if there was no planetary curve...it was, he reminded himself, big enough that no one could hope to see from one end to the other with the naked eye. He tested the ground lightly and frowned. It was scruffy, like ancient concrete; solid enough, to the touch, but constantly on the verge of breaking up or turning to dust. He poked at it gingerly, wondering if they could take a sample, then straightened and looked around. There were no traces of anything resembling buildings, no hint the debris had ever been part of something bigger. Colin wasn't sure if he should be relieved or worried. They'd have to keep probing the debris until they found something they could use.

His radio bleeped as the rest of the squad—four Marines, wearing spacesuits—joined him outside the shuttle. Chatter was light, almost subdued. Colin would have been more worried if he hadn't felt subdued himself. It wasn't the first time he'd poked through wreckage, and it wasn't the first time he'd seen alien installations and structures, but the shattered sphere was daunting even to him. Part of him was oddly reassured to look at the ruins and know the sphere's designers hadn't been all-powerful, the rest of him hated to think what could have destroyed the sphere. An accident would be the *best* answer, for humanity if not for the long-dead occupants. If someone was out there with both the power and will to destroy Dyson Spheres...

The thought mocked him as they fanned out, spreading across the landscape. His mind found it hard to grasp the sheer immensity of what he saw, reminding him of the time he'd heard a young LT read a map and confidently give directions that would have sent one platoon off a cliff and the other on a wild goose chase. Just because two places looked close on the map didn't mean they really *were*. The idiot had tried to get the squad to walk a hundred miles in less than an hour. Colin had been irked at the time, classing the map-reader as yet another stupid greenie lieutenant, but he thought he saw—now—how the mistake had been made. It was hard to believe they were standing, right now, on one of the smaller pieces of debris, from a structure so immense that it had more surface area than every known Earth-type planet put together.

And the fact I'm an LT myself now has nothing to do with it, he told himself, firmly. He allowed himself a flicker of amusement at his own hypocrisy. *That's completely beside the point.*

He put the thought aside as they collected more samples, picking sites at random. Whatever had destroyed the sphere had left the plates scorched, making it hard to tell if the Marines were on the verge of finding something useful or just wasting their time. He told himself the researchers would take a look at the samples, then probably send them out to get some more as soon as possible. It would be a long time if they wanted samples from *every* last piece of debris, even just the planet-sized ones. He wondered if they'd want to set up a base amidst the ruins. It wouldn't be too hard.

"That's the last of the sample tubes," he said, when they'd finished. The ashy surface…was it really *ash* or something like it? He looked up, picking out the star. Had it flared? Was *that* what had happened? It was a G2, unlikely to go nova—if the briefing papers were correct—but he could easily imagine it flaring. And then…? Had the interior shell been scorched beyond all hope of repair? Had it popped like a can of beans shoved into a microwave? "We'd better get on our way."

He took one last look at the landscape, another chill running down his back at the sheer *alienness*, then turned away. Something prickled at the back of his neck, a sense they weren't alone…he stopped, bracing himself as he looked back. Nothing moved and yet…he wasn't sure if he was imagining it or if there was something out there. He'd felt the same, during one cold march in Canada during advanced training. He'd later learnt the SAS had been keeping a covert eye on the recruits from a distance. It had been oddly reassuring and yet...he shook his head. The plate was dead and cold.

"Keep the suits on," he ordered, as they stepped into the airlock. The bioscanners weren't sounding the alert, but no one would take anything for granted. They were not going to have fun when they returned to the ship. "We'll be passing through biohazard screening before we go anywhere else."

He ignored the grumbling, although he supposed he should have scolded them. The risk of cross-species infection was much higher than it had been only a couple of decades ago. And that wasn't the only threat. For all they knew, they'd picked up some alien nanotechnology or something beyond their imagination, something that would infect the entire starship if they weren't careful. His lips twisted, sourly, as he felt the shuttle take off and head into interplanetary space. The Royal Marines might not *like* decontamination procedures—Colin had yet to meet anyone who did—but they wouldn't do anything more than grumble. A civilian might do something foolish and try to circumvent the procedure, rather than endure them to the bitter end. And if that happened...

It's bad enough when someone tries to lie their way through a security test, Colin reflected. *But at least they know they're lying. The dumb bastard who gets infected and doesn't even know it is going to be spreading his shit everywhere he goes, sure of his own innocence until it is far too late.*

He leaned against the bulkhead and waited. Tobias had read a *lot* of pre-space novels concealing alien contact and artefacts, what he'd called Big Dumb Objects. Colin hadn't been so interested, but...some of the stories had been eye-opening. The idea of some of the more dangerous ones getting loose were terrifying. He wanted to believe no one could be so stupid, but even experienced soldiers sometimes had negligent discharges. They were hardly *intentional*, yet...they could be tragic. And no number of threats of dire punishment could prevent them from happening.

The radio bleeped. "We'll be back on the ship in five minutes," Tobias said, calmly. He was in his element, flying a shuttle though empty space. "And then this shuttle is going to be fumigated. No one stays onboard."

"Better than the alternative," Colin said. It would be awkward and embarrassing, and there was no point in claiming otherwise, but it would just have to be endured. "Believe me, it's far better."

CHAPTER SIXTEEN:
HMS ENDEAVOUR, DYSON SYSTEM

STACI HAD ONCE WATCHED a pre-space TV show in which the main characters had insisted on holding meeting after meeting to discuss the problem-of-the-week, rather than the captain simply deciding what to do about it and everyone else simply falling in line. She'd thought it silly at the time. One didn't hold a meeting when the clock was ticking and missiles were screaming through space, aimed right at your ship. The captain was the sole master of his ship—or *hers*—and there was no way any of his decisions could be debated. Not openly, at least. Staci knew junior officers often debated orders from their seniors—she had, when she'd been a junior officer—and she would pretend to ignore it, as long as the debate didn't come into the public eye. And they carried out their orders without a fuss.

She frowned as the steward filled teacups and handed around biscuits, then withdrew silently to wait for the summons. It felt wrong to call a meeting, to even *hint* she was prepared to let her officers, crew and passengers influence her decisions, and yet she had very little choice. She knew what to do if the ship was under attack, or if it suffered a catastrophic failure or something—anything—that required quick action, rather than debate. But this...she honestly wasn't sure how to proceed.

Her eyes swept the room. "Doctor," she said. "What do we know so far?"

"Very little," Doctor Athena Gaurs said. "We have launched over thirty sampling missions in the past ten days, doing what we can to ensure they're taken from fairly separate parts of the sphere debris. We have recovered traces of biological matter, or what we believe to be such, but we have been unable to determine anything of value. The years in the cold, frozen solid, did a considerable amount of damage. The only thing we can tell you for sure, at least at the moment, is that the recovered samples are not related to anything in the database. We didn't bring viral samples onboard."

"Good." Staci knew the decontamination procedures were good, but she hadn't been able to keep from worrying. One mistake, so far from Earth, would be disastrous. "And the atmosphere?"

"The samples we recovered were Earth-compatible, to a degree," Athena said. "There were traces of other gases and elements mixed in, although I doubt we'd have any problems breathing it if it was unfrozen. Right now, of course, I wouldn't recommend it. That said"—she paused, meaningfully—"we may be wrong. Whatever shattered the sphere might have done enough damage to change the interior atmosphere beyond recognition."

Lady Charlotte leaned forward. "Do we know how the sphere was destroyed?"

"I do have some theories," Athena said. She keyed her terminal, projecting a holographic image of the sphere over the table. "In theory, there's no problem encasing an entire star—and therefore taking advantage of the star's entire output—if you have the raw materials. In practice, it isn't so easy. The structure would face a number of problems that would need to be addressed, from gravity stresses to waste output. The star would be heating the space inside the sphere and, eventually, the heat would grow intolerable. The Builders would have to overcome these problems if they wanted to actually build a sphere that wouldn't rip itself apart.

"I think, from what we've spotted in the wreckage, that our sphere started life as a swarm of plates orbiting the star. Bit by bit, the plates were linked together until the entire star was eventually enclosed. My gut feeling is that they brought in vast amounts of raw material from nearby star systems, then broke it down and fed it into their construction program. It would happen slowly enough, even by their standards, to let them compensate for any problems that became apparent during construction."

She paused. "I can't prove this, not yet, but I think they actually knew how to generate tramlines," she added. "Their gravity technology must be far superior to ours. They may have been able to use the tramlines to snatch a world from its system to theirs, then rip it to shreds with tidal stresses and channel the raw material into position. It would be...a construction program on a massive scale."

Staci frowned. "If they did something like that...how?"

"I don't know," Athena said. "This is a binary star system. They may have based something at the barycentre, the balance point between the two stars, to tap their gravity fields and turn them into planet-smashers. It's possible, at least in theory."

Jenner frowned. "I thought the power requirements were just too high."

"They are, for us," Athena said. "But they had access to the power of two entire *stars*."

Staci held up a hand. "We can speculate on precisely how the trick was done later," she said, quietly. "Right now, what do you think happened to the shattered sphere?"

Athena had the grace to blush. "I think they lost control of their gravity compensators," she said, "and the stresses on the sphere's underlying structure became intolerable. The pressure eventually reached a point where something snapped, setting off a series of minor disasters that collectively turned into a far greater disaster. I'm not sure why they didn't try to stop the process before it got too far to be stopped. They certainly should have tried."

"Perhaps they couldn't," Lady Charlotte said. "If they didn't realise there was a problem until it was too late…they might have had no choice, but to evacuate and hope for the best."

"Or they'd already died out by then," Paris-Jackson said. "How *old* is the sphere?"

Athena bit her lip. "We have done our best to date the rubble, and to calculate when the sphere shattered, but results have been inconclusive. Our best guess is that the sphere came apart nearly a million years ago… frankly, though, that might as well be guesswork. We lack the baselines we need for more precise guesses, let alone something reasonably accurate."

"Over a million years," Staci said, quietly.

She stared at her fingers thoughtfully. The span of humanity's recorded history—for a given value of recorded—was somewhere between five to six thousand years. The human race had probably been around longer—there were all sorts of tales of ancient civilisations, some of which had supposedly made it into space—but not much longer. Staci was fairly sure the more absurd stories were little more than myths and legends, at best. The idea there had once been a spacefaring civilisation on Earth that had fallen back into complete barbarism and vanished without leaving a single trace of its existence was about as sensible as the hollow world concept or magic existing in hidden parts of the globe. A fun setting for a story, perhaps, but hardly *real*.

Her mind tried to look back over the years. The sphere had been built and then left to die so far before humanity…

She put it out of her head and leaned forward. "Doctor, do you believe it likely we will discover anything of value, if we keep sweeping the shattered sphere?"

"Impossible to say," Athena said. "We've been trying to locate more intact sections of the shell, but…again, all we really have is wild guesswork. We might find a Rosetta Stone tomorrow, or next year, or a thousand years from now. Or…they might have stripped this sphere of everything useful. They must have had all the time they needed to pick up and remove everything they wanted to take."

Staci nodded. "Which leads to the next question," Staci said. "Do we proceed to the second sphere?"

Her words hung in the air. They'd spent *days* signalling the second sphere, using everything from simple radio to laser signals and pulsed gravity transmissions. There'd been no response. Staci had read the speculations from the researchers, all of which had veered between the signals being too primitive for the aliens to detect to there being no one left to receive and reply to them. She found it hard to believe a civilisation capable of building two entire star-encasing spheres would have died out, but who knew? Perhaps the second star had belched, wiping out their civilisation in the blink of an eye.

"We do need to determine if there's anyone alive in there," Lady Charlotte said, slowly. "This *is* their system. We need to find out if they object to our presence before we do something they'll choose not to overlook. So far, all we've been doing is scrumping."

Staci blinked. "Scrumping?"

"Stealing apples from an estate garden," Lady Charlotte said. "The local kids used to sneak into the garden and steal apples, then sneak out again. We tended to turn a blind eye to it, as long as no actual damage was done. It could be irritating at times, but we normally had more apples than we knew what to do with anyway. If they wanted to think they were pulling the wool over our eyes, why not?"

She frowned. "But the more we probe the wreckage, the greater the chance we'll do something they'll find offensive. What if we find a body? Or something of religious significance? Or even a piece of technology that will be incredibly dangerous in the wrong hands? We need to know if we need permission to probe further, both because its polite and because it's the right thing to do. We don't know how they'll react if they see us poking around in the rubble."

"They can't have missed us," Jenner said. "We haven't been trying to hide."

"We're pretty much the only active power source in the system," Staci agreed, although she knew Lady Charlotte's point couldn't be dismissed. "But if they're not answering our hails…"

"The gardener could be trying to get some sleep in the onion bed." Lady Charlotte smiled, as if lost in a happy memory. "He might not have heard the kids shouting for permission before they clambered over the wall and went picking apples. That doesn't mean the kids actually have permission, nor that the gardener won't come at them with a stick if he catches them in the garden."

Jenner snorted. "Wouldn't it be wiser to call the police instead?"

"The gardener would then have to explain what he was doing when he was meant to be on watch," Lady Charlotte said. "And then he'd wind up in hot water."

Staci shook her head in amused disbelief. It was a far cry from the world *she'd* known as a young girl, although she knew a few neighbours who hadn't hesitated to use force if they caught any shoplifters. It had been that sort of neighbourhood. The police weren't trusted to react reasonably and, if the shoplifter got arrested, the bastard's relatives could be relied upon to make life difficult for the one who reported him. If she'd needed proof Lady Charlotte was from a different world…

And we're both human, she mused. *How can we hope to predict how genuine aliens will react?*

She leaned forward. "We should at least *try* to get their attention," she said. "And quickly, while it is just *us* out here."

"There's another point," Paris-Jackson said. "We don't know how they did it, but we do know they elongated the tramline in some way. If we can open communications, or even get our hands on the tech ahead of everyone else…"

"True," Staci agreed. International agreements insisted alien tech had to be shared. No one really expected anyone to keep the agreement, if they got access to something completely unique. She was mildly surprised other governments hadn't demanded access to the Sphere. Did they think it was worthless? Did they think no significant discoveries would come out of it? Or did they want to bide their time until something *did*? "It's only a matter of time until someone else probes their way down the tramline and finds the two spheres."

She thought fast. There was a degree of risk, made all the worse—once again—by their complete inability to actually carry out a proper risk assessment. For all they knew, they were trespassing...or poking through the remains of a long-gone race. There was no proof, unless one counted the elongated tramline, that there was *anything* left to be found within the system. The other sphere might be as dead as the first, even though it seemed intact. Their long-range observations had certainly not spotted any way in—or out—of the sphere.

"Right," she said, centering herself. "We'll recall the survey crews and put them through decontamination. If we don't receive any answer to our hails by then, we'll launch two probes on direct trajectories and two more on fly-past. All four of them will be broadcasting their locations constantly, so the inhabitants will have no trouble spotting them."

"If they're looking," Lady Charlotte said, quietly.

"Yes." Staci bit down on the flash of irritation. "Assuming there's no response to the probes, we'll take the entire ship on a fly-past trajectory. We don't want any watching eyes thinking we intend to ram the sphere. If that doesn't get any response..."

She nodded to the display. "At that point, we might have to see if we can find a way into the sphere."

"Which might be dangerous," Lady Charlotte said. "There's a difference between stealing apples and actually breaking into the mansion."

"We do need to try to figure out how to ring the doorbell," Paris-Jackson said. "I knew someone who stared, completely baffled, at a doorknocker."

"There's a more serious concern," Jenner said, quietly. "If we open the door to get inside, how do we know we won't be letting something *out*?"

"There was a movie about an alien race that had its entire star system trapped in a forcefield bubble," Athena said. "Quite impractical, based on what we know of modern tech. If you have the power to encase an entire star system in a bubble, you have the power to do something more drastic. And why would you dismantle at least a dozen other star systems just to trap a race you don't like?"

Staci said nothing. She'd grown up in a world of strictly limited resources. Her family's budget had been very low. The navy budget was immense, but so was its expenditures. Even the richest human had limits…she doubted anyone would go to so much trouble to lock up an alien race, not when the technology used to build the spheres could have offered other—simpler—solutions. If one didn't want to commit genocide, one could put automatic weapons platforms in orbit with orders to fire on anything more advanced than a steam engine.

"We'll take every precaution," she said, finally. It was Jenner's job to play devil's advocate and point out possibilities that seemed absurd, or simply impossible. "And if the spheres are prisons, one of them has already broken and the prisoners have escaped."

"The virus," Jenner said. "We still don't know where it actually came from."

"No," Lady Charlotte agreed. "But it never showed the same technological mastery…"

"It wanted our worlds for itself," Jenner countered. "It could have wiped out most of the human race in an afternoon, if it hadn't wanted our worlds and our bodies."

Staci held up a hand, forestalling the discussion. "We will proceed as planned," she said, calmly. "Mr. XO, recall the survey teams. Doctor Gaur, prepare the probes for launch. Make them as obvious as possible. We don't want them to look like incoming missiles."

"I'll have them broadcasting the First Contact package," Athena said. "They'll be very noticeable."

"Good." Staci looked at Lady Charlotte. "I want you and your team drawing up possible approaches, based on what we know, for use if they do make contact. Don't be afraid to think outside the box. Update the old scenarios and add new ones if you feel the need."

Lady Charlotte nodded.

Staci kept her face blank. It was busywork. Did Lady Charlotte know it? She was no naval officer, but she was smart and insightful and a lot more cunning than she let on.

Staci thought she understood, now, why Mitch Campbell had been attracted to her. It wasn't her looks, but her personality. Lady Charlotte was capable of making someone feel like the centre of the universe, telling them what they wanted to hear to weaken their defences and manipulate them in the required direction. Perhaps that was why the PM had sent her a very long way from home. Given time, Lady Charlotte could convince anyone to back her.

And she really would make a good ambassador, Staci conceded. *As long as you can keep her pointed in the right direction.*

"Yes, Captain," Lady Charlotte said. If she knew she was being fobbed off, it didn't show on her face. "When do you think we'll reach the sphere?"

"We shouldn't hurry," Staci said. She wanted to *know*, but not at the cost of her ship. "We want to give them plenty of time to notice us. Say... five days, unless we get a reply earlier."

"We should," Paris-Jackson said. He sounded like a man who'd seen all the old certainties vanish like a soap bubble in the rain. "We're poking around their system. You'd think they'd want to tell us to leave."

Or to fuck off, Staci's thoughts added, darkly. She knew how she'd react to someone poking around the Sol System and it wouldn't be polite. *Do they know we're here? Do they care? Are they too scared of us to say a word? Or are they hiding from some greater threat?*

In truth, she reflected as she dismissed the meeting, there was no way to know.

CHAPTER SEVENTEEN: HMS ENDEAVOUR, DYSON SYSTEM

THE TENSION ON THE BRIDGE was almost palpable.

Staci sat in her chair and watched, numbly, as Dyson Two swelled in front of her. It was impossible, the stuff of nightmares, a solid wall blocking their flight…and yet it was there, dominating the system with its presence. She would have almost sooner believed it was a giant forcefield, or something built out of solid light, or even an illusion designed to hide an entire planet behind a curious cloaking device. The sphere was just too big. The more she thought about it, the more her mind shrank back from the abyss.

And everything else, she thought. The sphere had existed, if the latest reports were accurate, well before the human race itself. The Builders had been and gone well before Earth had finally given birth to a spacefaring race. She still found it hard to believe they'd vanished, but…where were they? A race so powerful and *old* should have filled up the entire galaxy and beyond, not scattered a handful of artefacts in hard-to-reach systems. *What happened to them?*

Time crawled. The starship was moving incredibly fast, on a human scale, but the system was still impossibly huge. Staci watched the displays carefully, monitoring the live feed from the sensor probes orbiting the sphere. The surface was as smooth as a baby's bottom, although—upon closer examination—it was clear it had collected layers upon layers of space dust. The sphere didn't have much of a gravity field and yet, over the years...she shook her head. The researchers had done the math. There was definitely something with roughly the same mass as a G2 star inside the sphere. They'd even hinted there might be a planet or two as well.

We didn't find any planets inside the shattered sphere, Staci reminded herself, dryly. *But whatever catastrophe destroyed the sphere could easily have sent the planet hurtling off into deep space.*

She tried not to show her tension. The sheer *scale* of the system was wearing her down. She wanted to believe that any rogue planets would crash straight into the second sphere, but it was unlikely. The sphere was small on a cosmic scale...her lips twitched sourly, unwilling to accept that anything big enough to encase an entire star could be considered *small*. And yet, it was true. She felt her heart start to race and calmed herself with an effort. She had to be alert, if something happened. It was impossible to believe the occupants didn't know *Endeavour* was approaching. The signals alone should have drawn their attention at once.

Staci frowned. The datastream from the probes was growing more detailed, but it really wasn't telling them anything *new*. The sphere's exterior provided all the land one could possibly want to set up industrial nodes, spaceports and whatever else a civilisation that operated on such a scale could possibly want, but there was nothing. The sphere was strikingly smooth, almost perfect. Staci was starting to wonder if she was caught in a nightmare. She wasn't the only one who'd wondered if they were dreaming. She'd spotted a handful of bridge crew pinching themselves when they thought no one was looking.

"Captain," Jenner said. "The probes have completed their sweep of the sphere's exterior."

Staci nodded, curtly. "Anything of note?"

"No, Captain," Jenner said. There was a hint of waspishness in his tone. She could rely on him to report, the moment they picked up anything that might be worth attention. "No sensor nodes, no weapons emplacements, nothing. They haven't even been able to find a way into the sphere."

Staci bit down on the response that came to mind. The tension was getting to them. All of them. She keyed her console, wishing she dared go to her ready room and take a nap. Or haul someone into her cabin for an hour of…she cut that thought off too, before it could take shape and form. She was the ship's commanding officer. There would be consequences if she invited anyone into her bed. God knew, it hadn't worked out well for Mitch Campbell.

"We'll assume orbit, as planned," she said, quietly. "And then we'll dispatch a landing party."

She leaned back in her chair, wishing—not for the first time—that she'd been assigned to a warship instead. She knew how to command a warship, how to do everything from patrolling semi-explored star systems to fighting alien battleships or bombarding targets on planetary surfaces. It would be *comprehensible*. She wouldn't have to worry about an alien megastructure that might hold billions upon billions of intelligent life forms or might be nothing more than a colossal interstellar tomb. Or…she felt like an ant, staring at something so huge as to be beyond her understanding. Perhaps she'd been wrong. Humans took no notice of ants unless they became a nuisance. The Builders might feel the same about humanity.

But ants don't build starships, she thought, numbly. *How advanced must one be, to regard building starships and exploring space to be nothing more than instinctive behaviour from creatures that don't truly think?*

"Captain," Atkinson said. "We are levelling out now. We'll assume the planned orbit in five minutes."

Staci deliberately exhaled. She'd been so sure the inhabitants would react…*somehow*. No one in their right mind would let something the size of *Endeavour* get so close without making very sure of her *bona fides*, if only out of fear of what would happen if she rammed the sphere. Staci was starting to think she could unleash the firepower of a battleship on the sphere and it wouldn't notice. God knew none of the researchers in Virus Prime had ever been able to take a sample from the Sphere located there.

Their sphere, she thought, tiredly. *We're going to have to sort out nomenclature now there's more than one sphere.*

Her lips twitched as the display steadied. It would give the researchers the impression they were actually Doing Something, without actually doing much of anything. What would it matter, if they tagged the spheres by number or attached names to them? It wouldn't get them any closer to figuring out anything useful, from what had gone into their construction to what they'd been intended to do. She shook her head, wondering if it would be wiser to go to bed first and send the landing party tomorrow. If the sphere truly was dead...

We may never know, she thought, tiredly. *If we can't get inside.*

"Captain," Jenner said. "Lieutenant Lancaster is ready to deploy."

Staci felt a pang of...something she didn't care to look at too closely. The commanding officer could *not* abandon his—her—post and go into danger. That only happened in bad movies and worse novels. She couldn't afford to take the lead and yet, she felt guilty for sending a young officer into danger. She couldn't even calculate just how dangerous the situation actually was. Back home, she could have been reasonably certain the young man would survive. Here...

"Tell him he has permission to launch," Staci said. "And that I said *good luck*."

...

I must be out of my mind, Colin thought. *I signed up for this...*

He lay in the launch tube, bracing himself for the boost. He had volunteered the moment he'd heard about the mission, if only to set a good example for his men. He'd served under commanding officers who'd stayed at the rear and issued orders from a safe distance, officers he hadn't regarded as particularly competent or trustworthy. They might have been good bootnecks or squaddies once, but they'd lost touch with military realities. Colin dared not let his men feel the same way about him.

His heart raced as a countdown timer appeared in his HUD. It was hardly the first orbital drop he'd made—he'd done suborbital insertions and HALO parachute drops during his training—and yet, it was profoundly different. Perhaps it would be better to use a shuttle instead—Colin was entirely sure Tobias could have gotten him to the surface without any trouble at all, then gotten the shuttle away from the ground before anyone noticed—but the logic was sound. Better a lone man than an entire shuttle. The aliens—if indeed there were any—might not notice the drop. If they did...

He grimaced. There'd been a time when an insertion could be done, on Earth, without anyone noticing. And then, as technology advanced, it had grown harder and harder to slip through the sensor grid without being noticed. Colin had heard tales from the old sweats, the ones who'd tried to land in American or French territory without being detected and snatched before they even hit the ground. It hadn't been easy. Sure, the whole operation had been planned in advance—otherwise, the jumpers would have been fired upon rather than allowed to land peacefully—and the old sweats had insisted *that* was why success had been limited, at best, but he had studied the records. The jumps would have ended badly, in a real war. And here, it could easily go the same way.

The timer reached zero. Colin barely had a second to brace himself before he was blasted into space. The automatics took control at once, rotating the suit so he could see the wall rushing at him. Colin nearly panicked, despite his training. The sphere...he knew it was a sphere, he'd seen the images from the probes, but he was so close to the surface that it felt like an endless flat surface. It was impossible to see the sphere's curvature underneath him. It was just too big. He had to turn his head, just slightly, to see the stars. His HUD insisted he was still over a hundred thousand kilometres from the surface, around a thousand times further away than LEO, but he refused to believe it. It was all he could do to keep from throwing out his hands to catch himself, in the certainty he was about to smash right into a solid wall.

His eyes ached, his head hurt, as he tried to make sense of what he saw. The surface was growing closer, yet...it felt almost as if he wasn't moving. There were no objects of reference on the surface, nothing getting larger and larger as he approached. He'd expected *something*, from alien buildings to writing, but the sphere seemed unmarked. He told himself not to be silly. The writing would have to be *incredibly* large to be visible from his distance with the naked eye, each letter bigger than an entire country. And if there had been something on the surface, the probes would have spotted it long ago.

The display pinged. The distance was shortening rapidly. Colin felt a sense of urgency and yet, as he watched the HUD update again, an odd feeling there was no point in worrying about anything. He was watching himself on the big screen, as if he were an actor in his own life. It was... he bit his lip hard, telling himself to concentrate. The absence of any visual cues felt deeply wrong. If the automatics hadn't been engaged...he'd been irked, earlier, when the mission planners had told him he wouldn't be in control of his own descent. Now, he knew they'd understated the situation. His training was worse than useless. Everything he'd learnt over the years, and then put into practice, was dangerously misleading. He might have gotten himself killed, if he'd relied on his own skills to handle the landing...

An alert bleeped. Colin took a breath as the retros fired, an instant before the ground came up and hit him. Dust billowed everywhere, moving in eerie slow motion before drifting back towards the surface. The sphere's gravity field felt little stronger than the moon's, despite its immense size. Colin didn't pretend to understand it. Surely, something big enough to encase an entire star must have a *huge* gravity field.

But the sphere is hollow, nothing more than a shell surrounding a star, he thought. *It might be as light, relatively speaking, as a ping-pong ball.*

He straightened, putting the thought aside for someone else to worry about later, and looked around. The sphere was flat. His mind rebelled against what he was seeing, his head spinning until he reminded himself that *Earth* looked flat too, if one stood on the surface. One didn't begin to see curvature until one took an aircraft high above the ground…he shook his head and took a step forward, feeling the dust shifting under his boots. The surface felt like packed sand, hard but something that could be kicked free very quickly. He tried, feeling like a child on a beach as he used his foot to dig down to the *real* surface. The thought made him feel oddly maudlin. Beach holidays had never been a thing for *his* family even before the virus had reached Earth and everything had been locked down.

The radio crackled. He looked up, half-expecting to see the starship high overhead. There was a light…the ship? He didn't know. The stars themselves twinkled oddly, as if the sphere had an atmosphere…he frowned, puzzling over the mystery until he realised the dust was drifting above him, the tiny gravity field slowly pulling it back down to the surface. He muttered a quick report, then started to probe through the dust with his armoured hands. The layers were too deep to move quickly. He suspected, as he pushed the sensors into position, that the sphere had been gathering dust for centuries. He'd had instructors who'd made the bootnecks clean everything until it shone, learning useful skills as they worked. One of them had told him off for leaving a speck of dust on his bunk. He wondered, wryly, what he'd think of the sphere. The Builders didn't seem to give a damn about housecleaning.

Which would be pretty much impossible, he reflected, as he started to walk across the surface. *It would be easier to count all the grains of sand on a beach.*

The sphere was just too big. The sheer desolation threatened to overwhelm him. It was hard to believe he'd barely moved at all, even though he'd walked and walked…his head hurt as he tried to wrap his head around the truth. He could walk for the rest of his life and he wouldn't be able to traverse the entire sphere. Even a starship would take time…he remembered, suddenly, a story he'd read about a man in a spacesuit who'd outrun a spacecraft by using an asteroid for cover. *That* wouldn't work here, unless he burrowed under the dust...no, it wouldn't work. A starship with modern sensors would have no trouble tracking him, then dropping a KEW on his head. It probably wouldn't even damage the sphere.

He looked around, feeling cold. He'd once spent a week helping the emergency services clean up, after a major flood. The homes, far too close to a river for comfort, had practically been *buried* in mud. He wondered if there'd been entire cities on the surface, once upon a time, that had been hidden under the dust. The sphere had been around for millions of years. In that time, the dust could have buried a structure the size of an orbital tower. The *real* surface could be hundreds of miles below his feet. It might take years to dig down to it.

And then we might go through and pop the structure like a balloon, part of his mind added, wryly. *Wouldn't that be a turn up for the books?*

The thought made him smile, but it was unlikely. He'd helped the researchers, back on Virus Prime, when they'd tried to take a chip from the Sphere. They hadn't even managed to scratch the surface, even when they'd applied plasma tools or bomb-pumped lasers. Colin had no idea what the alien structure was made of—neither had the researchers—but he found it hard to believe they hadn't applied the same protection to the bigger sphere. The sphere was old enough that the risk of something striking the surface—eventually—was dangerously high. It *would* happen, sooner or later. The only reason the Builders hadn't put a proper asteroid deflection system into place, as far as Colin was concerned, was that they'd thought they hadn't needed to bother. And that meant they thought the sphere was indestructible.

He looked up, towards the other star. It was invisible, probably hidden behind a piece of debris. It was all the proof they needed that the sphere was *far* from indestructible. Colin had no idea what had destroyed the sphere—and the speculations ranged from practical to truly insane—but it didn't matter. The Builders had been powerful and there was no denying it, yet they weren't gods. They made mistakes. They could be beaten.

On impulse, he knelt down and pressed his hand against the surface. There was nothing and yet...he had the sudden sense that something was watching him, that something was waiting for him on the other side. His heart started to race as he looked around, bracing himself to run or fight or...he saw nothing. He wanted to believe he was imagining it and yet, his instincts insisted he was being watched. If the Sphere was inhabited...

The radio bleeped. "Lieutenant," a voice said. "The shuttle is on its way now."

Colin nodded, and acknowledged the message. He'd go back to the ship and be put through decontamination, then write his report while waiting to be released from quarantine. And then...he looked back at the surface, frowning. The sense he was being watched was still there, nagging at the back of his mind. He didn't feel alone.

And yet, you can't see anything, he thought, numbly. *How do you write that into the report?*

CHAPTER EIGHTEEN: HMS ENDEAVOUR, DYSON SYSTEM

"THERE WAS A FIGHT IN THE CREW QUARTERS." Jenner said. "I dealt with it."

Staci scowled. It had been a week since they'd reached the intact sphere—Dyson Two, the boffins had called it—and, so far, they'd learnt very little. The sphere might not be dead—quite a few spacers and crewmen had insisted something was watching them—but it held its secrets close. She rubbed her forehead. The researchers were in heaven, but everyone else…drinking had gone up, minor disciplinary issues had soared and now there'd been a major fight. It was going to be a headache. She'd have to do something about it without making it look as though she was treading on her XO's toes.

"Good," she said. "How serious?"

"A couple of minor injuries, but it would probably have been worse if the senior chiefs hadn't stepped in," Jenner said. "The tension has been building for weeks. One little spark was enough to set it off, with fists flying before anyone realised they were crossing the line."

"Yeah." Staci understood, all too well. She'd been a junior officer once. It was easy for people to get more and more irritated with their bunkmates, the bunkmates utterly unaware of it until the first punch was thrown. And then…the tension pervading the entire ship didn't help. Tempers had been fraying ever since they'd made the jump into the system and come face to face with the shattered sphere. "Do you think the matter can be handled without my intervention?"

"I've assigned punishment duties to the perpetrators," Jenner said. "It should be enough, for the moment. But we really need to address the root cause of the problem."

Staci took a sip of her tea. "We can't," she said. "The spheres won't give up their secrets in a hurry."

She sighed, inwardly. The sphere was…odd. There'd been no answer to their hails. There was no way in or out of the sphere, giving rise to all sorts of rumours about the population being dead or imprisoned or both. One researcher had speculated the sphere had been intended to literally—and sadistically—cook an entire planetary population, although Staci felt it was unlikely. If you wanted an entire population to suffer and die, you didn't *need* to build something the size of the sphere. You could just throw asteroids at them from a safe distance. And yet…no, it made no sense.

But we still don't know why they're ignoring us, she thought. *They must know we're here.*

She glanced at the latest set of reports. The automated diggers had dug their way down to the sphere's surface, hundreds of miles below the dust, and tried to use sonic pulses to signal the inhabitants or determine what lay on the other side. There'd been no answer, no suggestion there was anyone listening who was capable of replying. The researchers hadn't even been sure what, if anything, lay on the far side of the wall. Their results hadn't quite made sense. Staci suspected they were wasting their time.

And we haven't found anything under the dust either, she reminded herself. *It might be years before we do. If there's anything there to find…*

"We may have to make some hard decisions shortly," she mused. "If we find nothing…when do we go home, report to our superiors and request a much larger team be assigned to the system?"

"We can remain here for several months, without pushing it," Jenner said. "After that, it gets a little more problematic."

Staci nodded. In theory, *Endeavour* could keep herself going more or less indefinitely. She could grow her own food and drink, mine whatever raw materials she needed from nearby asteroids and even produce spare parts and suchlike in her machine shops. In practice, the stress on the crew and passengers would start to grind them down well before the ship started suffering problems that couldn't be fixed without a shipyard. She'd kept a careful eye on Lady Charlotte and her team. She wasn't blind to the implications of them spending more and more time watching movies, rather than catching up on reports or studying for exams when they got home. They simply weren't used to feeling useless.

And she could presumably go for a ride on a pony back home, Staci thought. She had no idea how Lady Charlotte lived, but she was sure it included—or had included—a great deal of mindless hedonism. It might have prepared her well for a good match, yet not for naval service. Hell, she had it worse than anyone else. *Here, there's literally nothing for her to do that isn't busy-work designed to keep her out of my hair.*

The buzzer bleeped. Staci looked up. "Come."

She raised an eyebrow as David Atkinson stepped into the ready room. The helmsman had been on bridge duty...why had he come to the ready room, when most young officers would sell their souls for more command experience? Staci knew *she* would have killed for it when she'd been his age, in his rank...she leaned forward, suddenly convinced the helmsman had something important in mind. It *had* better be. She would not be amused if he'd passed command to the next in line and bunked off. He'd been meant to stay in command until she or her XO returned to the bridge.

"Captain," Atkinson said. His eyes flickered to Jenner, then back to her. "I...I think I have something I need to bring to your attention."

Staci kept her face under tight control. The chain of command had to be followed at all times, unless it was a major emergency. If Atkinson was trying to bypass the XO...it would have all sorts of repercussions, unless the shit had really hit the fan and the XO was nowhere to be found. Hell, if there had been an emergency, Atkinson should have called them both to the bridge rather than abandoning it to a low-ranking officer. No one would bother with a court-martial if he'd done anything of the sort. They'd just shoot him and be done with it.

"Go ahead," she said. She'd tear him a new asshole if he didn't have a very good explanation. "What have you found?"

Atkinson took a breath. "Captain, I think we can get inside the sphere."

Staci met his eyes. "You *think*...?"

Her mind raced. They hadn't found an entrance anywhere on the sphere. Given the sheer *size* of the megastructure, and the layers upon layers of dust coating the exterior, she had no real anticipation of finding one soon. They might be searching for years before they found it and then, they'd have problems trying to *open* it. Human airlocks were designed to be easy to open from the outside, so a spacer could get back into the ship before running out of air, but there was no way to know if aliens would follow the same logic. The entrance might be impossible to open without the proper keys...

"You think," she repeated. "What do you have in mind?"

Atkinson squirmed under her gaze. "The...ah, there's a line of gravitational force between two nearby stars," he said. "We can use them to jump from star to star..."

Jenner cleared his throat. "The captain is already aware of such details, David."

"Um." Atkinson flushed. "Yes. Sorry, Captain."

Staci hid her amusement. Atkinson was describing the *tramlines*. She damn well *had* better know they existed...

"There's a tramline between Dyson One and Dyson Two," Atkinson said. "We can use it to get inside."

"Clever." Staci kicked herself, mentally. She should have thought of that. Or at least considered the possibility. The Dyson Sphere was *hollow*. Of course it was. There should be more than enough room, between the surface and the star, for the entire navy to exist comfortably. "Are you sure we can use the tramline?"

"As far as I can tell, yes," Atkinson said. "We'd just have to move back to Dyson One, assume a position between the projected surface of the sphere and the primary star, then trigger the drive. It should drop us into the sphere. If it didn't work, we'd know at once."

"We know the tramline that brought us here was oddly extended," Jenner pointed out. "How do we know the tramline leading into the sphere will actually take us inside?"

Atkinson hesitated. "I...sir, as near as I can tell, the tramline we used to get to this system was artificially boosted. We're still working out the theory behind it, but the analysts think it was an alien-grade tramline beforehand, one that needed to be boosted anyway before it could be put to use. There are faint hints the tramline was boosted, visible within the gravitational substrate. This tramline is a standard tramline. We don't see anything to suggest it *doesn't* lead inside the sphere."

"We didn't see anything odd when we jumped into this system," Jenner reminded him, curtly. "Are you sure you're not missing anything now?"

Atkinson stood his ground. "We did see hints, sir," he said. "We just didn't understand what we were seeing. But there, the hints are simply not present."

Staci said nothing for a long moment. The only sign of *active* alien tech they'd seen within the system was the extended tramline. The analysts hadn't been able to determine if whatever the Builders had done was permanent, or if the tramline would snap back to normal when the power ran out, but either way...the nation that managed to duplicate the trick first would be in a very strong position indeed. Even now, decades after First Contact, nationalism was far from distasteful. They needed to get their hands on the alien tech and quickly, before other nations—and alien superpowers—started sending their own ships to the twin spheres. And they would. Staci was no naïf. She *knew* there was no way anyone would agree to stay away, if the rewards were so high.

"The civvies will be asking if we'll just slam into the sphere at superluminal speeds," Jenner pointed out, mildly. "You'd better come up with an answer for them."

"Later," Staci said. "For the moment, I want you to check and recheck your flight plan. If we do this, I want to proceed as quickly as possible."

"Yes, Captain," Atkinson said. "We should have no trouble getting inside."

"Good." Staci wasn't so sure, but she kept it to herself. "I want a report by the end of the day. Return to the bridge, inform the next in line that he has command, then put the flight plan together for me."

"Aye, Captain," Atkinson said.

Staci watched him go, then glanced at her XO. "What do you think?"

"It's workable," Jenner said, slowly. "But it would mean risking the entire ship."

"Unless we sent *Grantchester* instead," Staci said. *Grantchester* had very specific orders...she doubted, somehow, it would be easy to convince the corvette's CO to ignore them. It wouldn't be easy to get away with it, even though it made sense and the people who'd issued the orders were a very long way away. "No, she needs to watch from the outside."

She scowled, looking down at her hands. Atkinson's insight was brilliant, but there was no reason someone else couldn't come up with it for themselves. Sooner or later, someone would try and then...they'd be the ones who got the first look inside the sphere. Who knew what they'd find? Staci had no idea how they'd be greeted, if indeed there was anyone alive inside the sphere to do the greeting. The lack of a visible entrance made sense if the Builders had assumed they could use the tramlines to get in and out.

Her fingers touched her terminal, bringing up the system display. There were eight tramlines linked to Dyson One, but only one to Dyson Two. That made no sense, which suggested the Builders had somehow negated the other tramlines, the ones that *should* have been clearly visible. How? She couldn't even begin to imagine what it would take to manipulate gravity on such a scale. It would be stellar engineering on a godlike scale. Everything she knew about tech told her it was impossible and yet the evidence was right in front of her. The tramlines simply couldn't be natural.

Well, she thought, wryly. *You wanted to be Captain.*

It was her decision, she knew. No one would say anything, openly, if she declined Atkinson's suggestion and chose, instead, to remain outside the sphere. But there would be whispers that she lacked the fortitude to command a starship, whispers that would become shouts if someone else went into the sphere and found something they could use to reshape the galaxy. She wanted to take the risk—if she'd been in command of a corvette, she would have done it without hesitation—and yet, she hated the thought of losing her ship, her crew, and her civilian passengers. And the fact it was impossible to properly assess the risk didn't help.

"We can stay outside, with no guarantee we'd find anything and time slowly ticking away," she mused. "Or we can take the risk and jump inside."

"Yes, Captain," Jenner said.

Staci took a breath. "Supervise Atkinson's work. Check everything, and I do mean everything. Calculate where we'll materialise, inside the sphere, and do everything to ensure we don't materialise *inside* a solid object. And…if we don't find anything by the end of the week, we'll take the risk."

"Yes, Captain," Jenner said, again. "I'll see to it at once."

He stood and left the compartment, the door hissing shut behind him. He would have argued, Staci was sure, if he genuinely disapproved of the plan. Jenner had enough moral fortitude to say so, if he disagreed. An XO was meant to be completely supportive, at least in public, but in private… she smiled, although she would almost have preferred him picking holes in the plan. He was a survey officer, after all. The thought of being the first to see the interior of an alien megastructure had to be very attractive. And yet…

Staci's heart twisted, painfully. She dared not assume her own feelings didn't have their thumb on the scales. They'd spent too long wandering the alien system, unsure if the aliens had died out long ago or were simply watching, waiting and preparing a hammer to throw at *Endeavour* if she did something they didn't like. She wanted to do something to provoke a reaction, even though there was no guarantee her ship would survive the experience. There was no guarantee of a lot of things.

She tapped her terminal. "Lady Charlotte, please report to my ready room."

The hatch opened, five minutes later. Staci's lips twitched. Lady Charlotte looked cool and composed, but she must have run to get to the ready room so quickly. She was good at presenting the right impression, Staci conceded, yet...she had to feel about as useful as warship diagrams from the Age of Sail. There was nothing for her to do, no one for her to talk to...it had to have crossed her mind that she was wasting her time, that she was hanging around hundreds of light-years from Earth while her former husband and his political allies settled everything to their best advantage. Perhaps it would be better for her never to go home...

"Captain," Lady Charlotte said. "What can I do for you?"

"We've come up with a plan," Staci said, briefly outlining the concept. "If it works, we can jump right *inside* the sphere."

Lady Charlotte looked at her as if she was insane. "Wouldn't we just *hit* the sphere?"

Jenner called it, Staci thought. *Nice one.*

"No," she said. It was an understandable misconception, but a misconception all the same. "A starship doesn't *actually* travel faster than light when it uses the tramlines. It jumps from one position to the other, without passing through the space between them. We would not be so much as going *through* the shell as going around it. It will work."

"I'll take your word for it," Lady Charlotte said. "They may not be too happy to have us materialise in their sphere."

"No," Staci agreed. "We simply don't know."

She met Lady Charlotte's eyes. "We can transfer a few people to *Grantchester*. Not many, but a few. Do you want to go with them?"

Lady Charlotte said nothing, but her face went so blank Staci *knew* she was lost in inner turmoil. She didn't lack for courage or cunning, yet she hadn't joined the navy or signed up to jump into the unknown. The offer to let her leave the ship…Staci admitted, privately, that if she'd been in the older woman's shoes she would have seriously considered transferring to the corvette. It wasn't as if it would have done any real damage to her career. It was already beyond all hope of repair.

"No," she said, finally. "If there's someone waiting for us on the inside, you'll need me to do the talking."

Your aide could do it, Staci thought. Paris-Jackson had probably had a better idea of the risks than his nominal boss. Terrorists saw British diplomats as acceptable targets, despite a century of military activity to teach them otherwise. *You don't have to stay with us.*

She leaned forward. "There won't be another chance," she warned. "If you stay now, you're committed."

"I was committed when I boarded the ship," Lady Charlotte reminded her. "And now, I have to see it through."

"And so do we," Staci said. "I suggest you update your will, and any letters you want to write. There won't be a second chance for that either."

Lady Charlotte nodded, curtly. "Will do."

CHAPTER NINETEEN: HMS ENDEAVOUR, DYSON SYSTEM

"CAPTAIN," ATKINSON SAID. "We have reached Point Clarke."

Staci nodded, curtly. She'd never had to steer a ship through an immense cloud of debris in her entire career. She couldn't think of anyone who had, save—perhaps—for post-battle assessment teams. It wasn't a career choice she envied. Now...she cursed under her breath at just how close they'd come to hitting several pieces of debris, something that should have been impossible on an interplanetary scale. It was suddenly very easy to believe the Builders had dismantled a dozen or more entire star systems to build their spheres.

"Good," she said. "Hold position."

She eyed the display, her mind racing. It had been a week of waiting, then four days in transit, before they'd finally reached their destination. She hadn't been sure why she'd taken it so slow, although it gave her a chance to check and recheck the calculations and update *Grantchester* before making the jump. The corvette had strict orders. If *Endeavour* didn't return within a month, she was to return directly to Earth and report to the First Space Lord, who would decide what to do next. Staci suspected it would involve kick-starting the jump-capable probe program, spending whatever it took to take the concept off the drawing board and into real life. The Royal Navy was too short on hulls, after the war, to look kindly on any suggestion to send a second ship after the first.

Her heart started to beat faster as the seconds ticked away. Her crew had cheered up enormously, when they'd realised there was a way to get inside the sphere, yet...they could allow the thought of action to galvanize them, but she had to think past the moment and consider the future. The jump might work perfectly, or it might land them in hot water. The silence was ominous. There was no way to know if anyone was waiting for them, or how they'd react to her arrival. The Builders might greet them with a hail of fire. Hell, it was precisely how the Royal Navy would react to a cloaked ship trying to sneak past the defences and into the shipyards.

And we have tried and tried to get a reaction, she thought. They'd hailed the aliens on all radio frequencies, then tried everything from laser signals to sonics. There'd been no response at all, just eerie silence. *We can't leave the mystery unsolved.*

She sighed. It wasn't in humanity's nature to leave well enough alone. She'd watched countless horror movies where the plot wouldn't have got off the ground if the main characters hadn't dug too deep, or pushed a big red button, or simply ignored the warning signs until it was too late. She knew people who had pushed too far, simply because they wanted to be acknowledged, and others who'd gotten themselves into trouble because they refused to stop and *think*. Perhaps, if she'd been making the call, she would have been content to leave the sphere alone. But she knew the decision wouldn't be made by her...

And you do want to know what's inside, her thoughts mocked her. *If the ship and everyone on it wasn't your responsibility, you'd be leading the charge yourself.*

"Mr. XO," she said, putting her thoughts aside. "Report."

"All departments have reported in, Captain," Jenner said. "We are ready to jump."

Staci nodded. The drives were ready to recycle as quickly as possible, the moment they made the jump. The weapons were on standby, although none of them would be fired without her authorisation. She'd made sure of it. The last thing she needed was a war started when someone panicked and fired on an alien ship. And yet...she told herself, again and again, that it wasn't going to happen. Anyone with half a brain would be careful to avoid doing something provocative, wouldn't they?

Her lips twisted. *One man's peaceful signal is another's challenge to a fight.*

"Communications, copy our final logs to *Grantchester*," she ordered. "Helm, start the countdown."

"Aye, Captain."

Staci braced herself. Transiting was normal, but transiting into unexplored space was...unpredictable. A month ago, she would have laughed at the thought of running straight into a sea of debris. Now...she hadn't felt so nervous since her first combat jump, when she'd been a junior officer so young her seniors had asked if she was still in diapers. It had taken her longer than it should to realise what they'd actually meant, then...she shook her head, putting the memory behind her. Right now, she was as inexperienced as a young midshipman heading out on her very first cruise.

She glanced at the display. Lady Charlotte and her entire team had volunteered to remain on the ship, as had the researchers from Virus Prime. Staci had considered putting the majority of the diplomats off the ship anyway, but finally—reluctantly—decided to keep them onboard. If they did need to talk to someone, they'd need the diplomats. And besides, they knew the risks...the unquantifiable risks. She'd given them their chance.

A low whine echoed through the hull as the power built up. "Captain," Atkinson said. "We will jump in thirty seconds."

"Data dump complete," MacPhee put in. "*Grantchester* has acknowledged, and sends us her best wishes."

"Noted," Staci said.

"Ten seconds," Atkinson put in. "Nine...eight..."

Staci took a breath as the countdown reached zero. Her vision dimmed—for a moment, she had the impression her feet were about to take her right over a cliff—as the displays blanked, a low shudder running through the entire ship. Time itself seemed to slow down for a long chilling moment, as if the seconds were being stretched into hours, before it snapped back to normal. She felt something slap her, as if someone had smacked her right across the face, but the pain was gone almost before it registered. A ghost of a slap...the display rebooted with terrifying speed, red icons flashing in and out of existence far too close to her for comfort...a window popped up, showing the live feed from the hull-mounted optical sensors. Staci almost didn't believe her eyes. It was impossible.

"Status report," she barked. "Tactical?"

"No immediate threats," Lieutenant Commander Philip McDougall said. The tactical officer sounded unsure of himself. Staci understood. For all they knew, the alien tech could blow them away from the other side of a star system. "But the system...the *interior*...is very active."

"We're holding a stable position, as planned," Atkinson said. "Drives are cycling now."

Staci barely heard him. The scene before her was impossible. The starfield was gone. The ship was facing a giant wall of green and blue, a sight so far beyond her she had trouble recognising it even existed. They were inside the sphere, staring at the surface...her head hurt as she realised, dully, that she was staring at a sea. No, an ocean...an ocean so large it defied imagination. She'd grown up on tales of brave seafarers exploring the world and uniting it, building the first and second empires before the British had turned to the stars instead. She wondered how Drake would have coped with a sea so vast one could sail for years before sighting land. It was hard to accept the tiny wisps of white were storms so immense they were larger than Britain herself.

We calculated the interior would have enough land surface for every living human and alien, she thought. *But we didn't really believe it, did we?*

She forced herself to pull back. The interior of the sphere really *was* crowded. A network of giant shapes hung between the shell and the star, casting long shadows over the surface and providing artificial darkness for the population. If there *was* a population. A lone planet orbited the star, at roughly the same distance between the Earth and Sol. The original alien homeworld? Staci found it hard to believe anyone would want to dismantle Earth for raw materials. Even the asteroid settlements who hated and resented the Earth-based governments still regarded the planet itself with an almost religious awe.

More icons appeared on the display, objects moving around the interior on seemingly random courses. Spacecraft? Staci's eyes narrowed as she studied them. They darted from side to side, yet...the only things she'd seen that could do anything like that, at least in the known universe, were starfighters. She swallowed, hard. There was little hard data, but if the objects were being detected at such long range they were either immense or putting out a *lot* of energy. It suggested terrifying things about the sphere's technological base...

"Captain," MacPhee said. "They've made no attempt to contact us."

Staci exchanged a look with Jenner. The sphere was clearly very far from dead. The evidence was right in front of her. The more she looked at the interior, as it took shape on the display, the more she was sure someone was constantly monitoring the sphere and tweaking things to ensure the second sphere didn't meet the same fate as the first. And yet, a full-sized starship had just materialised inside the sphere and they hadn't tried to contact it, or even open fire? Either they were incompetent or they thought they had nothing to fear and...

A shudder ran through the ship. Staci looked up. "Report!"

"Unclear, Captain," McDougall said. "It doesn't appear to have been aimed at us."

"I think it was a gravitational surge, Captain," Atkinson said. "It happens, when a small ship brushes against a larger vessel's drive field."

"There are no vessels within range," Jenner pointed out. "Could it be a gravitational quake?"

Staci grimaced. The smaller bodies within the Sol System—Luna, Io, Ganymede and the others—suffered from regular earthquakes, caused by the tidal pull from the bigger planets and the sun itself. She'd been in the academy when a particularly nasty quake had caused real damage, although not as much as the alien bombardment during the first war. The sphere was certainly given to gravitational stress. Could a gravity surge reach out and touch them?

She looked at MacPhee. "Can you pick up any signals, any at all?"

MacPhee hesitated. "There are a *lot* of emissions," he said, finally. "But I can't tell what they're saying, if they're saying anything. The transmissions might not be artificial."

"I see," Staci said. It might be far too early to expect a breakthrough, but..."Can you locate any command centre, anything that might be in control of the sphere?"

"Not as yet," MacPhee said. "The radio sources don't seem to follow any predictable pattern."

Our datanets don't either, Staci thought, coldly. *We don't want the enemy picking out the flagships and targeting them for destruction.*

She forced herself to think clearly. The longer they stayed, without saying a word, the greater the chance they'd be taken for hostile. Staci knew what *she* would think about a mystery starship that came so close to her territory, particularly one that refused to identify and explain itself. They had to be monitoring the tramline, right? They had to. For all she knew, the aliens were just lining up their superweapon to be sure they blew *Endeavour* away with one shot.

"Communications," she said, finally. "Transmit the First Contact package, omnidirectional signalling."

"Aye, Captain."

Staci waited, keeping a wary eye on the display. The sphere was just too big for her to comprehend. She understood the realities of interstellar transmissions, as well as any other spacer, but it was hard to force herself to believe they applied *here*. The sphere was both very big, to her perceptions, and very small. She'd watched a movie, once, about a family who'd been shrunk down to microscopic size. She knew, now, how they'd felt. *Endeavour* was trapped inside a machine designed for giants.

There won't be any reply for a while, she told herself. *The signal will have to cross interplanetary distances before it reaches anyone who might be able to hear it, then their reply will take just as long to reach us.*

The display kept updating, picking out more and more objects orbiting the sphere or making their way around the interior. It was hard to wrap her head around what she saw. It looked as if a world had been turned inside out, as if satellites were now orbiting inside the world instead of outside it. She was amused to note they didn't seem to have any trouble remaining on station, no matter how much her mind kept insisting they should plunge to the surface and crash. The sphere's interior gravity wasn't that strong. Even on the surface, if the science team's assessments were correct, the gravity field would be little stronger than Mars's. If there was anyone down on the surface, they'd need genetic treatments to compensate for the low gravity.

Unless that's what they're used to, she told herself. *They might have grown up in a very different environment.*

Another shudder ran through the ship. She shivered, remembering the day she'd taken a speedboat out in a storm. The waves had slapped against the boat's hull, each one threatening to make the instability worse until the boat turned over and capsized. She'd enjoyed it at the time, but then she'd only had herself to worry about. Now...

"Captain," McDougall said, sharply. "One of the alien objects has altered course. It is now on an intercept course."

Staci leaned forward, a flicker of alarm banishing the cobwebs from her mind. The alien object was picking up speed at a terrifying rate. Its drive field should have been clearly visible...did it even *have* a standard drive field? She couldn't see any traces of a drive field and the acceleration curve was almost unbelievable. An object nearly twice the size of a battleship, she noted in disbelief, and it was coming at them with the speed of a starfighter?

"Evasive action," she snapped. The object was tightening its course, even as it kept picking up speed. It was right on the heels of the warning, pushing them so hard they didn't dare try to cycle the drive and jump out before it struck home. "Communications, kill the signal."

McDougall looked up. "Captain, I have a target lock."

"Hold your fire," Staci ordered. If the range kept closing, and the object kept adjusting its course, she would have to open fire and hope for the best. The Virus Prime Sphere had been pretty much indestructible. She suspected that even nuclear-tipped missiles wouldn't make an impression on the object and, if they did, they'd draw attention from elsewhere. Who'd ignore a nuke going off inside the sphere. "Helm, keep trying to evade."

"Aye, Captain," Atkinson said.

"The object is trying to ram us," McDougall said. "Captain, I request permission to open fire."

"Evasion successful," Atkinson put in. Another shudder ran through the ship. "The object missed us by a mile."

Which is pretty much point-blank range, on an interplanetary scale, Staci thought. The object could easily reverse course—probably, a starfighter certainly could—and come at them again. *What the hell is that thing?*

Jenner frowned at her. "It must have been drawn by our transmissions, Captain," he said. "It lost its lock on us the moment we cut the signal."

Staci nodded, slowly. The object...she couldn't see the logic in creating a weapon that rammed its targets, rather than shooting at them, but it didn't matter. It had been—it was, she reminded herself sharply—bigger and faster than *Endeavour*. If it had been guided by anything other than radio transmissions, it would have struck them before they could open fire. Hell, if it was as tough as the Sphere, shooting at it wouldn't have done any good.

"Keep a lock on the object," she ordered. "I want to know if it reverses course or if another one comes at us."

"Aye, Captain."

"This puts a dampener on our exploration program," Jenner said. He kept his voice very quiet. "That might have been an automated attack, or it might not."

"Yes." Staci thought fast. "We need to keep our distance until we know what is really going on."

Her mind churned. The aliens might have thought *Endeavour* was a piece of junk that needed to be deflected, before it struck the surface. Or they might have recognised the starship for what it was and sent the object to destroy it. Perhaps it had been a warning shot. Shooting at someone was *also* a form of communicating, after all. Or perhaps the entire system was automated, deliberately created to be too dumb to notice *Endeavour* until she started transmitting and then assuming the sudden silence meant she'd been destroyed. Or…

A new icon appeared on the display. "Captain," McDougall said. "I'm picking up a starship, a *human* starship, decloaking on the edge of engagement range."

"A *human* starship?" Staci blinked. They were alone, weren't they? Had *Grantchester* disobeyed orders? "*Grantchester?*"

"No, Captain," McDougall said. "Warbook says it's a Chinese cruiser."

"She's lasing us," MacPhee said. The communications officer worked his console, his fingers flying over the touchpads. "Standard protocols, all codes up to date. Authentication confirmed. She wants to talk."

Staci sucked in her breath. How the hell had that ship followed them? Had it seen *Endeavour* make the jump? Or had it gotten to the sphere and jumped inside before them? It would have been an important question, elsewhere. Here, it was mainly a matter of curiosity. The sphere couldn't be claimed by a single power…

"Establish a laser link," she said, quietly. "And then inform Lady Charlotte that she can use my ready room."

Jenner blinked. "Captain?"

"She's the diplomat," Staci said. "And right now, we're looking at a diplomatic crisis."

CHAPTER TWENTY: HMS ENDEAVOUR, DYSON TWO (INTERIOR)

"YOU'RE SURE?" CHARLOTTE WASN'T SURE she believed her ears. "A *Chinese* ship?"

She felt weirdly numb, as if the universe had shocked her to the point she no longer had the ability to be shocked further. The sphere's interior was just too big. She could grasp the sheer scale of it, intellectually, but her mind refused to believe something so large could possibly be real. She'd been told megastructures were just a matter of time, once a species climbed out of the gravity well, yet…she didn't believe anyone could *really* build on such a scale. And yet, the Builders very definitely *had*.

"Yes." Jenner seemed oddly relieved, as he escorted her to the diplomatic section. "She's very definitely a Chinese ship, unless she's doing a very good job of *pretending* to be one."

Charlotte shot him a sharp look. A number of international treaties forbade flying false colours. She was also cynical enough to assume the treaties were honoured as little as possible. And yet…she was no expert, but she was fairly sure it was harder to hide the mystery starship's true form than merely broadcasting a false ID. *Endeavour* would have made visual contact by now. If the unknown ship was Russian or American…

she shook her head. She had to assume it was Chinese. There was no point in considering any other possibilities, not now.

She stepped through the hatch and sat down, feeling oddly unsure of herself. The standard diplomatic protocols had been watered down to the bare essentials, when two starships met well away from Earth. There was no way to know if the Chinese had brought a high-powered diplomatic official with them…and, even if they hadn't, she could still treat with them. It wasn't as if she could commit Britain to anything that was legally binding, at least nothing that would last beyond the moment word reached Earth. She wondered, suddenly, if she should insist on Paris-Jackson talking, instead of her, then dismissed the thought with a flicker of irritation. Her enemies back home would pounce, if it looked as if she was setting a career diplomat up to take the fall. *She* was the legal ambassador. The buck stopped with her.

At least until we get home, she thought, keying the console. The Chinese would get a datapacket with her name, diplomatic credentials and limited biographical data. They'd run her name through their files at once, the moment they got the datapacket. She wondered, idly, what they knew about her. She hadn't been a major political figure until recently and, even then, she hadn't been particularly important. *There's no reason they should know much of anything about me.*

She waited, patiently. How long *would* it take them, to run her name through the files. It shouldn't take *that* long, unless they were drawing a complete blank and they wanted to try it again. Her lips quirked. She liked to think she was supremely important, and anyone who liked to think they were anyone knew her name, but the reality was rather more insulting to her ego. The Chinese were more likely to know Paris-Jackson than her. Hell, they might assume she was the puppet, with the experienced diplomat pulling her strings and writing her scripts. They might even assume she was just the fall guy, the person who would be scapegoated for the government's failure. And yet, what could they do about it? They couldn't ask to talk to Paris-Jackson directly without breaking diplomatic protocols…

The terminal bleeped, a countdown ticking down the seconds to zero. *Incoming call.* Charlotte gathered herself, trying not to roll her eyes at the mock drama. The two ships weren't *that* far apart. The time delay would be minimal. There'd be no danger of them accidentally talking past or over each other, at least not by accident. And yet...she supposed it made a certain kind of sense. The playacting made it impossible for one side to think the other had caught it by surprise.

She nodded, politely, as a face appeared in front of her. The Chinese official wore civilian clothes, which meant he was either a diplomat or a security officer or both. Charlotte evaluated him thoughtfully. He looked older than she did, although that was meaningless. He could easily have adjusted his appearance, ensuring he looked older than he was. Or...she told herself, sharply, not to judge by looks alone. The Chinese government was notoriously paranoid. It wouldn't send someone so far from home unless it trusted him to stay well within government-set guidelines. And there was probably someone looking over his shoulder too.

"Good morning," she said, calmly. "I am Ambassador Lady Charlotte Hammond, Special Representative of Her Majesty's Government."

"A pleasure," the Chinese official said. His English was very good, almost completely accentless. Charlotte suspected he'd studied in Britain or America. "I'm Representative Shen. I must say, we were astonished to discover so much so far from home."

"As were we," Charlotte said, coolly. She knew how to negotiate. Shen—she wondered, idly, if that was his real name—was probing, trying to determine how much she knew already. "We did not expect to find...*this*."

"No." Shen met her eyes, evenly. "On behalf of my government, I must lodge a formal complaint. The treaties are clear. Any hint of alien contact, even that of a long-dead race, must be immediately disclosed to the rest of the human race. The British Government's decision to conceal the evidence represents a serious breach of the treaty and so we demand recompense."

Charlotte thought fast. Technically, Shen had a point. Technically. But then, no one back home knew what they'd found. The British Government hadn't hidden anything from anyone. It wouldn't be until *Endeavour* got back in touch with London that the government would have the chance to decide what to do about it, let alone inform the rest of the treaty partners. She frowned inwardly as she felt sweat prickling on her back. Shen was pushing her. What did he really want?

"The British Government does not yet know about the existence of this system," she said, flatly. There was no way word could have reached Earth, unless the Chinese had found the system first and sent a ship home already. "It has not informed the other governments because it doesn't know it needs to inform them of anything."

"Regardless, the treaty has been infringed," Shen informed her. "I must insist on you and your ship withdrawing from the sphere until a multinational investigative team can be put together and dispatched."

Indeed, Charlotte thought, coldly. *And what do you think we know, beyond the bare fact of the sphere's existence?*

She studied Shen thoughtfully. The Chinese had ample reason to be concerned about what Britain might find, if it went poking through the sphere. There was evidence of alien technology everywhere. The...*thing*... that had been aimed at *Endeavour*, that had come far too close to crashing into the ship, was clear proof the sphere wasn't dead. And yet...Charlotte doubted the sphere would give up its secrets in a hurry. It was just too big. She suspected it would be quicker to develop the technology from scratch.

Charlotte leaned forward, allowing herself a friendly smile. "Can we speak bluntly?"

"Of course," Shen said, confirming her suspicion he'd studied abroad. "What would you like to say?"

"The blunt truth is that neither of us are high-level diplomats," Charlotte said. She wasn't sure just how much authority, let alone maneuvering room, Shen actually had. "We can come to whatever agreements we like, but our governments may renounce our agreements the moment they hear about them. And, if I may be honest, neither of us expected to find something like *this*. I feel as if I went fishing for minnows and caught a shark."

Shen smiled, so slightly Charlotte wondered if she'd imagined it. "It wasn't what we expected to find, if we're speaking bluntly."

And what did you expect to find? Charlotte didn't ask. She doubted she'd get a straight answer. *And how much authority do you really have?*

"There's nothing to be gained by shouting at each other," she said. "Our governments will determine how best to approach the sphere, when word reaches home. Until then, I propose a joint mission to study the sphere. All data will be shared, in line with our treaty obligations."

"It would still risk the treaty," Shen pointed out. "I must insist we both withdraw and wait for the multinational team."

"And we cannot withdraw, not without disobeying orders," Charlotte said. She had no idea how Captain Templeton would respond to a suggestion they left the sphere and waited for a follow-up team, but she doubted it would be kind. "There's little a new team could bring, beyond additional manpower, that we don't already have on *Endeavour*. She was designed for deep-space survey work."

Shen said nothing for a long moment. Charlotte wondered how his ship had even found them. Had she shadowed *Endeavour*? The survey ship hadn't really been trying to hide. Or had she reached the system first? She didn't ask. She wasn't sure she could trust the answer. And...what was he thinking? His government wouldn't be pleased, if there was a delay in studying the sphere. Who knew what there might be, waiting to be found? As long as they were sure the data really *was* being shared, the Chinese had good reason to go along with Charlotte's proposal.

But will it be good enough for him? Charlotte felt a twinge of sympathy. Shen would be in deep shit, if his government renounced his actions and turned him into a scapegoat. *Whatever choice he makes, he could wind up in hot water.*

She sighed, inwardly. In hindsight, it might have been better to formally approach the other governments and ask for liaison officers. Downplaying the Virus Prime Sphere—it occurred to her there were too many *spheres*—was one thing, but the Dyson Spheres was quite another. It could blow up in the government's face...she wondered, idly, if she'd find herself carrying the can for *that* disaster. It wouldn't have been her fault—she hadn't been the person who'd drawn up the mission orders—but it could all be blamed on her anyway.

"Your proposal is acceptable," Shen said, finally. "However, we must insist on complete access to your sensor platforms and communications networks."

"I'm sure we can share the live feeds with you," Charlotte said. She'd have to discuss it with the captain before making any solid commitments, but it wouldn't pose a technical problem. The various navies had learnt to make sure their ships could fight as a unit well before the virus had driven the human race to the brink of extinction. "I don't know about the communications networks."

Shen didn't seem surprised. "Our officials can sort out the details," he said, curtly. "It will depend, of course, on what my government says, but for the moment we will be happy to extend our full cooperation. Exploring the sphere could be beneficial to the entire human race."

"Agreed," Charlotte said, hoping her sigh of relief wasn't audible to him. "It opens up all sorts of possibilities for future research and development."

And settlement, she added, silently. *We could set up one hell of a colony here.*

The thought tantalised her. The sphere represented more land mass than every human-settled world put together. If it was safe to settle... she told herself not to get too invested in the concept. It would be a long time before they could confirm the sphere was uninhabited, let alone safe. The *thing* that had homed in on *Endeavour's* transmissions might have been an automated system or it might have been pointed at them by a hostile intelligence. Charlotte favoured the former. An intelligent enemy should have noticed the starship hadn't been hit, let alone destroyed. Hell, it should have noticed *Endeavour* was trying to communicate with the sphere's inhabitants.

"My staff will be in touch," Shen said. "I thank you."

His image vanished. Charlotte shook her head as the terminal bleeped again, confirming the link had been cut. Shen wasn't a *real* diplomat then... she frowned, wondering just what he *really* was. A security officer? A political commissioner? She vaguely recalled being told that China and Russia sent out commissioners to ensure their captains and crews stayed loyal, but it struck her as an exercise in futility. Treating someone as though they were disloyal was an excellent way to breed disloyalty. There were better ways to keep them loyal.

The hatch hissed open. Paris-Jackson stepped into the compartment, the hatch closing behind him. His face was artfully blank. "Did you notice what was missing?"

Charlotte frowned. "Missing?"

"No datapacket." Paris-Jackson said. "The Chinese didn't tell us anything about their ambassador."

He paused, waiting. Charlotte sighed, inwardly. He was testing her and he wasn't even bothering to hide it. She bit down hard on her irritation before it could show on her face. It was part of his job...and he was right. She *hadn't* noticed the missing datapacket. Proof, if she'd needed it, that Shen wasn't an accredited ambassador at all. He'd been thrust forward for the very simple reason the Chinese ship didn't have any better candidates.

Which suggests they had no idea what to expect, any more than we did, she thought. *Unless they want us to think that...*

"No," she said, finally. "Rude of them, wasn't it?"

"Yes." Paris-Jackson seemed oddly perturbed. "We can and we will file an official complaint, when we return to Earth. That sort of datapacket should be supplied as a matter of course."

"I doubt they expected to have to enter diplomatic discussions," Charlotte said. Starship captains had limited diplomatic authority, on the assumption they might encounter a new alien race without warning, but there were strict limits. Shen might have the authority to arrange a later meeting, when trained diplomats could be assembled, and little else. "They may have been concealing their own lack of preparation."

"Careless," Paris-Jackson said. "We are a *long* way beyond the edge of explored space."

Charlotte nodded, slowly. The odds of encountering an intelligent spacefaring race were very low, but…she frowned as she realised four, perhaps five if one counted the virus, spacefaring races had sprung into existence in the same general region of space. The humans and Tadpoles were so close together, on a cosmic scale, that they might as well share the same house. Perhaps the odds of encountering a new species were higher than she thought.

"They must have followed us," she said, finally. "Did they know why we travelled so far from explored space?"

Paris-Jackson shrugged. "Unknown," he said. "The Sphere was never a secret, not in any real sense. It was…it is an alien structure of unknown origin that seems reluctant to give up its secrets in a timely fashion. I think…I think it never drew as much interest as captured alien starships because it was so inexplicable. But…they might well have figured out that we were throwing a mission together at speed. We clearly expected to find *something*."

"They should have expected it too," Charlotte said. *Endeavour* hadn't been prepping for a routine flight into deep space, after all. "Why didn't they send a survey ship of their own?"

"A proper warship would have found it easier to hide," Paris-Jackson said. "We didn't have the slightest idea the Chinese were there, at least until they showed themselves. But they should have put a diplomat onboard…"

Charlotte frowned. The great mystery, the one the diplomats and xeno-specialists had debated over and over again, was what—precisely—had happened to the Builders. A species capable of such technological marvels was hardly going to vanish, yet…its mere existence should have precluded all possibility of human evolution. It should have settled Earth long before the human race's distant ancestors had crawled out of the muck and started to evolve into their current form. Humanity and every other known race should never have existed...and yet, they did. Perhaps the Chinese had assumed the Builders were dead and gone. It would have made a certain kind of sense.

And yet, we know the sphere is still active, she told herself. She would have felt less urgency if the sphere had been dead and cold, little more than a giant gravestone for a long-gone race. *Who knows what's waiting for us?*

She sighed, inwardly, as she reached for the terminal to write her report while the events were still fresh in her mind. There were all sorts of jokes about searching entire countries, or even *planets*, for a single person, but it was far from easy. A lone man who wanted to hide and knew how to do it could drop out of sight for a very long time. And the sphere was so much larger...she shook her head. It was just too big. London would vanish without trace on the surface. Even the biggest city on Earth would be little more than a grain of sand on a beach. It might take years to find something useful, let alone something the human race could duplicate and put into mass production. Or it might be immediate.

"The captain will want to speak with you, afterwards," Paris-Jackson said. "You'll need to be involved with coordinating with the Chinese."

"I can do that," Charlotte said. She'd finish her report first and then report to Captain Templeton. "The real question, of course, is what do we do if we do find something important?"

"It depends," Paris-Jackson said. He'd read the briefing notes thoroughly, just as she'd done. "But we have to think about it while we still can."

CHAPTER TWENTY-ONE: HMS ENDEAVOUR, DYSON TWO (INTERIOR)

"IT FEELS AS IF THE MORE WE LEARN, the less we know," Staci said, as she sipped her tea in her ready room. "And we still don't know how the sphere actually works."

"No," Jenner agreed. "But we do know there's something to find."

Staci nodded, curtly. A week of holding position, of monitoring the sphere with passive sensors and launching probes in all directions, had confirmed beyond all doubt the sphere was still active. The interior *thrummed* with life, from strange gravity pulses—the boffins thought they were signals—to automated craft humming around the sphere, carrying out missions none of the researchers—British or Chinese—had been able to define. And...she shook her head in disbelief. None of the automated craft, whatever they were, had any drive signatures. It was difficult to understand how they even *moved*.

Their gravity-manipulation technology must be light-years ahead of ours, she thought, numbly. *How did they even give something as big as a Dyson Sphere a gravity field of its very own?*

She sucked in her breath as she turned her attention to the latest set of calculations. The boffins insisted, loudly, that the sphere should not have had a gravity field. And yet, it did. The probes had passed close enough to the surface to calculate it exerted a gravity field slightly lighter than Earth's, which should have been flat-out impossible. And yet, it existed. The Royal Navy used artificial gravity, but...there was no way human technology could encompass something the size of a Dyson Sphere. Staci found it hard to comprehend why anyone would bother. If you could build something big enough to encase an entire star, you could build hundreds of smaller habitats and ensure your entire race couldn't be wiped out by a single technological glitch or unexpected flare from the star.

Unless they modified the star too, she thought. It wasn't impossible, if the boffins were correct. It was just beyond any known or theorised application of human technology. *Were they so sure of themselves, they put all their eggs in one basket?*

She took another sip of her tea. Dyson One was in ruins, nothing more than a halo of debris orbiting a star. It was oddly reassuring and yet... she dared not assume it had been a simple technological failure. What if something had attacked the system? She couldn't imagine a weapons system capable of cracking a sphere like an eggshell, but a few weeks ago she couldn't have imagined the sphere either. And yet, if the system had been attacked, why hadn't the attackers finished the job? Dyson Two was right next door. Anyone capable of cracking the first sphere could easily have cracked the second too.

Jenner cleared his throat. "Captain?"

Staci flushed. "I'm sorry," she said. She'd been wool-gathering and she knew it. "What were you saying?"

"The tactical staff drew up attack plans," Jenner said. "Their conclusion was that we *could* take the *Haikou*, if we caught them by surprise."

"If," Staci repeated. She fought down a hot flush of irritation. The tactical staff were just doing their jobs. It was their duty to consider how best to win an engagement, even if the diplomats had the situation well in hand. "I think the Chinese will have considered the same thing too."

She shook her head. *Haikou* was a cruiser. *Endeavour* was bigger, but otherwise the two ships were evenly matched. No...that was only true on paper. *Endeavour* wasn't designed for a close-range engagement and, if they started shooting at each other, *Haikou* would probably have the edge. Captain Yunan could decide if he wanted to blow *Endeavour* to dust or break contact, race back to Earth, and start a war. Staci suspected he'd do the latter. Captain Yunan had been standoffish, when she'd finally managed to talk to him, but he hadn't struck her as incompetent. He wouldn't put the urge to win ahead of the pressing need to inform Earth.

And then all hell will break loose, she thought. *Too many people already know about the sphere.*

"They haven't moved to attack us," Jenner pointed out. "As far as we know, they're alone."

"As far as we know," Staci said. The Chinese had refused to be drawn on how many other ships they'd deployed, so far from Earth. Lady Charlotte believed Captain Yunan was on his own and Staci suspected Charlotte was right, although she wasn't *sure*. "We might as well be on our own too."

She stared down at her hands. The situation was becoming too dangerous and unpredictable for her liking. They were inside a giant megastructure, crammed with alien technology of uncertain purpose, unable even to leave for fear the Chinese would find something useful when *Endeavour* was gone. The probes had answered some of her questions but raised others. And that meant...she felt tired and numb and wished, not for the first time, that someone else was in charge. She knew how to command starships. But the sphere was something else.

No wonder so many crew are turning to drink, or to sex, she thought, tiredly. *But there's no way I can do that, not as long as the buck stops with me.*

"We could send *Grantchester* home," Jenner said. "If she went for help..."

"We might have to," Staci said. "But I don't want to do that except as a last resort."

Jenner nodded. "Captain," he said, "we may have to face up to the fact we won't find anything during *this* voyage."

Staci suspected, deep inside, he was right. The sphere was just too big. The odds of finding something, anything, were just too low to be calculated. It was hard to pick out anything on the surface, let alone the planet or the giant sunshades...she wondered, again, what sort of minds would go to all the trouble of building a sphere, when there were so many other possibilities.

They might have been gods, to all intents and purposes, she thought. Her lips twitched in sudden amusement. She'd watched countless movies about godlike entities putting humanity on trial for being human. It had been a common plotline, once upon a time. *And if they're watching us now, what would they think if we started shooting at each other?*

"We'll continue the survey for the next few weeks," she said. "We need to try to communicate with the inhabitants, if there *are* inhabitants. If we find nothing, we'll rethink."

"The Admiralty will send out a far bigger survey team," Jenner said. "They know there's something here now."

"Yes," Staci agreed. "And so will everyone else."

She dismissed him, then settled back in her chair. The display updated again, as more probes reported back to the ship. They were gathering more and more hard data, but it wasn't information. Not yet. She frowned as she saw a road on the surface, a road so big...she shook her head, tiredly. It wasn't a road, but something far larger. A wall that made the Great Wall of China look like something a child might put together with building blocks, something that could be knocked down with ease. She wondered, suddenly, if the surface wasn't a single ecosystem, but a multitude. The builders could have taken biological samples from the planets they'd broken up to make the sphere, then seeded the surface after they'd put everything in place. And then...

It might be a zoo, she thought. *But who knows?*

• • •

"I must have been out of my mind," Tobias muttered. "What was I drinking?"

Marigold chuckled. "You were bored," she reminded him. "Remember?"

Tobias nodded, curtly, as the shuttle raced through interplanetary space. He'd been to a poorly run primary school and then a secondary school that managed to be even worse and nothing, not even the most tedious lesson on the leather industry, had dulled his mind as much as the sphere. It was hard to concentrate on anything, from his duties as a shuttle pilot to reading, watching movies and even the few moments they'd been able to snatch in a privacy tube. His thoughts felt sluggish, as if he'd been awake for so long he'd passed beyond tiredness and into a state trapped between wakefulness and deepest sleep. It was hard, so hard, to think clearly.

He kept his eyes on the display as the shuttle started to gain on the alien object. It was impossible to look at the sphere, at the green and blue wall ahead of them, without battling panic as his senses insisted the scene was *wrong*. It was impossible to escape the sense he was about to plunge into a planet's atmosphere and crash, even though cold logic and his sensors told him he was well clear of the surface. Hell, he was a *long* way from anything he could hit. And yet…he bit his lip, battling the fear reaction once again. He felt like a mouse running around inside a piano, constantly at the mercy of the player…of a player who didn't even know the mouse was there. The sense he could be crushed at any moment was overwhelming. And yet…

"Signal the ship," he ordered, carefully. "Inform them we are closing the range now."

"Got it," Marigold said. "Done."

Tobias nodded, counting down the seconds until he could be sure—or as sure as humanly possible—the laser signal had gone unnoticed. In theory, there was no way anyone could detect a laser beam in vacuum without crossing its path. In practice, it was impossible to be sure. The Builders were so advanced that the best estimates of their capabilities were little more than wild-ass guesses. For all he knew, they could sense human minds and read their thoughts. No one had proved telepathy was possible, outside bad fiction and worse movies, but Dyson Spheres had also been thought fictional until *Endeavour* had discovered one sphere and the remains of another...

He took a risk and raised his eyes. The alien object was coming into view, a shiny silver sphere...tiny compared to the Dyson Sphere, but still easily five or six times the size of *Endeavour*. Tobias felt a chill run down his spine. He'd seen battleships and fleet carriers and they'd lumbered along, easily outrun by starfighters and gunboats alike. The object in front of him had no drive field, no gas jets or rockets...no visible means of propulsion at all. And yet...it wasn't following a ballistic course. It was being steered and...and how? Tobias didn't know. He'd never seen anything like it.

"The passive sensors are clear," Marigold said. "I'm not seeing anything."

Tobias swallowed, hard. The Dyson Sphere was a megastructure, so vast as to defy comprehension, but it was understandable. The object in front of him...was it a spacecraft? Or...or what? How did it move? It was impossible. It was...

He glanced at her, mouth suddenly dry. The mission briefing had made it clear they'd proceed to the second part, if the passive sensors saw nothing the boffins could use to work out how the sphere flew, but...he knew, now, he'd never believed it would be necessary. They should have picked up something, even if they didn't understand what they saw.

"Bring up the active sensors," he ordered. His head felt as if someone had stuffed it with cotton wool. "Sweep her."

"Aye, sir."

Marigold's voice was calm, but Tobias knew her well enough to hear the hint of fear. Passive sensors were undetectable. Active sensors...sweeping active sensors over a moving target could easily be deemed a hostile act. The shuttle's popguns couldn't threaten a starfighter, let alone something that made *Endeavour* look small, but the Builders might not realise it. Hell, for all he knew, they had handheld pistols capable of blowing up entire planets. There was just no way to know...

"Nothing," Marigold said. "The sensors...*Jesus!*"

Tobias barely had any time to react. The sphere altered course, turning on a dime and barrelling straight at them. He'd never seen anything turn so quickly, not even a starfighter...no, it hadn't turned. It had simply reversed course and come at them, as if someone had thrown a car into reverse without slowing to a halt first...his mind yammered in panic even as he darted the shuttle to one side, dodging the smaller sphere by the skin of his teeth. The alien object was impossibly fast. It didn't seem to have an acceleration curve so much as an instant jump to top speed.

"Shut down the sensors," he snapped. The sphere came at them again, as if it was simply adjusting course and speed. "Now!"

"I did," Marigold said. "It's still coming!"

Tobias cursed as he dodged the sphere again. He could accelerate and try to put some distance between them, and normally it would have worked fairly well, but the sphere was just...*impossible*. Flying in a straight line would just get them killed, yet the longer they stayed close to it the greater the chance they'd simply be rammed. The sphere was moving so quickly their odds of survival would be precisely nil. And yet...he briefly considered jumping ship, donning their masks and launching themselves into space so they could be recovered by *Endeavour* as soon as the sphere was gone. He dismissed the thought a second later. There was no way to be sure the sphere would leave and, if it didn't, Captain Templeton wouldn't risk the entire ship to save them. He couldn't blame her.

"Prep a drone," he ordered, as he dodged another swing. "Launch her, then trigger her radio."

"Aye, sir," Marigold said. "Two seconds...drone away. I say again, drone away. Going live now..."

The sphere altered course the moment the drone started to transmit, swooping down on the automated drone like a hawk on a defenceless mouse. It moved so quickly Tobias feared, even as he swung the shuttle away and boosted the drives, that it would have time to polish off the drone and then turn to deal with the shuttle once and for all. The sphere didn't try to be clever. It just crashed into the drone and obliterated it. Tobias was too numb to feel any surprise, even though he *knew* the impact should have vaporised both craft. If the sphere had taken any damage, it didn't show it.

His heart raced as he watched the display, bracing himself. If the sphere came at them again...they might have to jump ship after all. He had no idea if that would succeed, if they would even live long enough to be recovered...he let out a sigh of relief as the sphere resumed its previous course and vanished into the distance. It was still quite impossible...he shook his head, feeling a flicker of cold amusement. They were going to have to get used to that word.

"Signal from the ship," Marigold said. The signal would have passed through a pair of relay stations, just to make sure it couldn't be traced. "They want us to sneak back, carefully."

"Got it." Tobias could *feel* the sweat trickling down his back. That had been too close. He'd been in engagements where the missiles had come so near he could almost see them with the naked eye and yet, those engagements had been understandable. The sphere was something else. "If we go ballistic, we'll be home in a couple of hours."

He leaned back in his seat, letting the autopilot do the flying. That really *had* been too close. It was sheer dumb luck the sphere had been fooled...he frowned as he considered the possibilities. The sphere had ignored the shuttle until they'd brought up active sensors, whereupon it had made a very creditable attempt to kill them. And then it had been fooled by a simple trick, one Tobias knew—without false modesty—would never have convinced a human sensor operator. He found it oddly reassuring. On one hand, the sphere—and the greater sphere—was the product of extremely advanced technology. On the other, it was clearly as bright as a box of rocks. It didn't seem capable of tracking drive fields, just radio and sensor signals.

Put that in your report, he thought, as the shuttle raced into the darkness. *See what the boffins make of it.*

Marigold let out a sigh. "You know, when we get home, it might be time to retire," she said, tiredly. "Find a place to live, a civilian job or two... even write books full of lies about our exploits. We could probably eat out for years on that story alone, when we get home..."

"Yeah," Tobias agreed. They'd needed a nest egg—it was why they'd agreed to stay in Virus Prime, then board *Endeavour*—but he was starting to think they'd done their bit. "After we get home."

"Yeah," Marigold echoed. Her thoughts were elsewhere. "They seem to like spheres, don't they?"

Tobias nodded. "Their style?"

"Perhaps," Marigold said. "Our starships look faintly aerodynamic. They look as if they could fly in an atmosphere, even though they couldn't. Theirs? They look like something a native spacer might build."

"There's no such thing," Tobias said. "Is there?"

"The universe is a very strange place," Marigold said. "For all we know, the Builders might have been born on a gas giant. They might be all around us, and far beyond explored space, and we simply don't see them."

Tobias frowned. "You should mention that in your report," he said. "But...why would they build a Dyson Sphere if they live in gas giants?"

"Good question," Marigold said. "I just don't know."

CHAPTER TWENTY-TWO: HMS ENDEAVOUR, DYSON TWO (INTERIOR)

CHARLOTTE HAD WORRIED, as the days started to turn into weeks, that she might have made a mistake offering to share everything with the Chinese. She'd seen no choice—she certainly wasn't about to condone an attack on the Chinese ship, which could easily spark a full-scale war—yet she'd feared, as more and more data poured into the ship, that they'd miss their chance to get exclusive access to a piece of alien technology. And yet, she was starting to suspect she was worrying over nothing. The sphere was extremely reluctant to give up its secrets.

She sat in the conference room and frowned as Captain Templeton called the meeting to order, then invited the holograms of Captain Yunan and Representative Shen to attend. Charlotte had spent enough time working with the latter to be *sure* he was out of his depth and probably completely on his own, facing a situation in which *Haikou* had to both stay with *Endeavour* and report home to her superiors. Charlotte suspected his inability to square the circle was grinding him down, made worse by the suspicion that whatever answer he picked—whatever he chose to do—would be the wrong one. His superiors would probably blame him for not doing the impossible.

"There have been developments," Captain Templeton said, calmly. "Doctor Gaurs?"

Doctor Athena Gaurs leaned forward. "As you know, we have deployed nearly every drone in our combined stores in an attempt to map the interior of the sphere," she said. "We brought nowhere near enough, a problem made worse by several drones simply dropping out of the communications link and vanishing. We don't know what happened to them, but it's probable they went too close to one of the rammers and got smacked into dust."

Charlotte sucked in her breath. The sphere's interior remined her of a giant piece of clockwork, built on an interplanetary scale. It was hard to believe the Builders had departed, or simply lost interest in maintaining their system, but…so far, there'd been no actual answer to any attempt to signal them. The rammers had been drawn to communications platforms, silencing them…Charlotte had a theory, and she knew some of the boffins agreed with her, that the Builders had simply lost control of their own defences. It was insane and yet…why would they program their defences to go after radio transmissions? Surely, they knew there were other intelligent races in the universe?

"We have yet to put together a detailed map," Athena continued. "There are limits to what passive sensors can tell us, as you know, and switching on the *active* sensors draws a sharp response. However, we have discovered something interesting."

She keyed her terminal. The display changed rapidly, zooming in on the south pole. "The sphere does not rotate," she said, quietly. "However, we believe this is the south pole—the lowest point of the sphere, at least from our vantage point. The interesting thing is that the south pole is surrounded by mountains, which reach all the way up to orbit. Or what we would *call* orbit, on Earth. The smallest mountain rises nearly two hundred kilometres above sea level, poking its head firmly out of the atmosphere."

"You mean, it's a space elevator," Jenner said.

"It could be used as one, yes," Athena agreed. She adjusted the display again. "The mountains surround a giant hatch, for want of a better term, that leads outside the sphere. Don't let the display fool you. The hatch appears to be big enough to take something the size of Earth, while the mountains provide an airtight seal to keep the sphere's atmosphere from rushing out into the vacuum."

Charlotte stared. It was so *big*. It was...she swallowed hard. "How... how long would it take to *open* the hatch?"

"Hours, at best," Athena said. "We think there are smaller hatches buried within the big one, hatches capable of handling smaller objects like starships and shipyards..."

"And Death Stars," an officer Charlotte didn't recognise said.

Athena smiled but otherwise ignored the verbal sally. "The system is relatively simple," she said. "It's just built on a very big scale. Given the amount of dust we saw outside, it's probable the sphere wasn't opened since it was put together and seeded with life. They wouldn't need to, not as long as they could use the tramline. However, that isn't the interesting detail."

She tapped the console, zooming in on the sphere's surface. "We found this, quite close to the mountains," she said. "We think it's a command centre."

Charlotte felt, more than heard, the excitement running through the compartment. No one wanted to admit it, but they'd started to give up hope of finding something important, something decisive, before they had to turn around and go home. The sphere was a treasure trove, yet the odds of finding anything that would put their names in the history books were growing steeper with every passing day. It didn't help that everyone knew, soon enough, that an even bigger team of xenospecialists would arrive and take over. She understood, better than she cared to admit. The majority of the crew were just sitting around, waiting for something to happen. And there was a limit to how much their officers could do to divert them.

Captain Templeton leaned forward. "Are you sure?"

"It is impossible to be sure, Captain," Athena said. "However, the station is quite close to the South Gate, as we're calling it, and we think there would be command and control links to the gate itself. We have yet to chart the entire surface, but we simply haven't found many other structures. This one sticks out."

"They have all the surface area they could possibly want," Jenner said. "Why don't they have cities?"

"They may have built them underground," Athena said. "Or they may have seen the sphere as little more than a nature reserve, with their population on the planet rather than the sphere's surface."

"We could also check out the planet," Paris-Jackson said. "If it is their homeworld…"

"It is surrounded by rammers," Captain Templeton said. "I doubt a shuttle could get through easily."

"There are stealth shuttles," Charlotte said. Her ex-husband had said something about them once, years ago. She wished she'd paid more attention now. "Aren't there?"

"The shuttle would have to make an insertion into a planetary atmosphere without being detected," Captain Templeton said, quietly. "The odds aren't good at the best of times."

"We think we can land on the sphere itself," Captain Yunan said. "I propose a joint diplomatic mission."

Captain Templeton scowled. "We have no idea what the team will find, when they land."

"No," Captain Yunan agreed. "But if there is anywhere on the sphere we might find someone, it is there."

"It would be risky," Paris-Jackson said. "We don't know…"

"Staying here is risky too," Athena pointed out. "The longer we stay here, the greater the chance one of the rammers will mistake us for a threat and attack."

"I intend to make contact," Captain Yunan said, firmly. "Captain Templeton, will you deploy a shuttle too?"

• • •

Staci kept her face under tight control as she thought fast. Captain Yunan was under a lot of pressure, both from his political commissioner *and* the simple fact his ship wasn't designed for long-term operations so far from his logistics chain. He'd already had to request a handful of items from Staci's stores, something he probably wouldn't have been allowed to do if his commissioner had realised just how much the mere act of *asking* would tell his rivals. He had good reason to want to speed things up, to try and make contact with the Builders before he had to head back to the nearest shipyard, leaving the British in sole possession. And yet, Staci wasn't convinced they *could* land on the sphere. Who knew what other defences it might have?

Her mind raced. She could try to block the Chinese, but they'd take that as an act of war. Probably. She could let them try it alone, but...who knew what they'd find? If they were the first humans to make contact with the Builders, or if they stumbled across an abandoned library or...she cursed mentally, caught between conflicting objectives. She could offer to escort the Chinese as far as Virus Prime, or...no, that wouldn't work. It was too late to make such an offer. They'd see it as a subtle attempt to block them and push back hard.

"A diplomatic mission," she said, slowly. "It will have to be volunteers only and..."

"I volunteer," Lady Charlotte said, quickly. "I'm happy to take the risk."

Staci fought down a flash of irritation. Lady Charlotte had nerve... either that, or she didn't understand the dangers. She wasn't flying into a terrorist-held town or even travelling into an enemy state under safe conduct, she was heading straight into the unknown. Staci had read the reports from the shuttle's close encounter with a rammer. The researchers had yet to figure out how the alien objects worked, but they'd all agreed they were incredibly fast and maneuverable. The shuttle had been extremely lucky to survive.

"We don't know for sure we can get anyone to the surface," Staci said, carefully. The simulations suggested it was possible, but the sphere was one big unknown. The so-called command centre might turn out to be nothing. "And you might not come back."

She sighed, inwardly. The hell of it was that she was boxed into a corner. She *had* to send a landing party, one that had a diplomat, or risk leaving it to the Chinese. And yet, if Lady Charlotte never returned...Staci knew the aristocrat had enemies, enemies who might be quietly pleased if she came back in a box or not at all, but that wouldn't stop the Admiralty from asking a lot of pointed questions about why Staci, the ultimate authority, had agreed to let Lady Charlotte go. She shouldn't. Sure, she was an ambassador—at least on paper—but she wasn't a special envoy who might be sent into danger at any moment. She had basic survival training and not much else. A proper envoy would have some military and survivalist experience as well as training.

"If you are prepared to go, then you can," she said, ignoring Jenner's sharp intake of breath beside her. "If not, please let me know as soon as possible."

"I can do it," Lady Charlotte said.

Staci nodded, lifting her eyes to the display. "If we put together the mission, we can launch tomorrow," she said. "Captain Yunan, is that acceptable?"

"Yes, Captain," Yunan said. "It is."

"Good," Staci said. "And with that, I think we can bring this meeting to an end."

She dismissed everyone, save for Lady Charlotte. The older woman looked galvanised by the prospect of action, even though she was making a jump into the unknown. Staci almost wished she was accompanying them. She couldn't, and yet...she sighed as the last of the attendees left the compartment. They'd be running sims and training exercises, making sure they'd accounted for all the unprecedented weirdness in landing on the interior of a sphere...she knew, somehow, they wouldn't be ready for everything. The sphere would find a way to surprise them. She was sure of it.

"Listen carefully," she said, once they were alone. "You'll be out on a limb. You and the rest of the crew might run into something you can't handle. You might be killed by a rammer or something else. There's no guarantee the structure we've found really *is* a command centre."

"I understand the risks," Lady Charlotte said, flatly.

Staci doubted it. She'd met her fair share of naval wives who assumed they shared their husband's rank and experience and none of them had struck her as any more experienced than the average cadet on his first day. Lady Charlotte wasn't *that* bad, to be fair, but she was ignorant of her own ignorance. Staci would almost have preferred to be able to pull rank and insist on Paris-Jackson going in her place, yet...she *was* the titular leader of the diplomatic staff. *Not* letting her go could easily be construed as an insult.

"I hope you do," she said, finally. "Go get some rest. There'll be a mission briefing tomorrow, before the launch. And if you change your mind, let me know."

"I won't," Lady Charlotte said. "Thank you."

She left. Staci sighed again, understanding—not for the first time—what Mitch Campbell had seen in her. Lady Charlotte was brave and determined and extremely capable, at least in her field of expertise. She was no soft aristo, unable to even think of roughing it...unable, even, to think what roughing it might be like. And yet, how would she cope when she was taken out of her element? Sure, there'd be direct links back to the ship, so she could consult with her staff, but...

We'll see, Staci thought. *And when this mission is completed, we may have to simply head home.*

...

"Well," Colin said. "Do you think you can land on the sphere?"

Tobias said nothing for a long moment. "I've reviewed all the images from the drones and we've gone through a handful of simulations, so as long as there are no unpleasant surprises, we should be fine," he said.

"There's some odd atmospheric disturbances that may pose an unexpected challenge…"

Colin grimaced. He was no stranger to flights through unfriendly skies, followed by landings deep within enemy territory. He'd been trained to cope with rough flights and rougher landings. His instructors had told him that any landing he could walk away from was a good one…of course, he reflected, none of them had ever been *quite* so far from support before. Tobias might talk about boldly going where no man had gone before, but Colin was starting to suspect it was overrated. He'd even been tempted to suggest the first landings be carried out by the marines alone, rather than the diplomats. But he knew it would be pointless.

And so might be trying to follow all the diplomatic rules in the book, he thought. *The Builders are so powerful they don't have to follow the rules.*

"As long as you can get us down and then up again," he said, finally. "Can you?"

"I think so," Tobias said. "It shouldn't be a problem."

Colin hoped he was right. He'd been told, years ago, that people had believed the Earth to be flat. It had made a certain kind of sense. You had to get very high if you wanted to see the curvature for yourself. The sphere was just the same. Its inhabitants might live on the inside of a ball, if indeed there were any inhabitants, but the ball was so large the surface might as well be flat. The land might curve up around them, yet from a human perspective the curve would be so slight it would be almost unnoticeable. They'd probably stop thinking of it as a sphere shortly after landing.

He turned away, inspecting the crates as the maintenance crew carried them into place and locked them firmly to the deck. Survival rations, translation gear, weapons…he suspected the diplomats would complain to the captain if they realised how many weapons he was bringing, but it was better to have the weapons and not need them than vice versa. They'd probably also complain about the food. Ration packs were good for you, but they tasted terrible. He had no idea why. It wasn't as if the food couldn't be improved.

"It shouldn't be a problem," Tobias said, from the cockpit. "And it will be one for the record books."

"First pilot to make a landing on Dyson Two," Colin said, without looking around. Tobias would be pleased. He'd wanted fame and never had a hope of getting it, before he'd wound up in the navy. Colin too, for that matter. "And first Royal Marine to set foot on Dyson Two."

He sobered. He understood making insertions on hostile worlds. He understood suborbital drops and parachuting and even long and boring flights from one military base to another. But this...there was no way to inform the inhabitants they were coming. The reports were clear. Anyone who broadcast a signal was asking to be killed. The rammers came for them at once. Indeed, if some of the reports were correct, the automated defences reacted faster than light itself.

They probably have a flicker network embedded within the sphere, he thought. He was no communications expert, but he was sure it could be done. Their control of gravity waves was so far ahead of humanity's that the flicker network linking Earth to the colonies was little more than a joke. *Radio waves would be too slow for them.*

Colin scowled. Accidents happened. It would be very easy for the inhabitants, or their automated defences, to assume the shuttles were hostile and blow them to atoms. He knew *he* wouldn't have been happy to discover a foreign shuttlecraft landing in London, certainly if it didn't have permission. Who knew? They might assume the shuttle was loaded with nukes or antimatter or something—anything—that might turn it into a devastating weapon. The more he thought about it, the less he liked it.

"If we break off," he said as he stepped back into the cockpit, "could we make it out of the atmosphere?"

Tobias hesitated. "It would depend," he said. "It should be possible. But if we were too deep within the atmosphere before we tried to break off, we might find it difficult."

"Fuck." Colin turned again. "If they're not feeling welcoming, we might be in deep shit."

CHAPTER TWENTY-THREE: SHUTTLECRAFT, DYSON TWO (INTERIOR)

"ALL SYSTEMS GO," Marigold said, as she took her seat. "The passengers are all buckled in, ready for the flight."

Tobias swallowed a joke about stewardesses as he ran the final checks. Marigold wouldn't think it funny. Nor was it, he supposed. He'd done hundreds of routine shuttle flights, since his assignment to Virus Prime, but Dyson Two was a dangerously unpredictable environment. There was no way to know if anything, from the gravity field to the terrain, would remain consistent as the shuttle flew to its destination. He'd simulated everything he could, since the alien command centre had been spotted, but simulations had dangerous limitations. If the programmers didn't anticipate something, they wouldn't include it in their simulations.

He ran his hand down the console, checking and rechecking everything one final time. The flight shouldn't be *that* dangerous, but…his imagination provided too many possible examples of things that could go wrong. He'd supervised the installation of more decoy drones, and a modified ECM suite, but he feared they wouldn't be enough to keep the shuttle intact if the rammers decided to destroy it. It didn't help they'd been given strict orders to avoid doing anything that might be taken as hostile by watching alien eyes.

And we might have already crossed that line, he thought. *They've made it clear they're not interested in answering our hails.*

He sighed inwardly as the shuttle was cleared for departure. He had too much experience over the years with people violating his boundaries. They'd never been respected and why should they? He hadn't had the strength or skills to protect them. The Builders had made it clear they weren't interested in communicating with the human intruders...it was possible, he'd been told, that they were dealing with automated defences, but he wasn't so sure. They were poking and prodding at the aliens, just as he'd been poked and prodded as a schoolchild, and he couldn't help fearing they would eventually draw a sharp reaction. If the Builders were still around, they clearly didn't want to talk. If...

Marigold glanced at him. "Ready?"

Tobias nodded, stomach churning as he undocked and guided the shuttle away from the mothership. The gas jets were meant to be undetectable, except at very close range, but it was impossible to be *sure*. Who knew *what* the Builders could see? They'd certainly had ample time to put together a baseline image of the sphere's interior. They would notice if something was even slightly out of place. Tobias frowned as he spotted the Chinese shuttle ahead, its drives already online. It wasn't a race, he'd been told, but the Chinese didn't seem to see it that way. Their ship couldn't remain on station indefinitely.

Nor can we, Tobias thought. *We'll have to leave the sphere sooner or later, just to resupply from the ruins of the other sphere.*

He kept his eye on the sensor display as the shuttle's drives came online. The drives were stepped down as much as possible, but they were nowhere near as stealthy as he wanted. It was the worst of both worlds. The odds of being detected, even with equal technology, were too high for his peace of mind, while their chances of escape if they came under fire were very low. They didn't *seem* to have been detected, but there was no way to know. The shuttles might already have been spotted, then tracked back to their motherships. And who knew what would happen then?

His heart thumped in his chest as the seconds turned to minutes and the minutes to hours. It seemed impossible they weren't already entering the atmosphere, already testing themselves against the sphere's gravity field. The sphere was...he shook his head, putting the thought out of his mind. He'd been told, when he'd started basic training, that ninety percent of military service was nothing more than boredom. He was starting to think his instructors had understated the case.

Tobias took a sip of juice, wondering how the team behind him was coping. He didn't understand how Colin could be so calm, even though his fate was out of his hands. Tobias had never coped well with a lack of control, although—to be fair—much of his life had never been under his control. Perhaps Colin could give up control on the grounds he'd regain it as soon as the shuttle hit the ground, or perhaps he was smart enough to know there was no point in panic. The diplomats seemed a little more inclined to be worried...not, Tobias knew, that it would make any difference. If a rammer came at them, their survival would be in Tobias's hands.

He frowned as he lifted his eyes and looked at the approaching wall. It felt *wrong*, as if he was trying to ram an entire planet. His head spun, his perspective shifting violently, every time he tried to comprehend what he saw. He was plunging towards the south pole...no, he was flying horizontally...he lowered his head, choosing to fly by sensors alone. The visual input was just too confusing. He felt spacesick just looking at the sphere. It was impossible to convince himself there were still millions of kilometres between the shuttle and the surface. They were perfectly safe. They wouldn't even hit the atmosphere for another twenty minutes.

"Dump the live feed to the relay station," he ordered, quietly. "And then prepare for entry."

"The Chinese will make the first entry," Marigold said. "They shouldn't have any problems. The atmosphere seems calm."

Tobias nodded, although he wasn't so sure. The sphere was just *impossible*...he put the thought out of his head as the timer ticked relentlessly towards zero. The sphere was coming closer. And yet, save for the command centre, his sensors weren't picking up any structures on the surface. It puzzled him.

The sensors can read newspapers from high orbit, he thought. *If they can't see anything, there's nothing to see. But why build a sphere and then not populate it?*

He frowned, again. The sphere was *ancient*. No one was quite sure *just* how old it was—their estimates were nothing more than guesses—but it was quite possibly millions of years old. Old enough to evolve intelligent life? Tobias had once gone on a dinosaur kick and discovered there were nearly sixty *million* years between the age of the dinosaurs and the human race. Was the sphere old enough to give birth to intelligent life? Or was it a great deal younger?

And if a race was born here, instead of a normal planet, they'd have come up with some pretty strange ideas about how the universe works, he thought. *How long would it take for them to realise they were inside a sphere?*

"The Chinese are angling for entry now," Marigold said. "No sign of any trouble."

Tobias nodded. The senior staff, the officers and the diplomats, might moan about the Chinese making the first entry into the sphere's atmosphere, but it suited *Tobias* just fine. He'd have ample time to adjust his flight path if the Chinese ran into problems or break off completely if all hell broke loose. It wasn't as if the Chinese could lay claim to the sphere simply because they were the first to land. Even if the Builders were gone, the sphere was too important—and too game-changing—for any one nation to claim it for itself.

"Five minutes to entry," he said. The Chinese didn't seem to be having any problems. Their flight path looked unchanged, even as they slid into the upper atmosphere. "Inform our passengers we're about to take the plunge."

He took a breath. They were supposed to be taking it slowly, taking care to ensure the Builders had plenty of time to see them coming. He would have preferred to get down to the surface as quickly as possible, just to minimise the time for something to go wrong. He wished, sourly, that he had a live feed from the Chinese shuttle. The sphere's atmosphere was still a dangerous unknown. There was just no way to be sure it wouldn't change in a hurry.

"Here we go," he said. "Brace yourselves…"

A shudder ran through the shuttle as she struck the upper atmosphere. Tobias kept a sharp eye on the sensors, even as a second and then a third shudder echoed through the craft. The atmosphere was thickening with astonishing speed, as if the Builders had done something to keep it from thinning out. He felt a flash of alarm. Why had they done that? Who knew what other surprises lay in wait?

An alarm howled. "Contact," Marigold said. A flashing red icon appeared on the display. "One object, unknown purpose. It appeared out of nowhere!"

Tobias cursed. The mystery object was well above their heads, moving into position to…the display flashed as a bolt of energy stabbed down, striking the Chinese shuttle and wiping it off the screen with a sudden, terrible finality. Tobias acted on instinct, throwing the shuttle into a series of evasive patterns that made the hull groan in complaint, even as a second bolt flashed past. The power was off the scale. A single hit would be enough to vaporise them.

"Shit!" The threat display was clear, suggesting the enemy weren't using any recognisable sensors, but it didn't matter. The object—some kind of stealthed orbital weapons platform, Tobias decided—didn't seem to have any trouble in tracking them. The only upside was that its targeting was far from perfect, making it harder for it to score a direct hit as long as he kept the shuttle on an evasive course. "Launch the drones! Quickly!"

He cursed under his breath as another bolt of deadly energy shot past. The cockpit flared with light. The atmosphere shuddered, waves of turbulence crashing against the hull and throwing the shuttle off course. Tobias heard someone being noisily sick in the passenger compartment, but there was nothing he could do. Hopefully, the passengers had the sense to keep themselves strapped in. The flight wasn't going to level out in a hurry.

"The drones don't seem to be drawing enemy fire," Marigold said, grimly. "The platform is targeting us."

Tobias forced himself to think. The platform had picked its moment well. The shuttles had been too deep within the gravity well to simply break off and run for space, yet too far above the ground to eject and hope for the best. Tobias knew there were military parachutists who jumped from low orbit, somehow making it to the ground, but the shuttle didn't have the equipment for the entire crew to bail out. Even if they did...Colin and his two fellows might make it; the others, Tobias and Marigold included, didn't have a hope. Their odds of survival would be zero.

We can't go up and we can't stay where we are, he thought, as another flash of light lit the skies. The atmosphere was turning nasty, a thunderstorm starting to build with terrifying speed. Tobias had flown through storms before, but this one was different. The energy sparking through the sky was an order of magnitude more powerful, and more dangerous, than anything recorded on Earth. *We have to go down.*

"Hang on," he shouted. "We're going down!"

The shuttle rocked, again, as he dived into the lower atmosphere. It was hard to tell if they were evading the platform or not. He suspected they weren't. A human tracking system would have no trouble following them through the storm and he refused to believe the Builders would have designed and built something less capable. They might manage to give an automated system the slip, but...for all he knew, the automated system was far more advanced than anything humans could build. It didn't have to be a full-fledged AI to be a dangerous opponent. He'd played enough computer games to know an enemy with computerised reactions, capable of spotting and exploiting a microsecond of vulnerability, was extremely hard to beat.

He cursed as something struck the shuttle, sending them spinning. For a moment, he thought they'd been hit...no, not by the orbital platform. It might have been a lightning bolt or...he saw a light swelling through the clouds, pulsing brightly before fading into the darkness. Lightning, he realised. It was never a simple flash of light, if one was in the clouds. Another followed, then another. The darkness seemed to part as they flew lower, coming out of the clouds. The landscape below looked as flat as Nebraska.

The air vibrated. The shuttle rocked, then tipped sharply to one side. Tobias swore—that really *had* been a near miss—then fought for control as the shuttle plunged towards the ground. There was no time to try to get everyone into parachutes and jump, not now. He had to put the craft down as quickly as possible, yet...he heard a drive node screaming in protest, the display lighting up with alerts and warnings as the node teetered on the brink of failure. If it failed...

"Brace for impact," Marigold ordered. "Brace for impact!"

Tobias gritted his teeth. They were losing height rapidly, the ground coming up to hit them...he looked, frantically, for a safe place to crash. The trees below looked utterly solid. He didn't want to try to put the shuttle down there, but he was starting to think there wouldn't be any choice. There had to be a clearing somewhere...if there was, he couldn't see it. He heard someone scream as the air flared again, the storm shaking the shuttle as it started to make its way south. Tobias cursed, again. If the platform was tracking them through optical sensors, which he supposed was quite possible, it would see them the moment the storm cleared and then...what?

He gripped the controls, throwing all of his remaining power into the drive nodes as the ground smacked them in the face. The shuttle crashed into the trees and tore through them with terrifying speed, the remnants of the drive field throwing pieces of sawdust and debris in all directions before the last of the drive nodes gave out. The gravity field flickered violently—for a horrified moment, Tobias thought the sphere's gravity had been grossly underestimated—before the shuttle's gravity collapsed. He breathed a sigh of relief, his thoughts wavering on the brink of unconsciousness as the gravity returned to normal. It actually seemed to be slightly lighter than standard gravity, something that puzzled him. But then, there were definite advantages to dialling down the gravity field. He'd visited asteroid settlements that kept the field stepped down or simply didn't have one at all...

Colin burst into the cockpit. "Get up," he shouted, tugging at Marigold's straps. "We have to move!"

Tobias felt woozy, as if he'd hit his head at some point without noticing, but forced himself to stagger to his feet. The shuttle lay at an angle, the consoles and displays dead and cold. He thought he smelled burning and cursed under his breath, feeling sick as he stumbled into the passenger cabin and saw the gash in the hull. The shuttle was tough...he couldn't help noticing, in his dazed state, that the craft had been oversold. But then, no one had envisaged a crash landing on a Dyson sphere.

A body lay on the deck, its head caved in. Tobias felt sick, his stomach rebelling violently as he saw the blood staining the seats. A diplomat, he thought; someone who'd been fool enough to take off his straps before they'd hit the ground and discovered his mistake too late to fix it. The poor bastard was beyond all help. He started to bend over, to pick up the body, then caught himself. They didn't have time. He'd done enough combat insertions, as a pilot, to know they had very little time before the enemy sent someone to check out the wreck or simply dropped a missile on it from a safe distance. They had to be gone before that happened or they'd be dead.

He caught Marigold's hand and stepped through the gash in the hull. The air stank of burning trees and sawdust, bringing back bad memories of woodworking in school. Fires blazed behind the shuttle, trees torched as the shuttle had crashed down. The flames were all too noticeable. Had they started a forest fire that would spread to the entire sphere?

"Keep moving," Colin ordered. The rest of the passengers were already well clear of the wreck, poking through foliage that wasn't as impassable as Tobias had thought from above. "Hurry!"

Tobias nodded, swallowing as the full implications of the disaster dawned on them. They were alive, and safe for the moment, but the shuttle was beyond repair. They were trapped on the sphere…

… And there was no way in hell, as far as he could tell, that they could escape.

CHAPTER TWENTY-FOUR: HMS ENDEAVOUR, DYSON TWO (INTERIOR)

"CAPTAIN," LIEUTENANT COMMANDER Philip McDougall snapped. "The shuttle is under attack!"

Staci stared, a wash of helpless fury flashing through her as the shuttle desperately dove into the sphere's atmosphere to hide. There was nothing she could do. The shuttle was already too deep within the atmosphere to escape, yet...could they get down to the ground before the weapons platform blew it to dust? Staci found it hard to believe the sensor records, even when they'd been taken by two remote platforms of her own. The orbital weapons platform was pumping out enough energy with each shot to slice a battleship in half.

And that means the situation has just become very dangerous, she thought. *Everyone is going to want to get their hands on that weapon.*

She shuddered. The Chinese shuttle hadn't stood a chance. It had been vaporised before the crew had even realised they were under attack. And...she saw her shuttle vanish into the clouds and shuddered. If the Chinese—or anyone—captured the orbital weapons platform and put the alien weapon into mass production, it would be the First Interstellar War all over again. Worse, perhaps. *Ark Royal* had been the most heavily armoured ship of her generation and the alien weapon could burn through her armour as if it were made of paper.

"Captain," Jenner said. "The last databurst from the shuttle indicated they were going to try to land."

Staci nodded, numbly. The shuttle pilot had no choice. They *had* to land before the platform blew them away...her mind raced, trying to determine what the platform might be thinking. If it was an automated system, it might have assumed the shuttles were little more than pieces of space junk that couldn't be allowed to strike the surface. The sphere might not be as indestructible as they thought. The wreckage of Dyson One was clear proof spheres *could* be destroyed, either through carelessness, age, or hostile action. And yet...

Worry about that later, she told herself. *Right now, you have to focus on the crashed shuttle.*

Her mind raced. It wasn't clear if the shuttle had even made it. The sphere's upper atmosphere was rolling with energy, a storm spreading at terrifying speed. The passive sensor platforms couldn't see through the muck, couldn't determine if the shuttle had landed or crashed or had simply been vaporised by the orbital defences. If they were down, they were trapped. *Endeavour* didn't have any stealth shuttles. Even if she had, Staci feared they couldn't sneak past the alien defences.

Jenner's thoughts were running in the same direction. "How the hell are we going to get them back?"

Staci had no answer. The alien weapons platform would shoot down anything she sent to pick the castaways up. Could the platform be destroyed? She had no idea. If it was built out of the same material as everything else, the platform might be effectively indestructible. She suspected she'd need to test it, before too long. Could it be diverted instead? Perhaps...she had drones configured to pose as starships and shuttles, but it wouldn't be too long before it managed to pick them all off and start looking for new threats. Perhaps...she wished, suddenly, that she'd insisted on leaving the command centre strictly alone. They could have jumped out of the sphere and waited for a larger follow-up team to take over.

"Captain," MacPhee said. The communications officer sounded worried. "Captain Yunan would like to speak to you."

"I'll take it in my ready room," Staci said. "Mr. XO, deploy four more passive sensor platforms to look for the landing party. If you find them, alert me at once."

"Aye, Captain."

Staci nodded and left the bridge. The odds weren't good. The platforms already on station hadn't spotted the shuttle, which meant...what? By the time the other platforms arrived, it might be too late. She briefly considered moving the entire ship closer, but...she knew it wasn't a good idea. The weapons platform could vaporise *Endeavour* as easily as the Chinese shuttle.

She sat at her desk and keyed her terminal. Captain Yunan's face appeared in front of her, so tightly controlled she *knew* he was deeply worried. There was no sign of Shen...she wondered, suddenly, if Shen had been aboard the destroyed shuttlecraft. If he was gone...she felt a twinge of sympathy for her counterpart. The Admiralty was not going to be pleased with her, if Lady Charlotte and the rest of the passengers were lost forever, but at least they wouldn't assume it was because she was ideologically unsound. They'd be much more likely to think she was simply incompetent.

Which isn't that much of an improvement, she thought, crossly. *There's bound to be at least one armchair admiral who'll argue I should have let the Chinese take all the risk upon themselves.*

"Captain," she said. "I'm sorry about your shuttle."

"Thank you," Yunan said. "And I hope your crew made it down safely."

Staci nodded, although she still had no idea how they could rescue the grounded shuttle and its passengers. The weapons platform was just too dangerous to treat lightly. They'd have to test it, to determine what—if anything—it used to decide what should be fired upon. The only upside,

ENDEAVOUR

she thought, was that it might draw attention from the Builders themselves. If they got involved…

"I intend to take out the platform," Yunan said. "It needs to be removed before we can land on the surface."

"Are we sure it's the only platform?" Staci leaned forward, willing him to listen. "We didn't have a hint it was there until it started to target the shuttles. Whatever stealth technology it uses, it is a long way ahead of ours."

"Which implies the platform is hostile," Yunan pointed out. "Why bother cloaking something if you don't expect it to be attacked?"

He had a point, Staci conceded. There was no logical *reason* to cloak the weapons platform unless you thought the platform was going to be attacked. And yet, it was right inside a full-sized Dyson sphere! Not, she reflected, that it was impossible for someone to get into the sphere. *Endeavour* and her Chinese counterpart had jumped inside without difficulty. For all they knew, the Builders had left the platform cloaked as a test. If the intruders assumed the sphere was defenceless and attacked, the Builders would know they were hostile.

"We don't know for sure," she said, carefully. "The shuttles were heading into the sphere's atmosphere when they were attacked. The defences might have assumed they were falling rocks or something else likely to do real damage."

"Particularly as that part of the sphere may be weaker than the rest," Yunan said, thoughtfully. "What would happen if a large asteroid fell on the South Gate?"

Staci had no answer, but she doubted the results would be good. "The fact remains, we don't know what we're dealing with," she said. "If we cannot locate the shuttle party, we should withdraw and seek orders from home."

Yunan cocked his head. "You want to leave your people behind?"

"No," Staci said. "But right now, we don't even know if they're still alive."

"No," Yunan echoed. "And that is why we need to capture or destroy the weapons platform."

Staci took a breath, wishing Lady Charlotte or Paris-Jackson were available to advise her. "I urge you not to do anything hasty," she said. "We don't know what we're *really* dealing with. We don't even know there are no other platforms waiting in stealth themselves."

"I have to try," Yunan said. "My shuttles will be dispatched ten minutes from now. You are welcome to dispatch a team to accompany them, if you wish. Until then…"

Staci briefly considered threatening to fire on his shuttles, before dismissing the idea as insane. They had enough problems without shooting at their fellow humans. Besides, Yunan was in deep shit. Losing the shuttle, and perhaps his political commissar, would reflect badly on him when he got home, particularly as he'd been the one pushing for a contact mission. He didn't have much time to recover, not when his ship was pushing the limits about as far as they would go. If he didn't act now, he might never have another chance to save his career.

And he might want to do something before another political commissar is appointed to look over his shoulder, Staci thought. The intelligence reports were vague on precisely how much authority commissars really had, but she suspected they had a great deal more than anyone would be comfortable admitting. *If they don't have the slightest idea how to run a ship or any understanding of the realities of space combat, they might fuck up very easily.*

"Good luck," she said. "We'll be watching."

Yunan's face blinked out. Staci cursed under her breath. She understood the urge to do something—anything—but she had a feeling that trying to destroy the weapons platform was a mistake. There might be more platforms lurking under cloak, ready to open fire on the shuttle sent to collect the landing party…assuming, of course, they'd survived. She stood and hurried back to the bridge, reassuming command. The platforms were still racing towards the South Gate.

"We haven't been able to locate the crash site," Jenner said, grimly. "But we have picked up traces of fire on the surface."

Staci nodded, biting down the sarcastic remark that came to mind.

The shuttle must have crashed, unless the weapons platform had accidentally set fire to the surface itself. It was certainly putting out enough power to do real damage, although she suspected—from the latest sensor analysis reports—that the weapon was actually *too* powerful to set fire to anything. It would turn its targets into dust, wiping out the fuel before the fire got started.

"The Chinese are planning to try to capture the platform," she said, instead. "We'll watch and see what happens."

Jenner frowned. "What if they *do* take the platform intact?"

"Good question." Staci didn't know. It would be tricky for the Chinese to reverse-engineer the weapons and put them into mass production before the rest of the human race forced them to share, but who knew? They might be able to do it. Or they might try to take out *Endeavour* to ensure the secret remained firmly in their hands, at least long enough to master the weapon and deploy it. Or…it might provoke a reaction from the Builders. "We may be about to find out."

She took her chair, feeling—once again—helpless. It had been a lot easier to decide what to do during the war, when there had been a very clear enemy and they'd had no choice but to kill or be killed. Now, she felt as though she was on a knife edge. The slightest misstep—or even the correct step, if luck went against her—could lead to utter disaster. She wanted to tell the Chinese to stop, to wait until they made contact with higher authority, but she knew Captain Yunan wouldn't listen. Hell, she didn't even know if her landing party was still alive. If they were dead, there was nothing to be gained by provoking the alien weapons platform.

"Captain, the Chinese have launched their shuttles," Lieutenant-Commander Philip McDougall said. "They're entering stealth mode now. I'm projecting their courses…"

"Put them on the big display," Staci ordered. She didn't want to watch and yet she had no choice. "Can the alien platform see them?"

"Unclear," McDougall told her. "We're not sure how they spotted the original shuttles either."

Staci nodded, forcing herself to watch and wait. If nothing else, the whole operation would hopefully lead to a great many pieces of useful information. The Chinese were approaching under stealth, which would reveal if the alien platform could see through the masking fields...interestingly, it might also hint at an ability to see through a full-fledged cloaking field too. And when the Chinese started to board the platform...she found herself caught between hope the Chinese would succeed and fear they wouldn't, fear they'd draw some kind of reaction from the sphere's unseen masters. What would they do? What sort of species explored vast tracts of interstellar space, then withdrew back into a pair of megastructures and fired on anyone broadcasting radio transmissions within the sphere? Perhaps they were all gone. It was the only explanation that made sense.

They certainly didn't do anything to save Dyson One, she mused, as the Chinese shuttles zoomed closer to their target. *Perhaps they all evolved into energy beings and vanished long ago.*

"Captain," McPhee said. "The lead shuttle is making its first approach now."

Staci nodded, curtly.

• • •

Up close, Specialist Li Xiu noted, the alien weapons platform looked decidedly odd.

She frowned as the shuttle drifted nearer to its target. She'd shut down the drive fields long ago, relying on gas jets to propel her craft across the final few kilometres between her and destiny, yet she had the uneasy feeling she was being watched. A human platform looked like what it was, a cluster of weapons assembled around a single datacore. Crude and functional, with nothing beyond the bare essentials. The alien platform... she couldn't help thinking of a geode she'd seen, back when she'd been a little girl, that someone had dug up and polished until it shone under the light. It looked like a hunk of polished rock, an asteroid that had been sliced apart with lasers and then abandoned to empty space. It wasn't

ENDEAVOUR

even symmetrical. There was no sense the aliens who'd designed it cared one jot about appearance and yet, there was something about it that was decidedly weird.

"Put us down," the trooper ordered. "And quickly."

Li kept her expression under tight control as she hurried to obey. The troops were in command. That had been made clear to her, from the moment she'd been given the mission. And yet...the more she looked at the platform, the more unsure she was. The platform had vaporised one shuttle—she'd mourn her friend later—and perhaps a second, yet she couldn't see any weapons on the rock. It was bare.

A dull thump ran through the shuttle as it brushed against the rocky surface. Li sighed as the troopers hurried to the airlock, snapping their masks into place as the hatches opened, closed and opened again. The platform had no gravity field, but that didn't slow the troopers as they spread out. They'd find a way into the platform and then...

Her eyes went wide as she saw a blue-white flash of light on the far side of the platform. The passive sensors bleeped an alert, a second too late. The troopers had been ordered to maintain strict radio silence, but now they were chattering frantically, reporting more lights on the surface. Li heard their CO barking orders, telling them to shut up as the lights grew brighter, an instant before their voices fell silent. Li hoped they were following orders, but she feared the worst. She could see blue light racing across the platform, heading right for her...

She jabbed at the controls, trying to launch the shuttle into space, but it was far too late.

• • •

"Captain, the platform took out the Chinese boarding party," MacPhee said. "The second shuttle confirmed the destruction."

Staci cursed. "Details?"

"Unclear as yet," MacPhee said. "The second shuttle is bringing its torpedoes online now."

"The platforms didn't get a good visual," Lieutenant Helen Yang put in. "They picked up a major energy surge, and an explosion, then nothing. If there were any survivors, they're keeping their IFF beacons offline."

"Which may be all that kept them alive," Staci said. An automated system might not be able to tell the difference between a lifepod's distress beacon and a homing device for an incoming missile. There were agreements not to fire on lifepods, but she knew from grim experience they were often mistaken for mines in the heat of battle and blown out of space before the other side realised their mistake. "But it also means they won't be found."

She sucked in her breath as the Chinese shuttle launched its torpedoes. They were pathetically slow compared to starfighter or ship-launched missiles, but the alien platform didn't seem to be moving. The Chinese, Staci decided, probably hoped the torpedoes wouldn't look as threatening as an actual antiship missile, although she suspected the platform was too dumb to care. It had let the Chinese get very close, even walk on its surface, before finally destroying them and their shuttle. The torpedoes might get very close indeed.

"Ten seconds to detonation," MacPhee said, quietly.

Staci leaned forward as the last of the seconds ticked away. The torpedoes detonated in unison, funnelling all the power of two nuclear blasts into a pair of ravening torrents of destruction. A battleship might have been able to take them, its heavy armour deflecting the beams into space, but a smaller ship would have been in real trouble. *Unicorn* would probably have been vaporised, Staci reflected, and *Endeavour* severely damaged. The alien platform seemed unharmed. The heat from the beams was already radiating off into space.

"Jesus," McDougall breathed. "It's undamaged."

Jenner looked at Staci. "Captain?"

"Hold position," Staci ordered. The alien weapons platform was going to make it impossible to sneak another shuttle down to the surface. If they couldn't destroy the wretched device, they'd have to work out how to slip around it. "Deploy the stealthed platforms to hunt for the landing party. If they're still alive, we can work on how best to extract them from the surface."

Sure, her thoughts mocked. *And how do you intend to do that when you can't get a shuttle down there, let alone back up again?*

CHAPTER TWENTY-FIVE: NEAR SOUTH GATE, DYSON TWO (SURFACE)

"KEEP MOVING," COLIN SNAPPED. One man dead, two more injured...he wished, suddenly, that his emergency training had been a little more imaginative. He knew what to do, if a shuttle or helicopter crash-landed, but normally he'd be surrounded by Royal Marines and soldiers rather than civilians. "Don't look back!"

He gritted his teeth. The landscape had been shattered by the impact. The wind shifted randomly, often blowing smoke into their nostrils. His imagination suggested the forest fire would grow and grow, like the legendary infernos that had devastated California, until the flames swept over the running party and burnt them to a crisp. Or the shuttle itself was blown away, the platform overhead blasting it from high orbit and leaving nothing but ashes behind. Colin had been on active duty along the edge of the Security Zone. He'd seen orbital weapons platforms firing on anything that came too close. The idea of being hammered himself, in the same way, was terrifying. He was uneasily aware they were probably all too visible from high overhead.

His fists clenched as he assessed the survivors. There were only nine of them, nowhere near enough to defend themselves, let alone establish a permanent settlement. Colin had thrilled to stories of castaways settling entire planets, after their starships had crashed out of hyperspace and landed on isolated worlds, but his instructors had pointed out that most of them involved a great deal of wishful thinking. The heroes of the books—handsome, brave and true—had always had the *right* skills, in the *right* number of bodies. Colin scowled in bitter frustration. Even if they worked together without hesitation, they were almost certainly still fucked. It was shaping up rapidly to become one of his worst nightmares.

The trees started to close in as they kept moving. Colin had expected a thin layer of soil covering the sphere itself, but it was impossible to tell they weren't on a planet. The distant horizon looked flat, yet not *too* abnormal. The air tasted of pollen...he thought he saw insects buzzing through the trees, suggesting—at least—that the ecosystem had taken root within the sphere. He frowned as he eyed the trees. There was no visible fruit... could they eat the tree itself, break it down in a food processor? He didn't know. The survival packs included test kits, devices that were meant to confirm if something was safe to eat, but they weren't always reliable. For all he knew, the sphere's biosystem was deadly poison. It might already be seeping into his veins.

Your sensors didn't pick up anything dangerous, he reminded himself, holding up a hand to order the team to halt. *The chances are good we can find something to eat before we run out of survival packs.*

He looked around, cursing under his breath. Tobias and Marigold...it struck him, suddenly, that being trapped on an alien world with *him* had to be one of Tobias's worst nightmares too. It hadn't been *that* long ago since Colin had gleefully predicted what would happen when they'd been reading *The Lord of the Flies*...he wished, bitterly, that he could go back in time and give his past self the proper thrashing he had long deserved. But he couldn't. His eyes lingered on Lady Charlotte, his heart sinking. Tobias and Marigold were in relatively good shape. Lady Charlotte was definitely past her prime.

We're stuck together, for the moment, he thought. *And we have to stay together until we can be picked up.*

"All right," he said, trying to sound reassuring. His eyes swept the group. "We made it down in one piece, which is more than can be said for the other shuttle. We're alive and reasonably well and the captain is no doubt already working on a plan to extract us."

"If she knows we're still alive," Tobias said, grimly. "She might not be able to get a platform close enough to find us."

"The captain will have seen us go down," Colin said, resisting the urge to tell him to shut his mouth before the civilians could get any more depressed. "She'll be looking for a way to get us out of here."

"We may have been fired upon by accident," Marigold said, looking towards the towering mountains. "They might have assumed that anything heading towards the ground is dangerous until proven safe. A shuttle taking *off* might pass unnoticed."

Lady Charlotte didn't look convinced. Colin suspected Marigold was right, although he had no idea how they'd get an intact shuttle down to the surface first. The crashed shuttle might be beyond repair. He didn't know. His watch insisted it had been nearly thirty minutes since they'd crashed and fled, but it didn't feel anything like so long. If the aliens intended to do something to the shuttle...he listened carefully, motioning for everyone to be quiet, but there was nothing. No helicopters, flying towards the crash site; no emergency services, sirens howling as they raced to the scene of the crime. The sphere felt deserted.

"We could walk to the command centre," Lady Charlotte said. "Right?"

Colin shrugged. He wasn't sure where they'd crashed, let alone where the command centre—if it *was* a command centre—was relative to them. The towering mountains surrounding the South Gate were their only point of reference, but without others they were of only limited use. His heart sank as he contemplated the sheer *size* of the sphere. They could walk for the rest of their lives and not see even a tiny fraction of the whole.

"We'll see," he said, vaguely. Navigating was going to be one hell of a pain. "Right now, Tobias and I are going to return to the shuttle. The rest of you are going to wait here. If we don't come back...Jones, you're in charge."

"Aye, sir," Jones said.

"Good." Colin looked at Tobias. "Let's go."

He was mildly surprised, as they started to walk back towards the crash site, that Tobias followed him without apparent qualms. But then, Tobias wasn't stupid. He knew as well as Colin that the shuttle might represent their only chance of getting off the ground, if the ship couldn't send someone to pick them up. Colin wrestled with the problem, turning it around and around in his head, but drew a blank. Everything that came to mind required tools and supplies they simply didn't have. It had been a lot easier in the books.

The shuttle came into view, lying half-buried in a muddy trench. Water was pooling under the cockpit, suggesting it was just a matter of time before the interior was flooded. Colin silently motioned for Tobias to stay back as he assessed their route back into the craft, then sighed and started down towards the gash in the hull. The shuttle looked relatively stable thankfully, even if she was trapped. It was all too clear she wasn't going to return to orbit in a hurry.

"I think its fine," he said, as he slipped into the shuttle. "Follow me."

His head started to pound as he looked around the interior. The body lay where they'd left it...Colin made a mental note to come back for it, if they had time. It went against the grain to leave a body behind, but he had to take care of the living first. Tobias joined him as Colin started digging through their supplies, sorting out what they needed and could carry quickly from the rest of the gear. Some things were just too heavy to take in a hurry. Others...

"The communications system appears to be intact," Tobias said, from the cockpit. "It shut down when we crashed, but I think we can boot it up again."

"Not when we're in the craft," Colin said. It would be a great deal safer to use the laser communicator, but it was useless as long as they didn't know where to point the beam. "Can you set up a remote communicator? Something we can use to control it from a safe distance?"

Tobias glanced at him. "What's a safe distance?"

Colin shrugged. He had no idea why the shuttle hadn't been bombed already, if the defences were so keen on preventing anything that might be dangerous from reaching the surface. It wasn't as if the Builders *couldn't* hit them. Perhaps they'd simply gone too low to be noticed. One of his training exercises had pointed out, very bluntly, that it was all too easy to assume that anyone who got through the wire *had* to be authorised to be inside the base. An automated defence system might be programmed not to engage targets below a certain level, even if they dropped from orbit rather than rising from the surface. Given the sheer size of the sphere, he suspected that was a must. There was no way in hell the occupants didn't use hypersonics, if not outright spacecraft, to get from place to place.

"Just set up the wire as far as possible," he said, finally. "And don't turn anything on until I'm finished."

He forced himself to keep digging through the supplies, carrying what he could out of the craft and dumping it on the edge of the clearing. The water was growing deeper, lapping at the hull and threatening to pour into the shuttle itself. There was no time to salvage anything else. Colin had once been trapped in an IFV that had turned over during a training exercise and that had been bad enough, with all the safety and recovery gear on hand. Here…he shouted for Tobias to get out before the shuttle was gone for good. Tobias joined him, carrying a long length of cable and a portable terminal. It looked as if he'd been busy.

"The main transmitter appears intact," Tobias said. "I put together a very basic location matrix before we departed. If the ship picks up the message, they should be able to steer a platform into position to pick up a laser signal. It should work."

"Good," Colin said, deciding not to point out that Tobias was clearly trying to convince himself. Back home, it would be easy to use the stars to determine their position. Here, there were no stars. "How far can we get from the ship?"

"A couple of hundred metres or so," Tobias said. "But we'd better hurry. If the shuttle sinks completely, it might break the wire."

Colin nodded and led the way deeper into the treeline, heading away from the rest of the team. There was no way to be *sure* they couldn't be tracked. Using cables rather than wireless transmissions was normally safe enough, unless the enemy dug up the cables, but here…he looked up into the clear blue sky, wondering if alien eyes were looking back at him. The storm was long gone. It was odd someone hadn't come to investigate the crash. If he'd shot down an alien shuttle, that would be the very first thing he'd do.

More proof we're dealing with an automated system, he reflected, as they reached the end of the cable. *And one not smart enough to make sure the shuttle really was destroyed with all hands.*

"I've set up a basic datadump," Tobias told him. "Do you want to record a message, too?"

"Please." Colin took the terminal and took a moment to compose a message. "If the captain can figure out a way to get us back into space…"

Tobias frowned. "What are our odds?"

"Not good," Colin admitted. "Can we repair the shuttle?"

"No." Tobias sounded very certain. "We don't have the parts, let alone the tools or expertise."

"Shit," Colin said. He'd half-hoped Tobias would come up with something. "Are you ready?"

"Yeah." Tobias keyed the console. "The signal will last only twenty seconds, but it will be very detectable as long as the transmitter is online."

"That long?" Colin tried not to wince. It wouldn't have mattered, much, if the signal lasted only a bare second. The sphere was so silent their signal would stick out like a jarhead in a platoon of bootnecks. "Send it."

Tobias tapped a switch. Colin silently started to count. Five seconds.

Ten. Fifteen…something glimmered high overhead, bright enough to make him yelp even as he shoved Tobias to the ground and landed on top of him. A wave of heat passed overhead, followed by a small earthquake. Colin rolled over, just in time to see a tiny mushroom cloud rising into the sky. It was…he swallowed hard, WMD training yammering at him that he should run or check for radiation or something—anything—other than stare helplessly. He'd never seen anything like it. The platform high overhead hadn't dropped a KEW to silence the shuttlecraft. It had used some kind of energy weapon.

"Fuck," Tobias managed. He stumbled upright, shocked. "The signal should have gotten out…"

"Unless it got jammed," Colin said. "Stay here. I'll be back in a moment."

He ignored Tobias's protests as he strode back to the crash site. It was gone, replaced by a crater that was already starting to fill with water. The edges were charred, the stench of…something hanging in the air. Ozone? He wasn't sure. The blast had been powerful enough to reduce the shuttle to atoms, destroying it so completely there was nothing left. He cursed under his breath. If the automated systems fired on radio transmitters…

We'd better hope the ship got the message, he thought, numbly. *We can't send a second signal. Not now.*

He walked back to Tobias, then led him around the crater and back to where they'd concealed the supplies. Colin silently blessed himself for making sure they'd been some distance from the shuttle when they'd activated the transmitter, even though he was certain someone was going to blame him for setting the shuttle up for destruction. Not that he'd had much choice. The shuttle had been steadily sinking, ensuring they had to use the transmitter or lose it. And hopefully, the platforms had picked up and relayed the message.

"They could perform a suborbital insertion," he said, as they walked. "That might be less detectable than a standard shuttlecraft."

"If they can adapt a shuttlecraft to make the landing," Tobias said. "They tried to build an aerospace fighter once, craft capable of fighting in and out of a planet's atmosphere. I remember the results were decidedly mixed."

Colin glanced at him. "What happened?"

"I think the craft was a jack of all trades and a master of none," Tobias said. "There was one experimental squadron, which was removed from service shortly after the war began. I don't know if there's anything attached to *Endeavour* that could be converted into the role."

"Perhaps not." Colin was fairly sure there was *some* commando gear that could be adapted, but getting it down to the surface would be tricky. "What if we build a hot air balloon and float all the way to orbit?"

"The balloons would burst, well before we entered orbit," Tobias said. "We might as well try using the tramline to get out of the sphere."

"I thought someone had done that," Colin said. The idea sounded plausible. "The tramline must run through the surface, right?"

"We'd need a flicker drive to make it work," Tobias said, dryly. "And the captain would never risk the entire ship. The odds of crashing would be far too high."

Colin nodded, curtly. He hated the thought of being expendable, although he knew—compared to the ship—they were *all* expendable. There was no way in hell Captain Templeton would risk her entire ship for them, not when she had nearly a thousand crewmen onboard. *Grantchester* was smaller, but it was unlikely her captain would feel any better about her chances. No, there was no way around it. They might be trapped on the surface for a very long time.

"If you set up the transmitter later, we might be able to make contact this evening," Colin said. "And then we'll see if they have anything to suggest."

"Got it," Tobias said. He shook his head. "Maybe they just want their privacy."

It took Colin a moment to realise who he meant. "The Builders?"

"Yeah." Tobias didn't look at him. "There are times when you just want to be alone. You don't want to talk, you don't want to play, you don't want to so much as set eyes on anyone, anyone at all. And then someone comes to talk to you and you feel...cross. Irritated. Even if it's something important, you don't want them to bother you. They cross your boundaries and don't give a shit."

Colin frowned. "And you think the Builders are hiding from us?"

"You remember the civics teacher?" Tobias went on before Colin could answer. "He had an example he used to discuss. If someone locks their door and someone else breaks in, and then falls and hurts themselves inside the house, it's their own stupid fault. Maybe you can complain if someone digs a hole in a public area, and you then fall into it, but not on their own land. There's no way we could have jumped inside the sphere without knowing what we're doing, so...anything bad that happens to us is our own fault."

Colin forced himself to remember the lesson. Truthfully, he hadn't paid much attention. The teacher had enjoyed neither his respect nor his fear. But if Tobias recalled correctly...

"I see your point," he said, finally. "They think they drew the line so clearly that anyone who crosses it is in the wrong."

"Perhaps so," Tobias said. He looked down as they reached the campsite. "This is their world. And we're uninvited guests."

CHAPTER TWENTY-SIX: NEAR SOUTH GATE, DYSON TWO (SURFACE)

WELL, CHARLOTTE THOUGHT. *You wanted to do something so spectacular the establishment couldn't sideline or simply ignore you...didn't you?*

She sat, hands wrapped around her knees, and stared into the campfire. She'd thought she knew what roughing it meant—she *had* gone on camping trips as a young girl—but she'd clearly been wrong. None of *those* trips had been far from help, if they ran into trouble; hell, the staff had made it clear they could leave pretty much immediately, if they needed to go. There had been no danger of running out of food and drink, let alone being stranded in the countryside or being attacked by wild animals or anything. Now... she cursed herself, mentally, for not accepting Paris-Jackson's suggestion *he* should take the lead on the diplomatic mission. It would have saved her from crashlanding on the sphere's surface.

Her body ached, feeling sore and unclean. There was no hope of relief. There were no diplomatic quarters, no showers or trained resort staff or any of the other luxuries she'd taken for granted. She didn't even have painkillers. The naval crew had said painkillers were to be held in reserve for the wounded, for the crewmen who'd been injured. Charlotte wasn't used to *that* either. Basic painkillers had been universal, until they weren't. They had only a limited supply and when they were gone, they were gone.

She looked up, into the darkness. The sphere's inner shell—she couldn't help thinking of them as blinds, although on a scale so vast as to be beyond her comprehension—cast a long shadow over the surface. She expected to see strips of light and darkness rising into the unknown, but the sphere was just too big. She couldn't even see any curvature. It just seemed flat. On Earth, she wouldn't even have questioned it. On the sphere, it just seemed subtly wrong. She supposed, given time, she might have to get used to it. The sphere was hardly the most alien environment she'd ever seen.

Just the only one I've ever been stuck on, she thought. She'd seen images and recordings from the alien homeworlds, watched documentaries put together by trained xenospecialists and spiced up by PR specialists who knew what the public wanted to see, but she'd seen all that in the comfort of her living room. The most advanced VR technology in the world still lacked a certain something, when it came to convincing the users that the VR setting was *real. I might never see home again.*

The thought tore at her, mocking her. There were all sorts of stories of castaways surviving long enough to be picked up, from starship crewmen landing on unexplored worlds to asteroid miners eking out a rough existence from rocks while waiting for someone to come looking for them. She'd never been sure how many of those stories were true, but it didn't matter. If the naval crewmen were right, and she'd seen the beam that had obliterated the remains of the crashed shuttle, they were stuck. *Endeavour* couldn't mount a rescue mission as long as the alien weapons platform was in position to shoot down the shuttles without warning. If anything trying to enter the atmosphere got fired upon...

She swallowed hard, looking around. The jungle was as subtly wrong as the rest of the sphere. Charlotte was no gardening expert, but she'd designed the gardens surrounding her stately home and she knew enough to be sure the surrounding biosystem was truly alien. There was a very good chance it wouldn't have what humans needed to live, even if it wasn't outright poisonous. She'd heard of a couple of alien plants that had found popularity, at least amongst the wealthy, but they'd never entered the mainstream. She wasn't sure why they hadn't. Perhaps they had been tasty but lacking in vital nutrients. Or maybe the population had been too conservative to accept them.

And what, she asked herself numbly, *am I going to do?*

She'd read stories in which the castaways had set up small towns and settled down for the long haul. She doubted it was possible on the sphere. There were only nine of them, two injured. And she had no idea if they could even eat the local vegetation. She'd heard insects…did that mean there were bigger animals in the sphere? Something they could kill, cook and eat? Or…her mind spun in circles as she gazed into the darkness, pooling just outside the campfire's light. Anything could be out there, anything at all. She dared not assume they were alone and yet…

I could die here, she thought. A shiver ran through her. She'd accepted the possibility of a violent death the moment she'd boarded *Endeavour*, but she hadn't really believed it. The odds had seemed in her favour. Now… she wondered, suddenly, if anyone would find her bones. The mothership was a long way away. If Captain Templeton didn't know where they'd crashed, her crew might wind up searching millions of kilometres from the crash site. *If I die…*

She shivered, again. She'd written letters for her daughters, and recorded messages, but…suddenly, she wanted to see them again. They were mad at her—and she supposed they had a right to be—yet she wanted to see them anyway. She wanted to take them in her arms and…she shook her head. It wasn't going to happen. She wasn't even sure she would survive long enough to record a final message. Her lips quirked, bitterly. Her ex would be relieved if she never came home. It would spare the family a prolonged and agonising divorce that would—inevitably—dominate the news for years. And who'd want to court the family's daughters if it meant they'd get caught up in the chaos?

No one, Charlotte thought numbly, answering her own question. *And yet...*

She looked into the flames, wondering if she'd live to see another day. How long *were* the days on the sphere? She wasn't sure. She'd certainly never thought to look it up. For all she knew, they were condemned to hundreds of hours of darkness before the shell allowed sunlight to fall upon the sphere once again. She'd spent so long preparing for a diplomatic meeting, or for a flight to nowhere, that she hadn't paid anything like enough attention to life on the sphere. She could have found out, but instead...she'd flown straight into a trap. In hindsight, it *would* have been wiser to let Paris-Jackson take the lead.

"They didn't fire on the shuttle until we started sending radio transmissions," Doctor Athena Gaurs said. She sounded slightly woozy. The naval crew had done what they could for her broken arm, but that hadn't been very much. Charlotte didn't begrudge her the painkillers. She was going to be in agony when they finally ran out. "That's...worrying."

Charlotte gritted her teeth, then looked at the younger woman. "In what way?"

"They act fast to squash all radio transmissions," Athena said. She looked, for a moment, as if she were going to be sick. "We should have expected it."

"I suppose," Charlotte said. "Why do you think that is?"

"Radio is one of the easiest ways to determine if a planet's technology has reached a certain level," Athena said, quietly. "Every time a survey ship enters a new system and locates a life-bearing world, it spends hours listening for radio transmissions and other emissions. If it doesn't spot them, it thinks there's little chance of encountering a species advanced enough to cause problems. It can enter orbit and carry out closer surveys without risk of detection. The Vesy, for example, passed unnoticed until humans actually landed on their planet."

She paused. Charlotte waited, fighting her impatience. Athena clearly had something weighing on her mind.

"It isn't just radio," she added, after a moment. "You can't have anything approaching a modern civilisation without radiating emissions into space. Human development didn't start to pick up the pace until we started to develop electric technology, whereupon we just kept accelerating until we ran into hard limits. Right now, Earth sits at the centre of an expanding shell of radio waves. There used to be old stories about aliens picking up speeches made by Adolf Hitler, as they were amongst the first to be broadcast on the radio. Someone could make a set of very good guesses about Earth just by monitoring our emissions."

Charlotte frowned. "And Hitler would be pretty much the worst ambassador we could send."

"Yeah," Athena agreed. Her lips quirked. "Although, to be fair, the aliens wouldn't understand much of the context. They might never realise just what sort of person he was."

She leaned forward. "The automated defences fire on any radio transmitters," she said. "What if they're programmed to fire on any signs of developing technology?"

"I…" Charlotte blinked. "You're being paranoid."

"Am I?" Athena waved a hand at the darkness. "The sphere is very far from dead. It has far more land surface than any planet, even the gas giants. It isn't impossible intelligent life could evolve here, perhaps even start developing technology that would lead it into space…unless something is in place to keep them from getting so far. How long would it take for development to stall if lightning bolts from above smash anything radiating a betraying signal?"

Charlotte swallowed. "Who would do something like that?"

Athena looked down at her hands. "It was discussed," she said, quietly. "The Vesy are no threat to us. Their society will have time to absorb human tech before they get into space and join us as equals. But what if we encounter a far nastier race, one on the brink of making the leap into interplanetary space? Imagine a world where Hitler or Stalin or one of their peers succeeded in their aims, turning the entire world into a fascistic dystopia. What should we do if we find a race like that, one that might turn into an immediate threat? Would it be wiser to quietly prevent them from ever getting into space?"

"Madness," Charlotte murmured. "I thought it was impossible for modern tech to develop without democracy and human rights."

"That's what we tell ourselves," Athena said. "But the truth is, democratic societies can develop tech that is then abused by undemocratic societies. It happened on Earth. And...for all we know, an alien fascistic regime will manage to push technological advancement despite its fascistic nature. The Nazis did lay the groundwork for a *lot* of technology, even if they were defeated before much of it came to fruition. What should we do, if we encounter a race advanced enough to be dangerous, if it manages to climb out of its gravity well?"

Charlotte said nothing for a long moment. "And you think that's what happening here?"

"It's possible," Athena said. "And I can't think of any other reason to set your automated systems to fire on radio transmissions."

"I see," Charlotte said. Her blood ran cold as she looked at the campfire. "What if...what if the *heat* draws their fire?"

"I doubt it," Athena said. "There must be a lower limit on what draws their fire. But..."

She rubbed her arm. "We might be stuck here. Forever."

...

The darkness felt like a living thing, Tobias decided, as he placed the laser communicator on the ground and attached his terminal to the control node. Colin and he had walked two kilometres before the shadow had fallen over them, plunging the landscape into darkness. It was easy enough to calculate that the sphere's 'days' were roughly thirty hours long, evenly split into day and night, but understanding didn't make it any easier to endure. He'd never liked being out after dark, not as a child, and he'd hated and resented the times he'd been forced to leave the house. The sphere was worse than the streets of his home. There were no brightly lit homes, no streetlights...not even any stars. The darkness was almost absolute.

He nearly jumped when the communicator bleeped its readiness to transmit. It was hard to be *sure* it wouldn't draw attention. The laser beam was, in theory, aimed at a platform, but he didn't *know* the platform was there. It had been the first thing he'd put in the datapacket he'd said... hell, he didn't know if it had been picked up and decrypted either. His hand shook as he keyed the terminal, activating the communicator. Normally, the laser beam would vanish into interstellar space if it missed its target. Here, there was a very real chance the beam would intersect the sphere's inner shell and then...and then what? The shell might just be covered with sensors that would pick up the beam, or it might pass completely unnoticed. He wished he could be a long way away—Earth sounded about right, or he'd settle for Virus Prime—as he sent the signal. There was too great a risk something lurking in the darkness would spot them and open fire.

Colin lumbered around the transmitter. "Any response?"

"Not yet," Tobias said. "There *is* a time delay, you know."

He did the math in his head. Assuming the platform was where it was supposed to be, it would be at least five seconds before it could pick up the transmission and another five seconds before its response reached the surface. Longer, perhaps, if it wanted to relay the datapacket to *Endeavour* first. It should send a simple acknowledgement if nothing else, but...it was quite possible the mothership had ordered the platform not to risk any transmissions, even laser signals, without its permission. He waited, counting down the seconds. If something was about to go wrong...

The communicator bleeped, again. Tobias allowed himself a moment of relief as he checked the terminal, even if it was just an acknowledgement. They'd signalled the platform and established a solid link. There didn't seem to be any incoming messages, but he hadn't really expected them. *Endeavour* might have thought they'd crashed hard until they'd sent the first message. The ship might not have had a chance to respond.

"Well?" Colin was pacing grimly. "Anything useful?"

"Not really, beyond the fact we can and we have signalled the platform," Tobias said. "They'll know for sure we're still alive now."

"Good," Colin said. "Shut down the link. We'll re-establish it tomorrow, as planned."

Tobias nodded and keyed his terminal, shutting down the communicator. It was hard not to feel as if he was cutting a lifeline—it was strange to be so isolated, so far from the planetary or shipboard datanet—but there was no choice. The longer the communicator remained active, the greater the chance of alerting the orbital defences. The sheer power of the alien weapons was terrifying.

He sighed as he folded down the communicator and stuffed it into his backpack, then stood to follow Colin back to the campsite. There was no way, as far as he could tell, for *Endeavour* to pick them up. There was no way they could sneak a shuttle down to the surface without causing *some* atmospheric distortion, something that would make it far too easy for the orbital weapons platforms to spot the shuttle—no matter how stealthy it tried to be—and blow it away. Tobias had no illusions. The alien weapons were powerful enough to slice a battleship in half. They'd been very lucky they'd made it down to the surface alive.

And so we might be trapped for the rest of our lives, he thought. *This could end badly.*

His heart sank. There had been a time that being alone with Colin had been his worst nightmare. Their relationship had improved, since then, but...the nasty, fearful side of Tobias's mind wondered what would happen, now they were a long way from any naval discipline. Colin might decide *he* should have Marigold and to hell with what she wanted. It wouldn't be the first time, if rumour was to be believed. There'd been all sorts of stories about him and girls, few pleasant. Tobias had once believed them without reservation. Even now, even after discovering Colin was a far more complex character than he'd thought, he wasn't so sure. His hand dropped to his pistol. Would it be better to shoot Colin in the back now? Or would that merely ensure his own death?

Wait, he told himself. *We may yet come up with something.*

"We'll need to start testing the local environment, looking for things we can eat," Colin said, as they walked. "If we can't eat, we may be in some trouble."

Tobias scowled at the understatement. By his calculations, they had enough ration bars and packs to last for two weeks at most. If they couldn't find something safe to eat, or get supplies from the ship, they'd starve. Hell, he wasn't entirely sure the water was safe to drink. Who knew what might be lurking in a single droplet of water? They would run out of purification tablets soon too, and then...

"Yeah," he said, finally. Survival was their first priority. "We'd better start testing stuff tomorrow."

"And see what we can catch," Colin added. "Do you recall the camping trip when we were fifteen?"

"I didn't go," Tobias said. The idea of tramping across hills and dales hadn't been appealing even without the trip being led by the sadistic gym teacher. "What happened?"

Colin laughed. "Trust me, everything that could go wrong did," he said. "This time, we are far better prepared."

"Great," Tobias said, sarcastically. "Why am I not reassured?"

CHAPTER TWENTY-SEVEN: HMS ENDEAVOUR, DYSON TWO (INTERIOR)

"CAPTAIN," MCPHEE SAID. "Platform Seven picked up a laser signal from the ground!"

Staci allowed herself a moment of relief. She'd moved *Endeavour* closer to the South Pole, in hopes of reacting to any windows of opportunity before they closed again, but she hadn't even been sure—until the first radio signal—that the landing party had survived. Even after that, she'd feared the worst. Simple human decency—and interplanetary treaties—forbade firing on distress signals from crash sites, but the Builders had evidently never heard of any of them. They'd fired on the shuttle as soon as it started to transmit. It was hard to be entirely sure—none of the platforms had been close enough to get a good view—but the alien weapons were powerful enough to vaporise the shuttle. If the landing party had stayed in the craft, or simply waited outside, they might not have lived long enough to realise their mistake.

"Send the prepared datapacket," she ordered. She had no idea if the landing party would get it at once, or—more likely—in several hours when they reopened communications—but at least they'd know *Endeavour* was trying to find a way to get them back to the ship. "And then deploy three more platforms. We need to ensure we don't lose contact again."

"Aye, Captain," McPhee said.

Staci nodded curtly, her eyes on the display. The passive sensor platforms had picked up two more alien weapons platforms, in position to fire on anything that came too close to the surface. Given the sheer power she'd seen, she feared they could target *Endeavour* from well outside her own range. Staci thought they were a safe distance from any enemy platform, but it was impossible to be sure. Her skin itched, a grim reminder they could be blown to atoms at any moment. The Chinese had agreed to keep their distance, to watch events and report home if something happened to *Endeavour*, yet who knew if *they* were at a safe distance? Or if they wouldn't do something creative to the sensor records before they handed them over to the Admiralty?

And they blasted an alien platform with the most powerful weapons at their disposal, her thoughts reminded her, grimly. *The platform wasn't even scratched.*

She shook her head in disbelief. If she hadn't seen the sensor records herself, she would have been *sure* someone had fucked with them. Laser warheads, channelling all the power of a nuclear detonation into a single beam of ravening fury, were the strongest weapons in humanity's arsenal. Even a battleship would have known it had been kissed, if the Chinese had hit it so badly. The alien platform hadn't even *noticed*. It certainly hadn't bothered to lay waste to the human sensor network taking shape nearby. Staci had no idea if the platform was too dumb to notice or if it was simply contemptuous of humanity's ability to do any real damage, but it didn't matter. All that mattered was that getting down to the surface—and then being able to escape—appeared to be impossible.

"Mr. XO, join me in my ready room," Staci said, standing. "Lieutenant Commander McDougall, you have the bridge."

"Aye, Captain."

Staci led the way into the ready room, then sat as Jenner poured them both coffee. She hadn't had a chance to sleep since the crash, though she was tired. It was hard not to feel naked, naked and vulnerable, although everything she knew about military technology told her there was no immediate danger. She had a nasty feeling that her training was going to be a major problem, the longer they remained in the sphere. It wasn't what they didn't know that would get them, she reflected as she sipped her coffee. It was what they knew that simply wasn't so. The Builders—or their automatic defences—might be targeting their superweapon on her ship even as she spoke.

"They're alive," she said, flatly. It was a relief, although it raised a whole new set of problems. "How are we going to get them off the surface?"

Jenner said nothing for a long moment. Staci felt her heart sink. She trusted her XO would come forward, if he had an idea. The fact he hadn't... Staci wondered, not for the first time, if they could sneak a stealthed shuttle through the orbital defences. Perhaps if the craft inched towards the ground, it would pass unnoticed. Perhaps...

Or perhaps we can trick the defences into firing on decoys instead of the real shuttles, she thought. She told herself she'd need to set up a brainstorming session, perhaps even pose the question to the entire crew. It wouldn't make her look very good, not to the old farts who thought a captain should have all the answers, but she found it hard to care. *I don't care who comes up with the idea, as long as we get the landing party off the surface before something else happens.*

"We could try to drop a shuttle to the South Gate," Jenner said. "Would they fire on something leaving the sphere?"

Staci considered it thoughtfully. "They would know the gates weren't open, wouldn't they?"

She keyed her console, bringing up a holographic image of the interior. Too much was still unknown, hazy icons surrounded by guesswork and disclaimers. The probes she'd dispatched towards the planet, and the inner shell, had vanished without trace, leaving her with little solid data. She wasn't even sure what had killed the probes. And the gate...she found it hard to accept something so large could even exist. The biggest structure humanity had ever built, the giant shipyards that churned out colonist-carriers, would vanish without trace against the alien gate, itself a tiny part of something far larger. It was impossible to believe the automated systems wouldn't realise the gates were closed, that the shuttle would crash into them unless something happened. And yet, if they were dumb...

We don't know what'll draw their fire, she thought. Radio transmissions, certainly. What else? *For all we know, they're programmed to ignore anything flying below a certain level.*

"We might have to try," she said, finally. "But we'll try with decoys first."

"Yes, Captain," Jenner said. "Do you want me to organise a probe?"

"Yes." Staci took a breath. "And then put the word out. If someone comes up with a viable solution, it will be entered on their permanent record; if someone comes up with one that actually works, they will be promoted as soon as we return home."

"Let's hope it isn't a junior officer," Jenner said, wryly. "That'll hang over their head for a very long time."

Staci shrugged, although she understood his point. There'd been no room on a frigate for officers promoted beyond their competence. The boundaries had been so low everyone had *known* their superiors could do their jobs, that anyone who got promotion—even a temporary boost in rank—thoroughly deserved it. It wasn't so easy on a bigger ship. Promote someone too fast and everyone would suspect something untoward, even if they *were* the genius who got a stranded landing party back to the ship. Staci had heard the backbiting, when she'd been a junior officer. Sure, a commanding officer had near-boundless authority when his ship was underway, but that didn't mean immunity from consequences. The rapidly promoted had to work extra hard, just to prove they deserved it. And even if they did...

She shook her head. She needed rest, not endless waiting.

"See to it," she ordered. "Under the circumstances, everyone will know they deserved it."

Jenner stood and left the compartment. Staci leaned back on the sofa, torn between a desire to go to her cabin and a grim awareness she might be needed at any moment. She wished, suddenly, that she'd pulled strings to bring a lover with her, although—her lips quirked—she didn't have anyone in the first place. The rules were a little vague about such things, if one happened to be on a survey ship. But it didn't matter. She hadn't thought to look for someone in quite some time. Now, it was too late.

She closed her eyes and waited. It felt like seconds before the terminal pinged, alerting her to her next shift. The timer insisted she'd slept for five hours—and she had only forty minutes before she was supposed to be on the bridge—but she refused to believe it. The treacherous part of her mind wondered if she should offer the shift to a junior officer, giving him more command experience. She told that part of her to shut up. It wasn't as if they were in interstellar space, with no real risk of running into something a junior officer couldn't handle.

The hatch opened, her steward bringing her coffee and breakfast. Staci sat up—she still wasn't quite used to having a steward—and accepted it gratefully, then keyed her terminal to read the messages while she ate. The crew had responded well, she noted. They'd come up with all sorts of ideas, ranging from the practical—if they had the tools and supplies they needed—to the downright *impractical*. Jenner had flagged a number for her consideration, but she doubted they'd work. Trying to drop a shuttle to the gate still seemed their best option.

Her lips quirked. Whoever had come up with the idea of dismantling a shuttle, dropping the components to the surface and then expecting the landing party to put it back together again was thinking a little *too* far outside the box. On paper, it would work perfectly; in reality, it would be pretty much impossible. Shuttles weren't *that* small. Some of the other ideas were simply impossible...she sighed, quietly noting a handful of names. They had promise, even if their ideas weren't practical. She'd have to ensure some of them were offered a chance to qualify as officers.

The hatch bleeped. Staci looked up. "Come."

She frowned as the hatch hissed open, revealing a blonde girl who seemed too young to be in naval service. She wore an unmarked shipsuit... one of the diplomatic support staff, Staci recalled, probably someone with enough family connections to get jumped up a rung or two fairly early in her career. Staci couldn't remember the young woman's name, although they'd met briefly. Katy? No, *Kari*. She made a mental note to read her file afterwards as the hatch hissed closed. Kari might be more influential than her formal role suggested.

"Captain," Kari said. She sounded shy, unsure of herself. The type of person, Staci knew, who'd be mocked and harassed relentlessly if she'd attended a state school. "I was wondering...can *anyone* suggest an idea for recovering the landing party?"

Staci nodded, slowly. Kari worked directly for Lady Charlotte. It probably wouldn't look very good on her resume if her boss remained trapped on the surface, even if there was no way anyone *reasonable* could blame it on her. Spacers and diplomats could be superstitious at times. Staci had once heard of an asteroid miner who'd been ostracised after experiencing four mining disasters in quick succession. They'd called him a jinx. They'd known they were being unfair and yet...

"If you have an idea, please feel free to suggest it," Staci said. Kari *could* have entered her suggestion onto the datanet. Staci had no idea why she hadn't. Did she think the idea would be stolen? Paris-Jackson had never struck Staci as the sort of person who'd steal ideas from junior staffers, but...she had met a few REMFs who would happily do just that, if they thought they could get away with it. "What do you have in mind?"

Kari took a breath. "The problem is that we can't get a shuttle to them, isn't it?"

"Yes." Staci bit down hard on her impatience. She already knew it. She'd been over it time and time again. "If we can't get down to them, we can't get them up."

"Yes, we can," Kari said. Staci had no trouble reading her expression.

Kari was torn between her brilliant idea and a gnawing fear it wasn't as brilliant as she thought. "They can climb."

Staci blinked. "What?"

"The South Gate is surrounded by mountains," Kari said. "It's really one giant wall, right? It stretches all the way up into space, like an orbital tower. So why don't they just climb up it?"

"I..." Staci stared at Kari. It couldn't possibly be that simple, could it? There was no way it would be an easy climb. The mountains reached up and up...for all she knew, the walls were vertical, leaving nothing for even the most experienced climber to use to get up and into orbit. And yet... it was the best idea anyone had come up with, certainly the only one that seemed remotely workable. "Good question."

She keyed her terminal, bringing up the sensor records. *Could* the mountains be climbed? She didn't know. She'd have to steer a platform towards the South Gate and find out. And then the landing party would need spacesuits, if they wanted to climb right out of the atmosphere. She silently applauded Kari for coming forward, in the certain knowledge some people would make fun of her. Perhaps *that* was why she'd come straight to Staci herself. Her superior might simply have rubbished the idea without forwarding it to anyone capable of determining if it was workable.

And it might be hard for me *to promote her*, Staci thought. *That* was a complication she hadn't considered, when she'd made her offer. *She's a diplomat. Her future career prospects don't depend on me.*

"It won't be easy," she said, finally. The sphere's atmosphere might look thin, little more than a wisp of gas, on the display, but it was over a hundred kilometres thick. Staci had no idea if they could climb so far, even if they overcame all the other problems. And yet...it was still the best idea they'd had. "Let me fiddle with it, see what the analysts make of it."

"Please," Kari said. Her hands twisted in her lap. "If it gets them out..."

Staci nodded, seeing nothing but earnestness on the younger woman's face. Kari didn't seem to be thinking about promotion, merely the chance to get the landing party home. Staci suspected she might be happier to keep her contribution off the record, given that Lady Charlotte had enemies who might not be happy if she returned to Earth. Or was that just paranoia? The Foreign Office was known for vanishing inside its own rectum from time to time, forgetting its duty to the country. But then, that could be said of almost every government department. In her experience, career civil servants often wound up putting their career ahead of their country.

"I'll see what the analysts say," Staci said. "And thank you."

Kari flushed, lightly. "Thank *you*, Captain."

Staci dismissed her with a nod, then keyed her terminal to send the concept to Jenner. The idea sounded good, better than the others, but the practical problems would have to be worked out before they committed themselves to anything. She wasn't sure how best to approach it, although now Kari had pointed it out she could see some advantages in using the mountains. Perhaps she could roll supplies—or even an ATV—down to them. It certainly made the idea of rigging up a skyhook sound a lot more practical.

She finished her coffee, then stepped onto the bridge. Jenner stood to greet her, dark shadows under his eyes. Staci bit down the urge to reprimand him for not passing command to another officer, even though she knew it wouldn't look good on his record if something happened. She knew an officer who had a black mark on his file because command had devolved on him, without him knowing about it until it was far too late. He certainly hadn't been shirking his duty. But what did it matter, when the post-battle reports insisted he had been in command of the ship? An active-duty officer would know shit happened. Someone stuck at the rear would assume that shit happening meant someone had screwed up.

"It looks workable, if they can climb the mountains," Jenner said, holding out a datapad. "I took the liberty of dispatching two probes to take a look at them. If it's a vertical drop…"

"We could still lower something down to them," Staci said. They'd pretty much *have* to drop supplies, unless the landing party found edibles on the surface. There was a very real risk the local foliage would lack something humans needed to live. "But we'll test the defences as well, so we know what we can drop them. If they can't wear spacesuits, they can't get out of the atmosphere."

And we still don't know what they use as targeting criteria, her thoughts added. *But they wouldn't be mad enough to fire on their own gates, would they?*

She frowned, suddenly unsure. The sphere was *tough*. If it was tough enough to shrug off a blast from the orbital weapons platforms, sweeping the mountains with energy weapons might seem a sensible tactic. And then...she shook her head. They'd cross that bridge when they came to it. They needed to determine if the plan was workable first.

"Get some rest, then check with the analysts," Staci ordered. How long would it take for the landing party to reach the mountains? Days, at best. More likely weeks. The landing party was hardly made up of the finest the Royal Marines had to offer. Lady Charlotte was reasonably healthy, for her age, but she couldn't keep up with the troops. They'd have enough time, she hoped, to work the bugs out of the plan. "If they think we can make it work, we will try."

"Yes, Captain."

CHAPTER TWENTY-EIGHT: NEAR SOUTH GATE, DYSON TWO (SURFACE)

COLIN AWOKE, SLOWLY.

If his old instructors had seen his camp, he reflected as he clambered to his feet and looked around, they would have failed him on the spot. Or taken him behind the barracks for some remedial training. There was no stockade, no protection…not even anyone staying awake and keeping watch while the rest of the landing party slept. They'd just been too tired for him to organize a watch, let alone anything else. Colin almost wished his instructors were there to berate him, if only because they could have taken command and lifted the burden from him. And if they'd brought more supplies too…

He took a long breath. The air tasted vaguely odd, something tantalisingly familiar drifting at the edge of his awareness. There were hints of rain in the air, but no sense there'd been any rainfall during the night. That would have woken them, wouldn't it? He made a mental note to ensure they set up a proper watch schedule before the end of the day. There was no way to be *sure* the sphere was uninhabited. For all he knew, the sphere had a population greater than every human world put together. It certainly had enough space for it.

Think about it later, he thought, as he poured water into the heater for coffee. *Right now, you have too many other problems.*

He sighed, wishing he had an entire platoon of bootnecks with him. *They* would know how to survive. His team...Jones had the full training, just like Colin, but everyone else had little more than the basics. Tobias and Marigold had never expected to find themselves stranded on an alien world, Doctor Gaurs was wounded and the rest of the team were civilians. Lady Charlotte didn't look healthy enough to last for long, not in a primitive environment. The nasty part of Colin's mind pointed out it might be time to start calculating who they'd need to leave behind.

It isn't that bad, he told himself, firmly. *Not yet.*

Tobias stirred and woke. Colin felt a flicker of envy. Tobias and Marigold had snuggled together and...Colin shook his head as he poured coffee into a mug and handed it to him. It wasn't as if he hadn't had his fair share of sex, from when he'd become aware of girls to now. He'd slept with girls at school, then spent hours in military brothels...he didn't have anyone permanently in his life, yet he'd never felt the lack. And yet...he sighed inwardly as he sipped his own coffee. Officers were encouraged to marry, but it was felt that unattached officers got the better assignments. Colin wasn't anything like high-ranking enough to tell if that was true.

"Fuck," Tobias managed. "What did you *put* in this?"

Colin smiled, remembering the disastrous school camping trip. The mountain rescue party had been *very* sarcastic, when they'd gazed upon the lost schoolchildren. In hindsight, Colin was surprised the gym teacher hadn't been unceremoniously sacked. There wouldn't have been any shortage of replacements, not for him. It wasn't as if running a football team, screaming at welshers and dispensing corporal punishment required qualifications. Colin could easily name a handful of older bootnecks who'd be damn good at the job. They could hardly be worse.

"It's ration pack coffee," Colin said. "It's designed to keep you awake."

"Oh." Tobias took another sip. "You want to check in with the platoon?"

"Go set up the terminal." Colin said. "Take Marigold with you, but make sure you carry your pistols and don't get *too* frisky."

He hid his amusement as Tobias blushed furiously. They'd have a few minutes together, while they waited for the platform to respond. He wasn't sure he was doing them any favours—they'd both be vaporised if the weapons platforms spotted them and opened fire—but he couldn't send Tobias alone. There was too great a chance of him getting lost or worse. He turned to give Doctor Gaurs her coffee, checking her arm with practiced eyes. The sling was far from perfect, but it would have to do. They didn't have the facilities to repair the broken arm.

And it could be fixed overnight, if we were on the ship, he thought, as he handed out the rest of the coffee. It would have to be rationed along with everything else, if they couldn't get supplies dropped from high orbit. That would have been easy, if the weapons platform hadn't been ready and waiting to kill. *What'll we run out of next?*

"I'm going to answer the call of nature," Jones said, curtly. "Back in a moment."

"Dig a hole for your shit, then bury it," Colin said, although he'd given up hope of concealing their presence. It wouldn't take a team of investigators to find the campsite and track them down. "And stay alert, even when you're shitting."

Jones nodded. "Yes, sir."

Colin turned to check the supplies, again. No one had taken anything during the night...he sighed, inwardly, as he drew the same conclusions once again. They had barely a week's worth of food, if they were lucky. He wondered how the civilians would cope. Lady Charlotte wasn't used to roughing it, not even on school-mandated camping trips designed to introduce kids to nature. Would she want more to eat than the others? Or would she be smart enough to ration herself?

"I need to pee, too," Lady Charlotte said. "Where do I go?"

"Behind a bush," Colin said. He'd have told Marigold to go with her, if she hadn't already left with Tobias. "And come straight back here."

He watched the older woman go, feeling a twinge of respect. The women he'd known as a child had been tough and crude, refusing to hide behind baby-talk, but he hadn't expected it from the aristocrat. Lady Charlotte had more steel in her than he'd suspected. Colin had no idea how many of the rumours were actually true—he'd learnt very quickly that rumours were about as trustworthy as a politician's speech—but he found it hard to care. As long as she behaved herself, he would have no problem with her.

Perhaps she's just smart enough to realise throwing a tantrum and asking to speak to the manager would be pointless, Colin thought. *There's no way we'll get off the surface in a hurry.*

Lady Charlotte returned, just in time to help Doctor Gaurs answer the call of nature. Colin was surprised *that* went so well, although—if he recalled correctly—Lady Charlotte had children. She'd probably changed their diapers a few times, even if she'd had nannies to do most of the work. Colin wondered, idly, how many of the hit shows about the aristocratic lifestyle were true. He didn't want to know. In truth, most of those shows seemed designed to stoke class anger.

Unless we're not meant to believe them, he reflected. *But right now, it doesn't matter.*

"Colin." Tobias returned, Marigold behind him. Colin pretended not to notice their lips were slightly puffy. "We downloaded a message from the ship. They have an idea."

Colin took the offered datapad and scanned it, reading the message twice to be sure he wasn't seeing things. The mountains were clearly visible in the distance, a *long* way away…the thought of even reaching the bottom was daunting, let alone climbing to the top. Colin had done his fair share of mountain climbing—he'd trained on the Brecon Beacons, then Ben Nevis—but the sphere's mountains made Mount Everest seem small. Could they climb to the top? It looked as if the mountains weren't a solid vertical wall, but…

"Are they mad?" Colin honestly didn't know. "Or do they think they can get it to work?"

Tobias's lips twisted. "The theory is sound," he said. "But I don't see how we can climb so high, even in spacesuits."

Colin nodded. He'd never gone climbing on Mars, but he'd heard stories about climbing Olympus Mons, the largest mountain in the Sol System. He'd certainly never heard of anything larger, until now. The climbers had to wear suits and carry emergency oxygen...he forced himself to think, evaluating the plan as best as he could. It wasn't going to be easy just getting to the slopes, let alone heading up to orbit. They'd be lucky if it didn't take them weeks.

"If they can drop spacesuits to us, we might be able to climb up," Colin said. There were some specialised mountain climbing vehicles—they looked like spiders—but he didn't know if *Endeavour* could put one together for them. He didn't *think* the ship routinely carried them in case of emergency. "If..."

He took a breath, then raised his voice. "All right, listen up," he said. "We have a plan. It isn't a very good plan, but it's all we have."

His eyes moved from face to face as he outlined the concept. Jones was the only one who looked openly doubtful, but then he was also the only other person who might appreciate how difficult the plan was going to be. Colin grimaced. It wouldn't be the first time a tiny military force had been ordered to attempt the impossible, or merely very difficult, and hope for the best...what other choice did they have? The Chinese had lost a shuttle and it was sheer dumb luck *their* shuttle hadn't been blown away too. There was no way in hell they could rely on getting another shuttle down to the surface, let alone taking off again.

"We'll start walking in an hour," he said, finally. "Doctor Gaurs, I want you testing plants as we pass, looking for things we can eat. If we're lucky, we'll be able to make our rations last longer."

Lady Charlotte leaned forward. "Can't the ship drop supplies to us?"

"They're still working on it," Tobias said. "There's no guarantee they can get *anything* down here."

And if Doctor Gaurs is right, the defences are configured to fire on any signs of developing technology, Colin thought, *so anything they drop to us might be destroyed before we can make use of it.*

His mind raced. There *were* possibilities. *Endeavour* had one hell of a machine shop, better than anything he'd seen on *Lion*. They could put together a simple aircraft, perhaps a battery-powered monoplane, and drop it to them...if, of course, the automated weapons systems wouldn't fire on it automatically. Colin scowled at the thought. There was no way to know, save for putting a plane together and trying to take off. What else could they try without drawing fire? Solar power? Or...or what?

Now you know how the poor bastards on the wrong side of the Security Zone feel, Colin's thoughts mocked. *And you're just as trapped as them, aren't you?*

• • •

Charlotte had *thought* she was relatively healthy, for her age.

She wasn't young any longer, of course, but she'd had the best enhancements money could buy spliced into her. Her body was designed to push the limits as far as they would go, although—she'd been told—military-grade enhancements were an order of magnitude more powerful than hers. And yet, as she walked, she felt her age pressing down on her so hard she feared that, if she stopped, she'd never be able to start again. Her legs hurt as she forced herself to keep moving, pride refusing to let her linger at the rear even though it was hard to keep up with the naval personnel. It was hard to stop long enough to let Athena test the plants as they passed.

"The local biosystem does appear to be loosely compatible with ours," Athena said, between breaths. "We should be able to find things we can eat."

Charlotte nodded, gasping for breath. "How can you be sure?"

"There's a simple procedure," Athena said, holding up a sensor. "Anything outside a set of parameters will trigger an alarm, cautioning us not to risk eating it. There's no guarantee that anything within the parameters will be edible, let alone tasty, but it's a start."

"Really." Charlotte found it hard to breathe. "How...how can that be possible? I mean...this *is* an alien world."

"Artificial world," Athena corrected her. "Realistically, a lot—and I mean a lot—of life-bearing worlds do tend to fall within the same general parameters, even the ones that gave birth to other intelligent life forms. The Tadpole biosystem isn't *that* different from ours—we can eat some of their meat animals and vegetation, as they can eat ours. The only life form we know that stands outside those parameters is the virus and even *that* isn't too different. For all we know, there may be only one template for life-bearing worlds and that's the one that gave birth to us."

"And that's why every known race is humanoid?" Charlotte wasn't so sure. "The same problem, the same answer?"

"Of course," Athena said. "If you do a sum, and I do the same sum, there's only one right answer. It doesn't mean you copied from me or vice versa. And if that's the answer you need to get through a bottleneck, there won't be much room for variation."

"I see, I think," Charlotte said. She'd had math teachers who'd acted as if two students getting the same answer was clear proof one of them was cheating. It wasn't as if there was much leeway when there was only one right answer. "But we are still quite different from the Tadpoles."

"Yeah." Athena shrugged. "But on a cosmic scale, we're practically twins."

Charlotte said nothing as they resumed the walk. The mountains hung in the distance, mocking them. How far away *were* they? Charlotte wasn't sure. The naval personnel had refused to be drawn on the question, which probably meant she didn't want to know the answer. And yet... she frowned, remembering the xenospecialist lectures she'd attended on *Endeavour*. An intelligent race would have to overcome numerous pitfalls before developing space travel, from the first stumbling steps towards intelligence to surviving its own technology. The human race had come very close to blowing itself back to the Stone Age over the years, with all its progress wiped out by a nuclear or biological disaster. And yet...

Her thoughts grew sluggish as they kept walking, the terrain changing from a jungle to a grassy hillside and then back to a jungle again. She thought she heard birds in the trees, but they were keeping themselves firmly out of sight. The ground seemed to turn muddy beneath her feet, water trickling through the earth as she splashed through it and onto firmer ground. It was hard to understand how the ecosystem truly worked. Geography hadn't been her specialty at school—her teacher's breath had stunk of rotten bananas, making it hard to concentrate on anything else—but she was fairly sure the planet's crust was thicker than the sphere. Was the ground below her feet little more than a scattering of earth on the sphere itself? Were there any underground water feeding the soil? How deep did the roots even go?

The sphere may be thin, on an interplanetary scale, she thought. *But it is still impossibly thick by ours.*

She looked up, sharply, as she heard something rustling in the foliage. Back home, that would have meant a small animal, perhaps a deer or a rodent or even a village dog that had slipped its leash and gone exploring. Here…she froze, horribly, as she remembered all the stories from the days of big game hunting in Africa, before hunting had been banned once and for all. There might be lions or tigers or their alien counterparts on the far side of the jungle. Colin had evidently had the same thought. He held up his hand, calling a halt as he raised his rifle. Whatever it was, it was coming closer…

Charlotte gasped as a green and yellow reptilian form burst into the open. It was…she thought it was an oversized dog at first, but it rapidly became clear it was something considerably more alien. Others followed, bursting out of the undergrowth. Their heads twitched back and forth so rapidly it was hard to get a good look at them, yet…they seemed more like birds than anything else. They were remarkable and yet…very alien. Her legs felt as if they'd turned to stone. She couldn't move.

Tobias gasped. "Dinosaurs?"

The word hung on the air. Charlotte stared. Were they dinosaurs? Or something akin to them? The Vesy were reptilian and they were very definitely intelligent, if primitive. Were the creatures in front of her intelligent too? It was hard to say. They acted more like pack animals than anything else, yet...did it matter? The Tadpoles were pack-like too. They very rarely acted alone. Hell, the very concept of a lone wolf to them was an oxymoron.

Very sharp teeth, she noted, dully. *But they're keeping their jaws firmly closed.*

Her mind raced. Was that a threat display? Or not? Or did the creatures simply not know what to make of the humans? Or...

A rustle ran through the pack. They turned and left, moving so quickly they were gone almost before Charlotte realised they were going. They merged with the jungle, vanishing so completely she couldn't trace their path. Her thought spun in circles. Were they intelligent? Or...or what?

"Fuck," Colin managed. His voice was stunned. "That was...*dinosaurs?*"

"They're probably not *our* dinosaurs," Athena said. She sounded more enthused than shaken. "I suspect they probably followed the same evolutionary path."

"And they can be dangerous," Jones said. "We need to be careful."

"Yeah," Colin said. "They weren't scared of us. Not at all."

Charlotte shivered.

CHAPTER TWENTY-NINE: HMS ENDEAVOUR, DYSON TWO (INTERIOR)

"DINOSAURS?"

Staci had heard a lot of strange reports over the years, from the plausible to ones she was sure had been dreamed up by men with too much time on their hands. Giant alien starships, somehow only visible to the naked eye; godlike alien entities who tested isolated humans to put the entire human race on trial; fleets of starships fleeing robotic enemies bent on exterminating all forms of biological life...they were not, in her view, anything other than tall stories told by spacers in bars. It was funny how there were no actual recordings of any such events. And yet...

She stared at the report in disbelief. The Royal Marines were not given to making up stories. Colin Lancaster had always struck her as remarkably level-headed. And yet...she found it hard to place any real credence in his report. If she hadn't seen the visual recordings, she wouldn't have believed it at all. Dinosaurs? They probably weren't *real* dinosaurs—there was no reason another planet couldn't have evolved something comparable—but it was still a shock. The sphere wasn't as dead as they'd thought. For all she knew, the dinosaur-like creatures had evolved there. God knew the sphere was old enough for evolution to bring forth quite a few intelligent races.

"Remarkable," Jenner said. "And they may pose a problem."

Staci nodded, curtly. The sphere's biochemistry wasn't *that* different than theirs. The landing party had already found plants they could eat, with minimal reprocessing. There was no reason to think the local wildlife couldn't eat humans, if indeed they hadn't already hunted down and consumed the landing party. Staci had watched movies in which dinosaurs chased bikini-clad girls, after they'd fallen back in time or some mad genius had resurrected the dinosaurs in the modern world. The idea of that happening in real life, without a sympathetic or patriotic scriptwriter, was just absurd. And yet, it might happen.

"Right now, we have other problems," she said. "Are the drones ready to deploy?"

"Yes, Captain," Jenner said. "*Haikou* has taken up overwatch position."

"Good." Staci would sooner have risked the smaller ship, but Captain Yunan had been reluctant to do anything more than wait out the clock. Besides, it was a *British* landing party on the surface. "Helm, prepare to alter course if we come under attack."

"Aye, Captain."

Staci took a breath. *Endeavour* was far too close to the alien defence grid for her peace of mind, even though they were well out of range of any human weapon. The alien weapons were a dangerous unknown. They could sight *Endeavour* and open fire and the first warning she'd get would be when the beam sliced into her hull. She'd done what she could to minimise the risks, but she doubted any of her precautions would make a difference. She might as well have carried an umbrella in a hurricane.

"Tactical," she ordered. "Launch the first set of drones."

"Aye, Captain," McDougall said. "Drones away...now."

Staci leaned forward as the drones sped towards the sphere on ballistic trajectories. There were no betraying emissions, nothing to reveal their presence to passive sensors. Her crew knew where to look and even *they* couldn't see them, not without bringing the rest of *Endeavour's* sensors online and drawing alien eyes to the ship. She hoped—prayed—the lead drones made it into the atmosphere, perhaps even down to the ground. If they worked out what would—and what wouldn't—draw alien fire, they might be able to drop supplies to the landing party too.

Sweat prickled on her back as the seconds ticked away. She'd been in the navy long enough to know, beyond a shadow of a doubt, that it took time for things to happen, but here...it was hard to wrap her head around the distances between their position and the alien weapons platforms. There was something about being inside the sphere that made her feel trapped, even though she *knew* it was an illusion. *Endeavour* was little bigger than a dust mote, compared to the immensity of the sphere. She wondered, suddenly, how an intelligent race would develop if they realised their entire world was the interior of a giant sphere. Would they dig down to see if they could break out? Or would they assume they'd been placed inside a protective wall by a god? Or...or what? How would a race develop if they found incontrovertible proof of a guiding intelligence shaping their world?

"Captain," McDougall said. "Drones one through five are approaching the atmosphere now. Drones six to ten are nearing the weapons platforms. Laser links are coming online."

And let's hope they can't track laser beams, Staci thought. So far, the landing party's laser communicators hadn't drawn fire. She hoped that would continue long enough to get them back into space. *If they can, they'll find us within seconds.*

"Links confirmed," McPhee said. "Datalinks going active...now."

Staci nodded, keeping her face under tight control. The drones were the most sophisticated human technology could produce, so expensive she *knew* the beancounters were going to make a fuss when they realised how many of them she'd deployed on a suicide mission. They were supposed to be capable of picking up whispers of energy from hundreds of thousands of kilometres away...if there were any betraying emissions within the sphere, anything that might help her crew unlock its secrets, they should be able to detect their existence and relay the details to the mothership.

But here...she didn't know. The alien technology was too advanced. It was like playing poker when everyone, apart from her, knew what cards everyone else held.

"No visible damage," Jenner said, as the alien weapons platform appeared on the display. "The Chinese didn't even *scratch* the paint."

"It looks that way," Staci agreed, grimly. She'd tried to think of a way to take out the platform, but if nukes didn't work...hell, she was alarmed the Chinese attack hadn't drawn a response from the Builders. A nuclear detonation within the sphere *should* draw attention, shouldn't it? Were they truly gone? Or was a nuke so meaningless to them they hadn't even bothered to find out what had happened? "If we can't..."

"The lead drones are entering the atmosphere," McDougall reported. "Drones one to three will bring their active sensors online..."

He broke off as his console bleeped an alarm. "Energy spike!"

Staci braced herself, even though she knew it was pointless. The enemy weapons moved at the speed of light. They'd hit the ship well before any warning could reach her. And yet...she cursed as four drones vanished from the display. The weapons platforms had wiped them out effortlessly. Her earlier thoughts came back to haunt her. Perhaps the Builders really *didn't* care about nukes in the sphere. They'd swatted the drones with enough firepower to vaporise a battleship.

"Drones one to four are gone," McDougall said. "Drone seven was badly damaged. Her sensors were overloaded by the energy spike."

"Steer her towards the platform, if possible," Staci ordered. "Drone five?"

"So far, seemingly unnoticed," McDougall said. "But she was on the edge of the atmosphere rather than a direct insertion trajectory."

"And they might not realise she's on a course to eventually hit the sphere," Jenner said, quietly. "If we slip very gingerly into the atmosphere..."

Staci frowned. *Endeavour's* shuttles weren't designed for a slow entry into a planet's atmosphere. There were some pleasure craft that were built to prolong the descent, so their passengers could watch the inky darkness of space giving way to the planet's atmosphere, but there were none of them on hand. She'd hoped to drop a capsule of supplies to the landing party, yet if the defences fired on anything that came in too fast...

"We can rig a drone to carry a supply capsule, then release it to parachute down to the surface," she said, thoughtfully. It would be a dangerously slow descent, and there was a very real risk it would land hundreds of miles from the landing party if the drone had to drop the package in a hurry, but it could be done. "See to it."

"Aye, Captain."

"Drone five is losing attitude," McDougall said. "So far, no reaction."

Staci felt a twinge of hope. Logically, the orbital defences shouldn't target aircraft. The sphere's inhabitants would need them to get around and that would be impossible, if the orbital defences shot them down. How smart *were* the defences? Anything below a certain attitude might be assumed to have launched from the ground, rather than dropped down from orbit. Unless the theory the sphere was really a *zoo* was actually true...

"We'll send the supply drone in on the same path," she said. "And hope for the best."

"Aye, Captain," Jenner said. "Or we might be able to land on the mountain."

And hope the climber works as advertised, Staci thought. Her crew had been producing mountain rescue vehicles, throwing them together out of spare parts, but they weren't purpose-built for the job. They were lucky they had ground vehicles that could be adapted for the role. A regular warship wouldn't have been able to do anything like as much to face the unknown. *If we can't get them off the surface, we may have to abandon them.*

The thought gnawed at her. The Royal Navy left *no one* behind. It was a tradition older than human spacefaring, a rule that was both idealistic and deeply practical. You couldn't expect your crewmates to give their all for you, she'd been told, if you weren't prepared to give your all for them. And yet, what choice would she have? They couldn't remain on station indefinitely. They'd need to return home, arrange for an entire *fleet* of exploration ships, and then return to the sphere. Could the landing party last that long? In theory, yes. In practice...

"Captain," McDougall said. "Drone seven is approaching the platform."

Staci leaned forward. Up close, the alien weapons platform looked like a rocky club, an asteroid out of a science-fantasy writer's imagination. She couldn't help being reminded of asteroid artworks from the belt, rocks that had been carved with lasers to bear mute testament to humanity's existence. It managed to look both natural and entirely artificial, something that made her head spin. The belters had once planned to turn asteroids into interstellar starships. The concept had been cool, from what she recalled, but impractical. The tramlines had put a stop to development before the ships could leave the drawing board.

Although the virus did something like it, she recalled. *And if we can't stop those ships, we'll be refighting the war a thousand years from now.*

"Impact in ten seconds," McDougall said. "Nine...eight...*energy spike!*"

The live feed went blank. Staci didn't need to look at the feeds from the stealthed platforms to know the drone had been vaporised, swatted like a bug. There'd been no warning. The shot had been fired at effectively point-blank range. She didn't want to think about the implications.

Jenner scowled at the display. "How did the platform even *spot* the drone?"

"Unknown," McDougall said. "The drone was as stealthy as we could make it."

Staci frowned. The drone had been tiny, on an interplanetary scale, and silent. It hadn't radiated a single betraying emission. The gas jets used to steer the drone should have been as undetectable as the rest of it. She would have understood the drone being targeted the moment it touched the platform, like the Chinese shuttle, but it hadn't even got close enough to touch the alien structure when it had been destroyed.

"Did the platform use active sensors?" She shook her head in disbelief. "Or did the gas jets touch the hull?"

"If it did, the drone didn't recognise them," McDougall told her. "None of the threat receivers were tripped until it was too late. The drone was destroyed so quickly half of them didn't even sound the alarm."

"It could be a very finely tuned gravimetric sensor," Jenner suggested. "The Builders manipulate gravity on a scale we can't even begin to match."

Staci frowned. Everything she knew about gravimetric sensors told her it was impossible. The drone hadn't been radiating drive emissions, nor had it been large enough to have a gravity field of its own. Its effect on the surrounding section of space-time had been so minimal one could reasonably argue it didn't have *any* effect at all. And yet, if someone *did* have sensors so sensitive as to be able to pick up something so tiny, the drone would have been as blatantly obvious as a punch in the face.

And they'll be able to see the rest of us too, she thought. It was a chilling thought. The Builders might know *precisely* where her ship was lurking, ready to blow her away whenever the whim struck them. *No cloaking device could hide us from their eyes.*

"Relay everything to the Chinese," she ordered, shortly. "And prepare to launch the supply drop."

"Aye, Captain."

Staci's mind raced as the second flight of drones was prepared for departure. It just made no sense. The Chinese shuttle hadn't been destroyed until it had actually dropped a landing party on the weapons platform, but the drone had been blown away as it approached the platform. Why had the Chinese been allowed to get so close? Had the platform gone on high alert, after the Chinese had landed? Or had the drone seemed a more immediate threat?

We don't have anything that can threaten the platform, Staci thought. *What the hell is it made of?*

Her mind raced, studying the reports from the analysis deck. They had thrown all sorts of suggestions around like confetti, from unobtainium to pieces of technobabble about atoms being held in place by forcefields, theories that veered between the practical to the downright insane and back again. Staci didn't know what to make of it. Until they managed to take a sample and subject it to proper analysis, they might never be able to find a proper answer.

"Captain," Jenner said. "The drones are ready to launch."

"Deploy them," Staci ordered. The second flight of drones were cheaper, designed to be expendable. "And activate the transmitters when the drones are in place."

She waited, counting down the seconds. The drones would draw fire—that was inevitable. She had no illusions about what would happen the moment the drones activated their transmitters. But...they needed to know what, precisely, would draw fire. Which transmitters would be fired upon first? And would a silent drone be ignored when there were loud targets just waiting to be blown away? She grimaced as the countdown reached zero, perfectly timed to draw the platforms away from the drone entering the sphere's atmosphere. If they were lucky...

"Energy spike," McDougall reported. "Four platforms went live..."

The drones started to vanish, one by one. Staci leaned forward, feeling another flicker of hope. They'd been programmed to go evasive, the moment they started to transmit, and it was becoming obvious the platforms were using the radio signals to target their weapons. The drones kept evading, letting bolts of energy slash past them...aimed, she noted, at where the drones had been a few seconds ago. The platforms didn't seem designed to spit out plasma bolts like a human point defence system, intended to maximise the chances of a hit by firing hundreds of pulses in a handful of seconds. They seemed to target, fire, retarget and fire again...

"Slow," Jenner commented. "There's a slight but very noticeable time delay."

Staci nodded in agreement. It wasn't much, but it was the first hint the alien technology wasn't all-powerful. She silently evaluated it as the last of the drones vanished from the display. The platforms had picked them all off, eventually, but it hadn't been easy. She had the feeling she could distract them again, perhaps even long enough to get a shuttle through the defences. Would the platforms fire on something that was clearly *leaving* the surface?

We need to find out, she thought. *And quickly.*

McDougall swore out loud. "Captain, they just blew away the supply drone."

Staci glanced at Jenner, who looked equally concerned. "Why?"

"I don't know," McDougall said. "They must have seen it. Somehow. They just shot it out of the air."

Shit, Staci thought. The rules had changed...or had they? Had it just been bad luck? Or...had they convinced the platforms to fire on *anything* that looked suspicious? The drone should have *looked* as if it was skimming the atmosphere, instead of trying to make a descent to the lower levels, but the platforms had blown it away anyway. *What the fuck are we dealing with here?*

"The third flight of drones is being prepped now," Jenner said. "Do you want to test the defences again?"

Staci hesitated. "We'll wait until the analysts have had a chance to evaluate the data from the first set of probes," she said. It was possible—unlikely, but possible—that one of the analysts would see something she'd missed. "And then we'll test the defences around the South Gate."

"Aye, Captain," Jenner said.

Staci turned back to the displays, thinking hard. How long did they have? If they couldn't unlock the defences, if they couldn't even predict what would—and what wouldn't—draw fire...she shook her head. They were in deep shit...no, the *landing party* was in deep shit. How long could they survive on the ground? If they were attacked by wild animals or worse...

We won't abandon them, she told herself. *We won't.*

But she knew, even as she keyed her console to view the next set of drone deployments, that she might have no choice.

CHAPTER THIRTY: NEAR SOUTH GATE, DYSON TWO (SURFACE)

SOMETHING WAS WRONG.

Colin couldn't put his finger on it, as they walked due south through terrain that seemed thrown together at random by a child-god, but it nagged at his mind. Something he was missing…something right in front of him, that he was missing. He kept one hand near his pistol at all times, ready to draw it in a heartbeat if the dinosaurs returned or if something—anything—else happened. The trees started to draw in again, forcing them to walk in single file as they made their way through the jungle. He thought he heard something crashing through the undergrowth, but—whatever it was—it refused to come into the light.

He scowled, wishing—not for the first time—that he had a full platoon under his command and no civilians to worry about. They were doing better than he'd expected—there hadn't been more than a little grumbling—but he doubted they had the endurance to keep going long enough to reach the mountains, let alone climb to the top. It was going to take at least two weeks to get there, by his most optimistic estimate, and *that* assumed the terrain wasn't going to get any worse. There was something so oddly *patchy* about the landscape that he felt as if he was walking through a dream.

The terrain changed, rising slightly as they made their way onwards. He wondered, as the air grew hotter, if the designers had sculpted hills and valleys as well as everything else, or if they'd just thrown down earth, water and seeds and settled back to see what would grow and develop. The human race had done that on Mars, he recalled, although the terraforming project had barely started when the tramlines had been discovered and everyone had gone looking for worlds that would be easier to settle instead. Mars had been left alone long enough for the new vegetation to take root, for a whole new ecosystem to flourish. It might not have been what the settlers had wanted, but it was a step in the right direction. And...

He held up a hand as he heard something up ahead. The team slowed to a halt, hands dropping to weapons. Colin hoped they knew what they were doing. Jones had been through commando training, and Colin had taught Tobias personally, but he had no idea about the others. Lady Charlotte had probably never touched a weapon in her life, unless she'd gone hunting or shooting on her estate. Colin hoped she had. They'd need another shooter soon.

"Stay ready," he said, as the sound came closer. More dinosaurs? The team had seen others, peeking at them from a distance before vanishing back into the undergrowth. Doctor Gaurs had insisted they weren't *really* dinosaurs, just something from a contingent evolutionary tree, but Colin couldn't think of them as anything else. It wasn't a reassuring thought. He had no idea if they had anything like enough firepower to ward off a pack of raptor-like creatures, if they attacked. "If they are..."

The trees parted, revealing...*humans*. Colin stared in disbelief. There were nine of them, wearing nothing more than loincloths. They couldn't be human and yet...his eyes flickered over them, noting the slightly tinted skin and lingering on a pair of bare breasts. There were no alien races so close to humanity, not close enough to pass for human. He swallowed hard, suddenly very aware of just how isolated they were. If the newcomers were hostile...

A young man stepped forward. Colin evaluated him quickly. There was something slightly *off* about him, something Colin couldn't quite place. It wasn't just the slightly greenish tint to his skin, but something in the way he held himself. He carried a simple wooden spear, slung over his shoulder. His comrades, including the women, carried simple bows and arrows as well as spears. Colin knew better than to underestimate them. There were special forces units that used crossbows for certain very specific missions.

The man spoke in an unknown language. Colin kicked himself, mentally. Of *course* the strangers didn't speak English. It might be the default language on Earth and the rest of the human worlds, to the point that nearly everyone spoke English as their primary or secondary language, but the natives might not have seen Earth for centuries. How the hell had they even reached the sphere? Colin had heard of survey ships that went into the unknown and never came back, or colonist-carriers that vanished somewhere in the darkness, but…he shook his head. There'd be time to worry about that later. Right now, they needed to make friends before the natives decided they were a threat.

"Doctor Gaurs," Colin said, quietly. "You're up."

The doctor nodded, taking her datapad from her belt as she stepped forward. The native speaker chatted to her, their voices rising and falling as they worked to build up a speaking vocabulary. Colin prayed, silently, that they could put something together before the natives ran out of patience. It should be easier than talking to aliens, right? He recalled the briefings, in which the xenospecialists had admitted the process hadn't been as easy as anyone had thought and shivered. The dinosaurs had been quite bad enough. If there were humans on the sphere…

He frowned as he looked at the natives. They seemed very human—the women in particular—and yet, they looked slightly *wrong*. How long had they been *on* the sphere? Long enough to diverge slightly from the human norm? Or…he felt his frown deepen as it hit him. The sphere's gravity was slightly lower than Earth's. If humans living in zero-g lost muscle tone and needed to regain it before returning to a normal planet's gravity well, what would happen if they lived permanently in a low gravity field? Would they evolve longer—and lighter—arms and legs? Or were his eyes tricking him and they weren't human at all?

Tobias moved up beside him. "How the hell are they even here?"

"Good question," Colin said. "And I don't know."

"There were stories about aliens kidnapping people," Tobias said, as if Colin hadn't said a word. "Did they bring them here?"

Colin shrugged. "Right now, we have more immediate problems," he said. "We can worry about their origins later."

Doctor Gaurs caught his eye. "We don't have their language in the datafiles," she said, "but we've put together a small vocabulary. They're inviting us to accompany them to their home."

"I see." Colin thought fast. They were in no position to refuse. Hell, for all he knew it was a demand rather than an invitation. "How long until we can speak to them properly?"

"It's hard to say," Doctor Gaurs said. "It's a human tongue, and it should be easier to understand than a truly alien language, but it may be weeks or months before we're sure of the autotranslator."

Colin nodded, curtly. He'd been cautioned the autotranslator software wasn't always reliable. It was one thing to literally translate English into a foreign tongue, another to translate the meaning behind it. Even something as simple as asking the way to the beach could cause confusion, if the autotranslator produced something that didn't make sense to foreign ears. Somehow, Colin doubted that repeating the question in a louder voice would get him anywhere. They were outnumbered, possibly outgunned and stranded a very long way from help. And there wasn't even any time to contact the ship. They were completely on their own.

"Tell him we would be delighted," Colin said. If the natives were friendly, it would even be true. If not...he doubted they could escape or hold out for long. Once they ran out of ammunition, they'd be fucked. "And that we will follow him when he's ready."

The natives seemed delighted, chattering amongst themselves in low voices as they turned and led the team through the jungle. They didn't *look* to be leading them into a trap, although Colin kept a wary eye on the surrounding foliage anyway. He'd been in too many jungles—natural and concrete—to feel safe, if there was plenty of cover for possible enemies. They could be enveloped by native soldiers, without even the slightest idea they were there. Who knew what the natives *really* wanted with them?

We have to look very alien to them, Colin thought. *Our skins, our clothes, our weapons...they must know we're not from around here. Or do they? For all they know, we could be from a settlement a few million kilometres away, rather than the old world. Do they even know where they came from?*

The jungle widened suddenly, revealing a stone city on a hill surrounded by patchwork fields. Colin stared. Natives—mainly women—were working the fields, while the menfolk patrolled the edges of the jungle or headed out on what looked like hunting missions. The city itself was surrounded by a solid wall, suggesting the natives had some reason to fear attack. Colin didn't like the implications. The natives might have enemies, enemies who might lurk between the team and the mountains. And that meant...he frowned as he spied a river, flowing through a gash in the walls and into the city. A handful of canoes made their way up and down the water.

"Fascinating," Tobias breathed. "It looks like a city from the ancient world."

Colin shrugged. Archaeology had never been his thing. Instead, he studied the defences as they made their way up to the gates. There was very little metal in evidence, just wood and stone. The walls had been laid brick by brick, bound together by something that might have been concrete yet probably wasn't, but it wouldn't stand up to a missile. He guessed the local enemies, whatever they were, didn't have anything more advanced than sticks and stones, although it was hard to be sure. Without reliable supplies of metal, could they even build a modern civilisation? Could they even climb out of the Stone Age?

He wrinkled his nose as they passed through the gates. The air stunk of piss and shit and too many humans in too close of a proximity. The city wasn't as dirty as a refugee camp, or some of the poorest parts of Britain, but it wasn't as clean as it could be either. The natives thronged around, staring at the newcomers as they were urged through the streets. Colin couldn't help noticing that women seemed to do all the work, save for hunting and fighting. It made a certain kind of sense. Men were inherently more expendable than women.

The smell grew stronger, the further they went into the city. Colin silently catalogued all the things the locals were missing, from basic sanitation to surprisingly simple pieces of technology like the wheel. There were no carts, no horses…he thought he saw a pair of domesticated dinosaurs, but it was hard to be sure. His lips quirked at the thought of a massed charge of knights in armour, riding dinosaurs as they mowed down their foes…it would be something out of a bad movie, yet…

"They'll need medical help, if nothing else," Tobias said. "We have things to trade."

Colin kept his thoughts to himself as the locals showed them into a large building, one that reminded him of a king's throne room. The stone walls were lined with carvings, from human faces to things that made no sense to him. Three women sat on raised chairs, wearing nothing but loincloths and feathered headdresses that fell to their shoulders…queens, perhaps, or princesses. Colin wondered, suddenly, if the local society was matriarchal. It was quite possible. If the men went to war constantly, as noblemen had done in days of old, the women would have to stay home and keep everything going. They probably hadn't had a choice.

Their escort stepped forward, bowed deeply, and began an explanation. The queens looked at the newcomers with thoughtful eyes. Doctor Gaurs kept an eye on her datapad, recording and translating the discussion. Colin hoped she'd crack the language sooner rather than later. He'd studied French in school, but he couldn't remember very much beyond a handful of words that couldn't be repeated in public. Doctor Gaurs was an xenospecialist. She *had* to be good with languages.

The queen motioned Doctor Gaurs forward and addressed her. The doctor answered, carefully. Colin kept his face under tight control as it dawned on him the natives might have assumed the women in the party were the ones in charge. It wouldn't have been unprecedented. There were plenty of human societies that assumed the man was always in charge, even in the modern day. And yet, the men clearly had their own spheres of responsibility. Perhaps they didn't impinge on each other as much as he'd thought.

Doctor Gaurs glanced at him. "They are curious about us," she said. "How much do we tell them?"

Colin hesitated. The rules for alien contact were clear. Ideally, no alien race was to learn anything about humanity until the human race was sure they weren't a potential enemy. In the real world, it was rarely so simple. The queens in front of him were human, or close enough. What would they do, if they were told the truth? Assume Colin was lying? *He* wouldn't have believed the story, if he hadn't known about starships or the sphere or anything else. Or decide Colin and his team could be safely eliminated? He didn't know.

"Tell them we're from a long way away, and that we're travelling to the south pole," he said, finally. It wasn't quite a lie, although it was devoid of anything useful. "Ask them if we can stay for a couple of days."

Doctor Gaurs nodded, then turned back to the queens. Colin watched, wondering if he'd just signed their death warrants. They didn't know *anything* about the natives. Were they friendly or hostile or…or what? The chatter rose and fell as the doctor pressed her case, arguing with the help of her datapad. Colin tensed. If there was a mistake now, even something that would barely cause a ripple of discontent on Earth, they might have to fight their way out of the city.

"They are offering to host us for a few days," Doctor Gaurs told him. "And they are asking for our help."

Colin grimaced. "What sort of help?"

"I'm not sure," Doctor Gaurs said. "We don't have a complete vocabulary yet."

"Understood." Colin forced himself to think. They were in no position to openly refuse the natives, not yet. What did they want? Technology? Medicine? Or military support? "Tell them we'll consider it."

"Got it." Doctor Gaurs spoke briefly to the queens, who nodded as one and spoke briefly to their attendants. "They'll take us to our apartments now."

Colin shared a look with Jones as they were escorted out of the hall and through the streets to a stone temple-like building. The sight set off alarm bells in his head. The building was comfortable enough, he supposed, but getting out without being spotted would be difficult, if not impossible. They looked too different from the locals to pass unnoticed, even if they did get out. The thought nagged at him as they settled into the chamber. It had a weirdly minimalistic vibe, reminding him of a Japanese traditional home he'd been shown by one of his teachers. Less cover, he noted. If the locals wanted to overwhelm and capture them, they'd have little trouble in doing so.

"They promised us food," Doctor Gaurs said. "Let me check to make sure we can eat it first."

"Got it." Colin looked from face to face. "Observations?"

"They're concerned about being attacked," Jones said, flatly. "We were lucky they didn't greet us with a hail of spears."

Lady Charlotte looked up. "We have guns."

"Spears can kill too," Colin said. "And once we run out of ammunition, the guns will be nothing more than clubs."

He glanced at Tobias. "If we get onto the roof, can we contact the ship?"

"If we can get up there, yes," Tobias said. "But they might take it as a hostile move."

"They didn't tell us *not* to go onto the roof," Doctor Gaurs said. "We can ask."

"And then we'd have to explain *why*," Marigold pointed out. "They might think we intend to spy on them."

Colin opened his mouth to reply, then stopped as a line of young women entered the chamber carrying trays of food. He glanced at Doctor Gaurs, who produced her test kit, then waited for her to check the food. The young women didn't seem inclined to leave. Colin guessed they had orders to wait on the guests hand and foot, while keeping an eye on them and probably trying to learn their language. It was what he would have done, if he'd been confronted by a group of very strange humans. Who knew? The women might be a *lot* smarter than they looked.

And they're topless, he thought. *How better to distract a group of mostly men?*

"It should be safe," Doctor Gaurs said, finally. "No guarantees about the taste, though."

Lady Charlotte took a bite of her food. "Tastes like French stew," she said, finally. "Not bad, but some flavours I don't know."

Colin shrugged. Ethnic food had been making a comeback before the virus had reached Earth, but he'd never really bothered with it. Pizza and curry was as far as he'd go...although, to be fair, he'd never had the money to experiment. Lady Charlotte, on the other hand, had probably eaten in a different restaurant every day. He wasn't sure if he should envy or pity her.

"It will do," he said. "Right now, we have to build up our vocabulary. And then decide how we're going to pay for our stay."

CHAPTER THIRTY-ONE: NEAR SOUTH GATE, DYSON TWO (SURFACE)

CHARLOTTE HAD ALWAYS PRIDED HERSELF on being *good* at languages.

It was a useful skill to have, she'd been told, and her experience had borne it out. The entire world might speak English, at least as a second language, but many of the foreigners she'd had to deal with over the years had preferred to speak in their own languages. The French and Russians were often more open to those who spoke their languages, while the Chinese insisted they would only honour agreements written in their official state-approved language. Charlotte had grown up speaking French as well as English, then added enough Russian and Chinese to get by. It had been wasted on the estate, but here...

She studied the datapad with one eye as she chatted to the maidservant. The young woman might look like someone out of an absurd male fantasy, but she was as smart as Charlotte herself...perhaps smarter. Charlotte suspected she had orders to attach herself to one of the men, probably to serve as a pillow dictionary. It wasn't impossible. The locals would want to keep a close eye on their guests, if only to determine why they were *really* making their way through the sphere. They didn't seem to believe the newcomers were really making their way to the southern mountains.

And they seem to know very little about their past, Charlotte thought. *How did they even get to the sphere?*

She frowned. They'd been shown around the city, after a restful night, and it had merely deepened the mystery. The city seemed to draw in elements from all over the world, from Ancient Greece and Rome to the long-gone Aztecs and Incas. Charlotte had seen some of those ruins, during her gap year before going to university. It was hard to deny the city looked as if it had been based on the ancient works, although it could be just a coincidence. And yet…how had the natives even gotten to the sphere? The question was unanswerable. However they'd been transported, if indeed they *had* been kidnapped from Earth, it had been so long ago they'd lost all memory of it. Did they have a recorded history? It didn't seem so.

Curious, she thought. It was hard to be sure they were telling the truth, as they knew it. They could easily be trying to mislead her. Charlotte had studied the contact protocols. Outright lying was a bad idea, but misleading one's listener was acceptable. Personally, Charlotte wasn't so sure about that—someone could easily take offense to being misled, even if they hadn't been lied to—yet she could see the logic. *Are they hiding things from us or have they simply forgotten?*

She kept the thought to herself as she did her best to hold up her side of the conversation. It was hard to keep asking questions, to try to build up an understanding of what was actually going on. She was grimly aware the mere fact she was asking specific questions would be quite revealing, when the maid reported back to her superiors. Why would she ask unless she felt she had a pressing need to know? And yet…Charlotte couldn't blame them for being concerned. Nine strangers, in their lands…it was lucky the native styles were so different. If they'd looked like enemies, they might have been attacked on sight.

"My Lady?" Charlotte looked up to see Marigold, her face pale. "You're wanted back in the main room."

Charlotte nodded and dismissed the maidservant, watching the girl thoughtfully as she left the room. If she was any judge, the maidservant's English was better than her grasp of the local tongue. It probably was. The locals didn't have written records, let alone recorders or computers or anything that would make it easier for them to study the language. The girl was dependent on her native wit and cunning, which probably meant she was *very* good at it. She'd never had a chance to get too attached to technology, to the point it blunted her ability to do things without it.

Marigold walked beside her as they made their way back to the main room. Charlotte didn't know the younger woman very well, although it was clear Marigold wasn't happy about being trapped on the sphere. She'd had plans for the future which had been derailed, perhaps permanently. Charlotte feared they'd have real problems climbing out of the atmosphere. If the ship couldn't get spacesuits to them, they'd run out of air before they could be rescued.

"We have a problem," Colin Lancaster said. His face was grim. "A big one."

Charlotte frowned as she sat and glanced around. "Can we talk openly?"

"I hope so." Colin sounded as if he didn't believe himself. "There's no one listening, as far as we can tell, but that might be meaningless."

"Might," Charlotte repeated.

"Might," Colin said. "First thing, we've confirmed the natives actually *are* human. Doctor Gaurs ran a blood test"—he nodded to Athena—"and they're just like us."

"Save for a little genetic drift," Athena said. "Not enough to be significant. I'll have to run our findings past the ship's doctor, when we get back in touch, but as far as I can see they really *are* human. The only real difference is skin colour, which is—pardon the expression—only skin deep. There's no reason to think we couldn't make babies with them."

Tobias frowned. "Why *greenish* skin?"

"I don't know," Athena said. "The course of human evolution is fairly understandable. Humans developed dark skin in sunlit places and lighter skin in darker places…but green? I think there must have been an issue, back in the distant past, that evolution gave them green skin to counter. But we may never know."

She paused. "The bad news is that our diseases will be less than friendly to them and verse versa. They might catch something from us, something they have no defence against…"

Charlotte swore. "You mean, like the Native Americans?"

"Yes." Athena said nothing for a long, chilling moment. "It shouldn't be an immediate problem. Our immune systems were improved, courtesy of the navy, and many of the nastier diseases were largely eliminated centuries ago. I don't think we can infect them and their diseases shouldn't be able to get at us. We'll need to implement full biohazard procedures as soon as we return to the ship, but otherwise…realistically, there's little we can do."

"So we just hope they don't all die if we cough on them?" Marigold sounded furious, her eyes flashing grimly. "Just by being here, we could cause a disaster!"

"We would have to be infected with something nasty, in order to give it to them," Athena said, calmly. "As far as I know, none of us is infected with anything. Right now, I'm more concerned about a different problem. We know, now, what they want from us."

She paused. "They're at war," she said. "And they want our help."

Charlotte hesitated. "*Can* we help them?"

"Yes." Colin was very certain. "We can do quite a bit to help them."

"But should we?" Tobias looked at the stone floor. "What about the non-interference edict?"

"This may be a primitive society," Charlotte said, "but it is not an *alien* primitive society."

"We're not supposed to get involved in fights beyond the Security Zone," Colin said. "If we interfere…what will it do to their society?"

Athena leaned forward. "They're insistent they're the ones being hammered by their enemies," she said. "They lose people every week to raids, captured and enslaved or simply killed."

"We don't know they're the good guys," Tobias said. "For all we know, they started the war."

"We don't know anything," Charlotte agreed. "But these are the people who helped us."

"Perhaps we should make contact with the ship," Marigold said. "And ask for orders."

"We're the people on the ground," Colin said. "It has to be our decision."

Charlotte said nothing. The rules were clear. There was to be no contact, no contact at all, with an intelligent race that had not started to climb out of its gravity well. Human history suggested that any contact between an advanced and a primitive race would be destructive to both sides, ruining their chances of meeting as equals. And yet, the one time humanity *had* met a primitive alien race, the rules had been thrown out the airlock. Charlotte understood the logic, but she still shuddered when she thought about the cost. The Vesy should have been left alone to develop in peace.

Her thoughts mocked her. *And should we kill ourselves now, to make sure we do no further harm to the local society? Or should we do whatever we must to survive?*

She turned the problem over and over again. If they meddled, they would be responsible for whatever chaos followed in their wake. If they didn't...if they refused, they might be chased out of the city or simply butchered by the locals. Hell, even if the locals let them go without a fight, they'd still have to get to the mountains. Who knew how many other cities were waiting, between then and now?

"We can offer limited military support," Colin said. "And we can give them some pieces of technology, the wheel in particular. I don't know why they never developed it for themselves."

"There's very little metal here," Tobias said. "It would probably put limits on just how far they could go."

Charlotte frowned. "No metal *and* orbital weapons platforms, ready to smash all signs of technological development?"

"They're caught like rats in a trap," Colin said. "They'll never be able to get off the surface. Not unless we help."

"Then we should," Tobias said.

"The truth is, our ability to intervene is very limited," Charlotte said. "What happens when we run out of bullets?"

"We die," Jones said, flatly.

"Yes." Charlotte met his eyes, evenly. "And what happens if we do nothing?"

"They kick us out, perhaps," Jones said. "Or, if they're desperate, they try to take our guns anyway."

"They wouldn't know what they were," Tobias said. "They don't *have* guns."

"They're metal," Colin pointed out. "Even if they don't know what they are, they'll know they're valuable."

Marigold cleared her throat. "This would be an interesting dilemma, back at school," she said. "The moral and ethical aspects of this problem would make for some *fascinating* debates. I'd enjoy the arguments myself, if I were back there."

She tapped the floor with one finger. "But the truth is, we're trapped here. We are interfering simply by *being* on the surface. We didn't mean to land here, but the truth is we did and now we're stuck. There's no way out, unless we *do* manage to get up the mountain and into orbit. And let's be honest. That's one hell of a long shot."

Charlotte felt her heart sink. "You think we're stuck?"

"I think we must accept that we may never see the ship, let alone Earth, ever again," Marigold said. "And that means our only hope of surviving is working with the locals."

"And giving them advanced technology," Jones said, quietly.

"Not *that* advanced," Tobias countered. "The orbital platforms will see to that, won't they?"

"We will still have an impact," Athena said. "Just introducing better medicine will cause a population boom."

Charlotte cocked her head. "Would that be a bad thing? There's an entire sphere for living space?"

"We have only seen a tiny fragment of the surface," Colin said, calmly. "For all we know, there are Tadpoles in the ocean and Vesy on the far side of the sea."

"My vote is to offer what help we can, in exchange for safe passage," Charlotte said. "And if we are stuck here, at least we'll have some friends."

She scowled as the discussion grew heated. Marigold had a point. It was not an academic debate, but a matter of life and death. Their superiors might expect the landing party to commit suicide, to ensure they didn't contaminate the locals any further, yet she knew she wasn't going to do it. They had to get to the mountains and that meant working with the locals and that meant interfering and...

Colin stood. "I need some air," he said. "Stay here. Try to decide what to do."

Jones looked surprised. "Sir...?"

"Stay here," Colin repeated. "I'll be back shortly."

• • •

Colin was not used to moral dilemmas.

There was little room for them in the Royal Marines, he reflected curtly. There was very little ambiguity about small-unit actions, from guarding a supply dump to storming enemy positions or even disaster relief operations. His superiors could worry about such issues if they wished, he thought. His role had always been to carry out their orders. And yet, right now, he was cut off from them at the worst possible time. There was no one who might tell him what to do.

It was...frustrating. The practical part of his mind agreed with Marigold. He wasn't ready to simply give up on getting home, although he had to admit the odds were against it. They would be better off, in the long run, to make alliances with the locals. And yet, if they took sides in a local dispute, would they choose the *right* side? Colin had studied the

Troubles, noting how easy it was to get entangled in local issues and how hard it could be to determine who was in the right. If indeed *anyone* was in the right. There'd been atrocity-prone factions on both sides of the war, some only considered the good guys because they were supposed to be allied. Colin was privately glad he'd never had to tackle such a battlefield. The advantages of backing the side that looted, raped and killed with impunity were outweighed by the disadvantages. Who would trust the side that backed such monsters?

They were desperate for allies, he thought. *And so are we.*

He frowned as he wandered the city, noting eyes following him. The city could easily have passed for a town on Earth, although it was strikingly primitive. The locals weren't stupid, but they were limited in what they could do. He peered at the marketplace, at temples raised to gods that meant nothing to him, then walked on to the battlements. The men on the walls eyed him curiously but made no attempt to stop him clambering up and peering into the fields. He wasn't sure if they had strict orders to leave him alone or if they simply didn't care.

This isn't a country, he told himself, numbly. *This is a city-state.*

He frowned. It was hard to be sure, but—if he was right—local women outnumbered the men four to one. Some of them would be out hunting, he thought, yet...all of them? It made him wonder how many men died, every year. The idea of women staying at home and doing nothing was ahistorical, even in the most patriarchal of societies, but here...women seemed to be involved in all levels of society. They were the leaders...*that* was rare, if he recalled correctly. He wished now he'd spent more time studying social history and less time playing sports at school. It wasn't as if he'd had a hope of climbing into the big leagues.

A drumming noise split the air. Colin looked up. Someone was beating a drum, the sound taking up by other drummers...the field workers, scrabbling to draw some kind of livelihood from the dirt, scooped up their tools and ran for the walls. Dark shapes burst from the jungle, throwing makeshift bolos at the women. A handful fell, hitting the ground hard. They couldn't get up before the men were on them...

The gates slammed closed as more enemy troops emerged from the jungle. Colin swallowed hard, watching helplessly as they dragged the captives to their feet. The women struggled desperately, but they couldn't break free. Colin caught a glimpse of their faces and felt his heart sink. They were going to die—or worse. He'd heard enough about local warfare to tell it wasn't conquest, not in the sense he know it. It was practically a game.

He unslung his rifle and took aim. The enemy didn't know they were in danger. They made no move to take cover as he squeezed the trigger, putting a bullet through a man's head. He fell. Colin didn't wait for his body to crumple to the ground. He moved to the next target, and the next, picking them off one by one. The enemy troops seemed to waver, unsure of what was picking them off, then broke and ran. A handful of captives were left behind, staring at their departing backs. Colin wanted to keep firing, but he knew he had to conserve ammunition. Once it was gone, it was gone. He didn't even think they could find the components to make gunpowder, not in a hurry. And without metal, how could they make guns?

Silence fell, like a thunderclap. Colin was suddenly aware of everyone staring at him. They hadn't known—how could they?—what he could do. They'd asked for help and yet...he knew, suddenly, that he might have made a mistake. He'd certainly be in some trouble when—if—he got home. And yet...he felt as if he'd done the right thing.

If nothing else, they won't be back in a hurry, he thought, as he made his way down to the streets. He had to get back to the guesthouse and quickly. They'd need to talk to the locals, to find out where the enemy had come from and take the war to them...and quickly. *And if we can put an end to their war, they might just be grateful enough to help us on our way.*

CHAPTER THIRTY-TWO: NEAR SOUTH GATE, DYSON TWO (SURFACE)

"YOU STILL HAVE TO LET ME TALK FIRST," Marigold teased. "Remember?"

Tobias flushed. It was hard to remember, sometimes, that the locals—they still didn't have a proper name, despite a week of fiddling with the translation software—were a decidedly matriarchal society. Their women stayed in the city and made all the decisions, while the men hunted for food and fought in wars. It was odd, to his eyes, but it seemed to work. The women worked together better than their counterparts on Earth.

He nodded as the locals gathered for a brief introduction to higher technology. It was a joke, at least to his eyes; wheels, catapults, improved bows and arrows, printing presses…there were limits, apparently, to what the locals could duplicate in a hurry. They didn't have much metal and what little they did was more expensive than gold, rarely used for any significant purpose. Tobias suspected the locals would never develop anything more advanced than a steam engine, even if they managed to find enough metal to build one for themselves. The orbital weapons platforms would see to it. A radio transmitter would be blasted with a thunderbolt before the operator could so much as say a couple of words.

And that means they're permanently caught in a trap, he thought. He didn't like the implications. The sphere seemed designed to keep its occupants alive, but not to let them climb above a certain level. Was it a zoo? Or was it just a way to protect intelligent races from their own technology? *How many other races are trapped on the sphere?*

He frowned, inwardly, as Marigold started her lecture. The locals might be primitive, by their standards, but they were far from stupid. Their woodworkers were brilliant. They'd already started improving their old technology and duplicating newer ideas. The wheel had gone into service faster than anything Tobias had ever seen, followed rapidly by several different makes of catapults…each successive version better than the last. They'd done a very good job, he noted. They could dismantle their catapults, move them to a new location and put them together at incredible speed. Tobias wasn't sure even the Royal Marines, trained to operate on a shoestring, could match them.

His heart sank as he watched the ideas sink into the audience's heads. They knew a great deal about their environment—they knew how to make best use of the resources around them—but there were limits to how far they could go. Tobias was fairly sure there was no way they could get into space, let alone escape the sphere. In theory, one could build a spaceship out of wood; in practice, it would never get out of the atmosphere. Perhaps they could figure out how to climb the mountains themselves…

And then die when they run out of air, he reminded himself. *They really are trapped.*

Marigold went on, her audience listening raptly. They didn't seem to pay any attention to Tobias, something that amused and depressed him at the same time. The majority of the audience were female, their bare breasts making it hard to look them in the eye—or, he acknowledged in the privacy of his own thoughts, to take them seriously. He knew he was being an ass and yet, he didn't understand how their society worked as well as it did. Perhaps the locals were just used to walking around in loincloths, and very little else. Nudity wasn't so interesting when everyone was nude.

He kept his thoughts to himself as the lecture came to an end. The craftsmen—craftswomen—asked a series of questions, each one surprisingly insightful. He told himself he shouldn't be surprised. They might know nothing about modern tech, but they knew their fields very well and understood the limits on a level none of the outsiders could match. Tobias had studied uplift techniques, theoretical until humanity had stumbled across the Vesy, and yet pretty much all of them had relied on an abundance of metal. He was mildly surprised Captain Templeton had authorised telling the locals *anything*, even though they couldn't possibly threaten the ship. If the sphere was little more than a vast zoo, where were the zookeepers?

"I saw you staring," Marigold teased, when they were alone. "Their eyes are above their necks, you know."

Tobias flushed. "I..."

"Better be careful," Marigold said. "We don't know how they'll react to you staring at them."

"Hah." Tobias shook his head. "How does this place even work?"

"It makes sense," Marigold said. "Men go out to fight. Some of them don't come back. The women have to do everything else, because women don't get killed so often."

Tobias grimaced. There was something oddly perfunctory about local warfare, as if it was little more than a bloody—in all senses of the word—game. Men got killed, women got carried off and forcibly inducted into enemy tribes...hell, there weren't any real nations on the sphere as far as they knew, just city-states and their surrounding villages. He was surprised no one had tried to unite the cities into a single country, but the technological limits had probably put a stop to it. They just didn't have the power to garrison their conquests, let alone keep them from revolting. Even taking the cities would be difficult. The stone walls were impregnable without better weapons.

Sure, his thoughts pointed out. *Like the ones you're giving them?*

Marigold frowned. "They asked me to stay," she said. "Apparently, I could have a place here...if I wanted it."

Tobias felt a twinge of alarm. "Do you want to stay?"

"No." Marigold snorted. "I don't know if they've worked out none of this is actually *my* innovations."

"True." Tobias had read, once, an *isekai* series in which the protagonist—a young woman trapped in a primitive world—had introduced everything from gunpowder to steam engines and railways, sparking an industrial and political revolution that had changed the world beyond repair. It had always struck him as impossible, if only because of the sheer unlikelihood of someone who knew how to do it surviving long enough to actually *do* it. "If they do..."

He scowled. *Endeavour's* analysts had sketched out dozens of ideas and were working on hundreds more, breaking down concepts from the distant past and reworking them so they could be put into practice without metal. The locals thought Marigold was the one doing all the work. What would they say when they realised there was a starship, high overhead, feeding them the innovations they wanted? What would they say when they realised they had cousins amongst the stars? What would they say when...he shook his head. Right now, it wasn't a problem. They had to get off the sphere before it was too late.

"Well, as long as they think you know something, they won't do anything to you," Tobias said, finally. The local rules of engagement were surprisingly simple. Men could be butchered at will. Women were taken prisoner and forcibly inducted into their captor's population. Oddly, there didn't seem to be any stigma attached to those who changed sides. It made no sense to him. "Me? I'll be lucky if they only bash me on the head and dump my body in a ditch."

"Looks like it," Marigold agreed. She winked at him. "Give us a week or two and we'll be on the move again."

"Yeah," Tobias agreed. He looked towards the wall—and the distant mountains reaching all the way into space. "And if we can't get back to orbit, we may be trapped here for the rest of our lives."

If she'd been younger, and less concerned about the dangers, Charlotte would have enjoyed watching the local men preparing for war. She'd done her duty—she'd put in appearances at military ceremonials, from passing out parades to funerals and everything in between—but it had never been anything other than a chore. Here...the young woman she'd been would have thrilled to the sight of naked men parading in front of her, carrying wooden spears, bows and arrows. She hadn't seen so much flesh since a brief—and ill-advised—visit to a carnival when she'd been a university student. And *that* had ended very poorly indeed.

She watched for a long moment, torn between envy and pity. The young men in front of her had no concerns, beyond making a brave showing in the coming fighting. The queens—it seemed the right word, although they appeared to be elected to the post—would pick and choose the bravest amongst them, then order the men to sire children. Charlotte hadn't quite worked out how everything worked, but it was clear neither the men nor the women had any great say in who sired and bore the next generation. She suspected the female side of the city was more communal than anyone would care to admit, with the older generation keeping the younger girls under strict control. It was a village, one that had little room for individuality. How could it? Survival came first.

And we're messing this society up, just by being here, she mused. It was hard to determine if the locals were actually smarter, on average, than the Earth-born, but they certainly had a hard core of solid common sense. *What's going to happen when the tech we gave them starts to spread?*

"We should be ready soon," Queen Alane said. She'd learnt English remarkably quickly, to the point she could hold a conversation without a translator. "And then we will move."

Charlotte nodded. It had been difficult to put together a clear picture of local politics—it didn't help that the locals didn't seem to be aware of anything beyond a few hundred kilometres from their city—but it was clear that one city had been dominating the others even if it hadn't brought them under its formal control. Charlotte was surprised the city hadn't tried, although—based on technical limitations—it might have been the wise choice. Better to threaten and bully rather than gamble everything on a trial of strength, one that could easily cost the bad guys everything even if they won in the short term. The locals couldn't regenerate their numbers either, not in a hurry. A costly victory might lead to a string of certain defeats.

"And then you intend to continue on your journey," the queen continued. "Why not stay?"

"We have to reach the mountain," Charlotte said. She'd been cautioned to say as little as possible about their ultimate destination. The locals didn't know about starships—they didn't even realise they were living in a sphere—and it was better to keep them in ignorance, at least until the governments back home decided how to handle the situation. Charlotte was uncomfortably aware they'd already bent the non-interference rules to breaking point. "It's a religious quest for us."

The queen said nothing. Charlotte sighed, inwardly. The locals had been tight-lipped on the subject of religion, something that surprised her. Did they even *have* a religion? She didn't know. It was impossible to say, although she suspected they did. But then, they didn't seem to have much of a history either. They—their ancestors—had to have been on the sphere for thousands of years, yet they didn't seem to be aware of it. Anything past a few hundred years or so ago was just a haze.

They are too focused on survival to develop anything that isn't immediately practical, she reflected. The locals knew a *lot* about using their resources to best advantage, from woodworking to medicine, but there were limits. *They don't even have much of a written language.*

"We understand," the queen said, finally. "But we would ask you and your fellow queens to stay."

Would you now, Charlotte thought. The locals seemed to have a strong taboo against killing women, although they had no qualms about kidnapping and forcibly integrating them into their new societies. They hadn't been very clear on how this was done, but Charlotte could guess. *And do you want us to stay because you want to keep us safe, or because you want hostages?*

She sighed inwardly. There was no way to know. She understood aristocrats, formal or informal, from right across the world. She had more in common, in some ways, with a Russian or Chinese oligarch than the average British citizen. But here...society had clearly developed along very different lines. It was impossible to predict how the locals would react to anything. Hell, she wondered—and she suspected some of the analysts on the ship agreed with her—if the women weren't provoking small wars, really nothing more than skirmishes, to keep the male population under control. It made a degree of sense. The wars would kill off the more aggressive men, the ones who might seek to challenge female control of their world...

Sure, her thoughts mocked. *Or maybe you're just being paranoid.*

"We have to stay together," she said, finally. "The men will do silly things if left unsupervised."

The queen smiled, then turned to leave. Charlotte watched her go, feeling decidedly dowdy. The xenospecialists swore blind the locals were *human*, with minimal genetic drift, but there was something about the way they moved that made her wonder. Their skin colour was understandable. Their movements...she shook her head, telling herself she was wrong. The locals had grown up in a very limited world, with no room for anyone—male or female—who couldn't pull their weight. The queens might be the leaders of the community, but they still had to work. Queen Alane was fitter than the average servicewoman.

And there's no way I could walk around so underdressed, she thought. *They'd probably laugh at me if I did.*

"Lady Charlotte!" Charlotte turned to see Colin hurrying towards her. "Did the queen agree to our suggestions?"

"I think so," Charlotte said. "I don't know how much she understood."

Probably more than you'd like to believe, her thoughts added, cynically. She'd noted how close the locals had gotten to their guests. Some of them made conversation, practicing their language skills; some had merely served in the background, listening to everything their guests said. Charlotte was unwilling to believe the locals couldn't remember everything they heard. *Once they picked up the basics, they could repeat what they heard and translate it.*

"As long as we stay together, we should be fine," Colin told her. "Unless you *want* to stay here?"

Charlotte shook her head. The locals had done what they could, but the accommodations simply weren't very good. The beds were little more than blankets, the food was very plain and the less said about the toilets the better. They understood the value of cleanliness, at least, but still... she had been told human waste could be used to make gunpowder, with the right knowledge, yet she found the thought disgusting. Besides, that might draw attention from the orbital weapons. They'd have to test them, when they got back to the ship, and see just *what* drew fire.

And besides, I wouldn't last long here, she reflected, ruefully. The soldiers might be able to blend in, but not the civilians. She was uneasily aware that, compared to the local women, she wasn't particularly healthy. *The environment will kill me even if the locals don't.*

"I thought not," Colin said. "You know they've been propositioning us?"

"Not me," Charlotte said. Her earlier thoughts haunted her. "I suspect they want a little more genetic diversity."

"If they understand the concept," Colin said. "Should we?"

Charlotte frowned. Her distant ancestors hadn't understood how diseases spread, but they *had* realised that spending time with the visibly infected was asking for trouble. They'd bricked up plague houses, leaving the infected in a form of primitive quarantine in hopes they would either recover or die without infecting others. It was quite possible the locals knew more about genetics than anyone thought, even if they didn't understand the concept. The incest taboo was pretty much universal, right across the globe. There weren't many societies that had ignored it and those that did had tended to come to bad ends.

Like all the old-time aristocrats who insisted on only marrying other aristocrats, she recalled, wryly. *Most of them ended up with hereditary disorders of one kind or another.*

Colin cleared his throat. Charlotte forced herself to think.

"I don't see any problem, as long as they don't mind the children being fatherless," she said, slowly. The locals did seem to segregate the sexes, as soon as the children were weaned. "It might be good for them."

"And if they do object?" Colin met her eyes. "They are quite blatant about it."

"Ask them," Charlotte said. Given what she'd seen of local society, there was no way it was an accident. The matriarchs had probably given their blessing, encouraging the younger girls to try to seduce the soldiers. "If they're fine with it, go ahead."

"Thanks." Colin grinned, then sobered. "Are we doing the right thing?"

"I wish I knew," Charlotte admitted. "We don't know anything like enough about the local situation to be sure we're on the right side. For all we know, our allies are just as bad as their enemies. Or they have habits we'll find repulsive. But do we have a choice?"

"No," Colin said. They'd discussed sneaking out of the city, only to decide it was impossible without starting a fight. "I think we were committed the moment we made contact with them."

"Yes," Charlotte agreed. There were academics, back home, who'd argue the question until everyone was thoroughly sick of it. But none of those academics were actually on the ground. They weren't the people who had to make the call—and then live with the consequences. "And that means we'd better ensure our allies win the coming fight."

CHAPTER THIRTY-THREE: NEAR SOUTH GATE, DYSON TWO (SURFACE)

COLIN HAD ASSUMED, RATHER NAIVELY, that the local warriors would march from one city to the next, mounting attacks that were little more than glorified raids. In that, he'd discovered very quickly, he was wrong. The locals could and did make their ways through the trees in ways that would awe a special forces soldier, but they used canoes to get around the region surprisingly quickly. Indeed, reading between the lines, the only reason the bad guys had become an overwhelmingly powerful threat—at least by local standards—was that their city rested on a lake, which was linked to nearly every river in the region. They didn't have to exert much force, he reflected, to overshadow every other city within a few hundred miles of the lake.

He sat in a canoe and watched as the local boatsmen steered their way down the river. The invasion fleet was laughable, compared to the giant seaborne forces that had invaded Europe in 1944 or retaken the Falklands in 1982, but the fifty or so canoes of various sizes were surprisingly mobile by local standards. The boatsmen had no trouble racing downstream, while archers scanned the horizon for possible threats. Colin's training told him he needed to be careful—one man with a machine gun could obliterate the entire fleet—but his intellect suggested otherwise. They were relatively safe as long as they stayed out of spear-throwing range.

Which might not be anything like as short as you want to think, Colin reminded himself, thoughtfully. *You used to watch professionals throw javelins for hundreds of metres, remember?*

He glanced back, eyes picking out Lady Charlotte and Doctor Gaurs in the rear boats. The locals had come close to flatly refusing to let them sail, although Colin couldn't tell if they were being overprotective or if they wanted hostages. Local society was decidedly odd by any reasonable standard. Colin had never imagined so many girls coming to him and asking for sexual favours, let alone to have his children. He wasn't sure if he'd done the right thing, when he'd slept with them. The thought of leaving his children behind to be raised in such a weird society was fundamentally *wrong*. And yet, he'd had no choice. They couldn't risk offending their hosts.

At least they weren't interested in Tobias, he thought. *That would have put the cat amongst the pigeons.*

The boat shifted as it hit an eddy, the water picking up speed as it flowed down to the lake. Colin thought he could smell humans on the air, the wind blowing the scent to him...the city was dead ahead of them, even if it was still hidden by the jungle. The baddies—they hadn't been able to work out their name, or even the name of their city—had gotten lucky. They'd had two cities which they'd merged into one, giving them a considerably greater level of resources than their more distant enemies. Colin had to admit they'd done well, given the technological limitations. They might not be able to create a formal empire, let alone a country, but they'd put together an informal alliance that put the Athenian Empire to shame.

He braced himself, holding his rifle at the ready as the boats steered towards the shore. It was hard to believe they hadn't been spotted, although it was actually quite possible. The locals didn't have radios or landlines, not even trained carrier pigeons. The fleet might well outrun any warning of its presence. He told himself not to be overconfident as the first canoes hit the shore, the warriors darting onto land with a striking disregard for their own safety *and* for that of their boats. It wasn't as careless as it looked—the locals could cut down trees and produce new canoes with a few hours hard work—but it still bothered him. The next wave of canoes landed moments later, the crews hastily unloading the supplies and dumping them onto the beach. It looked like organised chaos, but they'd practiced time and time again until they could practically do it in their sleep. Colin smiled, despite the growing tension. He hadn't realised how hard it was to train soldiers until he'd had to do it himself, training men who already thought they knew everything. If he got home, he promised himself he'd find his instructors and take them out for a beer. They'd done a very good job with unpromising material such as himself.

And the locals have no real concept of organised war, Colin though, as the first scouting parties set out into the wild. *They really think this is just a glorified raid.*

He scowled, remembering how the attackers had tried to drag off the women. He'd saved them and…he'd heard, in the aftermath, stories of how prisoners were broken and integrated into their new communities. It sounded like brainwashing, only worse. He'd never heard of anything like it, not on Earth. There'd been a vague report of a soldier who'd gotten lost on patrol, in the Security Zone, and somehow found himself adopted into a community, but he'd always assumed it was little more than army rumour. He certainly hadn't heard any confirmation. But then, it was the sort of thing the brass would try to keep from the troops.

Sweat prickled down his back as he took one final look at the coolies—it had been hard to convince the locals to carry more than their weapons, but worth it—and joined the next force as it headed into the jungle. The trees seemed thinner, as if a number had been taken out…they probably had, he decided. The locals had chopped down hundreds of trees, but they just didn't have the technology to make a *real* dent in the jungle. Deforestation wasn't a threat, not yet. He hoped that wouldn't change in a hurry, even though the locals needed better roads to circumvent the rivers and lakes. Now they had the wheel, they'd need roads to put it to good use.

And shake themselves to bits, without suspensions, he reflected. The first carts had been miles better than anything the locals had developed for themselves, but their suspension was practically non-existent. *They'll have to come up with something to compensate or simply put up with it.*

The trees parted suddenly, revealing a lake. It was bigger than any lake he'd seen back home, big enough to pass for an inland sea...he frowned as he saw the giant city, resting on islands in the middle of the water and linked to the mainland by a single giant causeway. The wind shifted, blowing the stench against his nostrils as he surveyed the scene. The city's stone walls looked strong in places, surprisingly weak in others. He couldn't help thinking of the Tower of London. The Tower had places for boats to dock, too.

And this city sits at the heart of a trading network, he noted. The waters were alive with canoes, bobbling on the waves. *They have to let people dock all the time.*

He barked orders, sending the troops rushing to the causeway. A howling note echoed across the waters, followed by a grinding sound as the enemy hurried to raise the drawbridge. Colin was surprised they even *had* a drawbridge. He hadn't seen anything like it in the other city, although it would probably have been pointless. The locals hadn't even thought to dig a moat in hopes of protecting their walls...why bother? It would be difficult without metal tools and, if they were surrounded, would be just as dangerous to them as the enemy.

Jones came up behind him. "One missile and the city walls would be rubble."

"We don't have any missiles," Colin said. The ship was too far away to drop KEWs and, even if it did, the orbital defences would vaporise the projectile before it hit the target. "And..."

A thought crossed his mind. He considered it briefly, then placed it in reserve. "Watch the assault force," he said. "We need to get across that bridge, if possible."

It wasn't going to *be* possible, he realised a moment later. The assault force was good, but the defenders had a slight edge. They held the line long enough for the drawbridge to rise completely, then dived into the water and swam like hell. Colin sighed inwardly—he hadn't planned on the assumption they'd take the causeway but failing would damage his side's morale—and then turned his attention to the archers. They'd been practicing with their new weapons for the last week. Would they be enough to give the enemy a very hard time?

He leaned forward, watching as enemy canoes formed up to hurl spears at the shore. It was an odd tactic, although he had to admit it had its uses. The canoes were fast enough to make it harder for anyone to hit them with a spear, though they clearly hadn't prepared for bows and arrows. Colin smiled grimly as they recoiled in shock, bodies falling into the lake as they tried to retreat. The arrows were an unpleasant surprise. They'd need time to come up with a countermeasure.

Or simply put them into production for themselves, he thought. He had no illusions. The baddies had seen the bows in action. They'd have their own designs within the day, then start putting them into mass production. *Given time, they could yet turn the siege around.*

He glanced at Jones. "Set up the catapults," he ordered. The local troops looked as if they expected to be ordered to turn and leave at any moment. It made a certain kind of sense—they didn't see any point in taking heavy losses for nothing, and the enemy city was largely untouched by the fighting—but he had no intention of letting the attack turn into a rout. "We need to batter them into submission."

The enemy canoes retreated, followed by hissing arrows. Colin studied them through his optical sensors. They looked shocked beyond words. They probably hadn't believed what had happened to their raiding party, not if so few warriors had returned home to tell the tale. How many of them *had*? Colin didn't know. They should have made it back by now, if his rough calculations were accurate, but there was no way to be sure. Anything could have happened to them, in a jungle teeming with dinosaurs and other creatures. Or they might have been reluctant to return home and face the music.

He sighed inwardly, forcing himself to watch and wait as the catapults were shoved into position, then primed to fire. The local warriors still looked as if they expected to be ordered home at any moment, something that irked him. No *wonder* none of the local cities had been able to build a proper country, let alone an empire. They just didn't have the tech to take a well-defended city. The walls he could see, on the far side of the water, were strong enough to ward off anything that might be thrown at them, at least until now. Bombarding the walls with spears would be an exercise in futility.

They don't think like us, he reflected, as the first of the catapults was finished. *They don't take family ties seriously. They don't fight to defend their women and children, but their city. And they don't think there's any such thing as ultimate victory.*

"Fire," he ordered.

The catapult jerked as it hurled a rock towards the enemy city. It crashed against the wall, cracks appearing against the stone. The warriors stared, torn between shock and awe. They hadn't really expected it to work, Colin noted, even though they'd practiced assembling and firing the catapults over the last week. The idea of a stone damaging the great walls...he wondered, numbly, if the warriors truly understood everything that had happened in less than an eyeblink. The nature of war on the sphere had changed forever. If walls could no longer keep out armies, who knew what would happen next?

It shifts the balance of power, Colin reflected. *And it makes an empire possible for the first time.*

He nodded to the warriors, directing them to continue firing. The city was largely built out of stone. It was unlikely it would collapse in a hurry, but a prolonged period of bombardment would do a hell of a lot of damage. Who knew? It might convince the bad guys to surrender while they had a city left. If the damage went too far, they might find themselves unable to rebuild before it was too late. The survivors would be jumped and slaughtered by the massed armies of the cities they'd bullied over the years.

The men will be slaughtered, Colin corrected himself, as the next salvo of projectiles flew through the air. *The women and children will be integrated instead.*

He frowned, noting their accuracy could be improved. Ten projectiles, four of which had hit the water. Waves splashed against the walls, but did no significant damage. He wasn't surprised. The remaining projectiles came down within the city, yet it was hard to tell how much—if any—damage they'd done. The city was big enough to absorb a few blows. His earlier thoughts came back to mock him. There was a way to do far more damage in a single blow, but the risks would be considerable.

"This could go on for quite some time, sir," Jones said, quietly. "They might not even be *able* to surrender."

Colin winced. The defenders wouldn't surrender if they thought they'd be slaughtered out of hand. Even if they wanted to, how *could* they? There was no conception of raiding a whole city, let alone a universally understood way to surrender. No white flags, no deactivating the drive field and hoping the enemy realised what you were trying to do before they blew you away…he kicked himself, mentally, for the oversight. The plan had been to force the city to surrender, or batter it into ruins that could be stormed easily, but he was starting to think it wasn't possible. The enemy just didn't have the concept of surrender.

"We'll continue the bombardment for the moment," he said. "And then we can at least *try* to convince them to surrender."

Jones snorted. "Good luck, sir."

"Cheeky bastard," Colin said. "Get back to work."

He gave orders for the boats to be brought around to the shore, so they could launch an assault on the city itself, then settled back to wait. He wasn't sure how they could convince the enemy to surrender and… he wasn't even sure their allies would *accept* the surrender, even if it was offered. There *had* to be limits to how many enemy personnel they could integrate at any one time and they'd be reluctant to try to integrate men... he shook his head in disbelief. The whole idea of integrating enemy prisoners was just bizarre. He had no idea if it had ever worked, in the long term, on Earth.

The warriors grew more and more restless as the day wore on. Colin tried to keep them busy, prepping the boats or patrolling the surrounding region to make sure the enemy didn't land an army some distance away and try to take them from the rear. His lips quirked at the thought as another round of crashes echoed across the lake, then faded. The walls were steadily weakening, but the damage wasn't great enough—yet—to allow them to storm the city. At close range, all their advantages—as slight as they were—would be minimised. The enemy might have a chance to bleed his force white.

And then we might not be able to continue the offensive, he thought. *What will happen then?*

His mind raced. They could mount an offensive against the drawbridge and try to bring it down. If it fell, he could get troops across the river and into the buildings...and yet, that would still leave them with the problem of *storming* the city. He briefly catalogued the modern weapons at their disposal, but there were nowhere near enough to make a serious difference. They didn't have the ammunition, nor did they have the time to put some of the nastier ideas from the ship into production. And that meant...

He waved to Lady Charlotte and Doctor Gaurs, who'd been watching the affair from a reasonably safe distance. They looked as tired and worn as Colin felt, even though they'd done little beyond riding in the canoes and watching the display. Colin reminded himself, savagely, that neither of the women had expected to find themselves trapped in a primitive war zone. They'd thought they'd meet the Builders themselves. Colin wished, not for the first time, that they'd been able to land near the supposed command centre. It would be nice to determine, if nothing else, what it *was*.

"My Lady," he said, as Lady Charlotte approached. The locals seemed adamant that men should always offer the proper respect to women. "Are you interested in trying to make overtures to the enemy?"

Lady Charlotte blinked. "Are you serious?"

"Yes," Colin said. "The bombardment hasn't been as effective as we'd hoped. Storming the city is going to be costly as hell. And if we prolong matters, our allies are just going to turn and go home."

"Which will make things worse, as their enemies will duplicate their new weapons," Doctor Gaurs said. "Right?"

"Right." Colin let out a breath. "There's one other thing we can do. But it will be risky. If we can convince them to accept terms…"

"I'll try," Lady Charlotte said. Her face was very pale. The locals might revere women, but that didn't mean she'd be safe. "And if it doesn't work?"

"Then we gamble," Colin said. "And we might lose."

CHAPTER THIRTY-FOUR: NEAR SOUTH GATE, DYSON TWO (SURFACE)

IF THIS GETS OUT, BACK HOME, Charlotte thought, *I'll never be able to show my face in polite company again.*

She stood in the prow of a canoe, stripped to the waist. She felt naked in more ways than one, even though the only thing standing between her and a spear to the chest was the enemy's awareness she was female. Offhand, she couldn't recall any ambassador being asked to strip down to underwear before attending an important diplomatic meeting, not even in the most paranoid parts of the world. The closest she could think of was human ambassadors wearing bathing suits when they spoke with their Tadpole counterparts, but the Tadpoles found human biology as bizarre as humans found theirs. Here...

They used to make surrendering prisoners strip naked, when it became clear some of them were ready to break the laws of war and use surrender attempts to cover for a final suicide attack, she thought. *And people stopped making a fuss about it after the number of reported attacks dropped to zero.*

Charlotte clasped her hands behind her back, uneasily aware of eyes watching her. She knew how to swim—she'd been a very capable swimmer, back in her youth—but she doubted she could jump into the water in time to evade an incoming spear. The enemy could throw their spears quite some distance, to the point she was probably already well within their range. There weren't many men in the open—the bows and arrows had driven most of the defenders into cover—but there were quite enough to kill her. Charlotte felt her skin crawl as the canoe nosed towards the jetty. The mission would either boost her career to the point *no one* could ignore her again or end with her dead body floating in the waves.

Her eyes narrowed, just slightly, as an older woman stepped into view. She was as underdressed as Charlotte herself, but she held herself in a manner that suggested she didn't feel remotely vulnerable. Charlotte wondered just how much of that was an act. The city had taken less damage than they'd thought, from what she could see as the canoe bobbled against the jetty, but it shouldn't have taken any damage at all. Her counterpart had to be all too aware there was no shortage of stones, just waiting for the attackers to dig them up and hurl them at the city. Given enough time, there wouldn't be anything like enough of the city left to rebuild.

Charlotte clambered onto the dock—no one moved to help her, something she wasn't sure was local custom or calculated rudeness—and nodded politely to the older woman. The woman studied her for a long moment, her eyes lingering on Charlotte's paunch, before rising to meet her eyes. Charlotte tried not to flush. She'd had two children and never quite recovered her old figure. She bit down the urge to point out that her eyes were above her neckline, gritting her teeth as the woman frowned at her. Local custom was clear. The host got to speak first.

"Greetings," the woman said, finally. "Why have you come?"

No name, Charlotte noted. *And no politeness either.*

"I represent the forces laying siege to your city," Charlotte said, through the autotranslator. It was a calculated risk, but there was little choice. Her grasp of the local tongue was frustratingly weak. And repeating the same thing over and over again in increasingly loud and angry tones would accomplish precisely nothing. "We wish to come to terms with you."

The woman looked, just for a second, completely astonished. Charlotte understood, all too well. The locals had never really been able to do more than skirmish with each other, not until now. Their walls were impregnable. Charlotte looked past her, at the spiderwebs of cracks covering the stone walls. Now, the walls were no longer invulnerable. It was just a matter of time, when the bombardment resumed, before they came tumbling down.

"Terms?" The woman shook her head. "Terms?"

Charlotte resisted the urge to rub her forehead. The woman was too old, too set in her ways, to realise things had changed. She supposed the human race had had the same problem, when it first encountered intelligent alien life forms. The Tadpoles had come very close to winning the war within a few short months of starting it, simply because they represented a threat no one had bothered to prepare to meet. How could they? They'd never considered—seriously considered—a hostile encounter with an alien race.

"You submit to us," she said, flatly. "You stop taxing boats passing through the lake and you stop sending raiding parties to other cities. In exchange for this, we will refrain from pushing our advantage and destroying you."

The woman eyed her thoughtfully. Charlotte suspected she knew what was going through her counterpart's mind. Breaking down the walls would take a long time, long enough—perhaps—for the enemy to start putting together their own bows and arrows. It wouldn't be that long before they had catapults too. And if they surrendered, even on terms...how could they expect the attackers to keep their word? The locals simply didn't have a custom of surrender. They'd expect...

"You cannot have brought enough rocks to batter us into dust," the woman said, finally. "It will take you time to replace the rocks hurled at us."

That was true, Charlotte reflected. It would take time to either find a quarry nearby—it was astonishing how many planets looked like gravel quarries—or have stones shipped down from the city. The defenders weren't going to return the rocks that had been hurled at them, after all. And there was a very real danger the warriors would give up and simply go home. They didn't seem to have any concept of long-term deployments either. The defenders could win simply by sitting tight and waiting.

Or so they think, Charlotte thought. *We have an ace in the hole.*

"This is the one chance you have to come out of this a living city," she said, flatly. If the stories she'd heard were true, the city in front of her had stirred up a *lot* of hatred. "If you refuse to concede now, you'll face our full force."

The woman stared at her coldly. "You will not break our walls," she said, curtly. "And all your tricks will avail you nothing."

Charlotte wanted to scream at her, to tell her she had no idea what she was dealing with, but she knew it would be pointless. The woman didn't comprehend—how could she?—that there was a world beyond the sphere. She didn't even know she lived in a sphere! Her world was a few hundred miles in all directions, if indeed she'd ever left her home and gone exploring. To her, the world was flat and Charlotte—for all the difference in skin colour—was just someone from a distant city. She would find it easier to believe that than the truth.

"When you change your mind, hoist a white flag," Charlotte told her. "Goodbye."

She turned and clambered back into the boat, her back prickling. Colin was watching from the shoreline, she'd been assured, ready to open fire if the enemy tried to take her prisoner, but she hadn't been convinced there was anything he could do. She was lucky they hadn't invited her inside the city, although they would have wanted to keep her from discovering just how badly damaged the city truly was. The canoe rocked as the boatsman steered them away from the shore; she picked up the transmitter in one hand, bracing herself, then keyed the switch and dropped it in the water. Colin had told her what to do, but...

It's the only way to get through the defences in time, she told herself. It wasn't very convincing. Not to her. *We don't have a choice.*

She cursed under her breath as the boat picked up speed. Darkness was approaching, a wave of shadow washing across the land. The moment night fell, she'd been cautioned, the enemy would try to counterattack. They'd never have a better chance. The attackers had to work fast and yet...

We could sail past the city and head to the mountains, Charlotte thought. *And leave the locals behind to fight it out.*

But she knew, even as she thought, that there was no way they could abandon their allies now.

...

Tobias felt oddly discomfited as he watched the boat making its way to the shore. He'd been told what Colin had in mind, from the moment it became clear their shock and awe campaign had failed, but...he still felt as though there should have been a better way. The enemy should have surrendered...he knew, intellectually, that the locals didn't even have a *concept* of mass surrender, yet it was hard to believe. Surely, they weren't complete fools.

The boat hit the muddy beach. Lady Charlotte stood, looking faintly ridiculous in her best approximation of local clothing, and allowed Colin to help her to shore. Colin seemed unbothered by the older woman's appearance, something that left Tobias unsure if he should be amused or annoyed. Perhaps Colin had had too many women, over the last few years, to be impressed by an older woman. Or perhaps he'd just had too many local girls. Tobias was quietly relieved the locals hadn't tried to approach him. It would have been awkward as hell.

Colin caught his attention. "Time?"

"Twenty minutes," Tobias said, checking his wristcom. He would have preferred to use a radio detonator, or a simple microburst transmitter, but the former would have been certain suicide and the latter probably the same. "If you're wrong about this..."

"I understand the risks." Colin gave him a hard look. "And I take full responsibility for them."

I doubt you'll be allowed to take all the blame upon yourself, Tobias thought. He'd silently totaled up the number of laws, regulations and international treaties they'd bent—if not broken—and the number was frighteningly high. *We'll be lucky if we just get told we're being retired from the navy, without any further ado.*

He kept an eye on his wristcom as the troops were pulled back from the shoreline and ordered to get into the trenches, giving the enemy city a respite. They seemed oddly amused by the whole affair, joking and laughing as if they didn't *know* they'd been raining stony death on an entire city. Tobias knew the damage hadn't been as great as they'd hoped, but most of the stones *had* landed somewhere within the island…God alone knew how many people had been killed. Tobias had never had any qualms about firing on enemy starships and starfighters, but a city? How many innocents, women and children too young to be dangerous, were inside the walls? How many of them were about to die?

The wristcom bleeped an alert. He raised his voice. "Get down!"

He threw himself to the ground, Marigold right beside him, an instant before the air lit up so brightly he could see it even though his closed eyes. The shockwave hit a second later, a wave of heat and pressure that passed over his head and vanished into the distance. He heard the sound of falling trees, followed by screams. The troops had been warned not to look at the blast, but they might not have listened. How could they comprehend the hell that had been unleashed on the enemy city?

Tobias rolled over and forced himself to stand. The sky was darkening rapidly, but the night was illuminated by flames billowing up from the lake. Tobias stumbled forward, tripping over fallen branches and nearly walking into smashed trunks, until he was in place to look at the city itself. It was burning brightly, the entire northern side of the city so badly damaged it was difficult to believe it could ever recover. The buildings beyond looked almost melted, as if the heat had been so great it had turned the stone to lava. Even the more intact buildings looked charred, scorched by a heat the locals could not have hoped to create.

"Jesus," someone said, behind him. Tobias glanced back to see Colin. "It looks as if it was hit by a baby nuke."

"Yeah..."

Tobias found it hard to speak as the wind rose, fanning the flames. He saw a burning boat, drifting on the lake before capsizing and sinking under the water. Had there been someone on the boat? He couldn't tell. He felt sick even thinking about it. How many people had died in a single terrible second? How many people had he just helped kill? He knew he'd killed before, always at a distance, always infected zombies who would have killed or infected him too if they had a chance. Now...

He turned away and retched, heedless of who might be watching. He wasn't a killer. He *wasn't*. He'd killed icons on the display, not living breathing humans. He'd killed...they'd been dead already, their bodies hollowed out and turned into hosts for the virus...it wasn't the same. And yet...how did he come to terms with what he'd done?

"It wasn't your fault," Colin said. Tobias realised, suddenly, he'd said that out loud. "We didn't have a choice."

"We murdered hundreds of thousands of people," Tobias snarled. "We did!"

"I doubt it was anything like so many," Colin said. "The city might be the biggest in the region, but it wasn't *that* big."

"We killed them all," Tobias protested.

"Yes," Colin said. "And do you think we had a choice?"

Tobias glared at Colin's back as he hurried to rally the troops. It was easy for *Colin* to do awful things. It was easy...no, he knew better. Colin had seen a simple way to get rid of an obstacle in his path and...and it might even have been merciful, compared to what the locals would have done. They hated the lake city. They'd wanted it gone. He supposed, numbly, they'd gotten their wish. Even if enough of the city survived to be rebuilt, its power had been broken forever.

"They would have killed us, if they'd had the chance," Marigold said. He couldn't see her face in the growing darkness, but she sounded as disturbed as himself. "They'd have killed all of us."

Not you, Tobias thought, although he wasn't sure that was true. The ones on top were the ones who had the most to lose from any sudden change in the balance of power, to the point they might break their normal rules and kill a handful of women to maintain their stranglehold on power. *If they'd killed you too...*

He took her hand and held it tightly, wondering if he'd ever stop feeling guilty. It was one thing to win or lose on a level playing field, but quite another to cheat by convincing the alien weapons platforms to open fire on the city. The blast had been stronger this time, he thought. Were they programmed to do more damage to cities, in hopes of killing whoever had devised radio transmissions? Or had the city simply been more flammable? The stone had melted and the wood had caught fire and...he felt sick, again. The people had probably caught fire too.

...

Colin couldn't understand everything the troops were saying to each other—his grasp of their language wasn't as strong as he wanted—but he could tell they were scared. He didn't really blame them. The catapults might be new concepts, but they were hardly beyond their comprehension. A good look at a working device would be enough to tell a skilled craftsman how they worked, allowing him to start constructing his own. But the orbital weapons platforms? To them, it must look as though the enemy city had been smote by the hand of God.

He moved from trench to trench, doing what he could to encourage them. They'd cross the lake tomorrow to take possession of the city, and what survivors there were. Colin dreaded to think how many innocents had been killed, even if the locals *did* believe the city was a blight on the land. He had no qualms about killing terrorists, and the infected needed to be put out of their misery as quickly as possible, but innocents? It was easy to argue, he supposed, that the women hadn't been innocent...somehow, he was sure that argument would cut no ice with the inquiry. The only point in his favour was that he hadn't realised the blast would be *that* big. He wasn't sure what had changed. Had it been the city? Perhaps it had been more flammable than the shuttle and the surrounding area? Or… the orbital weapons had noted, and fired upon, two radio transmissions in less than a month. They might be programmed to raise the force used with every shot. Given enough time…

There has to be an upper limit, he told himself. It was impossible to be sure. He had no idea how the orbital weapons actually worked. Were they merely hyped-up plasma cannons or something else? Fission beams? Antimatter cannons? Or what? *Can they keep raising the power levels until they burn a hole through the sphere itself?*

He frowned as a thought struck him. It seemed impossible and yet… *Was that how the other sphere died?*

"I'll keep watch, sir," Jones said, as he finished his rounds. "You get some rest."

"Thanks," Colin said. "I'll see you in the morning."

But in truth, he knew as he found somewhere to sleep, it was unlikely he'd get much rest at all.

CHAPTER THIRTY-FIVE: HMS ENDEAVOUR, DYSON TWO (INTERIOR)

"IT DIDN'T WORK," Jenner observed, as the icon vanished from the display. "They killed the drone before it reached the mountaintop."

Staci nodded, too tired to feel anything but numb. They'd spent the last week poking and prodding at the orbital defences, in hopes of finding a way through them or for the defences to alert someone a little higher up the food chain. Staci was sure they could talk to an *intelligent* entity, one smart enough to look at the situation and determine the sphere's surface wasn't under threat of bombardment, but so far they were just dealing with automatic systems that were extremely perceptive and terrifyingly trigger-happy. Every attempt to get something down to the surface had failed.

She scowled as the display blanked, then refocused on the next probing attempt. Her crew—and the Chinese—had come up with all sorts of ideas, from cloaking devices to stealth coatings and even heavy armour in the hopes the probes would survive long enough to reach the surface. The Chinese had even taken a piece of debris from Dyson One and turned it into a shield, but the alien energy weapons had sliced through the unobtanium as effortlessly as it had cut through everything else. Staci was *sure* there had to be limits—no one in their right mind would want the orbital platforms firing *that* sort of energy at the surface, it would be like firing a gun inside a life support bubble—but where were they? It was starting to look as if the whole plan was a non-starter.

And we have worse problems, because we've already meddled with the native society, she thought, numbly. She was either going to be rewarded or put in front of a court martial when she got home and, right now, she honestly wasn't sure which. *If our people are stuck down there forever, do they have a choice?*

"The second drones are being deployed now," Jenner said. "They'll cross the engagement line in twenty minutes."

Staci nodded, although she had little hope any of them would reach their target. The alien sensors were just too good. They saw through cloaks and stealth coatings as if they simply weren't there, to the point she suspected that trying to hide the probes was a waste of effort. The moment the drones crossed the engagement line, they'd come under fire. And none of them would survive long enough to reach the surface.

The shuttle reached the surface, she mused. *It crashed, but it got down intact. Did it survive because there were living people riding it down?*

She dismissed the thought a moment later. The Chinese shuttle had been crewed too and *it* had been vaporised with a single shot. Hell, the British shuttle had been targeted too. Had it survived because it had managed to get into the safe zone before the orbital platforms could retarget and blow it away? Or because it had flown through a crack in the enemy defences? Perhaps they were programmed to ignore anything below a certain level until it started broadcasting radio transmissions. The more she looked at how the sphere was set up, the less she liked it. She was starting to think the analysts who thought it was a zoo for intelligent life forms were correct.

And that is a terrifying thought, she told herself. *If this is a zoo, where are the zookeepers?*

The thought plagued her waking moments and haunted her dreams. The Builders had dismantled a number of star systems to build their spheres. Had they intended to do the same to Earth? They might have decided to preserve something of the planet's native life, if they'd put it on the list for destruction. And yet, they clearly hadn't done anything of the sort. Earth had survived long enough to give birth to an interstellar civilisation. She wondered, idly, just what would happen when *that* little titbit got home. There'd been stories about alien civilisations kidnapping people, back in the Crazy Years. The sphere's civilisations was proof there was some truth to those stories.

And the world will go crazy, when the truth comes out, she thought. *Perhaps the Admiralty will try to convince the government not to share the news with anyone...*

She shook her head. That wasn't going to happen. The other governments might not go along with it. Even if they did, something would leak out...and probably grow in the telling, if it became clear the government was hiding *something*. The virus had undermined a great deal of trust in the government, ensuring any cover stories would be treated with great suspicion...she sighed, inwardly. What choice did they have? The sphere was clear proof there were races with technology light-years ahead of humanity's best. The culture shock alone would shake the human race to its foundations. There would be riots and chaos and all for nothing.

"Mr XO, you have the bridge," she said. "Inform me if anything changes."

"Aye, Captain."

Staci stood and walked the decks, moving from department to department. Her crew were on edge. She understood, all too well. They were in an alien environment, a dangerously unpredictable realm. They might be blasted at any moment, without warning, or simply ignored until they gave up and went home. It was being ignored, she suspected, that was really getting to her crew. No one in their right mind would let a survey ship potter around their system, gathering all sorts of intelligence, without making at least *some* attempt to communicate. Staci had seen the contingency plans. An unknown alien starship that entered the Sol System without permission would be greeted by a multinational task force, then—if it refused to communicate—stopped by force. The planners weren't blind to the risks—the starship's masters might be far more advanced than humanity—but letting the ship gather intelligence and go was not on the cards. And yet, the Builders seemed content to do just that.

She frowned as she made her way into the engineering department. They were steadily running out of supplies, even though—technically—they could remain on station for several months if necessary. The Chinese had been pressing for both ships to withdraw and return to Earth, to arrange a multinational effort to explore the sphere. Staci suspected, reading between the lines, that Captain Yunan was pushing his ship's crew to the limits. She was surprised he hadn't asked her for assistance. It wasn't as if she couldn't deduce his problems for herself. She'd spent most of her career on small ships. He *had* to be pushing his operational limits as far as they would go.

"Captain," Chief Engineer Daniel Barnett said. "We have the mountaineering vehicle ready for launch."

Staci frowned. The mountaineering vehicle looked like a cross between a worker bee and a giant mechanical spider. The army had experimented with walkers, if she recalled correctly, although they'd never gone into mass production. She wasn't sure why the army had discarded the concept. Walkers could go places tanks couldn't, not without leaving one hell of a trail. And yet...she felt her frown deepen as she studied the vehicle. It was perfect, save for one problem. They couldn't get it to the mountaintop, let alone down to the surface.

"Good," she said, finally. "But right now, we can't deploy it."

"I was thinking about that," Barnett said. He handed the final checks over to his crew, then led the way to his office. "I think there may be a way to spoof the enemy sensors."

Staci frowned as she took the offered chair. The engineer's office gave the impression of being cramped, even though it was only a little smaller than her ready room. The bulkheads were covered with starship diagrams, the desk littered with datapads and engineering models; the air thrummed with the steady beat of the drives, somehow louder here despite the sound baffles worked into the design. She had the feeling Barnett had been sleeping in his office, as he tended to the drives, designed the mountaineering vehicle and studied the sphere's interior. His holographic projector was displaying everything the passive sensors had been able to discern about the sphere.

"The Builders had—have—far more advanced gravity manipulation technology than ourselves," Barnett said, as he poured them both coffee. "They clearly went to a lot of trouble to ensure the sphere had a gravity field of its own, as well as"—he paused—"I think they must have been generating near-permanent tramlines, perhaps even wormholes. The power required to capture a single planet, let alone dozens or hundreds, is incredible, but they could do it. They probably brought the planets here and used focused gravity beams to tear them apart."

Staci sipped her coffee. "I thought that was supposed to be impossible."

"Our gravity beams are…puny, compared to theirs," Barnett said. "The theory is sound. There was a lot of chatter about earthquake generators, back in the day. The only problem is pumping enough power into the beam to make it work. I think the Builders solved the problem and used it to gather enough raw material to build the spheres."

"Right," Staci said. The concept of just how the spheres had been built would have fascinated her, if she wasn't trying to deal with a more immediate problem. "How does that help us now?"

"Their ability to scan the fabric of space-time must be light-years ahead of ours too," Barnett said. "It must be, because they cleaned out entire star systems. If you can do that, to the point there's nothing left bigger than a chunk of rock, you'd have no trouble adapting your sensors to pick up cloaked ships or probes nearing the surface. I think that's why none of our probes got anywhere near the surface. As long as they looked as if they were going to crash, they were targets."

"And got blown away," Staci said. "Why did the shuttle make it down?"

Barnett grinned. "I think the shuttle's destabilising drive field confused the alien sensors," he said. "For a few vital seconds, the sensors couldn't pick out the shuttle's exact location. They may even have thought it was in pieces, and that it didn't have a hope of getting through the atmosphere anyway. It wasn't until the shuttle sent a radio transmission that the defences knew precisely where it was and opened fire. I think we can use our own gravity systems to make it harder for the defences to pick out the mountaineering vehicle, just long enough to land on the mountain. And then it should remain undetectable as long as it doesn't make any transmissions."

Staci met his eyes. "Are you sure?"

"No," Barnett said. "There's a lot we don't know about how the alien technology functions. We know so little that even our best estimates are nothing more than guesses. But it should be doable, at least for *just* long enough to get the vehicle to the mountaintop."

"Very well." Staci felt a twinge of hope, which she ruthlessly suppressed. "Prepare for deployment. If it doesn't work…"

"There's a second possibility," Barnett said. "And it might give us a better than even chance of getting them off the surface in one piece."

Staci listened to his idea, then returned to her cabin for a nap before heading back to the bridge. There was a new energy in the air as the crew went through the final checklist, readying themselves for the deployment. It was a chance, if nothing else…Staci knew, if it didn't work, they'd have to leave the landing party to its own devices until they could figure out how to crack the defences or make contact with the intelligence behind them. The thought of abandoning the landing party was galling—the navy *did not* leave people behind—but she was starting to think she had no choice. Captain Yunan had a point. They needed to pull out, report home and put together a more specialised team to explore the sphere.

"Captain," Jenner said. "The landing craft is ready for deployment."

"Good." Staci studied the display carefully. Technically, the mountaineering vehicle was a spacecraft in its own right, but it was no quicker than the average worker bee. The engineering crews had rigged up an automated shuttle to carry it, giving the craft a marginally better chance of survival. Staci feared it wasn't likely to work as well as they hoped. If at first the alien defences didn't hit their target, they could just try again until they blew it away. "Deploy."

She took her seat and watched as the shuttle—and its cloud of drones—separated itself from the ship. The seconds crawled by, each one feeling like an hour as the shuttle inched towards the invisible line marking the point it would draw fire from the defences. Staci had to admit the Builders had done a good job. They'd left themselves plenty of room to operate in space, while making sure *nothing* could slip through the atmosphere and strike the sphere. It was hard to believe *anything* could punch right *through* the shell, but who knew what would happen if a rock struck the surface. Would it damage the shell? Or would it set off a series of tremors that would eventually tear the sphere apart? It seemed impossible and yet... she understood, now, why so many of her crew had turned to drink. She suspected Yuri Gagarin or Neil Armstrong would have done the same, if they'd gazed upon *Endeavour*. It was so far beyond them it might as well be magic...

"The drones are going live in twenty seconds," Jenner reported. "There's no hint they've been detected yet."

Staci nodded, curtly. The alien weapons platforms didn't have to orient themselves on their targets. She'd slipped drones close enough to watch them firing and it was clear the pulses could come from any point on their hull, rather than obvious energy weapons or missile tubes. The first shot would come without warning...she felt her heart start to race as the gravity haze took shape and form, a field that might—that *might*—mask the landing craft long enough to let it touch down. If it worked...

A warning light flashed on the display. "They fired," McDougall said. "They missed!"

Staci leaned forward as another pulse of enemy flashed through space. The weapons platforms hadn't taken long to realise their error. The haze hadn't faded, which meant...she shivered, inwardly, as a third pulse wiped one of the drones from existence. The gravity haze twisted, making it easier—suddenly—for her to pick out the real shuttle. The automatic systems took control a second later, launching the spider towards the mountains while angling the shuttle towards the sphere itself. She could almost *see* space boiling with gravity waves. The enemy weapons platforms took the bait, firing an entire *stream* of pulses towards the shuttle. It wasn't very accurate, but it didn't have to be. The shuttle vanished in a flash of light.

She switched her attention to the landing craft. The spider had slowed as it approached the mountains, then landed neatly on the rock and waited. Staci felt her breath catch in her throat. The spider was tiny, compared to the mountains. They'd provide all the cover it needed…in theory. Would the weapons platforms fire on the mountains? Or would it contact its superiors and request orders? Or…or what? The seconds ticked away, the spider not daring to move. It was an easy target, if the platforms knew it was there…

"No contact." Jenner said. "Captain, I think we made it."

"Contact the spider," Staci said. "Deploy the drone."

"Aye, Captain."

Staci waited, again. The drone's orders were simple. Leave the mountains and fly back into interplanetary space. A test, to see if the platforms would fire on something *leaving* the sphere. She wouldn't have, if she'd been programming the platforms, but if the sphere was designed to serve as a prison it would be odd if they *didn't* engage anything trying to escape. She'd been told the guards around Colchester had permission to shoot anyone who got over the inner wall, before they could get any further. She wasn't sure it was true, but it didn't matter. The drone barely got a couple of hundred miles from the mountaintop before it was vaporised by the platforms.

Shit, Staci thought.

She took a long breath, calming herself as the spider started the descent to the surface. There was no reason to think it would come under fire, no reason to think it would be taken for anything other than a native vehicle if it was spotted at all, yet...she cursed under her breath as the implications sank in. The engineers had come up with a good plan, but it was one she was *sure* would draw attention. The Builders would react and she had no idea *how* they'd react. What would happen, she asked herself, if they took it badly? They might have good reason to think the humans were trespassers. It wasn't as if they'd programmed the weapons platforms to open fire on passing starships.

If someone breaks into your property and you shoot him, it's their own stupid fault, she reflected. It was a point of law, one settled long ago. *And if they get injured on your property, it's their stupid fault too.*

"Mr. XO, inform the landing party of the spider's approach," Staci ordered. If nothing else, the landing party would have more tools and supplies. "And then start emplacing the drones for Plan Omega."

"Aye, Captain," Jenner said.

Staci took a breath. If it failed, the landing party was dead. If it succeeded, it might draw attention—hostile attention—from the Builders themselves. And who knew what would happen then?

We have to try, she told herself. *And if they do show themselves, we can at least try to talk to them.*

CHAPTER THIRTY-SIX: NEAR SOUTH GATE, DYSON TWO (SURFACE)

IT WAS A TRUTH, Colin had been told during basic training, that humans from different parts of the world reacted differently to different things. A friendly greeting in one culture was a deadly insult in another. A piece of slang in one country could be extremely offensive in another. A loud and brash person might be the boss in one corporate environment, but a childish and immature brat in a second. One person's friendly accent might grate on another person...he'd been cautioned, time and time again, not to assume he knew what someone was feeling, let alone thinking, if they came from a very different society. It was something he hadn't truly grasped until he'd met his first aliens.

And yet, the local queens—there was no better term for them—seemed stunned and horrified by the devastated city.

It was hard to blame them. The northern side of the city was a melted nightmare, as if someone had put a plastic toy in an oven and let it melt before taking it out and leaving it to cool. They hadn't found any survivors, nor any traces there'd been humans within the city before the alien weapons platforms had opened fire. The centre and southern sides had been devastated, first by the blasts and then by the firestorms. It was hard to say how many people had lived in the city, but they'd only pulled a few hundred survivors out of the wreckage. A number were so badly injured they were beyond anything the locals could do for them, save mercy kills. In hindsight, Colin feared they'd made a terrible mistake.

His stomach churned. The baddies had done horrific things to their enemies. They'd killed men with abandon, kidnapped and brainwashed women and children...they'd controlled the trade routes, using them ruthlessly to keep their enemies from banding together against them. They'd even turned war into a game, blooding their warriors without ever pushing so far they couldn't withdraw pretty much effortlessly. They'd been horrible people. And yet, did they deserve to be broken so completely?

It was a hard question to answer. Colin had grown up in one of the roughest parts of the country. He had few illusions. The idealists might believe in the primacy of law, but the law meant nothing when it wasn't enforced. Colin knew, through grim experience, that people couldn't always wait for society to act. He knew a bunch of terrible neighbours who'd been hounded out of their community, he knew a child molester who'd been castrated by a mob after the police had refused to act. He wasn't blind to the downsides—the neighbours had bought their house in good faith, the molester might not have been guilty at all—but what did it matter, when people felt they were on the edge? The rich and powerful and *safe* could afford to take chances. The poor and weak, permanently one missed payment away from total disaster, couldn't. Colin understood the horror Tobias and Lady Charlotte felt at the devastation they'd wrought. He just didn't share it. Some people acted so badly they forfeited all rights to consideration. Or to protection.

Sure, his own thoughts mocked. *And five years ago, Tobias would have thought you were one of them.*

The feeling of unease grew stronger as he—and the warriors—poked through the rubble for survivors. It was clear none of them had ever expected to actually *win* so completely there was little left of their enemy.

Colin understood—the warriors hadn't had the technology to win until the outsiders had arrived—but it still bothered him. He could see a handful talking amongst themselves in hushed voices, glancing at Colin when they thought he wasn't looking. It felt as if he was being singled out for a beating. He kept one hand near his pistol as they made their way from building to building, dragging out survivors and dead bodies alike. Some looked unharmed, as if they'd simply expired from heartbreak. Colin suspected they'd suffocated as the flames ate the oxygen.

He frowned as they opened a building, discovering a number of women and children. The warriors pointed them towards the centre of the ruined city, where the prisoners were being processed. The women stumbled off, looking as if they were too badly stunned by everything that had happened to make any protests, even small token ones. Colin reflected, numbly, that there were a *lot* of them, even if they were only a small percentage of the original population. It was not going to be easy to integrate them into a single community.

I'm sure they'll come up with something, he thought, as they probed through the charred ruins of another building. *And...*

He ducked instinctively as someone came at him, swinging a club the size of a rifle. Colin darted back, then slammed a hand into the man's chest. The warrior struck the ground hard, choking violently. Colin held up a hand to keep the other warriors from grabbing the stunned man and beating him to death, then sent him to the makeshift POW camp. He had no idea what was going to be done with the men, let alone the boys on the verge of manhood. The local practice—slaughter them all—was unacceptable. And yet, could it be stopped?

His heart sank as he reached the edge of the city, docks broken beyond easy repair, canoes little more than scorched wood or piles of ash. A handful of friendly canoes were speeding through the water, bringing warriors and ambassadors from other cities. Colin wondered, idly, what the locals would do, now that the enemy city was broken. Share out the prisoners? Rebuild the city under joint control? Or burn what was left of it and salt the ground? He sighed, inwardly, as he spied the bodies bobbing in the waves. It was quite possible they'd backed the wrong side, or that the good guys—if given the opportunity—would become as bad as the formerly bad guys. They just didn't know enough to be sure.

But you heard all the stories from the Troubles, his thoughts mocked him. *The good guys were only good because they were on your side, weren't they? There was no real difference between them and their enemies...*

He turned and led the warriors back towards the centre. The female POWs were sitting in rows, looking grim and yet determined to survive and prosper in their new homes. The menfolk, kept well apart from their women, looked broken. Colin rather suspected the fact they *hadn't* been killed was wearing on them. He'd seen that attitude before. He'd even held it himself, before his instructors had knocked it out of him. Where there was life, there was hope. And yet, what did the men have to hope for? Slavery? Or slaughter, without even a chance to defend themselves...? Who knew?

We can't stay here, he thought, as he waved to Tobias and Marigold. They might have gone too far, too fast. The catapults were, as far as the locals were concerned, quite understandable. The alien weapons platforms were an outside context problem. Did they even know what had happened? How could they? *We may have overplayed our hand.*

...

There had been times, in Charlotte's long career as a society beauty—and then as her husband's business manager when he was away on naval business—when she'd *known* she, or others, was losing the respect of High Society. It was subtle, hard to perceive, unless you were precisely attuned to the ebb and flow of a world where one raised eyebrow could mean the difference between being in or out, but it was there. It had been hard, back then, for anyone to exclude her permanently, but...she'd known when she wasn't welcome. And she wasn't welcome now.

She watched the queens—from a dozen different cities talking amongst themselves, sometimes throwing sharp glances at her. Everything had been surprisingly polite and yet, they were on edge. She could feel it. They were acting as if they expected the other shoe to drop, rather than celebrating their victory. She hadn't felt so out of place since she'd been a child, trying to talk to the older teenagers. There was a sense they were just waiting for her to go before starting *serious* discussions.

I think we've outstayed our welcome, she thought, as she bowed to the inevitable and went to find the rest of the team. The enemy city was a nightmarish mess, despite the warriors searching for bodies and the craftswomen hastily throwing together a new bridge to replace the one that was now nothing more than ash. *And they're unsure if they want anything to do with us any longer.*

A chill ran down her spine. She'd never experienced it for herself, not until she'd made the decision to leave her husband, but she'd watched social climbers get excluded for the dread sin of being too blatant about it. They were cut out, left off invitation lists…sometimes, if they didn't get the hint, they were told bluntly they were not welcome. It felt like that, as if the locals no longer wanted them around. She'd known social climbers who were immensely rich, climbers who were disliked even though they couldn't be dismissed easily. It felt as if they were on the verge of getting the same treatment and that meant…

Colin nodded to her as she stepped into their guesthouse, a building that had been scorched by the firestorms, but was otherwise largely intact. There hadn't been any bodies left inside, as far as Charlotte knew. She couldn't help thinking the real owners might return at any moment, although she doubted it. The city's population was either dead, taken prisoner or on the run. Who knew? They might find a place to build a new city and, eventually, come back to take revenge. It might not have happened on the sphere, but it had certainly happened on Earth.

She glanced at the cracked walls, wondering if they could be overheard. There were no servants within the chamber, but that was meaningless. The entire structure could be designed to channel their words to listening ears.

Or…she told herself, sharply, the locals didn't have access to electronic bugs. Back home, there were bugs so tiny they couldn't be seen with the naked eye. Here…

"I think we've outstayed our welcome," she said, pitching her voice as low as possible. "They're unsure what to do with us now."

"I think so too," Colin said. "We might need to leave in a hurry. Tobias is calling the ship now."

Charlotte frowned. On Earth, attacking an ambassador and her staff was a declaration of war. It was taboo. No one would fault Britain for launching punitive strikes on a country that either attacked British ambassadors or failed to protect them properly. Everyone knew the steady breakdown of international law and order had started when a country attacked an embassy and took the staff hostage and got away with it. Diplomats could be kicked out for any—or no—reason, but attacked? It didn't happen. Here…she wasn't so sure. It wasn't as if the locals could understand what *Endeavour* could do.

And she won't, if she doesn't know what happened to us, Charlotte thought. *We could just vanish.*

She turned as she heard someone approaching, just in time to see a young woman enter the room and bow deeply. "My Lady, you and your servants are invited to a formal dinner this evening to celebrate the end of the war."

Charlotte frowned as the woman hurried away. "It's a trap."

"It looks that way," Colin agreed. "I think we need to plan our escape."

Tobias entered, looking oddly hopeful. "Colin, the ship managed to land a climbing machine," he said, holding out a datapad. "It's making its way down the mountains now."

Colin nodded as he scanned the orbital images. "We should be able to get there, if we borrow a couple of canoes," he said. "Tobias, tell everyone I need them back here. Quickly."

Tobias nodded back. "Got it."

Charlotte let out a breath. "Can't we just tell them we're leaving?"

"I don't know," Colin said. "But we scared the piss out of them. And people who are scared make bad decisions."

...

Tobias couldn't say he was surprised, when he was told the locals were preparing to turn on them. He'd grown up in a place where showing gratitude was a bad idea, to the point he could help someone one moment and have them shoving his face into the toilet and flushing it the next. Indeed, like it or not, the locals had every reason to worry about the newcomers and no reason to comprehend how much devastation might be wrecked on them, if they slaughtered the landing party. It was clear, from Jones's explorations of the city, that they were preparing their warriors to rush the party and kill the outsiders before it was too late.

His mouth was dry as he checked his pistol, then glanced at Marigold. She looked as nervous as he did. The locals might believe the outsiders suspected nothing, that they would step into the trap as casually as someone might walk into their own house, but they were about to commit themselves. It would be an utter disaster for one of the landing party to remain alive long enough to make a radio transmission, calling down another strike from the orbital weapons platforms as a final desperate *fuck you* to the locals. Tobias was sure Colin intended to do just that, if they had no hope of escape. It would, if nothing else, take the traitors with them into the next world.

Colin caught his eye. "You know the way?"

Tobias nodded, not daring to speak. The city was a shattered ruin. There was little, as far as they knew, between the handful of inhabited buildings and the docks on the far side. The locals didn't seem to like the dark very much, to the point they kept their cities lit up constantly. He thought he knew how they felt. Back home, going out after dark had been a very bad idea. Who knew *what* might be lurking in the shadows?

"Good." Colin turned to watch the darkness sweeping across the land. "We'll move as soon as its dark."

"They're expecting us shortly," Lady Charlotte said. "As long as they think we're walking into the trap, they shouldn't do anything to stop us."

"Quite," Colin agreed.

Tobias squeezed Marigold's hand as the edge of darkness swept over them. It was the strangest thing about living on the sphere. The inner shell didn't produce twilight, just an instant switch between light and darkness. He slipped his goggles into place, testing the night vision function. The city took on a grey sheen, as if it was displayed on an old television. He felt his heart starting to pound as he led the way onto the streets. They were disturbingly empty.

They did march the prisoners away, once they finished searching the city, he reminded himself. The northern side of the city was lit up by controlled fires, but the south was dark and cold. *Do they want to destroy the remains of the city as soon as they've finished looting?*

The thought mocked him as they slipped down the streets, hiding within the shadows as best as they could. He wasn't sure how well they were hidden. The locals had very good night vision, even without goggles. Colin moved up and past him, rifle at the ready even though he'd told the team he wanted to get them out without bloodshed. There was just too great a risk of them being overwhelmed and slaughtered by sheer numbers, particularly in a confined space. Tobias found it hard to believe—they had pistols and rifles, while their opponents had nothing more than spears and bows—but Colin had been insistent. An arrow through the head could kill them as easily as a bullet.

He smelt dead bodies—and worse—as they neared the docks. A handful of canoes had been brought up on the jetty, then abandoned. It looked oddly insecure to Tobias, although he supposed the canoes weren't particularly expensive. He'd seen a local craftsman carve one out in less than a day. A lone guard stood on watch, swinging around to face them. Colin darted forward, grabbing hold of the guard and pressing something against his face. He stumbled, then hit the ground. Colin checked his pulse, then waved the rest of the team forward. Tobias hurried to obey.

"Get the canoes in the water," Colin hissed. "I don't know how much time we have."

Tobias nodded. The local feasts were loose affairs, with no set start and finish times, but they'd notice if the guests of honour didn't show up soon. If they hadn't already...he put the thought out of his head as he helped move the canoes to the water, then drop them into the lake. Thankfully, Colin had insisted they spend time learning to row during the preparations for war. It wasn't something Tobias had ever thought he'd need back home.

Behind him, he heard a sound. A trumpet...or something like it... joined, a moment later, by drums. A call to war.

"Shit," Colin snapped. He shoved the first canoe away from the docks, then jumped into the second. "Get paddling. We have to move."

Tobias nodded and scooped up the paddle, trying not to shiver at how the boat twitched under him. He'd never gone in a boat before, not even a simple ferry. He knew how to cope with shuttles, but this...it didn't matter. The trumpets, and drums, were growing louder. They'd just run out of time.

"Paddle harder," Colin ordered. "Quickly!"

CHAPTER THIRTY-SEVEN: NEAR SOUTH GATE, DYSON TWO (SURFACE)

COLIN PADDLED AS IF DEATH ITSELF was hard on his heels.

Sweat prickled on his back as he forced himself to paddle even harder. The darkness made it hard to see, even with night-vision goggles, but it was just a matter of time before the locals worked out what had happened and came after them. If he'd had more time, he might have taken the opportunity to set fire to the rest of the canoes, but he suspected it would have been pointless. There were canoes on the far side of the lake, as well as the rest of the docks around the ruined city. There simply hadn't been any time to get it done.

If we can get into the right river, we should start heading south towards the mountains, he thought. The orbital imagery wasn't very clear—and he was painfully aware there were things it wouldn't pick up until it was too late—but the outline seemed doable. There didn't *seem* to be any cities along the river, something that struck him as odd. The river was certainly wide enough to navigate. *Is there something more dangerous down there, waiting for us?*

He glanced back, seeing the city slowly starting to come to life. Lights darted along the ruined buildings, probably torches carried by searchers. How long would it take the locals to determine the outsiders were no longer within the city. Not long, if he was any judge. The locals had to suspect their plans had been rumbled, which meant…the outsiders would have to be insane to stay in the city. They could always just swim, if they couldn't find canoes or one of the sailing boats. How long did they have until the locals came after them?

They might just assume we're someone else's problem now, Colin thought. *If we're lucky…*

He shook his head and kept paddling hard. They couldn't be that lucky. The locals had crossed a line. They might not comprehend the true size and power of the orbiting starship—they didn't understand the concept of rockets, let alone starships—but they had to suspect the outsiders came from a distant, far more advanced city. Letting the outsiders get home, after planning their murder, would be suicidal. He tried to tell himself the warriors might look to the north instead, assuming the outsiders had come from the north rather than the skies, but it was impossible to be sure. They certainly knew the outsiders had been heading south.

And we don't even have time to take a look at the control centre, if indeed it is a control centre, he thought. *We might have to save that for the next voyage.*

"Shit," Jones muttered.

Colin glanced back. The goggles weren't optical sensors, capable of pulling an astonishing amount of data from almost nothing, but they were sharp enough to spot the canoes leaving the city and coming after them. He cursed under his breath as the sound of drumming intensified, drawing the canoes to the drummers like flies to honey. How the hell had they even spotted the canoes in the dark? They weren't lit up…did they think the outsiders were still heading south? Or were they concentrating on uninhabited rivers in hopes the cities further up the settled rivers could block their escape…

We really did scare the shit out of them, he told himself, sardonically. *Bravo.*

"Keep going," he muttered. The river was directly ahead of them—and flowed south. If they could get into the river mouth, they could get the rest of the way. "Hurry."

Jones looked grim. "We're not experienced sailors, sir."

Not all of us. Colin thought. The Royal Marines had made sure he knew how to handle a boat—in hindsight, he deserved a kicking for sneering at the old tradition—but he and Jones were the only ones with any real experience. *They can probably catch up with us, given time.*

He watched the enemy canoes as they picked up speed. The locals knew how to get the best from their craft, more than his team could do. He wished for an outboard motor, or even a proper sail. The range was closing with terrifying speed. He was starting to think they wouldn't get into the river before it was too late.

"Grab the flares," he ordered, grimly. It was probably their last chance to escape before someone got hurt, or killed. "On my command, prep them for two seconds detonation and fire."

"Aye, sir."

Colin glanced at the rest of the team. They were still rowing, but too many of them were glancing back at the approaching enemy. He gritted his teeth—he would have sold his soul for a platoon of Royal Marines—then leaned forward as something *hissed* through the air and hit the water. An arrow, he guessed. The irony of being threatened by weapons he'd introduced was chilling.

"Keep your eyes forward," he said, keeping his voice calm. Tobias and Marigold flew shuttles and gunboats. They weren't used to fighting on the ground. Everyone else was even worse off. "When I give the order to fire, shut your eyes and count to five."

He glanced at Jones. "Fire!"

Jones nodded, launching the flares. Colin braced himself, counting the seconds. It was one hell of a gamble. If the orbital weapons platforms decided the flares were the mark of a developing civilisation and dropped a hammer on them...he shuddered, helplessly. It had to be done. He didn't want to slaughter hundreds of his former allies if he could help it. The light flared, so brightly it hurt even through his closed eyes. He waited for it to fade, then looked at the enemy canoes. Some were scattering, some were…continuing the chase, even though night had turned to day for a few brief seconds. Thankfully, the flare didn't draw attention from the orbital platforms. They didn't seem to notice.

Or they're asking for orders from the higher-ups, he thought. He'd used remote systems himself, but they were never considered entirely trustworthy. The smarter ones were designed to alert their human overseers if they encountered something they didn't understand or couldn't handle. *Will they react or will they just sit back and watch?*

Another arrow hissed through the air. "Take aim," he ordered, reluctantly. "Target anyone holding a weapon and preparing to fire."

"Aye, sir," Jones said.

Colin peered through his scope, cursing under his breath. The warriors were gaining again, paddling their canoes at astonishing speed. They were probably used to water engagements fought by spearmen…he wondered, suddenly, if they'd take the newer and better designs for boats and turn them into something their distant ancestors would recognise easily. The Romans had used catapults and slingshots on their warships, if he remembered correctly. The locals could do the same…

He spied a man drawing back to throw a spear and shot him through the head. The target toppled and fell. Colin hoped the rest would get the message. He couldn't surrender and if they refused to let them run, he'd have to keep shooting and hope for the best. A thought crossed his mind a moment later and he kicked himself, mentally, for ignoring the obvious. The canoes were made of wood. They could put a bullet right through the hulls.

"Aim to sink the boats," he ordered. "They can swim home."

"Aye, sir."

The lake seemed to shift, the water pulling them forward as the river mouth yawed open in front of them. Colin had a sense of rapids, even though he couldn't spot any tell-tale signs as they picked up speed. He fired twice more, silently relieved the canoes were so fragile. Even if the locals started patching them up at once, they'd have problems getting them back on the water in time to make a difference. He saw a man fall and hit the waves, his body vanishing inside a plume of water. Colin told himself, firmly, that the poor bastard could swim.

"The waters are dragging us onwards," Jones said. "And they're getting choppy."

"Paddle carefully," Colin said, grimly. Perhaps the river wasn't as navigable as he'd thought, when he'd seen the orbital images. He'd paddled down the rapids during his training, but it had been in a proper boat with comrades who knew what they were doing. This time...he shuddered, wondering if Lady Charlotte and the others could even swim. He hadn't thought to ask. "We have to get out of the way before they come after us."

He peered into the distance. As long as they stayed in the canoes, they could probably outrace any locals on foot. There were no cars or aircraft... were there horses? Or domesticated dinosaurs? He hadn't seen any locals riding dinosaurs, but it was a possibility that couldn't be ignored. Or maybe the dinosaurs were too wild to be tamed. If he was any judge, young men from all over the region would be putting their lives on the line to try. It would be as good a way to win glory as fighting, perhaps even safer. The older women would be wary of any young man who was *too* aggressive.

"They don't seem to have followed us," Jones said, finally. "Perhaps they've given up."

"Perhaps," Colin agreed. "And perhaps they know something we don't."

•••

Charlotte woke, to bright sunlight.

She wasn't sure quite when she'd drifted off to sleep. Colin had told her and the others that they could stop paddling, now the current was pulling them onwards, but it had been a long time before her tiredness had dragged her down into the darkness. The water below the keel was strikingly blue, filled with shoals of fish that seemed undisturbed by their passing. It was so clear she could see the riverbed, at least five or six metres below. It felt almost like a tropical paradise.

Charlotte looked around, feeling her stomach growl. It *did* seem like a paradise. Birds flew through the trees or stood by the river and dipped their beaks in the waters. Some looked oddly familiar, although not quite the waterfowl she recalled from her childhood; some seemed so alien she had no idea where they'd come from, if indeed they hadn't evolved on the sphere itself. She saw an oversized pelican-like bird dive into the water, scooping up fish in its beak before flying away into the distance, spied a dog-like creature sitting by the river, watching the world go by. None of them showed any real fear of humanity. Charlotte didn't know why, but it bothered her. She knew there were humans only a few short miles to the north.

Perhaps the locals really don't use this river, she thought, as she nibbled a ration bar. *Or perhaps there's just so much wildlife up north they don't have to hunt down here.*

She lifted her eyes to the mountain as it rose in front of her, dominating the skyline even though it was still miles and miles away. It was so big, just like the rest of the environment, that it was hard for her to comprehend what she saw. The mountain looked like a solid wall, too big and strong for her to believe they could climb it…she'd been told a vehicle was waiting for them, but really…it was impossible. She was so small and the mountain was so big its peak was lost somewhere in the bright blue sky. It was hard to believe they were inside a sphere…

Athena stirred and sat upright. "Why did they try to kill us?"

Charlotte was almost glad of the diversion. "We scared them," she said. "And they decided we were too dangerous to keep around."

She sighed, inwardly, as she accepted a ration bar. It was easy to be wary of someone who had the demonstrated ability and *will* to do something destructive, even if they didn't do it to you. Bullies were loathed by all because they could so easily turn on someone else, someone who'd thought the bullying was funny until it happened to them. The catapults had been understandable, improvements of tech the locals already had. The orbital weapons platform was so far beyond them…she sighed. She wouldn't have called down fire on friendly cities. She wouldn't. But she knew the locals wouldn't take that on faith. How could they?

The boat shifted as Colin paddled towards the riverbank. "Give me two minutes to check the area, then we can answer the call of nature," Colin said. "And then we'll resume our journey."

Charlotte nodded and helped him steer the canoe to shore. She wasn't entirely unfamiliar with boats—boating had been part of her education, when she'd been at boarding school—but then, she'd had life jackets and teachers who knew what they were doing. Here...she let Colin do his duty, then answered the call of nature herself before returning to the boat. The local wildlife seemed undisturbed by their presence...

Something flickered, at the corner of her eye. A spear flashed through the air and slammed into Colin's chest. He grunted and stumbled back, just as Jones popped up from the boats—pistol in hand—and shot the warrior. Charlotte shook herself out of her trance and forced herself to go to Colin, hoping and praying the enemy taboo against hurting women still held true. They didn't *know* she'd been the one to carry the radio transmitter to the destroyed city. Colin looked sore, but there was no blood. She stared at him in astonishment as he staggered upright.

"What...?"

"Body armour," Colin said. His breath came in fits and starts, as if he were having trouble breathing. "We have to move."

Jones fired twice more as they dived back into the canoes and cast off, paddling further down the river. Charlotte stared back at the enemy warriors on the riverbank, staring at them as they made their escape. How the hell had they caught up so quickly? It should have been impossible. Or had they simply run into another hostile tribe? It wasn't impossible...

Marigold let out a yelp. Something had lodged itself in her shoulder... Charlotte blinked in shock, then motioned for everyone to get down as she realised it was a tiny dart. A blowpipe? She braced herself, then carefully pulled at Marigold's uniform, hoping desperately the dart hadn't broken her skin. Her heart sank, a second later, when she saw the drop of blood.

If the dart was poisoned, Marigold might be dead before they could get her to the ship.

"Hold still," Charlotte told her. It had been a *long* time since she'd had to do any actual first aid. She kept her voice stiffly formal as Colin opened fire, forcing the tribesmen to scatter and run back into the treeline. "Doctor Gaurs, can you test the dart against the database?"

"Check." Athena took the dart and inserted it into her scanner. "If they're human, or very close to human, it's likely…"

Charlotte glared her into silence. She'd already worked *that* out. The tribesmen wouldn't be using something *useless*. She vaguely recalled a story about a detective who'd chased a man with a blowpipe and poisoned darts…she couldn't remember what had happened, but it didn't matter. Marigold would have been given military broad-spectrum antibiotics, right? Perhaps, just perhaps, some of them would be enough to protect her from the poison…

"A fairly simple poison," Athena said, as the scanner bleeped. "I think she'll be fairly safe."

"You think?" Tobias looked ready to strike the older woman. "Are you sure?"

"I think so," Athena said. She didn't sound confident. "It should be countered by the military enhancements."

"Keep an eye on her anyway," Colin ordered, curtly. "We need to keep moving."

"I'll be fine," Marigold said. She looked shaken, but otherwise unhurt. "What would it do to one of them?"

"I'm not an experienced toxicologist," Athena said. "I dabble a little, as its part of xenospecialist training, but I'm not an expert. My best guess"—she carefully wrapped the dart, then placed it in a sample bag—"is that it would cause limited, perhaps complete, paralysis. I'm not sure how long it would last. If the victim didn't receive proper care…"

"Thank you," Charlotte said, tartly. She looked at the shoreline, suddenly very aware of just how easy it would be for attackers to hide in the shadows. They might not be able to risk landing again, for anything. There could be anything waiting for them. "I get the picture."

"If we get home, I think I'm going to stay there," Tobias said. He reached over and squeezed Marigold's hand. "And to think I *wanted* to be something special."

Charlotte laughed, although there was a bitter edge to it. That remark was closer to her—to her truth—than she wanted to admit, even to herself. Everyone wanted to be special. They just didn't want to accept there was a price.

I wish Mitch was here, she thought, wryly. *No, I wish we were both home, telling each other about our adventures.*

"A common desire," she said, finally. She wondered, suddenly, just what would happen when they got home. She had neither made contact with the Builders nor sat in her cabin doing nothing while *Endeavour* explored the ruins. The PM wouldn't be sure if he should reward her or quietly sideline her, which might be easier if she didn't have a solid success under her belt. "But let's get home first, shall we?"

CHAPTER THIRTY-EIGHT: SOUTH GATE, DYSON TWO (SURFACE)

TOBIAS FELT COLD.

Marigold was fine, as far as he could tell, and yet he fretted. The poison could easily have done long-term damage, even if the vaccines she'd been given when she'd entered the military seemed capable of warding off the effects. She'd been shot with a dart, a primitive weapon that could have been just as lethal as a bullet through the brain or a plasma bolt burning through a gunboat. He felt sick to think of what might have happened to her, condemned to paralysis or death or worse. He wasn't surprised the locals had violated their custom of never harming women. In his experience, such taboos were more than a little flexible, no matter who claimed otherwise.

He kept an eye on the riverbank, and his hand on his gun, as they sailed onwards. The mountains ahead of them rose and rose, seemingly close enough to touch even though they were a long way away. They passed through the endless jungle, broken only by clearings that might—might—have been proof of intelligent life, sleeping in the canoes night after night rather than risk the shore. He overheard Doctor Gaurs talking about altering course, to go find the wretched alien command and control centre, but

Colin—thankfully—overruled her. They had to get back to the ship before it was too late. They'd worn out their welcome on the sphere.

And they turned on us, because they feared what we could do, Tobias thought, darkly. The nasty part of his mind wanted to return with guns or drop rocks on the villages and cities from a safe distance. He knew it was a bad idea, and he would never put it into practice, but it was tempting nonetheless. *We could have done a lot more for them if they'd given us the chance.*

The river widened suddenly, sweeping them into a lake...Tobias had seen it on the orbital maps, when they'd plotted their flight from the ruined city, but the sheer size of the lake still took him by surprise. It looked more like an ocean than anything else, a body of water that would have seemed impassable were it not for the mountains on the far side. Colin muttered a curse, too tired to be loud, as he struck out for the mountains. Tobias bent his back and started to paddle, trying to ignore the shapes in the water below. The orbital sensors hadn't spotted any traces of intelligent life so near to the mountains, but he wasn't reassured. They hadn't spotted the cities either until the landing party had literally stumbled into them.

Marigold caught his eye. "The water must have gathered at the bottom of the sphere."

Tobias shook his head. His head spun as he tried to tell himself that the water *hadn't* flowed downwards until it had pooled around the southern mountains. It was impossible and yet, the mental image was surprisingly hard to get out of his mind. More proof, if any were needed, that an intelligence was quietly monitoring and maintaining the sphere. He wondered, idly, what sort of technology could remain in working order for thousands of years, then shrugged. His father had owned an ancient car he'd lovingly maintained, replacing components as they wore out...Tobias had asked, once, if it was still an ancient car if everything had been replaced at least once. Perhaps the Builders had done the same. They might simply have automated servants repairing or replacing their systems as they wore out, over the years. It wasn't as if it would pose any challenge to them.

"When we get home, I think we should stay there," he said, instead. "I've had my fill of adventure."

"If they let us simply retire," Marigold said. "They'll want to debrief us thoroughly when they hear about the sphere."

Tobias's heart sank. There was no denying that they'd broken the non-interference laws beyond repair. They'd had contact with the locals, they *had* given them new technology...worse, perhaps, they'd done something that had shaken the locals so badly they'd turned on the outsiders. Who knew what they'd make of it, as the stories grew in the telling? Would they assume the outsiders were gods? Or devils? Or...or what? He had a nasty feeling they'd be charged with breaking the rules, even though Captain Templeton had given her blessing to the whole affair. The Russians who'd first introduced modern technology to Vesy had been tried and shot, when they'd been returned home.

Although they were really shot for desertion, he reminded himself, as the wind started to pick up. *They weren't charged with breaking international law.*

The mountains grew and grew until they dominated the skyline, a wall so high they made the Great Wall of China seem tiny. Tobias could believe the locals regarded the wall with awe and fear, if they realised what it was. The scale was so immense they might think it was *just* a mountain, a mountain so high they couldn't hope to reach the top. How could they imagine there was a giant gate on the far side, large enough to take an entire planet? Tobias felt his head swim, again, as they grounded themselves on the far side of the lake. It was just too much to accept, even though he knew it was true. The locals might be happier not knowing the true nature of their world.

"There," Colin said. "It's where they promised."

Tobias nodded, following his pointing finger. The spider-like vehicle was waiting for them, looking oddly out of place against the mountainside. He gazed past the mountaineer, looking up the slopes until they vanished into the clouds. Why *were* they slopes, rather than a solid and utterly unbreakable—and unclimbable—wall? It made no sense. The Builders might have assumed their pets—he shuddered at the thought—might not have been able to climb right out of the atmosphere, but...

Colin was clearly thinking along the same lines. "If they had spacesuits in the command centre, they might have been able to climb out if they found themselves stuck on the surface."

"If they needed to breathe at all," Doctor Gaurs said. "They might have been capable of surviving in space without a suit."

"Perhaps," Colin said. "Tobias, take the wheel."

Tobias nodded and stepped up to the spider. It looked weirdly crude—it had been put together in a machine shop, rather than a proper fabricator—but the hatch opened when he pressed his fingers against the sensor. They'd taken a shuttle cabin, he noted, and turned it into a life support pod, linking the former control systems into the spider legs rather than drive nodes. They'd taken the latter out completely, he noted, leaving only the gas jets. He understood the logic, but suspected it was a waste of time. The last updates from the ship had suggested the weapons platforms were perfectly capable of tracking objects on purely ballistic trajectories.

He glanced over his shoulder as he took the driver's seat. "Get in and get strapped down," he said. It had been a long time since he'd driven anything remotely comparable. He hoped the automated systems were up to the task. "This is going to be a bumpy ride."

"Got it," Colin called back.

Tobias keyed the console, frowning as he triggered the laser communicator. The ship would be waiting for them...he hoped. There was no way Captain Templeton would risk bringing the entire ship any closer to the South Pole than strictly necessary. They might be rescued by a shuttle instead, once they got well clear of the weapons platforms. In theory, they shouldn't shoot at anything *leaving* the sphere. In practice...he thought they were about to find out. It might not end well.

A low hum echoed through the spider. Tobias raised his voice. "Everyone strapped in?"

"Yep," Colin said. "Get us out of here."

Tobias nodded, then tapped the console. The hum grew louder as the spider came to life, spinning around to orient itself on the mountainside before starting to practically glide up the slope. Tobias had expected to feel unwell, perhaps even carsick, but the ride was surprisingly smooth. He wondered, idly, how the spider knew where to put its legs. There was no way it could risk using radar, not on the sphere. Perhaps it was a form of sonar. He didn't *think* that would draw thunderbolts from high above.

He turned his head to peer out the portal as they climbed higher. The sphere still looked as flat as a board, but as he stared it slowly—very slowly—started to curve. The landscape looked green and pleasant, endless jungles broken only by rivers, lakes and seas. He couldn't see any trace of intelligent life, but that was meaningless. The locals didn't have anything resembling modern technology. They hadn't even had the wheel a few short weeks ago. It would be a long time before they made any great impression on the sphere.

The spider rocked, the gravity field seemed to shimmer around them. Tobias braced himself. Leaving the atmosphere was never easy, never routine, even on a planet. Here…who knew? The sphere's atmosphere was surprisingly even—probably because of the artificial gravity field—but there was no way to be sure. He remembered stories from men who'd launched themselves into the atmosphere, gliding from the orbit to the surface. They'd told him the upper levels could be dangerously unpredictable. Right now, he believed every word they'd said.

"Fantastic." Doctor Gaurs sounded stunned. "Who could *build* something like this?"

"We'll be back," Colin told her. Tobias wondered, rather sardonically, if Colin was sweet on the doctor. She was intelligent as well as pretty… the former something the *old* Colin would have rejected without thought, although the more mature version might have learnt to appreciate. "And next time, maybe we can find that wretched command centre."

If it really is a command centre, Tobias thought. The skies were darkening now, wisps of atmosphere brushing against the portal. *For all we know, we were wasting our time.*

He sighed inwardly. He'd never really wanted adventure, for all that he'd wanted to be something special. It wasn't that he was a coward—or so he told himself. He'd just wanted to be safe and comfortable and respected. And...

Colin cleared his throat. "Are we there yet?"

Tobias smiled, glancing at the display. It didn't *feel* as though they'd been climbing for nearly an hour. He didn't blame Colin for being surprised. A regular shuttle took less than ten minutes to reach orbit, which was halfway to pretty much anywhere. The spider was alarmingly fast, disconcertingly so, but it still crawled compared to a shuttle. Or a rocket. Or something else that might draw attention from the orbital weapons. Better to take their time than be blasted without warning...

"We'll be there when we're there," he said. He laughed, despite himself. He knew precisely how Colin was feeling. "Slow and steady wins the race."

"Only if your opponent is fool enough to go for a nap when he thinks he's won," Colin said, although there was no heat to his words. "Can *I* take a nap?"

Tobias shrugged. "If you like," he said, with the private thought it wouldn't matter *what* Colin did. Either they escaped the sphere without being noticed or they got blown away. He didn't think there was any middle ground. If the orbital weapons were powerful enough to cut a starship in half—he found it hard to believe, but the analysts insisted—even a glancing blow would be enough to vaporise the shuttle. "I'll wake you when we get there."

He checked the display, then peered out of the portal. It was clear, now, that they were escaping the interior of a sphere, not a planet. His head hurt as he stared at the scene, spinning in confusion at the sheer *wrongness* of the sight. He looked up as darkness fell over the spider, the inner shell blocking the sunlight and casting a shadow over the land. His head pounded as he turned his attention back to the controls. It was just impossible. He'd seen Venus and Mercury from Earth, but they'd just been flickers of light, no bigger than the twinkling stars. Here...he told himself, firmly, that his imagination was filling in the details. The shadow was clear proof the sun had been eclipsed by the inner shell.

And we're still only halfway to orbit, he thought, numbly. He felt as if he'd fallen into a trance, as if the world around him had taken on an eerie dreamlike quantity that made it impossible to think clearly. *How much longer do we have to climb before we can make the leap into space?*

He checked the display. They had thirty minutes before they reached the peak and jumped into open space. The passive sensors couldn't track the orbital weapons platforms—they were as silent as stealthed recon probes—but he knew they were there. Could they track him? The spider was tiny, compared to the mountain, yet it was moving at a speed that could *not* be natural. Tobias feared, now, they'd been wrong to assume the platforms wouldn't fire on anything below a certain level. If the Builders wanted to keep the locals under lock and key, they'd want to make sure they never built aircraft. It seemed excessive to him—the locals probably couldn't build anything more dangerous than a glider, if they ever developed the concept of flight at all—but who knew? His instructors had told him to be very careful, to check and recheck everything before taking flight. Better to waste time on the ground than deal with a crisis in space.

The spider seemed to jerk as the gravity field twitched, again. Tobias suddenly found it harder—much harder—to determine which way was actually *down*. His head ached again as he glanced back, noting how Marigold had gone to sleep while Doctor Gaurs was drinking in the scene and Colin looked twitchy. Tobias supposed he was feeling helpless. It was hardly the first time he'd been in a shuttle, let alone the first time he was flying through unfriendly skies, but now...there wouldn't be any warning if the orbital platforms targeted them and opened fire. No chance of survival either. The only thing that might keep the platforms from blasting them was the simple fact they were on the mountain, which might be badly damaged if the platforms struck the spider. Tobias wasn't so sure. The mountain walls couldn't be any less tough than the sphere itself and the orbital platforms hadn't hesitated to fire on radio transmissions, regardless of the risks. They might simply not be capable of doing any damage to the shell itself.

"Five minutes to space," he said, quietly. The landscape was smoothing out, becoming a wall. He wondered, suddenly, if dirt and rocks had been drawn to the original wall before the gravity field had come online. Or perhaps it was a deliberate choice. The mountains would make a good storage point for raw materials until they were needed. If one had the power to dismantle entire star systems...he shook his head. It was just too big. "Are you ready?"

Colin snorted. "Do we have a choice?"

"Not really." Tobias wasn't sure *he* could stop the spider from leaping into space, even if the platforms opened fire. The automatics were in full control. "Unless you want to try crawling down the other side instead."

"Bad idea," Colin said. "It might as well be a bottomless pit."

"It does have a bottom," Tobias said. There didn't seem to be a gravity field inside the mountain, one more impossible trick in a sphere full of them, but it didn't matter. There was a closed gate at the bottom, a gate they had no idea how to open. "That's the problem."

He shook his head in disbelief. A gate, a door into the sphere, big enough to take an entire planet? It was just impossible. The analysts were sure there were smaller doors—hatches—built into the bigger one, allowing smaller ships to come and go without opening the biggest hatch... Tobias couldn't wrap his head around it. What sort of ships did the Builders use? Something that made the Death Star look small? The biggest ships the human race had ever built were the giant colonist-carriers and *they* were tiny compared to the Death Star. Who in their right mind would build a starship the size of a small moon?

The spider picked up speed as it neared the peak, preparing itself for the leap into space. Tobias glanced back at the surface, a blue, green and white haze, then turned his head to look forward as the spider jumped.

The gravity field snapped out of existence. Tobias felt a flicker of surprise, even though he should have been expecting it. A gravity field might have been enough to draw attention, if the platforms were looking for targets. And that would be the end.

He gritted his teeth as the stars spun in front of him. They were moving at incredible speed and yet, compared to the sheer immensity of the sphere, they might as well be crawling. It was hard to accept...he knew what it was like to fly through space, yet they were inside the sphere...he told himself not to think about it as they glided further into empty space. If they were lucky, they might just evade detection long enough to be picked up. And then they could rest, before they had to spend the voyage home writing down everything they could recall from the trip...

An alarm sounded. Tobias blanched. "Oh, no."

CHAPTER THIRTY-NINE: HMS ENDEAVOUR, DYSON TWO (INTERIOR)

"CAPTAIN," MCDOUGALL SNAPPED. "Platform Two is targeting the spider!"

Staci swore under her breath. She'd thought things were going too well, despite everything they'd done to smooth the spider's flight as much as possible. The tiny craft didn't have that much propellant, certainly not enough to evade multiple blasts from the platforms until it got out of range. Hell, she wasn't even sure what the platform's upper range *was*. The only thing making life hard for the enemy gunners was the gravity shadows and *they* couldn't be relied upon to keep the spider safe, not when the platforms could simply fill space with blasts until they hit their target.

She took a breath as the first energy blast darted through space, passing so close to the spider that it was probably visible to the naked eye. The energy surge alone would have proven disastrous, if the spider's systems hadn't been hardened. Even so...it was just a matter of time before the platforms got lucky. And then the spider would be vaporised.

"Tactical, trigger the modified probes," she ordered. "And boost the signals as much as possible,"

"Aye, Captain," McDougall said.

Staci glanced at Jenner, who glanced back. The plan was relatively simple, but...she was uneasily aware it might not work. The platforms were *tough*. Worse, they could fire in all directions and engage multiple targets with ease. She suspected the boffins back home would be scratching their heads for years, trying to figure out how the trick was done. If she was wrong, if the platforms didn't react as she'd predicted, the entire plan would be worse than useless. The only upside, as far as she could tell, was that the automated systems *might* send an alert up the chain to someone who could actually think for himself. She might just have a chance to plead her case...

"Going live...now," McDougall said. "Signals pulsing..."

Staci waited, bracing herself. The probes were too close to the weapons platforms to be targeted...she hoped. It would have worked, if she'd tried the same trick on one of the platforms defending Earth. The platforms could no more fire on the probes than she could punch a fly sitting on her nose. But was that true of the alien systems? They'd blown away a Chinese shuttle that had actually *landed* on the platforms, then survived two bomb-pumped lasers at point-blank range...

The first platform exploded, the blast frighteningly powerful for such a small structure. The second died a moment later, the probes caught in the blast, wiped from existence. Staci smiled as the crew whooped, even though she knew *they* hadn't fired the fatal shot. The probes had tricked the platforms into firing on each other, more proof the systems were automated. An intelligent controller would probably have hesitated to fire if they'd realised the other platforms might be hit. Staci had seen starfighters ducking under point defence weapons to evade fire, but here...the platforms didn't seem to be programmed to avoid friendly fire.

"Captain, both platforms have been destroyed," McDougall said, confirming what she'd already seen. "There are a handful of pieces of debris radiating out from the blast zones."

"Mr. XO, dispatch a shuttle to collect one or two pieces," Staci ordered. If they could figure out what the platforms were made of, they might be able to find a way to destroy them that didn't require another platform to do the honours. "And then dispatch another shuttle to pick up the spider."

"Aye, Captain," Jenner said.

Staci glanced at the display. So far, it didn't *look* as though anyone had noticed the destroyed platforms, but that would change in a hurry. How long? She didn't know. The sooner they picked up the shuttles and ran, the better. She'd take her ship back to Earth, report to the First Space Lord and then hopefully get a few days of shore leave before the inevitable Board of Inquiry. It was going to be one hell of a mess for the politicians. Hopefully, the lure of advanced alien technology would keep their minds concentrated.

"Helm, prepare to take us back to the tramline," she ordered. "I want to be underway as soon as the shuttles are docked."

"Aye, Captain."

McDougall looked up. "Captain, long-range sensors are detecting a rammer heading towards us," he snapped. "It'll be here in ten minutes."

Which is pretty much impossibly fast, Staci thought. They *had* attracted attention, although she had no way to know if their enemy was intelligent or just another automated system. She'd played games against computer-generated enemies who weren't intelligent, in any real sense, but still dangerous opponents. *What the hell are we dealing with here?*

"Stand by weapons," she ordered. If they were lucky, a simple kinetic projectile would be enough to take out a rammer. "And use gravity shadows to conceal our exact position."

"Aye, Captain," McDougall said.

"Captain, I recommend we use radio transmissions to draw the rammer onto drones," Jenner added. "We might be able to buy ourselves some more time."

Staci nodded. "See to it."

She gritted her teeth as the rammer came closer, barrelling through space and somehow picking up speed even though it had no visible means of propulsion. No rockets, no drive fields…she couldn't imagine something building up speed so quickly if it was propelled by nothing more than gas jets. They were for manoeuvring, not…she shook her head. It was just one more impossible thing in a sphere *full* of impossible things. The human race would unlock the secret eventually, now that they knew it was possible. She might not live to see it—she conceded the point without rancour—but it would happen. She was sure of it.

"Captain, the shuttles are docked," Jenner reported. "The passengers are entering decontamination."

"The drive fields are coming online now," Atkinson added. "We're heading straight for the tramline."

"We'll try to make the jump at our arrival coordinates," Staci said, grimly. Anywhere else, it would be fairly safe to jump *anywhere* along the tramline. Here, with Dyson One nothing more than an impossibly huge cloud of debris, there was a very real risk they'd make the jump and crash straight into a piece of junk. If they actually interpenetrated…she didn't know for sure what would happen, but she doubted it would be pleasant. "We don't need to take any more risks."

She glanced at McPhee. "Communications, signal *Haikou*. Copy all our files from the sphere to her, then advise Captain Yunan to leave. Now. We might not get out in time."

"Aye, Captain."

Staci nodded. It would be irritating as hell if *Haikou* was the only ship to make it out of the sphere—and there was no guarantee she'd share her records with the rest of the human race—but it was their best shot at making sure *something* got back to the homeworld. Next time, she promised herself, they'd come with an entire fleet of starships and a small army of explorers, with all the tools they needed to sneak down to the surface and back again without drawing attention. Perhaps they'd been looking in the wrong place, she told herself. They could land on the planet, if they could get though the orbital defences, or even explore the inner shell. The sphere's surface was starting to look more like a zoo—and a trap—than somewhere the Builders had intended to live.

Perhaps they were taking samples to ensure something would survive, if they turned our worlds into raw materials, she thought. *Or perhaps they had something more sinister in mind.*

"Captain," McDougall snapped. "The rammer isn't being diverted by the probes."

Staci scowled. The rammer *should* have altered course, *should* have gone after the probes. It hadn't...and that meant it was bearing down on *Endeavour*, altering course slightly to ensure it struck the starship. Staci had no illusions about what would happen, if something that size crashed into her ship at a respectable fraction of the speed of light. The resulting explosion would probably light up the entire sphere. Who knew what the humans on the ground would think of it?

"Deploy kinetic projectiles," she ordered. "Helm, prepare for evasive action."

"Aye, Captain," McDougall said.

We need a smaller ship, Staci thought. A frigate or a corvette could have played tag with a rammer. *Endeavour* was too big and too ungainly to survive for long if she tried. *And we need more ships to back us up.*

Her console bleeped. "Captain, this is Chang in Analysis," a voice said. "I think I know how the rammers fly."

Staci gritted her teeth. "How?"

"They don't have drives of their own," Chang said, as if her CO wasn't already aware of it. "I think they ride gravity beams, used to push and pull them around the sphere."

"Like a laser sail, but more powerful," Staci said. She'd seen the concept discussed for sublight probes, although—as far as she knew—no one had ever put it into practice. Why bother, when one could use the tramlines to get from star to star within seconds? "And that means...?"

She cursed under her breath as the kinetic projectiles struck the rammer and exploded. It should have been enough to vaporise the rammer, as well as the projectiles themselves, but nothing happened. The rammer flew through the blast, unscratched as far as she could tell, and kept heading straight towards her ship. Staci found it hard to believe her eyes. It should have been impossible, but…if the rammer was really nothing more than a solid lump of metal, riding focused gravity beams, it might just be effectively indestructible. And then…

"Deploy the gravity shadows," she ordered. If they could keep the rammer guessing about their exact location, they might just be able to stay ahead of it until they reached the tramline. "Sensors, if it really *is* riding on a pair of gravity beams, try to track them back to their source."

"Aye, Captain," McDougall said.

"The Chinese just activated their radio transmitters," Jenner said, sharply. "They're hailing the sphere."

Staci blinked. There hadn't been any answer, back when *Endeavour* had tried to make contact with the Builders…unless one counted a rammer that had tried to destroy the entire ship. Shooting at someone was also a message, she recalled, one that said—very clearly—they wanted you dead. And yet, the Chinese were transmitting openly…were they mad? Or did they think someone would reply? Or…

"Captain, the rammer altered course," Yang reported. "She's heading straight for *Haikou*!"

"They're drawing the rammer onto them," Jenner breathed. "But why?"

Staci smiled as she saw it. "*Haikou* is right on top of the tramline," she said. "They'll draw the rammer right to their position, then jump out the moment before they get hit."

She felt her smile widen as the rammer picked up speed. The Chinese were cutting it very fine, even though they'd bought *Endeavour* a few more minutes. Her eyes narrowed as she realised more rammers were setting off, launching from the inner shell towards both starships. The automated defences were taking note of their presence, then moving to engage them. Staci felt her heart sink. It was turning into a race.

We don't have time to project another safe place to jump, she thought, grimly. One more time their imagination had failed them, when it came to encompassing the sheer scale of the alien technology. She asked herself, not for the first time, if it wouldn't be wise to keep the sphere a secret. The culture shock alone would upset the entire human race. The discovery that aliens had taken samples from Earth, thousands of years ago...she shuddered to think what *that* would do. *If we can't reach the safe jump coordinates, we might have to cross the tramline randomly and hope for the best.*

"Captain, the Chinese just jumped out," Jenner said. "The rammer seems to be looking for them."

Staci frowned. The Builders *had* to know about the tramline leading in and out of the sphere. Their grasp of gravity technology was light-years ahead of humanity's. They had to know what the Chinese had gone... unless their automated defences weren't intelligent enough to work it out. She shook her head as the rammer gave up looking for the Chinese and reversed course, heading straight towards *Endeavour*. It was going to be a very close-run thing.

"I've adjusted the tramline sensors," Yang reported. The display updated, showing beams of light intersecting with the rammer. "I think they use two tramlines to generate a gravity nexus around the rammer, directing it where they wish. It may also be how it survived an impact that should have killed it. If it was wrapped in a gravity shell, we might as well have fired on a black hole."

"I see." Staci swallowed a curse as a nasty thought crossed her mind. "Does this interfere with *the* tramline?"

"I don't think so," Yang said. "It's so far beyond us that it may be hard to be sure."

Staci stared at the display. The tramlines were fixed. The relationship between two stars was impossible for anyone, even the Builders, to change...wasn't it? And yet, if the Builders were somehow adjusting and tapping the star's gravity field, would it change the tramline? The Chinese had jumped out...hadn't they? What if they'd materialised on the other side and crashed straight into a piece of debris, because they'd appeared in the wrong place? What if…?

"Prepare a focused gravity field of our own," she ordered, finally. It would be puny, compared to the fields pushing the rammers towards her ship, but it might just interfere with the enemy projectiles. "And trigger it when the rammer makes its final approach."

"Aye, Captain."

"It's adjusting its course to match ours," MacDougal warned. "There's no way we can escape."

Staci was inclined to agree. Nothing human, save perhaps for a starfighter, could have turned so effectively on a dime. It was impossible and yet, given the sheer power the aliens had displayed, perhaps she should consider herself lucky the rammer hadn't come at them at just under the speed of light, arriving within seconds of any warning signal. Was there an upper limit? Or were they concerned about damage to the sphere? Or…

We built devices that could turn asteroids into projectiles, she remembered, from the final battle of the war. Oddly, the thought made her feel better. The alien tech wasn't *that* advanced over hers. *They did the same, only they didn't need to use pushers. They could just focus gravity beams to have the same effect.*

"Impact in fifty seconds," MacDougal said.

"Trigger the gravity field," Staci ordered. "Now!"

The rammer seemed to stop dead, then span off into space like a balloon that was suddenly venting air. *Endeavour* shuddered, something that should have been impossible, as the alien gravity beam brushed against her drive fields, then let go. Staci breathed a sigh of relief. The beam could have done real damage, if the automated systems had been smart enough to realise the opportunity. Instead…it had let them go.

Endeavour leapt forward as the helmsman gunned the drives, throwing the starship at the tramline. Staci braced herself as alarms howled, warning the crew they were going to make the jump at speed…they'd be vomiting on the decks, throughout the entire ship, but it was better than the alternative. The rammer was slowing as the alien system regained control, coming around and back at them. They had bare seconds to make the jump...

The world went dark, her eyesight going dim. She felt, absurdly, as if she was about to sneeze, an instantly before a *crash* echoed through the entire ship. The alarms grew louder. For a moment, she thought they actually *had* hit something even through the explosion would have wiped them from existence before they knew something was wrong. The display blanked, then lit up with red icons. An entire enemy fleet? It took long seconds for her to realise she was staring at the ruins of Dyson One.

"Jump completed, Captain," Atkinson said. Beside him, MacDougal looked as if he wanted to be sick. "We put immense strain on the jump nodes. I'd recommend taking the time to inspect them before we set out for home."

Staci nodded. "See to it," she ordered. "Communications, locate *Grantchester* and update her."

"Aye, Captain," McPhee said.

"And well done, all of you," Staci added. "We did very well."

She leaned back in her chair, silently cataloguing everything they'd need to do before they headed home. It shouldn't take that long to get underway. And then...she'd have to spend the month writing her reports, followed by detailed recommendations for further exploration missions. There was no way the sphere would be left alone, despite the dangers. The human race *had* to know how the alien tech worked.

"Signal from *Haikou*, Captain," McPhee reported. "Captain Yunan sends his compliments, and wishes us to know he's setting off for home."

"Give him our best wishes," Staci said. The Chinese ship had been a complication—and would be a greater one, when they got home. God knew what sort of report Yunan would make. He'd lost a shuttle and his watchdog...Staci feared he'd be blamed, even though no one had known about the alien platforms until they'd opened fire. "And we'll see him when we reach Earth."

"Aye, Captain," McPhee said.

Staci grinned, tiredly. They'd done one hell of a lot, even though they'd barely scratched the surface. And when they got home...

They'll probably turn the ship around and send us right back out here, she thought. *We'll be lucky if we get any shore leave at all.*

CHAPTER FORTY: LONDON, UNITED KINGDOM

"I MUST SAY, IF YOU HADN'T HAD sensor and visual records to back up your report, I would have wondered if you were pulling my leg," Admiral Lady Susan Onarina said. "The statements you made are quite unbelievable…"

Staci nodded, without taking offense. She had few illusions about how hard the Admiralty, let alone the government, much less the media and the rest of humanity, would find it to believe her report. Two Dyson spheres; one in ruins, the other inhabited by humans and dinosaurs and God alone knew what else, both demonstrating highly advanced and *working* technology capable of doing things everyone *knew* were impossible. Staci had read the reports from the analysts, as they worked their way through the sensor records on their way home. She'd been there, she *knew* the sphere existed, yet she found it hard to believe some of their more far out conclusions. The idea the weapons platforms were somehow bound together at the atomic level, rendering them effectively indestructible…it was hard to accept. She didn't blame her superiors for finding the report unbelievable.

"We must, of course, accept it," Admiral Onarina continued. "And that does raise a bunch of worrying questions."

"Yes, Admiral," Staci agreed. She'd read the lists of unanswered questions and speculation, ranging from the sane and reasonable to the downright insane. "What were the Builders doing here, thousands of years ago, and where have they gone?"

"Good questions," Admiral Onarina said. "If they were here, and it seems they were, why did we never find any trace of their presence?"

"If they left something in the asteroid belt," Staci said, "we might simply not have stumbled across it yet."

"Or they may have done something to ensure we literally *couldn't* find it," Admiral Onarina countered. "We know they were capable of hiding their installations from the virus. Why couldn't they hide them from us too?"

She stared at her hands. "And if they kidnapped humans and took them to the sphere...why? And who *else* did they kidnap?"

"We don't know," Staci said. "The sphere is huge, Admiral. We didn't so much as scratch the surface. We were incredibly lucky we were able to get the team off the surface and back home without further injury or death."

"There could be anyone, or anything, on the other side of the great oceans," Admiral Onarina said. "Tadpoles. Foxes. Cows. Even Vesy, or the races the virus turned into puppets and effectively destroyed. That might be all that's left of their former culture and society."

"If the Builders intended to keep them safe from the virus..." Staci shook her head. "They could have stopped the virus, if they wished."

"Perhaps," Admiral Onarina cautioned. "We know very little about them, save for the fact they were around thousands of years ago and much of their technology continues to function, even now. And they don't like us trying to talk to them."

She frowned. "Was there no response? None at all?"

"Unless you count them trying to kill us, no," Staci said. "The analysts went through the sensor logs with a fine-toothed comb. There was no hint the Builders ever tried to signal us—or anyone, including themselves. We don't know if the sphere is still inhabited by their descendants, or if they all died out centuries ago and their automatic systems are just following their last orders. We simply don't know."

Admiral Onarina studied her dark fingers. "It seems hard to believe a civilisation so powerful, one known to have spread over thousands of light-years, simply vanished."

"We know very little about them," Staci said. "They might have evolved and passed beyond our ken. They might have died out. They might have retired or left the galaxy or...we simply don't know."

"We don't know an awful lot, it seems," Admiral Onarina said. "And we need answers."

She looked up, meeting Staci's eyes. "Word is seeping out, despite our best efforts. The political issues will be handled by our lords and masters, but the military issues are quite serious. The Builders entered our system thousands of years ago, kidnapped our people and then left without leaving any trace of their presence. *Then* they may have shown us the way to the sphere...why? The implications of a race capable of dismantling an entire star system—more than one—are quite disturbing."

"Yes, Admiral," Staci said.

"I fear the truth will shock the world, when it gets out," Admiral Onarina said. "Nothing has been decided yet, but I think you'll be heading back to the sphere. We're already started quiet discussions about a multinational flotilla, perhaps even a multispecies one. I don't think the rest of the known universe will be happy leaving the sphere to us, when they realise what we've found. It could easily restart the wars once again."

Staci grimaced. "I'm sorry to hear that, Admiral."

Admiral Onarina smiled. "The wars, or going back to the sphere?"

She leaned forward. "There have also been some quiet discussions about charging your crew, and you, with breaking the non-interference laws. My personal opinion is that you did what you had to do, particularly given the need to get the landing party through the human settlements and reach the mountain as quickly as possible. I think the politicians will likely go along with it, unless it blows up in our face in some manner.

The people on the sphere were human. One can claim a loophole there."

"I knew what I was doing, when I did it," Staci said. "Admiral, I…"

Admiral Onarina held up a hand. "Right now, you have a week of shore leave. Your crew has passed every check we've put them through, including some we came up with specially, and we're fairly sure you didn't bring anything nasty back with you. I suggest you spend that week relaxing, as once the shock wears off they'll probably start deciding what to do about the situation. Your ship is in good hands, so relax."

Staci nodded. "Yes, Admiral."

"You did well, given what you faced," Admiral Onarina told her. "Captain Campbell would be proud of you. I have no doubt there will be armchair admirals aplenty, who will point out mistakes you made, but most of those assertions will be made with the benefit of hindsight. You will do better next time, of course, as will anyone else. We know enough, now, to think we can continue to explore the sphere safely."

"We don't, Admiral," Staci said. "The sphere is a vast unknown."

"I agree," Admiral Onarina said. "But I'm afraid there's no way we can convince the rest of the known universe to leave the sphere alone. The lure of advanced technology will draw them to the sphere, like flies to honey. And so we have to get into the race too."

Staci said nothing, but she feared the admiral was right.

"Go. Enjoy your leave." Admiral Onarina stood, dismissing her. "I'll see you in a week."

"Aye, Admiral," Staci said. She felt oddly rudderless, as if she was no longer sure of her place in the world. "I'll see you soon."

• • •

Charlotte could not tell, in all honesty, if the PM was genuinely pleased to see her or if he was simply putting a good face on things. He'd thought, reading between the lines, that Charlotte would either spend months cooling her heels on *Endeavour* or hand any serious diplomatic discussions to Paris-Jackson as soon as possible. Instead, Charlotte had crashed on the interior of a sphere, made an alliance with a local faction, helped them win a war, then run for her life when the faction had turned nasty. Charlotte had no idea what he intended to do with her, now that she was famous for all sorts of reasons. The only real consolation, she decided, was that he probably had no idea what to do with her either.

"Your report made interesting reading," the PM said, as she sipped her tea. "Do you believe the Builders are still around?"

"I find it hard to believe the automated systems would be allowed so much of a free hand, if there was someone there to supervise," Charlotte said. "Even our remote burglar alarms call the police if they detect someone trying to break into the house."

The PM nodded slowly. "And so you think the sphere is uninhabited?"

"I know it *is* inhabited," Charlotte said, bluntly. "But, as far as we could tell, none of the humans we met knew they lived on a sphere. They thought the world was flat. I think their universe was really little more than a hundred or so miles surrounding their home cities and villages. If the Builders themselves are still around..."

She shook her head. "They made no attempt to contact us. Their automated systems largely ignored us, unless we crossed the line. They reacted badly to anything broadcasting radio signals, or on a trajectory that might impact the sphere. Either they didn't consider another spacefaring race finding the sphere, which is unlikely, or they simply didn't care. Or they're gone. My personal feeling is that they abandoned the sphere a long time ago."

"But you don't know," the PM said.

"I find it hard to believe anyone *intelligent* would fire on an unknown starship that wasn't doing anything openly hostile," Charlotte said. "It could start a war. An automated system, on the other hand, one designed to keep the inhabitants firmly on the ground, might engage the starship without thinking of possible consequences."

"Or they see themselves as being too powerful to care," the PM pointed out. "Compared to what we've seen of their technology, ours is little more than sticks and stones."

"I don't think the gap is *that* wide," Charlotte said, although she knew she might be whistling in the dark. "It's more a matter of scale than anything else. We can figure out how they do things even if we can't, yet, duplicate them."

"Perhaps so," the PM said. He leaned forward, suggesting he was about to come to the point. "There have been intensive discussions over the last week, concerning how best to approach the sphere. The other powers are not happy we didn't bring them in right at the start, although we countered by pointing out they *did* know about the Virus Prime Sphere."

He smiled, rather dryly. "There are too many *spheres* in this affair."

"I agree," Charlotte said.

The PM nodded. "Anyway, they have demanded a multinational team be sent to continue the survey. Given that all alien contacts are meant to be handled on a multinational basis, we have no legal right to refuse and no way to prevent them from sending ships of their own to the sphere. It's quite possible some vessels are already on their way. Regardless, we will be putting together a team as quickly as possible. *Endeavour* will be attached to the flotilla, as will you."

Charlotte blinked. "Me?"

"You are the most experienced diplomat we have, when it comes to dealing with the settlements on the sphere," the PM said. "You will also serve as our representative to the system council, when we put one together, and perhaps even political head of the team. I think it will not be long before hundreds of ships start heading to the spheres, to see what they can draw from the ruins of Dyson One even if they don't dare go into Dyson Two. And there will be little we can do about it. The Great Powers will not act in unison on this matter and even if they did, their—our—power is not what it once was."

"Because the war hurt us badly," Charlotte said, flatly.

"Yes." The PM met her eyes. "This could be the most important posting of your professional career, if you intend to remain in government service. You will have a staff, of course, but you will be in command."

Charlotte said nothing for a long moment. Her vaunted experience was laughable. She'd barely seen anything of the sphere. She might as well stand on the Shetlands and proclaim herself an expert on Great Britain. What little she did have was hardly a secret, hardly something that couldn't be duplicated in a hurry. And yet…she wasn't blind to the implications. If she accepted, she'd be heading away from Earth—again—for over a year. If she declined, it could be used as an excuse to push her onto the sidelines and eventually get rid of her.

And if I'm the one in charge when we make contact, it will be to my credit, she thought, coldly. The odds weren't that high—or the PM would have sent one of his cronies instead—but they were better than zero. *Mitch would tell me to gamble everything on it, wouldn't he?*

She smiled, finally. "It will be my pleasure," she said. "I look forward to returning to the spheres."

"Very good," the PM said. If he was surprised by her acceptance, he didn't show it. "As soon as the team is assembled, you will be on your way."

Charlotte nodded and stood. She'd have time to make some arrangements of her own, to check with the lawyers and try to make contact with her daughters and perhaps even to see what else she could do. And then…she'd be on her way back to the spheres. It would make or break her career, once and for all.

She smiled. She hadn't lied. She was quite looking forward to it.

• • •

END OF BOOK NINETEEN
HMS Endeavour Will Return In:
The Lone World
COMING SOON.

AFTERWORD

The usual example of an Outside Context Problem was imagining you were a tribe on a largish, fertile island; you'd tamed the land, invented the wheel or writing or whatever, the neighbours were cooperative... and you were busy raising temples to yourself and the whole situation was just running along nicely like a canoe on wet grass... when suddenly a bristling lump of iron appears sailless and trailing steam in the bay and these guys carrying long funny-looking sticks come ashore and announce you've just been discovered, you're subjects of the Emperor now, he's keen on presents called tax and these bright-eyed holy men would like a word with your priests.
—*EXCESSION*, IAIN M. BANKS

WHY THIS STORY?

One of the problems with writing an expanding series, of course, is the need to break new ground. I did my best to avoid some of the problems with ever-growing series by crafting a set of trilogies, each one following a different starship and crew even as they built on aspects of the previous universe. This had its limits, however, and I thought the series was starting to brush up against them. How much further could it go? I decided, after much careful thought, that it was time to try something a little different.

I have always enjoyed stories about 'Big Dumb Objects,' in which a human spacecraft encounters a giant and completely enigmatic alien artefact. They are rarely character-based stories, because the *real* star of the book is the alien artifact itself. They represent both new worlds to explore—sometimes literally, in the case of *Ringworld*—and a giant temptation to human factions, some of whom see the prospect of alien technology as either a chance to make themselves supreme or a potential threat. It is not a coincidence that Iain M. Banks coined the term *Outside Context Problem*—as quoted above—in a book where the super-advanced Culture found itself confronting evidence of technology so far above their own that it might as well be magic. They found it hard to cope.

These books do tend to run into a problem, as they develop. There's only so far you can push the mystery aspect before people start demanding answers, and those answers are often unsatisfactory. *Rendezvous with Rama* worked very well as a self-contained story, even if it offered no final answers; the sequels didn't work so well because the answers were unsatisfactory. The same could easily be said of *Ringworld*, while *Excession* ended with the titular 'Big Dumb Object' leaving as enigmatically as it came. And yet, while they last, they bear testament to the writer's imagination and humanity's ability to awe at the wonders of a long-gone civilisation.

So I asked myself, why not put such a story in *Ark Royal*?

It fitted, I decided, for two reasons. First, it would be a suitable homage to the books I read and loved in my youth. Second, it would provide a new setting *and* a reason for political storms that would kick off more action-orientated storylines. How would we react, to proof there was once an advanced alien race that visited Earth, well before the human race evolved to the point it could grasp the concept of alien life? How would we react to advanced technology, capable of things we thought impossible? Would we react maturely and study the technology carefully, or would we embark on a massive treasure hunt on the assumption the country—or world—that reverse-engineered and put the technology into mass production first would be the dominant power for decades to come? And how would other nations react to the suggestion that their rivals would get a shot in the arm? How would we cope?

I wrote this book to set the stage. The story is far from over.

And now you've read this far, I have a request to make.

It's growing harder to make a living through self-published writing these days. If you liked this book, please leave a review where you found it, share the link, let your friends know (etc, etc). Every little helps (particularly reviews).

Thank you.
Christopher G. Nuttall
Edinburgh, 2022

APPENDIX: GLOSSARY OF UK TERMS AND SLANG

[Author's Note: I've tried to define every incident of specifically UK slang (and a handful of military phases/acronyms) in this glossary, but I can't promise to have spotted everything. If you spot something I've missed, please let me know and it will be included.]

Aggro—slang term for aggression or trouble, as in 'I don't want any aggro.'

Beasting/Beasted—military slang for anything from a chewing out by one's commander to outright corporal punishment or hazing. The latter two are now officially banned.

Beat Feet—Run, make a hasty departure.

Binned—SAS slang for a prospective recruit being kicked from the course, then returned to unit (RTU).

Boffin—Scientist

Bootnecks—slang for Royal Marines. Loosely comparable to 'Jarhead.'

Bottle—slang for nerve, as in 'lost his bottle.'

Borstal—a school/prison for young offenders.

Combined Cadet Force (CCF)—school/youth clubs for teenagers who might be interested in joining the military when they become adults.

Compo—British army slang for improvised stews and suchlike made from rations and sauces.

COBRA (Cabinet Office Briefing Room A)—UK Government Emergency Response Committee.

CSP—Combat Space Patrol.

Donkey Wallopers—slang for the Royal Horse Artillery.

DORA—Defence of the Realm Act.

Fortnight—two weeks. (Hence the terrible pun, courtesy of the *Goon Show*, that Fort Knight cannot possibly last three weeks.)

GATO—Global Alliance Treaty Organisation

'Get stuck into'—'start fighting.'

Head Sheds—SAS slang for senior officers.

'I should coco'—'you're damned right.'

Jobsworth—a bureaucrat who upholds petty rules even at the expense of humanity or common sense.

Kip—sleep.

Levies—native troops. The Ghurkhas are the last remnants of native troops from British India.

Lorries—trucks.

Matelots—Royal Marine slang for sailors.

Mocktail/Mocktails—non-alcoholic cocktails.

MOD—Ministry of Defence. (The UK's Pentagon.)

Order of the Garter—the highest order of chivalry (knighthood) and the third most prestigious honour (inferior only to the Victoria Cross and George Cross) in the United Kingdom. By law, there can be only twenty-four non-royal members of the order at any single time.

Panda Cola—Coke as supplied by the British Army to the troops.

RFA—Royal Fleet Auxiliary

Rumbled—discovered/spotted.

SAS—Special Air Service.

SBS—Special Boat Service

Spotted Dick—a traditional fruity sponge pudding with suet, citrus zest and currants served in thick slices with hot custard. The name always caused a snigger.

Squaddies—slang for British soldiers.

Stag—guard duty.

STUFT—'Ships Taken Up From Trade,' civilian ships requisitioned for government use.

TAB (tab/tabbing)—Tactical Advance to Battle.

Tearaway—boisterous/badly behaved child, normally a teenager.

UKADR—United Kingdom Air Defence Region.

Uriah Gambit—a deliberate bid to get a husband killed so you can score with his wife.

Walt—Poser, i.e. someone who claims to have served in the military and/or a very famous regiment. There's a joke about 22 SAS being the largest regiment in the British Army—it must be, because of all the people who claim to have served in it.

Wanker—Masturbator (jerk-off). Commonly used as an insult.

Wank/Wanking—Masturbating.

Yank/Yankee—Americans

HOW TO FOLLOW

Basic Mailing List—http://orion.crucis.net/mailman/listinfo/chrishanger-list
Nothing, but announcements of new books.

Newsletter—https://gmail.us1.list-manage.com/subscribe?u=c8f9f7391e5bfa369a9b1e76c&id=55fc83a213
New books releases, new audio releases, maybe a handful of other things of interest.

Blog—https://chrishanger.wordpress.com/
Everything from new books to reviews, commentary on things that interest me, etc.

Facebook Fan Page—https://www.facebook.com/ChristopherGNuttall
New books releases, new audio releases, maybe a handful of other things of interest.

Website—http://chrishanger.net/
New books releases, new audio releases, free samples (plus some older books free to anyone who wants a quick read)

Forums—https://authornuttall.com
Book discussions—new, but I hope to expand.

Amazon Author Page—https://www.amazon.com/Christopher-G-Nuttall/e/B008L9Q4ES
My books on Amazon.

Books2Read—https://books2read.com/author/christopher-g-nuttall/subscribe/19723/
Notifications of new books (normally on Amazon too, but not included in B2R notifications.

Twitter—@chrisgnuttall
New books releases, new audio releases—definitely nothing beyond (no politics or culture war stuff).

BONUS PREVIEW

AND NOW, CHECK OUT *Desert Clash* by Leo Champion:

One Day In The Desert…In the intercontinental desert of Arkin, where the Confederated Union and its allies are locked in war with the fundamentalist Zinj, a lot can happen between sunrise and sundown…

A cavalry crew will lose their vehicle—and retaliate by seizing one much larger…

A platoon of wartime volunteers will find their baptism in violence…

A pair of incorrigible screwups will become accidental and reluctant heroes…

A unit of elite Janissaries will get wise to a Western deception…

And a trap will be sprung that may shift the tide of the war…

CHAPTER ONE

"Shaker, Chaser," came Ground Control, "you are cleared to launch."

It had only been six weeks, but, as Ensign Egan 'Chaser' O'Connor pushed his Viper's throttle forwards, it felt like six years since he'd last flown. The fighter's vibrating engines greedily accepted the power he was feeding them, their sound even within the cockpit growing from a low expectant rumble into a full-on roar as the jet picked up speed along the runway, and *airborne!*

The plane shook slightly from side to side as he pulled the stick back and leftwards, angling up into a clear pale-blue morning sky, empty of clouds and everything else except the dark shapes of circling aircraft. His wing leader James 'Shaker' Jamison was the closest of those, as O'Connor took the Viper into formation on Jamison's five o'clock, at a distance of about three hundred yards.

Jamison in turn was holding position to the five o'clock of B Flight's leader Jane 'Sauron' Mordar; Mordar's wingman Francis 'Messy' Murkowski was on her left, her seven o'clock. Another five hundred feet above, A Flight was circling, and now the Vipers of C Flight were launching two at a time and forming up at twenty-five hundred feet.

Arkin's massive orange sun glared at him through the cockpit's polarised canopy, warm but not blinding thanks to the polarisation. Above was endless pale-blue sky; below were rough volcanic hills, descending and smoothing out as you went east, and right now smothered with a dusty blur thrown up by the wheels and treads of thousands of Confederated Union and allied vehicles.

Everything, O'Connor imagined, from the modified civilian jeeps and buggies that the Khalsans and local volunteers used as makeshift cavalry, through the real cavalry of Raider and Lancer armoured cars; troop trucks, tanks, self-propelled artillery, right up to battalions of the gigantic kiloheavy Graf landcruisers. Rumour said three whole divisions were attacking right now, everything Lady Odin could assemble on the ground with twenty full squadrons covering them in the sky.

"B Flight," came Mordar's calm, low voice. "Follow me up to angels six, stay on me for now, and weapons live if you haven't already. Spearheads are due to make contact any minute now, so get ready for our signal."

O'Connor turned the plane rightwards and up toward six thousand feet, sticking on Jamison's five. He hadn't had flying time in over a month but there'd been plenty of simulator practice; the movements, the necessary instinctive twitches to the stick and miniscule adjustments to the throttle, came easily and reflexively. A glance at the weapons status indicators on his dashboard showed that, yes, everything was armed and live.

God damn was it good to be back.

• • •

"Contact!" Sergeant Jimmy Newland snarled as incoming fire suddenly erupted around his Raider, lines of bullets kicking flumes of dry orange dust into the air. It was wild, inaccurate shooting although, as one round did *spang* off the front of the armoured car, not *completely* inaccurate. "We have made contact!"

As Trooper First Class Barocce kicked the Raider into reverse and began a three-point turn, Corporal Reiss returned fire with the big six-wheeler's mantlet-mounted .50 and Newland raised his binoculars. *Where*, amidst the low rolling hills to their east, was the fire coming from?

Turning in his shotgun seat to keep his eyes on what had been forwards, he scanned, looking for movement. Muzzle-flashes would have given the enemy location away at night, but right now was a little past nine thirty in the morning. If the Zinj had any sense they would have held their fire until Bronze One was closer and more vulnerable—he *could* tell from its wild inaccuracy that they had to be a ways away, probably somewhere on the ridgeline.

"You see 'em, Reiss?" he shouted up at that man.

"Nah." Reiss let loose another long burst from his fifty anyway, turning it himself as the Raider did.

"Then stop shooting and look!"

Suddenly Newland did spot movement—a technical coming forwards over the ridge about a mile and a half away, followed by another one. Immediately both technicals started firing, one of them starting to accelerate downhill toward them.

Yup. Definite contact.

"Sir," Newland keyed the radio mic on his headset, "we've found them!"

• • •

Lieutenant Ojibwe was about four hundred yards away, his troop's six Raiders spaced in pairs, sections, about two hundred yards apart—although on these boulder-strewn hills that formation had been easier to maintain in planning than reality. He was a very tall, very lean, midnight-black man in his early twenties, and he hadn't needed Bronze One's report to know they'd engaged—because as it came in, wild fire erupted around his own vehicle. It was followed a moment later by its distant staccato chattering, and his driver followed standard operating procedure by hitting reverse.

"Three here. All three of my sections have found 'em," Ojibwe told the company command network as, on the troop channel, Sergeant First-Class Miser—Silver One—reported the same. "Techs and they seem to have something dug in, pretty sure it's not just a patrol."

"Disengage," came the company signalman. "Say again, disengage."

Sometimes it wasn't cavalry's job to fight the enemy. Sometimes it was just to locate them.

• • •

Captain Steve Bradford was a heavily-built man in his mid-forties, a prior-enlisted officer, and like Newland and Ojibwe he was riding shotgun in his own armoured car. The difference was that his was a Lancer with eight wheels, more armour, and a significantly better gun than the Raiders.

"Sir, all three of our Raider troops are being engaged now," reported company RTO Jimmy Wales from the back seat. "And Four wants to move up and fight."

Fourth was the company's Lancer troop, who with Bradford's own four-Lancer company command element had been tagging about half a mile behind the lighter, faster Raiders. Spaced two hundred yards apart from one another, the company's three Raider troops in their nine sections covered about a mile of front between them—and India Company was just part of the attack's screening element, the tip of the task force's spear.

"Tell Four to get ready but not just yet," said Bradford. His own driver was looking expectantly at him as well, tense and ready. "Then tell Regiment that we've got definite contact at…" He gave the coordinates. "Have them confirm and then"—he turned to his driver—"move up."

• • •

"Copy that, India," said the RTO, and another series of red contact indicators lit up on the digital map in front of Colonel Kara Vincent, operations officer of the 75th Cavalry Regiment. She was a short, stout woman with a blonde pageboy haircut, and right now—with some junior officers of her section and a handful of RTOs—she was sitting, tightly belted down, in the back of a command-fitted all-wheel drive five-ton truck.

"Definitely more than just patrols," her assistant remarked. Twelve companies, along that many miles of front, had now found Zinj. Not to anyone's surprise, of course—as the task force probed into the hills west of Barbiero the probability of that had been approaching one.

"Yeah, we've hit their pickets," Vincent replied absently, her fingers typing rapidly as she dashed off a summary. She hit Enter, transmitting the data dump upwards...

. . .

Brigadier-General Raoul Montiguez slowly nodded, his hands clasped tensely behind his back, as the screens in the task force's mobile command post lit up with contact indicators along what was now thirteen miles of front. Symbols told of the type of contact—light vehicles and troops in foxholes, apparently no fortifications more serious than a little bit of digging. Colours told that the density was low, definitely no more than the Zinj's outer pickets and patrols. And westward-pointing arrows showed that the enemy were behaving exactly as they were expected to—attacking what they, individually, would think were just Confederated Union patrols.

He only hoped they'd keep cooperating. There were any number of ways this plan could potentially go sour, any number of underlying assumptions that might be disastrously disproven in the battle to come. But for now, the initiative was his.

"Lancer troops are moving up in support?" he asked. He could see perfectly well, on one of the secondary digital screens here, that they were doing exactly that, but... part of being a flag officer was to follow these kinds of confirmation procedures.

It was part of why he'd initially resisted the promotion. As a regimental commander he'd had the chance to spend time in the field with his troopers, riding along in his personal Lancer with just a couple of cross-trained signalmen for personal security. General Brodie, for all his faults, had been a fighting man himself who'd understood the motivation.

But once they gave you a star you didn't get to do that kind of thing; Air Vice-Admiral Jaeger had made that point very, very clear. Too much of a coup if the Zinj killed you—or, Lord forbid, take you prisoner. The former black operator had quietly told him of some of what the Zinj did to prisoners they wanted information from, or who had simply aggrieved them enough; the details still sickened him to think about. So instead of leading from the front, he was in the rear of an artillery-variant Graf ten miles back.

"Lancers are moving up and the first main echelons are accelerating, ETA to engagement distance three to eight minutes," a staff sub-colonel reported crisply.

"Get the spearheads forwards. Tell them not to wait. We've got them off balance," Montiguez ordered, "so let's *get* them!"

...

More Zinj technicals had come across the ridgetop facing Newland's Raider, and more infantry had emerged, or at least their heads and shoulders had from foxholes on the ridge. The techs, five of them now, had advanced downhill—firing their machine-guns in irregular, ineffective bursts at Bronze Section. The infantry had mostly held their fire, although Newland could see dozens of heads moving in their foxholes. A couple of rocket-propelled grenades arcing ineffectually through the air was proof of their presence, even if the nearer of the RPGs had exploded more than a hundred yards short of Bronze One.

Reiss on the .50 had fired back at the advancing technicals with short, measured bursts, stopping one of the vehicles with what looked like an engine kill—its crew, through Newland's binoculars, had bailed out except for the gunner, who'd kept firing while his friends advanced down their side of the rocky hill. A mile and a half was extreme range even for heavy weapons, though, and the exchanges of fire hadn't achieved much else for anyone.

Now Captain Bradford's voice came over the company radio channel.

"Regiment says to press the attack. Armour's speeding up, let's stay ahead of them—follow me forwards!"

"You heard the captain," said Lieutenant Ojibwe.

"Copy that, LT," said Newland into his mic, and turned to Barocce. "Lancers coming up, tanks speeding up, skipper says *go!*."

The fourth man in the Raider, Sub-Corporal Mark Wagner, was loading forty-millimetre grenades into the six revolving cylinders of his launcher, carefully checking each grenade before pushing it into its cylinder. On Newland's own lap was a SI-7a carbine, a round chambered and ready as Barocce drove the Raider forwards.

Forming up alongside them was Bronze Two; Newland gave Corporal Patel, that vehicle's commander, a thumbs-up and gestured forwards. Patel responded with a nod and a thumbs-up and the two Raiders started to accelerate downhill.

Bouncing along the rocky ground, Bronze Two holding position about twenty feet to their left, Newland was glad for his seatbelt and his helmet. The Raider had six big wheels and decent suspension, but... all the same, as Barocce floored it downhill, picking up speed as wild incoming fire spattered in around them, there were rocks everywhere and the ones too small to bother going around, you had to bounce over.

"It's Meyer!" Wagner shouted from the back seat, gesturing backwards. A glance in his rear-view mirror showed two of the company command Lancers coming up fast, side by side; Lieutenant Meyer, India Company XO, his car identifiable by the three radio antennae sticking up from it. The other one would belong to company flag sergeant Hayden.

Where the Raiders had simple mantlets for their .50 machine-guns, the Lancers had proper stabilised turrets for their 25mm autocannon, and as they opened up on the Zinj technicals the difference was clear. At less than a mile's range now, Hayden's gunner blasted a line of tracers across two of the technicals, sending one of them skidding sideways and tumbling, men thrown from its tray. The other simply stopped dead—and, after a moment, flames started to flicker under the hood.

One of the remaining three paused, maybe to fire more accurately with long, sweeping bursts that pinged and pattered into the rocks around the oncoming armoured cars, one nearly-spent round bouncing off the hood of

Meyer's Lancer. The other two were turning sharply back uphill, fleeing.

"Get 'em!" someone shouted over the radio net, and Newland didn't need to encourage Barocce to keep his foot on the accelerator. They raced downhill; a glance to his left showed more pairs and foursomes of armoured cars, surging forwards amidst the rocks. He envisaged the whole spread-out screening force attacking like this along ten miles of front, hundreds of similar vehicles pushing forwards.

There was a hard bump and Newland was thrown forwards in his seatbelt as the car hit the gully at the bottom of the slope, a narrow sandy crevasse that probably torrented with water during rainy season. Barocce shifted to first gear and forced the Raider forwards up its other side, its all-wheel-drive tires pushing for grip and finding it. More incoming fire whipped over their heads and Reiss gave some back, firing a couple of bursts uphill as they got going again.

Boom! A rocket-propelled grenade exploded forty feet to their right, its blast sending a storm of dust and pebbles into the side of the Raider. Rifle fire began to drizzle around them as the Zinj in the trenches opened up, not all of them deterred by the sweeping bursts of suppressive fire the Raiders and Lancers were sending their way.

Wagner readied his grenade launcher, braced his boots on the back seat and emerged through his roof hatch. Newland heard the launcher *burp-whir, burp-whir, burp-whir* six times as the man emptied all six cylinders. He was firing at a high arc for maximum range, and by the time the first explosions bloomed around the general vicinity of the ridgeline he was strapping himself in again, already starting to reload his weapon.

The last of the Zinj technicals had disappeared over the ridge, fleeing and apparently making it—there had been five, and three of those were now smoking wreckage. The others would be warning their friends, but that was a given—besides, it was completely reasonable to assume that the Zinj infantry in their foxholes would have a radio or a telephone system connected to one anyway.

As the Raiders and Lancers surged uphill, closing to within four hundred yards, three hundred and fifty, three hundred, the dug-in Zinj started to get more enthusiastic about shooting—the attackers were getting inside effective range of the rifles most of them seemed to have.

"RPG! RPG!" came over the radio network as one Zinj emerged, leveling the shoulder-mounted weapon—

Reiss and another of the gunners focused on him, tracers lashing out—but, perhaps figuring that he was dead anyway, this man didn't seem deterred by the storm of suppressive fire slashing along the picket trench. He kept his cool and fired, the rocket streaking out toward the oncoming cavalry; Barocce swerved left hard, cursing as the Raider almost sideswiped one of the Lancers, who was reacting the same way in the opposite direction. The Zinj disappeared back inside his foxhole, apparently unhurt for now, but his rocket swept ineffectively between and past the armoured cars.

Suddenly a *big* explosion hit the centre of the Zinj positions, blasting a fountain of red dirt, rocks, and human body parts up into the air. Then another one, twenty feet left of the first, and a third twenty feet to the right. Accurate, precision fire from something big, bigger than anything the cavalry had...

"Armour's shown up!" someone cheered over the radio net. And yes, a glance in the rear-views showed the forms of several ARH-4 Junker main battle tanks coming over the ridge behind. As Newland watched, another of them fired its main gun with a great big muzzle-flash; a couple of seconds later the 120mm high-explosive shell tore up another part of the Zinj picket trench.

One Zinj vaulted out of the trench and ran, fleeing for the ridgeline and momentary safety. He made three steps before being cut down.

Barocce slowed the Raider as they neared the remains of the Zinj positions, which five minutes ago had been a line of trenches along the military crest of the ridge. The tank shells had blasted those to a line of gaping craters, shredded tents and bedding everywhere amidst a few trashed crates and more than a few robed human bodies or pieces of them.

Not all of the bodies were dead—Newland spotted movement as they drew up in front of the devastated positions, Barocce following protocol like the other drivers and keeping the top of their vehicle well below the actual ridge crest. There would be more Zinj on the other side of the ridge, an unknown number at an unknown distance but aware of the cavalry's presence and possibly with weapons trained on the ridgeline and ready for the first Raider or Lancer to enter their sights.

The top-mounted guns of those vehicles were certainly pointed in the other direction in case enemy showed up, although if there'd been Zinj on the immediate east side of the ridge then Newland's money was on them fleeing right now, not preparing a counterattack. In his experience so far, the damn firebugs were fanatical enough when they thought they had the advantage—but once broken, they tended to stay that way for a good long while.

"Silver, Bronze," came Lieutenant Ojibwe. "Hold up a few minutes for the armour behind us—sweep what's left of those trenches while you're waiting."

"Roger that," said Newland. "Wagner, you heard the LT."

Dismount procedure when in contact or when it was expected, involved only two men, the grenadier and the vehicle commander. Driver and gunner stayed in their places ready for action, to move or shoot rapidly if needed. What that meant right now was that Newland released his seatbelt, gave his rifle a last quick check—yup, round in the chamber and fire-select set to single-shot—opened his passenger-side door and swung his boots out to crunch on the scorched sand.

Wagner, getting out of the Raider's rear passenger-side door, had exchanged his grenade launcher for a SI-7a carbine of his own; the launcher wouldn't be much use in a close-up fight like anything they'd encounter right now.

He was a small man, Sub-Corporal Mark Wagner, with a trace of black hair underneath his helmet and little darting green eyes; right now he'd pushed his goggles up onto his forehead out of the way. Like Newland he wore heavy yellow-brown camo that included fifty pounds of bulky, heavy body armour; like Newland and the other experienced, spur-wearing veterans of India Company, the discomfort of that—even in the present ninety-something degree heat—was so normal that it barely registered.

"Sweep the trenches?" Wagner asked, mostly rhetorically. He'd heard the lieutenant.

Newland replied to the unnecessary question with a curt grunt, then made a decision: one of them was about to have to do some thoroughly dirty, entirely unpleasant work and a good NCO led by example.

"Cover me," he told Wagner, and without looking back at the grenadier for confirmation leapt into the shell-blasted remains of the trench, about a five-foot drop into a mess of ragged canvas that had probably been tent material until the tanks had opened up. The trench went on for about seventy feet and had originally been perhaps three feet wide, enough for two guys to pass but not much more. It wasn't zig-zagged or reinforced in any way. Zinj were lazy; they didn't like digging more than they absolutely had to and this picket had probably just been a formality for them. Looked like there'd been at least a couple of dozen here, maybe more.

It was hard to tell, because between the raking machine-gun fire and the tank shells there wasn't much left of them. Bile rose in his throat as he felt something soft squish under his boot; there was blood and messy tissue everywhere, a headless corpse on the bottom of the trench, a legless torso collapsed against the side of one of the blast craters. He kept focused, the rifle raised and ready at his shoulder, as he advanced down the trench.

Movement! A robed figure not quite dead, sprawled and bloody face-down and twitching. Before Newland could fire Wagner did from above, putting a neat double-tap into the robed guy's head. There was a final twitch and no more, but Newland was still cautious as he passed the corpse—two 6.6mm rounds to the noggin meant the fucker wasn't going to be playing possum, but wounded Zinj also liked to play cute games involving unpinned hand grenades.

Carefully he made his way along the messy trench, aware of limited time. Corporal Patel and Trooper First-Class Haney, the dismounts of Bronze Two, were coming along from the other direction, with big blond Haney the one in the trench and tiny Patel covering him from above. He had to be conscious of Haney's location, not raise his gun too far along the straight trench, but they also had to be thorough. Another cute stunt the Zinj enjoyed playing at was to hide until attackers had passed and then pop up behind them with a rocket-propelled grenade or some such, often against second-echelon or support elements. Wartime lessons had been learned the hard way in how to deal with those behaviours.

Soon, though, Newland met up with Haney around the middle of the trench; the two men nodded to each other, not wasting energy in the dry morning heat. Growling, grumbling engines were getting closer—from the west, the tanks arriving. Wagner reached down and took Newland's rifle so that he could use both hands to pull himself up.

"Bronze," came Ojibwe over Newland's earpiece, "get ready to move again. Soon as they get here, Delta Company"—the Junkers and Ritters—"will lead us over the ridge, and then we'll be going all-out."

"Check," Newland replied as he took his rifle back from Wagner, then accepted the canteen that tiny Surendra Patel handed him. Took a long swig of lukewarm but welcome water, grunted in thanks, and gave it back.

"LT says we're moving out again the second those tanks get here to take the brunt of it," he told Patel. "And the next lot aren't going to be as dumb or unprepared as these poor bastards were."

CHAPTER TWO

"B Flight," came Mordar's calm voice in Egan O'Connor's ears, "time to move out. Follow me to eleven thousand feet and keep your eyes open!"

O'Connor's hand on the Viper's stick, his boots on their pedals, instinctively made the plane obey, nosing upwards on Jamison's five o'clock; Jamison in turn was on the flight leader's five, with Murkowski flying a little less steadily on her seven, her left-hand side. His body was obeying but his heart was pounding and, in his brain, insecurity was clashing with eagerness.

The last time I was in a fight, I was shot down. I almost got killed. I lost the last fight I was in and cost the Air Force a fifty-two million dollar fighter jet.

He'd thought he was good—he'd had a rookie's clueless confidence, never believing that it could happen to *him*. Hadn't he scored four kills, just one short of ace? *He* was what happened to *others!*

And then—in the same desperate furball that had killed caustic, abrasive 'Cock-Eye' Castle—it *had* happened to him, out of nowhere. Not even a fair fight, just... suddenly his wing burning, his plane starting to augur, and no choice but to hit the Eject button. What if that happened again and he wasn't so lucky? What if he fucked up again?

Shut up, he told that part of his mind. He just needed to keep his head together. If it was going to be his time then it would be his time, and the *other* part of his mind wanted to get even for when it'd almost been—especially against the son of a bitch he'd rescued from a burning Murad and dragged to safety, only to be repaid by getting shot in the back, stripped of his survival kit, and left for dead. *That* asshole was probably flying again, possibly in a Murad, and next time O'Connor wasn't going to be so merciful. Zinj weren't honourable warriors or worthy opponents; they were pond scum to be exterminated and he was ready to do his part.

"Gentlemen, let's make a final review of plans and expectations," came Mordar. "Intel and recon tell us that the zigs have been heavy on combat air patrols right now—we're not going to catch too many of them on the ground. We think it's not because they're expecting us to hit them pre-emptively like this, but mostly because they've got a lot of new pilots in-theater who they figure could use all the practice hours they can get before *their* offensive kicks off."

"So we kill their rookies," said Murkowski. "Sounds like easy shapes."

Murkowski was new to Vipers but not to flying; from the Academy class a year before O'Connor's, he'd been flying Freightlifters until getting a transfer—by everyone's standards, a promotion—to fighters as a loss-replacement measure after last month's casualties. He'd been shot at but never had much chance to return fire, and was eager to prove himself in that department. In the Skulls—and every other squadron O'Connor had heard about—you did that by earning vehicle-kill scratches and air-kill shapes.

"Don't get complacent, Messy," Mordar said. "Some of them might be rookies, but not all of them—and they're going to have numbers, at any rate. So now, our timing is going to bring us, at present speed, over the battlefield's leading edge at around the time our first serious ground elements will be mixing it up with theirs. They're going to be calling for air support; our job is to fuck with that, protect the tanks and the infantry, establish air superiority and maintain it over this battlefield. We clear on that? Ake ake?"

The Skulls' chant. It meant 'Upwards upwards' in the language of the 28th's Maori ancestors.

"Kia kaha!" O'Connor cheered back; its response. Be strong.

"Now keep your eyes wide open and your trigger-fingers ready," the flight leader finished, "because we *are* going to see some action today!"

. . .

Bullets ricocheted off the heavy front armour of the Junkers and Ritters as the thirteen-strong tank company surged over the ridge ahead of India Company. The tanks' main guns boomed in reply and then, as they reported over the general radio net that there was nothing more in-depth than a few technicals "and what looks like something under construction in the valley about a mile away", it was the cavalry's turn to move.

Newland nodded at Barocce, who'd been looking expectantly at him for a tense couple of minutes. The driver hit the gas pedal and accelerated past the shot-up trench and over the ridge, Patel and Bronze Two sticking to their left and the rest of India Company moving forwards on either side of them, gone from having spread out across a mile's front to gathered inside a few hundred yards.

On the other side of the ridge the terrain was steeper slope-wise and messier in terms of more, bigger boulders that obstructed lines of sight. There were still few enough of them for Newland to see, as the Raiders accelerated past the slower-moving tanks, what the 'something under construction' was.

Hundreds of Zinj, it looked like, had been working with the assistance of some big portable cranes and various other heavy vehicles that looked to include at least two cement mixers, to build what was obviously a fuel dump. Four great big circular tanks had been assembled already, each of them thirty feet high by about the same in diameter, built on top of concrete foundations and still surrounded by arrays of rickety scaffolding as crews worked to cover them with white paint. Two more were under construction, skeletal frameworks only half-covered with unpainted metal plates.

The Zinj would have been hard at work less than ten minutes ago—now most of them were running like panicked ants. Mostly.

Yeah well, CU combat engineers were well-armed and it was reasonable to expect enemy to be similar. And there *were* armed vehicles around—fire came in now not at the steadily-advancing tanks but at the faster cavalry moving up ahead of them. Those two escaped technicals hadn't gone too far, and—Newland saw as the Raider bumped forwards toward them at forty-five miles per hour—they'd met up with friends, because there was a different one, this guy with a machine-gun on top of its roll bar, moving now.

"Disrupt their construction and don't let 'em dig in!" Bradford ordered. "Follow me, forwards!"

One of the tanks behind them fired, and an explosive gout of debris erupted a moment later near one of the rapidly-moving technicals—near miss, not a direct hit, and the vehicle kept moving. Streams of machine-gun and autocannon fire from the advancing cavalry were more effective, knocking out a fourth technical the moment it appeared.

"RPG!" someone shouted. "Multiple RPGs from the construction!"

Yes—trailing fire, several rockets were coming from the direction of the upper scaffolding. Reiss turned his machine-gun on their source, while Bronze Two's grenadier popped up out of his hatch and sent three grenades flying in that general direction.

The expanses between Arkin's continental plates were seismically unstable and at some points relatively close to the dry planet's molten core. Not only were minor earthquakes practically an hourly occurrence but big ones were fairly common as well, and energy release from bubbling lava filtered through the superconducting minerals in the ground had a chaotic, destructive electromagnetic effect on electronics themselves and a disruptive one on radio communications.

What that meant right now was that you *didn't* build long-term except on the more stable rock islands, because one big quake would turn the ground underneath into temporary quicksand and bury your construction. This depot wasn't on a rock island; it was out in the open, which meant the Zinj weren't planning on it being a long-term thing. It was preparation for the offensive they'd been rumoured to be building up for, and proof of those rumours.

"Get around them! Troops One and Two, take left—Three and Four, take right!" Bradford ordered calmly.

Yeah, that was what cavalry *did*—use their speed to outflank and bypass when possible.

Barocce had heard the captain; so had the drivers of Troop Three's other Raiders. They and the Lancers drove downhill, spaced apart and bumping hard over the rocks, rightwards with their gunners firing occasional bursts. Wagner popped up from his roof-hatch and let loose a couple of grenades before ducking down; they or someone else's exploded amidst the construction works and a man toppled from the scaffolding.

"Oh *shit!*" someone ahead of them yelled. "B-4! They have one—no, two, no, *four* B-4s!"

A moment later the first of the Zinj light tanks came into Newland's own line of sight—they'd been concealed behind the construction works, but now as the cavalry began to come around those, they became visible. The B-4 was an oversized rectangular turret on top of a relatively small chassis, and the cannon it mounted was usually a 75mm—not big enough to really do much more than scratch a Junker's paint, but a lethal threat to Raiders and Lancers. Especially at this distance, half a mile and closing...

Two of the B-4s now fired at the Raiders of Troop Three, their cannon booming as Barocce and the other Raider drivers started to swerve, making themselves harder targets. Tracers lashed back in their direction, machine-gun fire peppering them. Wouldn't do a thing against their armour, and it looked like they were already buttoned-down, their gunners and commanders safely inside.

• • •

Captain Ahmed Merza was buttoned up tight in the commander's seat of his ARH-9 Ritter heavy main battle tank as D Company thundered downhill: three troops of three Junker main battle tanks, one three-strong troop of the bigger, meaner Ritters, and his own company-command Ritter. The thirteen tanks were charging forwards, downhill over the rocks at twenty-five miles per hour, their treads crunching the smaller ones and bumping over the larger ones.

From the evasive swervings some of the cavalry screeners were starting to make, they'd run into something they considered a threat—although given the kevlar-and-aluminum excuses for protection Raiders and Lancers had, Merza supposed that pretty much *anything* constituted a valid threat from their perspective. He for one *liked* having a foot of reinforced steel between his muscular bodybuilder's ass and enemy guns.

Besides, the view was *better* from the inside, where the digital screens surrounding him showed not just the naked-eye view of the tank's surrounds but an augmented-reality perception from cameras and sensors elsewhere. For instance—as his electronic warfare specialist fed the filtered data to one of those screens—he could see that there were five B-4 light tanks engaging his cavalry, trying to keep the half-constructed fuel cisterns between themselves and the advancing armour.

He could also see that the cisterns were made of thin steel plating—their purpose was to hold fuel, not stop shells. With a tap of one muscular finger, Merza transmitted that particular data point to one of the screens in front of his gunner and got, in response less than a second later, a thumbs-up icon in confirmation.

Two seconds of adjustment later and the Ritter's main gun went *boom*, which Merza's noise-cancelling headset meant he felt as a brutal vibration more than he heard as a sound. Indicators on the company tracking screen showed other D Company gunners and commanders coming to the same conclusions from the same data and reacting the same way, a rippling fusillade of cannon fire blasting out from their main guns inside the space of a couple of seconds.

It was overkill. A dozen 120mm and 165mm shells tore through the cisterns like so much tissue paper and eviscerated the five Zinj tanks hiding behind them, punching through the B-4s' side armour and turning them into momentary fireballs on Merza's sensors. More than momentary ones, as the shells in turn set off the light tanks' fuel and ammunition in rippling secondary blasts.

Overkill was not a concept Merza had a problem with. Not when *he* was the one inflicting it.

. . .

"Suck on *that*, bitches!" Wagner smirked from the back seat as the burning shell of the nearest of the Zinj tanks, threats until five seconds ago, went up in a secondary explosion that threw its boxy turret tumbling twenty feet into the air. Cheers echoed across Third Troop's radio network; Barocce and a couple of the other drivers blasted their horns enthusiastically and Newland knew full well his own face was a bare-toothed grin.

The shells that had ripped through the fuel cisterns—*concealment but not cover*, as those tank crews had terminally learned—had done a number on the rickety scaffolding around them, knocking much of it away. The Zinj left around the construction site seemed to be going for cover—or running like hell, as two hundred of them were now doing as Bronze One and the rest of the Raiders passed around the fuel dump to its south side.

One of the figures, wearing dark robes spattered everywhere with white paint, turned at the sound of the engines to see the oncoming armoured cars. He pointed and screamed; some of his friends turned while others in the fleeing mob tried to redouble their speed. None seemed to be armed, and as the Raiders moved past the Zinj and then ahead of them, a couple of them waved empty hands in the air.

"Hold fire!" came Captain Bradford over the radio. "Say again India Company, *hold fire!*"

Ordering needlessly—although Reiss and Bronze Two's gunner were both keeping their fifties pointed at the Zinj, nobody was shooting. This possibility had been mentioned in the briefing: these ragged, paint-spattered, unarmed fuckers weren't Zinj combat engineers, they were low-caste slave labor.

As the cavalry drew ahead of the fleeing Zinj, cutting them off, more of them stopped running and began waving their hands in the air, shouting. A couple of them fell to their knees, pressing their hands together in desperate prayer.

"Ignore them," came Bradford. "India Company, spread out and keep moving!"

"We're just gonna leave 'em?" Wagner asked from the back seat. "They're running *now*, Sarge, but do we really want those guys getting their shit together to fuck around in our rear this time tonight?"

Newland shook his head curtly.

"Wagner, you remember a certain company formation last night?" he asked dryly. "Where the skipper and a couple of Regimental staff guys... *explained various things*?"

The sub-corporal was silent for one, two, three heartbeats before he grunted a tentative "Uh—yeah?"

Fucking E-3s, thought Newland with a roll of his eyes. Wagner hadn't even been pretending to pay attention during the briefing, and it crossed Newland's mind now to just leave the man hanging as a lesson to listen better going forwards.

Except that the little man from Murphysburg would just keep pestering until he got an answer, if not from Newland then from Barocce or Reiss simply to shut him up. First Sergeant Willis liked to mentor his NCOs with little tests and lessons, but that style of leadership development didn't work so well with guys you were stuck inside a Raider with.

"We're first echelon, scouting and screening," Newland said very slowly to the man. "Right behind us, *as you may have noticed*, are some treadheads. And behind those guys are...?"

"Grafs?" Wagner guessed after a moment.

"Legs," Barocce put in. "Bunch of Khalsan legs to mop shit up for us."

"So that we and the tanks don't have to slow down," Newland finished. "We've got surprise, zigs weren't expecting *us* to come knocking on *their* front door, but... that's not going to last forever. But while it does, while they're still warming up their engines and getting their shit together, we do not stop and we do not slow down."

Because even if neither their pickets nor that construction crew got off a warning, Newland thought, *their friends will have heard the shooting.*

On the other hand, even Zinj with their shit together were going to have a bad damn time against the force Cav was presently screening. Didn't matter if your engines were warm or not when Freiherr super-heavies and kiloheavy Grafs the size of apartment blocks showed up to kick your door in—and behind India Company were three full divisions.

CHAPTER THREE

Battalion-Colonel Rashaad Malouf al-Mutlali scowled slightly as he took another sip of coffee. Despite being a fine espresso made at double the usual strength, despite this water having been boiled and recondensed three times over, a faint metallic tang remained to irk his tastebuds.

In the recliner across from him, Mullah Reza gave an easy smile—not quite insolence, but more than one of Malouf's officers would have dared. Certainly the three such—two majors and one captain—presently occupying the tent's other folding recliners *didn't* dare; Major Ali was pretending to tolerate the metallic-tasting coffee, while the other two had entirely declined morning refreshments. Captain Habib, in fact, had the loyalty to give Reza the angry scowl it would have been undiplomatic for Malouf himself to give the Front-General's liaison.

"You get used to it," the mullah observed. "Think of it as tasting riches—the minerals that seep into the aquifers are worth more than gold, refined."

"*You* might get used to it," Malouf growled. There was enough else about this wasteland to irk him beyond its metallic-tasting water: chaotic electromagnetic pulses that had turned his insufficiently-hardened personal devices into scrap the first day. Infernally fine sand that made its way into engines and gearboxes, not to mention all through your clothing.

Seismic instability that meant the ground under your feet might at any moment shake and jolt like a yanked rug....

Most frustratingly of all, this Allah-be-damned intercontinental wasteland's threats and discomforts had *not* so far included the one he'd actually come here to face: the infidel.

In the three weeks since his regiment's arrival, despite the Fifth Selkot's persuasive and well-connected commander successfully arranging for them to be encamped as far west as permissible and practical, as close to the enemy as was allowed... neither Malouf nor any of his men, nor in fact anyone in the Fifth Selkot's other battalions, had so much as heard a single shot fired with intent.

Oh, Malouf and his officers had heard enough stories *of* the fighting that had opened the war, as years of simmering escalations had finally bloomed into open conflict and the infidel forces had been driven back, chased east like running dogs—until they had chosen to stop running and strike back.

Just stories from those who had—tales of death and bravado that were probably wild exaggerations from members of the Djegouni and al-Rafsa tribes, and self-serving excuses from the al-Sayidis, who had lost their flagship carrier to a Confederated Union pinprick in their war's first hour. That had upset a tenuous power balance between the three tribes, and factions within those tribes, enough to spark an internal struggle lasting almost a month—tribes and factions at one another's throats while, no doubt, the infidels watched and laughed.

On the other hand, Reza was a mullah, who had taken fire oaths renouncing clan, sept, and tribal loyalties in order to serve Allah of the Flames through the Council of Eleven as an impartial observer, adviser, judge and sometimes enforcer of faithful observance, often diplomat and no doubt always spy, since it would make no sense for Allah's advocates *not* to report their own observations and opinions up through the shrouded, denied, but inferrably real organisational structures inside the Faith.

To Malouf, who had been raised to a practical and literate family of the lower nobility and in his forty-six years of life developed a sensible understanding of the world's realities, that did not make Reza—or any other holy man—the impartial and absolute voices of Allah that they claimed to be.

For one, mullahs were whole men who had taken their vows by choice at maturity. Nobody simply wiped away loyalties of blood that had defined fourteen-plus years of childhood and upbringing. They were neither eunuchs nor Janissaries. Two, they sometimes disagreed with one another, those disputes to be settled by prayer and appeal.

And three, in the field they had their own hierarchies of precedence and seniority; Reza had several underlings reporting to him within the battalion, for instance, in addition to likely secret informers. He in turn *had* to operate in the context of some bigger power structure or dynamic, whose higher levels in turn would by necessity overlap with the secular affairs of clans and tribes.

It was relevant that mullahs swore to serve Allah of the Flames *through* the Council of Eleven—as opposed to how the eunuchs and Janissaries swore to serve the Council directly. Ambiguities in Allah's will had to be resolved through prayer and interpretation; the Council could simply be asked to clarify any specifics needed.

What that meant in practice was that Mullah Jalil Reza had to have *some* agenda, some angle, some perspective he wanted the commander of Malouf Battalion, Fifth Selkot Regiment, Selkot Red Division to behave assuming the reality of. But it wasn't the slimy self-justification of the powerful but humiliated al-Sayidis; neither was it the transparently self-aggrandising entreaties of the al-Rafsa factions, nor Djegouni manipulation. The mullah's descriptions of infidel behaviour were probably something close to truth... except that they made no sense.

The soldiers of the Confederated Union and their Khalsan allies were, Reza said, faithless in some ways. That they'd simply abandoned their holy city of Barbiero without a fight was clear proof of that.

Except that they were not in every case the abject cowards that Malouf's three decades of experience in holy war had proven faithless to be. An example of that had been Ganff Rock, where a regiment-sized unit had rejected fair surrender terms. Rather than live as dhimmi with the possibility of eventual exchange, the Confederated Union soldiers at Ganff had chosen to fight and die to the last man. Like New Canaanites on holy ground, except—without faith.

Sometimes these Western infidels were frightened sheep; other times they were cornered she-wolves, and they did not even seem to agree *with themselves* on a single set of truths. Family seemed to mean little or nothing to them, only a few of them seemed to recognise tribal allegiance in even the broadest ethnic-racial sense, and yet... somehow they worked together anyway, often at levels of selflessness and trust that no Zinj would give or expect beyond immediate family and not always then.

Suddenly, breaking the silence in the tent, Captain Habib tilted his head.

"Do you hear that?" he asked sharply, lowering his teacup.

Malouf swung his boots down from the recliner as his own ears picked up on something above the general ambient sound of the camped battalion, tools and voices and the occasional engine. Another layer, a sound that his experience in the wars of conquest on the Great Continent had taught him at an instinctive level to prioritise.

Dull booms, distant but growing closer.

Cannon.

"It's practice," Major Ali said dismissively. "Someone got bored."

"It is not practice," said Mullah Reza sharply, lowering his own cup and rising to his feet with surprising speed. "The enemy is known to be unpredictable. That is not the sound of our cannon."

The battalion had ammunition but, beyond a few test and calibration shots earlier, had not been allowed to fire any. They were part of a vast force at the end of a still-being-developed supply line and, the orders had been clear, shells could not be spared. The mullahs would be enforcing that order.

Suddenly a teenaged messenger pushed open the flaps of the tent, bowing at Malouf and the other officers.

"What is it?" This young boy was assigned to the battalion watch officer.

"Battalion-Colonel, Captain Mamnoon says that the forward engineers have just been overrun! They got out a call for help and a warning—Captain Mamnoon says to tell you, Battalion-Colonel, that a large enemy force is attacking!"

The wait was over? The enemy had been kind enough to come to them?

Handbells began to ring through the camp as, obviously on Captain Mamnoon's own initiative, the alarm was raised. There was shouting, yelling, engines starting up.

Malouf pushed his way through the tent's flaps, followed by his officers and the mullah. The camp had erupted into a state of furious action; crews were pulling on helmets, adjusting harnesses and equipment, running for their tanks while shouting mechanics performed last-minute adjustments. Engines were starting to throatily roar into life. Sergeants and junior officers bellowed amidst the still-ringing handbells, and—

Cannon fire closer. Close enough to be heard *over* the din of the camp!

The men were eager. They'd spent weeks listening to stories of how the westerners fought while bored, idle, waiting for the big offensive to finally begin.

They were ready. They wanted to see for themselves what the Western infidel were like in battle, prove the excuses of the inferior tribes who had failed here earlier to be just that, excuses.

The al-Mutlali tribe would have no need to make excuses.

"Get them! Counterattack!"

• • •

As O'Connor and the Skulls had finally turned east to join the fight, the hills below them had flattened out into a wide—sixty-five or so miles, according to the maps—valley, on the other side of which began the hills to Barbiero's immediate west.

In the valley, kicking up huge dust plumes that after three hours had reached well up to the Vipers' present eleven thousand foot altitude, were more Confederated Union vehicles than O'Connor had *ever* before seen in a single place. It was a bit hard to tell from all the dust they were throwing up, but his plane had image-enhancing and -clarifying software that could make up for some of that, and… Lugh, were there a lot of them!

Passing below, he saw the unmistakable shapes of Graf kiloheavies: huge boxy things a hundred and fifty feet long and fifty wide, double-gunned turrets that *on their own* were as big as Junker main battle tanks. You didn't *need* image enhancement to make them out even from this height; even from two miles up they were massive, and there were *dozens* of them spread across the valley below, advancing east surrounded by companies of Freiherr super-heavies, Ritters and Junkers.

Behind and amidst the tanks were trucks loaded with infantry and the smaller, boxier shapes that O'Connor knew were armoured fighting vehicles. The CU's own forces didn't include those—unless you counted the dismounts of Raider and Lancer crews, when they were fighting from outside their armoured cars—but the Khalsan military did, and there were Khalsan armoured infantry in this attack.

The sixteen-strong Viper squadron, a fingers-four arrow of fingers-four flights, flew east toward the sun, which O'Connor's canopy could only polarise to some extent. Below them the ground started to crease and fold, steep hills emerging and vehicles moving across them. Flashes from some of them as they fired—they were flying over a battle!

And holy *shit* were there a lot of vehicles on the far side of the flashes! Vehicles and tent encampments passed below O'Connor too fast to count, gathered into clusters of fifty, sixty, a hundred-plus large tents… battalions?

The hills became steeper, channeling traffic into valleys that were thick with Zinj, and on the other side of the passes…

So. Many. Zinj!

Their encampments were everywhere. The radar was starting to show bandits emerging from the airfields west of Barbiero, and…

"Charlie Flight, follow me!" came Hauraki. "Delta, you're with Sauron. See if you can get a few ground kills!"

"Bravo, Delta Flights," came 'Sauron' Mordar's dry voice. "Stay tight and—attack!"

It was hard for O'Connor to keep his eyes on the sky, and not just because they were still flying into the sun—his instruments were less blinded, and they were showing a whole swarming beehive of Zinj aircraft in the sky above Barbiero, some of them starting to come west toward them.

It was hard because he wanted to look at the ground, an endless sprawling expanse of Zinj encampments. For an attack to succeed, he'd heard, you ideally wanted to outnumber the defenders three to one… it looked like the Zinj here outnumbered the attacking Western forces by ten or more to one! There had to be hundreds of thousands of them here!

And then, as his threat indicator lit up and Jamison shouted "Murads at eleven o'clock!", he had other things to think about.

Like staying alive when it looked like they were outnumbered even worse in the sky!

. . .

"Look at them," an al-Mutlali battalion-colonel remarked to Major Daoud Aboud, pointing down from the second-floor balcony of what had been Barbiero's finest hotel and was now field headquarters to Front-General Najit Jafar, the Emir of Khalat.

A battalion of men in grey uniforms were marching slowly down the avenue, huge-wheeled jeeps driving slowly here and there amidst them. The men in grey marched six abreast in perfect step, and from what Aboud could see—mostly their faces and ungloved hands—they were mostly of lighter complexion. "All discipline. No spirit."

"And their officers have no balls," Aboud smiled as the Janissaries passed by.

It was an uneasy party, but less so than the ones two or three weeks ago, when Aboud's father the Sheikh of Zakhif had been forced to make peace with his enemy and nominal, until his rebellion, liege the Emir of Khalat. Officially the two men had mutually agreed to cease their war at approximately the status quo ante bellum, with gifts of equal value being exchanged to cement the peace.

In reality it had been ordered by senior mullahs. One of the elements of compromise was that Aboud himself—and some others—would be assigned to Khalat's staff in Barbiero, alongside officers from the Djegounis and al-Sayidis, and representatives from the six divisions of al-Mutlalis who had arrived in-theater more recently.

The Emir of Khalat had thrown parties every day, with support said to come from the Council of Eleven so that his new senior and staff officers might form bonds and make peace. Zakhif's rebellion had been expensive for the Emir's prestige, and the fighting itself had been a closer-run thing, Aboud had heard from both his father and from Khalat's people, than many had expected. It was time to turn a forced peace into a genuine one and win this war against the real enemy, the West.

There would be time enough to overthrow Khalat's worthless ruler when the Confederated Union was beaten. To achieve that, the plan involved a mighty punch toward the Date Line and across it. The immediate objective was the Western force built up on the far side of the valley around Des Laam, which would be overrun—then across the Zero-Three-Sixty Meridian, the Planetary Date Line, and on to Sand Harbor. That independent city—formerly independent city, effectively now a Confederated Union military base and staging area—would be secured, supply lines established, and the next push would take them still closer to the enemy homelands.

Every square mile of intercontinental desert secured in the meantime would give the Zinj better control of the priceless minerals, the superconductors and so on that the spacers would pay richly for, and deny those to the Westerners.

The problem was that a force the size that had been assembled required logistics to simply exist in the bare desert—which in turn required a supply pipeline to be constructed, the infrastructure for gasoline and water and food and ammunition and all the thousands of items a fighting military needed, to be brought forwards. That was taking time to build up, but in a week or two... they would be ready for the first push.

A buzz came around the gathering, which at its perimiter consisted of highborn field-grade officers like Aboud and the Mutlali battalion-colonel, and at its centre consisted of the Emir with his two eldest sons and the family mullah; his nominal deputy a Mutlali front-general with the social rank of First Sheikh; two Rafsa corps-generals; and one scowling al-Sayidi corps-general. Outer layers of division-generals surrounded the top men, followed by their deputies and a few of the regiment-colonels commanding actual regiments, those located within Barbiero itself. Past those were deputies, staffers, flunkies, hangers-on and so on.

"What was that?"

The Mutlali battalion-colonel turned to whisper with another man, exchanging words Aboud couldn't hear. He tried to, while outwardly he kept his eyes on the balcony watching the Janissaries pass. Apparently a full battalion, marching with a strange Western discipline most Zinj would have considered beneath them.

If our ways honor Allah as most think, he thought, *then why has Allah given the infidel victory so far?*

"The Westerners have lost their minds," the battalion-colonel remarked to Aboud. "They're attacking. We're getting reports coming from the front that *they're* attacking *us*."

"A nuisance raid," Aboud said dismissively. The Westerners were godless infidels. They were not *morons*.

"No—overflights have confirmed kiloheavies and troop-carrying trucks behind their spearheads. It's the real thing."

The party had erupted into chaos, commanders tailed by aides running out while messengers and scribes rushed in to gather around the Emir.

"Counterattack!" pronounced Front-General Najit Jafar as though it had been a decision. "Have everyone counterattack!"

"Lord Emir," an aide reported, "they already are."

・・・

For more, go online NOW!

Printed in Great Britain
by Amazon